Excalibur Rising
Book One
Arthur

Eileen Enwright Hodgetts

ISBN-97-806-9-222005-4

Eileen Enwright Hodgetts

PRELUDE

The One-Eyed Man
London

The one-eyed man stepped out of the mist under the light of a waning moon. He had timed his arrival to coincide with low tide on the River Thames so that he would step ashore onto a dry shingle beach. The hour was late, and the boy should not even have been there. Who, he asked himself, allows their kid to walk alone on the Thames Embankment so late in the evening? The boy had seen him. Briefly he considered killing the kid, but he decided a killing would attract too much attention. He was here to kill, but the killing would be subtle and secret, and should remain undiscovered for many days.

He consulted his watch, pleased to see that it had started to work again. On the other side of the mist, the watch was no more than an ornament, but here it told him what he needed to know.

He had allowed himself five hours. Just enough time to kill the man, reroute the victim's phone calls, steal his car, and drive to Heathrow Airport. If all went well, he would be on the flight to Vegas with time to spare.

He slipped the dagger out of his pocket and admired the way the cold moonlight played upon the jeweled handle. The kid was still looking at him. He climbed the ancient steps from the riverbank up to the Embankment, where the light of the streetlamp played full on his face. The kid took one look and then turned and ran.

The one-eyed man strode purposefully through the moonlit streets. He was on his way to end a life. The thought gave him no particular pleasure, but it also gave him no particular pain; killing was what he did. He would kill many more times before he could return to the place he called home.

1

CHAPTER ONE

Doctor Marcus Ryan
Las Vegas, Nevada

Marcus Ryan pounded angrily on the elevator button, but the doors to the staff elevator remained firmly closed. He reluctantly conceded that the Out of Order sign actually meant what it said and the elevator was truly not working, a rare event in the well-oiled machinery of the Mandretti empire. He was left with no choice but to leave the privacy of the Mandretti Treasure Vault and go out onto the Strip and around the corner to the main hotel entrance.

All he wanted to do was reach his room on the twentieth floor of the Mandretti Resort Hotel and get himself out of his work clothes and into a stiff drink. What he didn't want to do was parade himself through the Las Vegas Strip, where someone might recognize him as Marcus Ryan, the once youthful doctor who used to have a network television show about historical treasures. Of course, that was before cable had destroyed the networks, and before the passage of time had blurred Ryan's youthful features.

Unfortunately, Ryan's boss was still determined to cash in on the remnants of Ryan's popularity and insisted that Ryan should dress the way he had dressed for the TV program. Kitted out in full explorer gear, including snake proof boots, khaki shorts, safari jacket, and an Australian bush hat, Ryan felt like a caricature of his former self. The only really useful items in the ensemble were the bush hat that protected his head from the heat of the desert afternoon, and the thick-soled boots that protected his feet from a sidewalk that was roughly the temperature of a bed of burning coals. As for the rest, he had no useful items in the multitudinous pockets of the safari jacket, and in real archaeological conditions, his neatly pressed shorts would be of no use at all, too short, and too tight for any real work.

He hurried as fast as his long legs would carry him along the Strip, through the hotel lobby, and over to the bank of elevators serving the thousand rooms. A small group of newly arrived tourists had gathered in front of the elevator, clutching their keycards and suitcases.

"That's him," he heard a woman say.

"No, it isn't," came the reply. "He's bigger than that."

"They all look bigger on TV," the woman argued. "I'm telling you that's him. He's doing some kind of show here. I saw his picture in the brochure."

The man tapped Ryan on the arm. "Are you him?"

Ryan removed his hat and pasted on his best TV personality smile. "Welcome to Vegas."

The elevator doors opened, and he welcomed the rush of super-cooled air. They all stepped inside, the tourists with their suitcases and Ryan in his ridiculous explorer outfit.

The woman addressed her husband as though Ryan was invisible. "It's him," she reiterated, "but he's looking much older." She turned to him. "I used to watch you on TV every Sunday night. Me and the kids loved Treasure Hunt. You found such interesting stuff. I was sorry you was cancelled."

"So was I," Ryan said, and breathed a sigh of relief as the doors opened onto the twentieth floor.

"Nice to meet you," the woman said as the doors closed again.

Ryan made his way along the corridor to his room, where he immediately stripped off his safari jacket and flopped down on the bed in his shorts. How are the mighty fallen, he said to himself, although to be honest he knew that he had never been mighty. He had only been a fairly well-known TV personality, never a major star.

The message light was flashing on his room phone, and he picked it up, punched in his code, and listened to a recorded message telling him that Professor T.Q. Peacock would like Doctor Ryan to call him as soon as possible. His room number was 21112. He replayed the message to be sure that he had heard correctly. Professor T.Q. Peacock was here at the Mandretti? What on earth, he wondered, was Taras Quentin Peacock doing in Las Vegas?

Intrigued, he dialed the professor's room number and was greeted by the unmistakable upper-class British accent of the man who had been his freshman history professor during his first terrifying year at Harvard.

"Good news," said the professor. "Great news. Call room service, my boy, and order something decent, none of that revolting California swill, something French. I'll be with you in a tick."

"But how did you know I was here?" Ryan asked.

"I know everything," Peacock said. "I know all about you, my boy. You certainly haven't lived up to your earlier promise. How old are you now?"

"Forty-five," said Ryan.

"Forty-five," Peacock repeated. "That's what I thought. You're still young but don't have any time to waste. I think I have something better for you. Stop asking questions and order the drinks. I'll see you in a minute."

Peacock broke the connection and left Ryan to wonder what on earth his old professor could want with him after so many years, and just how and why he intended to revive Ryan's flagging career.

Before he picked up the phone to order room service, Ryan shuffled through his mental filing system until he arrived at the image of T.Q. Peacock sitting at his desk and pouring red wine into a whisky tumbler. The year was 1990, the place was Harvard, and the wine was a French Châteauneuf-du-Pape served at room temperature. He called room service and ordered a bottle of Châteauneuf-du-Pape at a somewhat alarming price, and then he took his own bottle of Jack Daniel's from the minibar. He had several bottles of Jack Daniel's in that refrigerator. For the past few years, Jack Daniel's had been his only friend.

He slipped into jeans and a tee shirt, and was searching for his sneakers when the professor knocked at the door. He greeted Ryan with a bear hug and then stepped back to look him up and down. "You've grown taller," he said, "and thinner."

Ryan shook his head. "No taller, and no thinner. Six four and one eighty."

"Five six and twenty stone," Peacock said in reply. "That's two eighty to you Americans, and I'm proud of every pound of it."

The professor stepped into the room rubbing his hands together in delight. His hair, which had been peppered with gray when Ryan first met him, was now a mass of snowy white curls. His rotund body was stuffed into a heavy Harris Tweed suit that may well have been the same suit he had worn as Visiting Professor of History all those years ago. His eyes had the same old twinkle, and his nose was the same cheerful red.

"Look at this, look at this!" Peacock exclaimed, waving his arms expansively to encompass the room, the view, and the whole of Las Vegas. "Fallen into clover, that's what we've done, lad. We've fallen into clover. Do you know how much money there is in this town, lad? Do you?"

For a moment, Ryan was a student again, forced to admit that he didn't know the answer. "Not exactly," he muttered.

"Neither do I," Peacock shouted, slapping Ryan on the back, "but I reckon there's enough to go around, and then some to spare."

"Do you mind telling me what you're doing here?" Ryan asked. "Of course I'm glad to see you, but …"

Peacock silenced him with a peal of jovial laughter. "Don't get upset, lad. I'm not here to get in on your act, not that you've been doing all that well lately. Lost the TV show, so I hear."

"Ten years ago," Ryan admitted. "My simple little Sunday night specials couldn't compete with the Discovery Channel and the History Channel, and all the rest."

"So now you're here authenticating treasures for a hoodlum," Peacock said.

"Not exactly," Ryan protested. "I mean, they are genuine treasures, and I have made it very clear that I will have the final say on whether or not they are authentic. He has some pretty amazing stuff, and being his curator is not so—"

"Oh, don't mind me," Peacock said. "You were my star pupil and you made such a good start, but I know times change and you have to do what you have to do. I can quite understand you prostituting your name; we all have to do it from time to time. I've put my name on some research papers that were just …" He stopped in mid-sentence, shrugged his shoulders, and sat himself down in an armchair. "Did you call room service?" he asked.

Ryan nodded his head.

Peacock drew a cigar from the depths of his appalling tweed jacket. "Fine wine, fine cigar, and a fine student, what more could I ask for?"

"This is a no-smoking room," Ryan protested as Peacock clipped the end of the cigar.

"I should hope so," Peacock said. "A fine Havana cigar is not something that should be smoked in the company of any lesser leaf."

"They're not legal," Ryan said. "Havana cigars are not legal in this country."

"I'm not a citizen of your petty-minded country," Peacock said. "I am a guest, and as such I am entitled to certain ethnic comforts. Anyway, this is Vegas, and as I understand it, what happens in Vegas stays in Vegas. Now stop frowning at me and sit down. Let's get down to business. I really don't like to say much before I have a glass of something in my hand, but no doubt room service will make its way up here before too long."

"No doubt," Ryan agreed, and sat down on the sofa.

"I've found something," Peacock said, "that goes beyond your wildest dreams, and you and I, Marcus, are going to sell it to the man who owns this hotel."

"Michael Mandretti?"

"Michael Mandretti, yes, that's right. He's going to give us a great deal of money for what I've found. Maybe everything he possesses."

Ryan smiled and kept his doubts to himself. In addition to cataloging and curating Michael Mandretti's collection for the past twelve months, he had also been instrumental in finding new treasures for Mandretti's hoard. He had no idea what was behind his employer's hungry search for rare and irreplaceable treasures, or why the man would spend hours at a time in the air-conditioned treasure vault, simply staring through the armored glass at the jewel-encrusted relics of lost civilizations. Nonetheless, Ryan had personally bargained with treasure hunters, divers, wreckers, and private collectors for whatever historical artifacts appealed to Mr. Mandretti's eclectic taste. When it came to collecting, Mandretti was like a butterfly landing greedily on whatever attracted his attention. He was not a discerning collector, but on any given day, Mr. Mandretti knew what he wanted and Mr. Mandretti got what he wanted, at the price he wanted to pay. Every single time. Ryan could not imagine for one moment that Professor Peacock could have found anything that Michael Mandretti could not have found for himself, if he truly wanted to.

Peacock puffed contentedly on his cigar. "You don't believe me, do you?" he asked.

Ryan said nothing.

Peacock looked around for an ashtray. Seeing nothing suitable, he hopped to his feet and trotted off to the bathroom, returning with the bathroom wastebasket. "You used to smoke," he said accusingly. "I suppose that wife of yours talked you out of it."

"She's not my wife any longer," Ryan said. "Hasn't been for years."

"Yes, yes. I read about it in one of the London rags," Peacock said. "Sorry to hear it. Oh well, onward and upward, my boy, onward and upward. By the time I'm finished with you, you'll be able to buy any woman in the world."

"I don't want to buy a woman."

"Figure of speech," Peacock said. "Don't be so damned touchy." He blew a cloud of pungent smoke into the air and looked at Ryan through the haze. "What," he asked, "would be the greatest treasure anyone could find?"

Now there's a question, Ryan thought. "The greatest?" he repeated.

"Yes," said Peacock, "the find of finds."

Ryan rose to his feet and looked out of the window. Below him the Las Vegas Strip slashed through the desert. Tall buildings reached for the sky, and inside the buildings, desperate men and women threw their money into the gaping mouths of one-armed bandits or onto the hungry green fields of the playing tables.

"Money?" Ryan asked.

"More than money," said Peacock, "a find of such historical value that no museum could ever afford to buy it, a find that could be housed here in this hotel. People would come from every corner of the world just to see it. What would Mandretti pay for something like that?"

"I don't know," Ryan said. "I don't know what it is."

"Of course you don't," Peacock agreed. "I'm just asking you to use your brain. You're the expert. You're the television personality. You're the man Mandretti trusts with his treasures. So what would that treasure be?

Think, lad. Think."

Ryan was a freshman again, being harassed by the eccentric bullying Englishman. "You don't change, do you?" he said sullenly.

"No," Peacock agreed. "I don't change. I don't want to change. So what do you think I've found?"

Ryan answered off the top of his head. "The Holy Grail."

"Yes, that's right, the Holy Grail."

Ryan stared at him. "You've found the Holy Grail?"

Peacock shook his head. "No, of course I haven't found the Holy Grail. I can't find something that doesn't exist. I'm using a metaphor. What is the holy grail of treasure hunters?"

Determined to impress him, Ryan reeled off a list. "The Lost Dutchman Mine, Atlantis, Noah's Ark, the Fountain of Youth."

"No basis in fact," Peacock said impatiently. "Think rationally, Marcus."

Ryan glared at his tormenter. "Just tell me. I know you're dying to tell me."

"Excalibur," said Peacock.

Ryan's heart sank. For a moment, he had thought that the old man had really found something, but apparently, he had only come to torment his student.

"The sword of Arthur," Peacock declared. "What would Mandretti pay if he could own Excalibur?"

"I thought we were talking rationally," Ryan said.

"We are," Peacock insisted. "I'm telling you that I have found it. I have seen it with my own eyes."

"Excalibur?"

"Yes."

"Impossible."

"Why?"

"Why?" Ryan asked. "Why is it impossible that you've seen King Arthur's sword? Because it never existed, that's why. King Arthur never existed, ergo his sword never existed."

"Who taught you that?" Peacock asked.

"You did," Ryan replied.

Peacock shook his head. "I never taught you any such thing. I taught you that the Arthur we hear of in legends was probably a creation of medieval romances, but he was rooted in fact. I know I taught you that, didn't I?"

"No, you didn't. You taught us that there is absolutely no historical record of Arthur, and the Arthurian stories seemed to be formed out of thin air and ancient legends sometime in the twelfth century."

The old man grinned engagingly. "Well," he said, "maybe that was before I had my change of heart on the subject. Don't tell me, Marcus Ryan, PhD, that you have never ever considered the possibility that somewhere in this great round world—I did teach you that the world was round, didn't I?"

Ryan laughed and nodded.

"Have you never considered," Peacock asked again, "that somewhere in this great round world, the sword of Arthur may exist?"

Ryan was reluctant to join in his game, but honesty forced him to say that yes, he had considered it. Of course he had considered it. "Historians are all romantics at heart," he said, "and if it was ever found—"

"It is found."

"—if it was ever found," Ryan continued, "it would obviously be priceless."

"We could get a price."

"I could never authenticate it," Ryan said. "I could never put my name to such an outrageous claim."

"I've seen it," Peacock said.

Silence filled the room. Ryan lowered himself slowly onto the sofa and stared at Peacock. He was looking for the sudden wink, the slight lifting of an eyebrow, the twitching of his lips, anything that would tell him that the aggressive little Englishman was joking. The silence hung heavily between them, and Peacock's face gave no sign.

"I've seen it," Peacock said again with a note of awe in his voice. He leaned forward, fixing Ryan with the hard stare of his pale eyes. "I've seen it," he said yet again, as though he could hardly believe it himself. "I've touched it." He stretched out his hand and touched something that only he could see. "It's nothing fancy, just a smattering of jewels. It's not well-formed, rather primitive, pre-Saxon, possibly Roman or early Celtic; very heavy. It was made for a big man."

"You're serious, aren't you?" Ryan asked.

"Yes."

"And you've told Mandretti already?"

"Not everything, but I've hinted. I've told him enough to whet his appetite. I told him that I had something very special and that you would authenticate it, and he invited me to come here."

Ryan thought about Michael Mandretti seated behind his enormous desk in his enormous office in the Mandretti executive suite. He tried to imagine himself wading across the sea of white shag carpet to stand in front of that desk and tell Michael Mandretti, who was without a doubt the most frightening man Ryan had ever met, that he, Doctor Marcus Ryan, was willing to throw the whole weight of his professional reputation behind a fairy tale.

"He trusts you, Marcus," Peacock said. "He doesn't trust me."

"I'm not surprised," Ryan replied. "I don't even trust you, not this time."

"I've seen it," Peacock said again.

"Where?"

Peacock smiled beatifically. "It's well protected but not well guarded," he said. "Its protection is its anonymity. No one realizes what it is. We can get our hands on it."

"Is it in a museum?"

"Not exactly," said Peacock. "That's why it's safe for the time being."

He fell silent and then took a deep breath as though he had decided to launch into an explanation. Ryan waited, admiring the professor's showmanship. He didn't believe a word Peacock was saying, but somehow the old professor had managed to hook him, and Ryan was eager to listen.

"Let me show you something," Peacock said at last, delving into the pocket of his tweed jacket. He produced something wrapped in a white handkerchief. He unfolded the handkerchief and revealed a small gold pin set with an unusual dull red stone.

"What is it?"

"It's a companion piece to the sword," Peacock said, "which I managed to liberate. The sword stays where it is, but I give you my word that they belong together." He handed Ryan the pin. Ryan turned it over in his hand and stared at it for a long time. "It has you stumped, doesn't it?" Peacock said.

Ryan continued to examine the pin in silence.

"Have you ever seen anything like it?" Peacock asked.

Ryan shook his head. "I can't place it. At first I thought Saxon, but it's not quite right. It's not Roman and definitely not Celtic, and there's something strange about the metal."

"And the stone," Peacock added. "Have you ever seen a stone like that before?"

Ryan turned the pin over and over in his hand. On first glance the stone was dull red like something that had been shaped by the sea and washed up on a pebble beach, but on closer examination it seemed to glow with an inner fire as though heat had been sealed into the very center of its being.

"What is it?" he asked.

Peacock shook his head. "No idea, but it's quite soft. I dropped it on the bathroom floor this morning and a piece broke off."

"You dropped it?" Ryan exclaimed.

Peacock pointed a stubby finger at a corner of the setting. "There was another small stone set in metal prongs. They broke."

"For heaven's sake," Ryan said, "what are you thinking of? This shouldn't be wrapped up in a handkerchief and stuffed in your pocket. This should be in a padded case. I don't know what it is, but it's ancient and it's valuable."

"Which is the very reason why I am carrying it in my pocket," Peacock said. "No fuss, no big fanfare, much the safest way."

He handed Ryan a twisted scrap of paper. "I wrapped the broken piece in here. I thought you might want to take a look under a microscope."

Ryan took the paper from him and put it into his own pocket.

"The gold's strange," Peacock said. "It's not actually gold. It's a kind of crystal."

"It can't be."

"But it is," Peacock insisted. "You'll see what I mean when you put it under the microscope, and there's a document—"

"A provenance?"

"Not exactly. To be honest, I don't know what it is. I've lodged it in a safe place, but I brought a sample to show you. It's in my room; I'll go get it in a minute, and you can see what you make of it. It's a bit of a puzzler."

They were interrupted by two firm raps on the door. "Room service."

The dreaming look faded from the professor's eyes and was replaced by an anticipatory twinkle. "About bloody time," he declared. "I hope you ordered something decent."

"Châteauneuf-du-Pape," Ryan said as he crossed the room to open the door.

Peacock raised an appreciative eyebrow. "Very good, lad. You have a good memory."

The waiter was a tall well-built man who looked supremely discontented with his career choice. He wore the Indiana Jones themed costume issued to all workers to complement the emerging theme of the Mandretti, including well-worn jodhpurs and soft leather boots. His hair was light brown with sun-bleached streaks and definitely needed to be styled, or at least washed, and he wore an eye patch. Ryan made a mental note to tell the management that eye patches were the preserve of pirates not treasure hunters. The waiter deposited the tray on the coffee table. An elaborate pseudo-gothic goblet accompanied the wine.

"Compliments of the management," he said. He picked up the wine bottle. "I took the liberty of opening the wine, sir, to allow it to breathe."

He spoke clearly, but Ryan found his accent unusual. Scottish maybe.

The professor beamed delightedly. "Excellent, excellent. I see there is some culture in this benighted town."

"Just a little," said the waiter.

Ryan leaned forward to look at the goblet. "I haven't seen these before," he said. "They're very good replicas."

The waiter's hand shot out, seizing the goblet before Ryan could look closer. "They've only just arrived," he said. "I didn't bring one for you. You didn't order anything."

"No," Ryan said. "I have my own supply."

He took his billfold from the nightstand and gave the waiter a tip. "I have to get some ice," he said to Peacock. "There's an ice machine at the end of the hall."

"Ice!" the professor bellowed. "I don't need ice! Philistine!"

Under the professor's eagle eye, the waiter lifted the wine bottle to pour the wine into the goblet. Peacock held out a restraining hand. "For goodness' sake, you can't put a good wine into that … that … thing. Heaven knows what it's made of and what it will do to the bouquet. Marcus, do you have another glass?"

"Yeah, sure," said Ryan. "But it's just a water glass."

"So long as it's glass," said Peacock.

Ryan held the glass out to the waiter, who poured a generous measure of wine that he then handed to the professor.

"Let me look at the goblet again," Ryan said to the waiter. "I want to see what it's made of."

"No, really, it's okay," said the waiter, setting the goblet on the cart and preparing to leave.

Peacock took a sip of the wine. "If it's just some cheap metal," he said to the waiter, "you'll have everyone in the restaurant sending back their wine."

"Not in Vegas," Ryan said. "Not everyone's a connoisseur."

"I'll tell the restaurant manager," the waiter said. He sounded more angry than anxious and was making small movements toward the door.

Ryan reached over, lifted the goblet from the cart, and carried it to the window. After the first judicious sip of the wine, Peacock was taking hearty swallows and seemed to be really relaxing into the chair. Ryan assumed that he was very tired from his journey.

He tried to concentrate on the object in his hands, but his mind was full of questions. He really didn't know where to begin or how to assess the professor's outrageous claim to have found the fabled Excalibur. He put his hand in his pocket and touched the twist of paper, feeling the hard outlines of the stone. Much against his better judgment, he knew he would have to find out more. Given the strangeness of the dull red stone and the certainty of Peacock's own conclusions, he would have to do something.

"Sir," said the waiter anxiously, "you need to give me the goblet."

"Yeah, sure." Ryan turned from the window and reined in his wandering thoughts. He noticed that Peacock held the water glass but he was no longer drinking. He seemed to be struggling to breathe. Ryan fell on one knee beside the chair, dropping the goblet into the professor's lap as he reached forward to loosen the old man's tie.

"Sir," said the waiter, hovering in the doorway.

"Get help," Ryan said.

"Just give me the goblet."

"To hell with the goblet. Call down to the front desk, get an ambulance."

Peacock drew in a strangled breath and dropped the water glass. The wine spilled across his lap and spread in a red stain across the floor. His eyes were fixed on the goblet that lay in his lap. He lifted it in both shaking hands. "It's not a fake," he murmured. "Early Saxon."

"Forget about it," Ryan said, lifting Peacock's chin and seeing that his face was waxy white and that he was gasping for breath. Behind him he heard a faint click and turned in time to see the door closing behind the waiter.

"Hey," Ryan shouted, "get back in here."

Peacock drew in another strangled breath, and his body began to convulse. The goblet slipped from his lap to the floor.

"I'll get you an ambulance," Ryan said. "Just hang on."

But Peacock could not hang on. His hold on life slipped away. Even as Ryan lifted the phone to call in the emergency, the professor stopped breathing.

The One-Eyed Man
McCarran Airport, Las Vegas

The one-eyed man sprinted through the airport. He had wasted precious time at the baggage check-in. Of course, he should have known sharp objects such as jeweled daggers would not be permitted in his carry-on. He should have known, but in the excitement of the moment, it had slipped his mind. Travel by air, although very efficient for long distance, was not as simple as stepping through a gate. But that was an unfortunate fact of life. There were no gates in the Americas, how could there be?

His lingering elation at the successful completion of his mission was somewhat mitigated by the indignity of airport security. Why did they have to look beneath his eye patch? Surely they should have understood that the bearer of such a wound would not want to reveal it to anyone. Oh, how shocked they had been to see the extent of the damage. I told you not to look, he thought. The young pretty one had been especially shocked at the scarring. That's what it looks like, he wanted to say, when you have your eye gouged out in a world where there are no antibiotics, no plastic surgeons, no ambulances, and no laws. Don't worry about it pretty young woman, I had my revenge, very much more than an eye for an eye.

He made certain his eye patch was firmly in place as he joined the shuffling line of passengers boarding the London flight..

CHAPTER TWO

Marcus Ryan

Ryan was not surprised to find that Michael Mandretti was well acquainted with the Las Vegas Metropolitan Police Department. Obviously, Mandretti and the police understood each other's needs. Mandretti needed to keep his hotel running smoothly, and the police needed to deal quickly and quietly with the suspicious death of a foreign tourist. Within an extremely short space of time, the mortal remains of Taras Quentin Peacock had been examined, photographed, zipped into a plastic body bag, and sent to the morgue, without any interruption to the river of money flowing into the casino.

Ryan's own meager possessions were bundled up by a couple of chambermaids and removed to a vacant room on the seventeenth floor while a cleaning crew arrived to tackle the stains on the carpet.

Ensconced in his new room, Ryan was allowed twenty minutes to shower and shave before he was summoned into the "presence."

It seemed to Ryan that the executive offices of the Mandretti occupied about an acre of prime real estate on the ground floor. He made his way through the vast lobby of the hotel, which rang with the beeping and buzzing of thousands of slot machines. The décor echoed the intrepid explorer theme, with ruined temples, fallen statues, and a fifty-foot-high waterfall. The entrance to the executive suite was concealed within a cave-like opening, but once through the doors, any illusion of ancient architecture was instantly banished. The hub of the Mandretti organization was all twenty-first-century efficiency, with the coming and going of men in suits and beautiful young women in power dresses.

Ryan found Mandretti alone behind his massive desk and waded across the carpet to sit in the white leather guest chair that Mandretti indicated with a wave of a manicured hand.

Michael Mandretti was a young man, or at least a man of Ryan's own age, and Ryan still liked to think of himself as young. He had the dark hair and dark eyes Ryan expected from anyone whose last name sounded so specifically Italian, but there was a certain unexpected sympathy and warmth in the way he rose from his seat and patted Ryan's shoulder as Ryan sank into the chair.

"I'm sorry," Mandretti said. "He was an old friend, huh?"

Mandretti's accent betrayed his youth somewhere in New York City, Brooklyn, Bronx, Queens; Ryan had never been able to tell the difference. All he knew was that Mandretti sounded like an average New York gangster from central casting, but his eyes told Ryan that he was far from average.

"He was my professor at Harvard," Ryan said.

"Your … er … mentor?"

Ryan wasn't sure if the question related to his relationship with Peacock or the correct use of the word mentor. Lately Mandretti had been trying to improve his vocabulary and fill in the many gaps in his education, and Ryan had become his unwilling tutor.

"Would you like a drink, Doctor?" Mandretti liked to address Ryan as "doctor." He seemed far more impressed by Ryan's title than Ryan was himself.

"No," Ryan said.

Mandretti returned to his seat. "My guess is poison," he said.

Ryan nodded his head. It was hardly an impressive guess, particularly in the absence of bullet holes, knife wounds, or other glaring evidence to the contrary.

"In the wine," Ryan said, "brought up by room service. Have the police talked to the waiter?"

Mandretti shook his head. "That wasn't one of our waiters."

"No, I suppose not."

Ryan waited.

"Our waiter, the one who should have brought you the wine, was found in the wine cellar," Mandretti said.

"Dead?" asked Ryan.

"Alive. Trussed up like a pig but still alive. He didn't know nothing."

"Neither do I," Ryan said. "I don't have anything else useful to tell you."

"Don't you?" Mandretti looked him in the eye, and Ryan could swear that he grew bigger. He was an average-sized man in a well-cut suit, no enormous gangster shoulder pads, no huge muscled neck, but when his eyes met Ryan's, Ryan felt his strength.

"Professor Peacock wrote me a letter," Mandretti said, "a genuine old-fashioned letter, pen, paper, stamp. Don't get them very often. He said he had something to offer me, something of great value, and he said you would vouch for him."

"I don't think I can do that," Ryan said.

"He said you would."

"That's before I knew what he thought he had."

Mandretti nodded his head. "So he did have something, Doctor?"

"No," Ryan insisted, "he didn't have anything. He had a wild idea, that's all."

Mandretti pulled a letter from a drawer and laid it on the pristine oak surface of his desk. Ryan recognized Peacock's flowing handwriting and distinctive turquoise ink. Mandretti made no pretense of reading fluently, and Ryan concluded that he was probably not used to reading cursive writing. No doubt his world was all e-mails and text messages. He stumbled through the words, tracing a path with his forefinger.

"'The treasure I can offer you is one of such great notoriety and such fame that owning it will make you the greatest collector of all time. In the history of Europe, maybe even the world, there has never been such a treasure, and it can be yours.'"

Mandretti looked up from his reading. "What did he find?" he asked.

"He didn't find anything."

Mandretti stared at him for a long moment, and Ryan found himself hurrying to explain. "Professor Peacock was a very entertaining man, a great teacher, but very, well, flamboyant."

Mandretti raised a questioning eyebrow, and Ryan reminded himself not to use three syllable words.

"He was a show-off. He'd do anything to get our attention and keep our interest. That's all he was doing in that letter, Mr. Mandretti. He was showing off."

Mandretti looked at the letter. "Your friend wasn't rich," he said.

Ryan shrugged his shoulders. "I don't know."

"I do," said Mandretti. "When a man writes me a letter like this, I look into it. I look into him. He didn't have no money. He didn't have no money, and he had a pile of debts. So this man with no money and lots of debt buys himself a ticket to come and see me."

"I thought that you—"

"I invited him; I didn't pay for him," Mandretti said. "That's a lot of money he spent just to show off."

He looked at Ryan for a long moment, and Ryan felt his blood temperature drop.

"So what did he find?" Mandretti asked.

"A sword."

Mandretti snorted contemptuously. "We got swords."

"We got lots of swords," Ryan confirmed, abandoning his usual grammatical care. "This was a king's sword."

"Ah, I see. King what? King who? King of where?"

"King of England."

"Nah," Mandretti said. "Them English royals don't go around losing their swords. Prince Charlie and Prince Willy, I bet they know where their swords are."

"It was a long time ago," Ryan said. "It's just a myth. There are people who choose to believe in King Arthur—"

Mandretti leaped to his feet. "Excaliver," he shouted.

"Excalibur," Ryan corrected.

"Whatever." Mandretti's eyes were bright with delight. "Excaliver," he said again.

Ryan let it ride.

"Jeez," Mandretti said. "The Excalibur Hotel, just down the road."

"I know it," Ryan said. He could see the place from his bedroom window. It was a somewhat shabby Disney-like confection of towers and moats with not even an attempt at historical accuracy, an attraction whose time was long past.

"If I had the sword, I could put them out of business," Mandretti said.

Ryan considered telling him that he could probably buy them out of business if he sold just a handful of the treasures he was keeping in his vault.

"I saw the movie, you know," Mandretti said. "Excalibur, the movie. Yeah, I saw it when I was a kid. Knights in armor, and the queen sleeps with her husband's best friend. He throws the sword in the lake."

"I've seen it," Ryan said.

Mandretti was round in front of his desk now, pacing so excitedly that his polished Oxfords were barely touching the upper levels of the carpet.

"The stuff they did with their armor on," he said. "You're the historian, Doctor; can a guy really do that in armor? I mean, wouldn't the woman get real squashed?" He waved a hand and laughed at himself. "Don't answer that. But I always wondered. I always wondered."

He perched himself on a corner of the desk. "Jeez," he said, "Excaliver." He shook his head and grinned at Ryan. "I know, I know, it's Excalibur, but when I was a kid that's what I used to say while I was running around with a stick in my hand. So he found Excalibur?"

"Excalibur doesn't exist," Ryan said. "Arthur never existed and neither did his sword."

"You sure?"

"Quite sure. King Arthur was an invention of medieval poets. There is no evidence that he was ever a real person. People made him up because they needed a hero. It's a beautiful story but it's not true."

Mandretti looked at him. The fire was still in his eyes. "This ain't really your area, is it, Doctor? I mean, you ain't no advanced English history expert, right?"

"Well, no."

"That's okay." He patted Ryan on the shoulder. "You do just fine for what I want. You're the best. That's why I hired you, but you ain't no English history expert. Now this Professor Peacock, he was the best at his game, right?"

"He was good," Ryan said.

"And he was from Oxford," Mandretti said. "That's one of the oldest universities in the world, ain't it?"

Ryan nodded.

"And it's in England," Mandretti added. "He has to know more about what's going on there than you do. Stands to reason."

"Nothing's going on," Ryan said.

"Then why is he dead?"

Ryan closed his mouth. Everything he had planned to say disappeared from his mind.

"Someone believed him and someone tossed his room," Mandretti said. "Went through his suitcase, clothes, everything. You have any idea what they were looking for?"

"He said something about some papers," Ryan admitted.

"Well," said Mandretti, "there ain't no papers now." He rose to his feet and walked around behind the desk. He opened a drawer and pulled out a plastic bag, from which he extracted a replica goblet similar to the one brought in by the waiter with the eye patch, the one Peacock had rejected because it could taint the flavor of the wine. "What do you think?" he asked.

"They're good," Ryan said. "They fooled the professor. Must have cost a bundle."

"They didn't cost me nothing," Mandretti said. "This is the only one, and it doesn't belong to the hotel."

"That's part of the crime scene," Ryan exclaimed. "Why did the police let you keep it?"

"They're finished with it." Mandretti tossed the goblet across the desk, and Ryan caught it clumsily. "I told them you'd be the one to find out where it came from, because it ain't a wine glass from our restaurant."

"The waiter said it was," Ryan protested. He looked carefully at the silver object in his hands. It was about eight inches tall and appeared to be genuine silver, recently cleaned and polished, and with no signs of tarnish.

"That ain't from our restaurant," Mandretti said. "It ain't fancy enough."

Ryan swiped his sleeve across the goblet to remove the light coating of fingerprinting dust. He took his time. "Peacock said it was Saxon," he said eventually. "I think he was right. Possibly from a church." He set it carefully on the desk. "It's old, but not really valuable. With the dissolution of the monasteries under Henry VIII and later under the Puritans, all kinds of church artifacts found their way into household use. It's interesting; probably worth a couple of thousand."

"And they left it behind," Mandretti commented. "Hey, maybe it's to show us they don't care about money. Maybe someone just wanted to make a point. It's very classy, you know; very classy way of doing business. Kind of royal, wouldn't you say?"

"What do the police say?" Ryan asked.

Mandretti dismissed the police with a flick of his wrist. "We ain't waiting for them. I got my own way of doing things."

He pressed the intercom on his desk, and within ten seconds a tall and beautiful young woman in a white blouse and short black skirt was at his side. Mandretti barely glanced at her, and Ryan was too distracted to take much interest in her as she swayed across the room, clasping an iPad to her bosom.

"I'll need the plane," Mandretti said. "File a flight plan to Key West. We'll be ready in an hour."

She nodded, smiled, and was already tapping the screen as she left the room.

"Go get packed," Mandretti said to Ryan. "Go, go; get out of here. I gotta make some calls."

"You want me to go to Key West?" Ryan asked.

"That's where you're from, ain't it?"

"I used to have a house in the Keys," Ryan confirmed, "but I'm not exactly welcome there these days. I wasn't planning on going back yet. Are you getting rid of me?"

"I'm coming with you," Mandretti snapped. "Didn't you listen to me? I said 'we.' That's you and me. There's someone we gotta see."

"In Key West?" Ryan asked, feeling stupid.

"That's where she lives. We don't have time to mess around persuading her to come here, so we go to her," Mandretti said.

"Mr. Mandretti," said Ryan, "who are you talking about? I know every treasure hunter in the business, and not one of them lives in Key West."

"I don't need no treasure hunter," said Mandretti. "I got you and you're good, Doc, I'll give you that, but this woman is different. My brother told me about her. He was doing some business, you know, in the Keys, and he lost something, and this woman found it for him. He says it's like voodoo."

"Voodoo?" said Ryan.

Mandretti warded off Ryan's protest by picking up the phone. "I talked to her already, told her we was coming. Go pack your stuff. Bring that network jacket you used to wear."

"That was years ago," Ryan protested.

"Bring it. I don't know nothing about this woman, but most people are impressed by your connections."

Ryan backed away across the acres of carpet, but before he reached the door, Mandretti raised a hand to stop him. "The police want to talk to you, seeing as how you're the only witness."

"Not really. The waiter saw everything."

"Yeah, well," said Mandretti, "that guy ain't gonna tell us nothing. He's long gone."

"I suppose so," said Ryan. "I wonder if the eye patch was real. Well, obviously it was real, but I mean, I wonder if he really had a fake eye or if he—"

Mandretti raised a hand to silence him. Ryan knew he was babbling, but somehow he was unable to stop himself. Events were moving too fast. He was a historian accustomed to sifting through the slow accumulation of centuries.

"It's not a good idea to give a waiter an eye patch," he babbled. "You know, depth perception and—"

Mandretti raised his hand again. Ryan lapsed into silence, and in the silence, he replayed the sound of Peacock's last shuddering breaths.

"Talk to the police," Mandretti said, "and then call the next of kin."

"Me? Why me?"

"You knew him, and it's kinder than getting a call from some 'don't care' Las Vegas cop telling you your dearly beloved has departed. You know how it is."

No, I don't know, Ryan thought, but I'm sure the Mandretti clan is used to getting that kind of calls.

Taras Peacock's next of kin as listed in his passport was Crispin Peacock with a London telephone number. Not surprisingly, he was not available to answer the telephone at two in the morning, London time. Ryan recorded a message delivering the bad news along with his own phone number and the phone number of the Las Vegas police. At the prompting of the detective working the case, he added that an autopsy would be necessary before the remains could be returned to England for burial.

He knew that his message sounded cold and impersonal, and he wondered what kind of relationship Taras had with Crispin. Was Crispin a brother or a cousin? Could he be a son that Taras had never mentioned? There was no way of knowing. Would someone weep? Ryan wondered. Would someone care?

He returned to the hotel, packed a bag, and included his old network blazer. When the bag was packed and the last of the Jack Daniel's was gone, he made a call to his ex-wife, Veronica, on Marathon Key.

"Hi."

"Marcus?"

"Yeah."

"What do you want?"

The passion, Ryan reflected, had truly gone out of their relationship.

"I'll be in Key West tomorrow," he said. "I'd like to see the girls."

"I don't think it's a good idea."

"I haven't seen them in months," he protested.

"More like years," she countered.

Years, he thought, had it really been years?

"They're settled Marcus. They're used to Erik now. They don't need to see you. You'll just confuse them."

He wondered how he had ever loved this woman, or how he had ever imagined that he could spend the rest of his life with her in that pretty little house in the Keys. But then he thought about his daughters. Surely he was entitled to see his own daughters.

"Just for an hour," he said.

"Alright," she said grudgingly, "but don't even suggest taking them out to eat. They're both on a new diet."

"I eat healthy," he lied. "I even stopped eating meat."

"We're only eating vegetables," his ex-wife informed him.

"For heaven's sake," he snapped. "You'll starve them to death."

"Don't be ridiculous," she snapped back. "They're teenaged girls; they're very body conscious. Do you want to see them or not?"

"Of course I do."

"One hour. At the house."

"Okay." He felt like a whipped puppy and decided that he might as well whine a little. "Taras Peacock died."

"Oh no. Oh, I'm sorry." Suddenly she was Veronica again; the woman he had loved and who had lived with him and loved with him all the way through four different colleges and two changes of major.

"How did it happen?"

He told her.

She was silent for a moment, and then she said, "How do you know they meant to poison Peacock? How do you know it wasn't meant for you?"

With that comforting thought in the back of his mind, Ryan walked out into the cool of the desert night and climbed into the back of Michael Mandretti's stretch limo for the ride to the airport.

Mandretti's personal Gulfstream taxied out onto the runway and rose smoothly into the star-studded desert sky. Hours later it dropped out of the clouds and began a long descent following the necklace of tiny islands leading from the mainland to Key West. Mandretti had slept for the entire flight and only awoke when the cabin attendant came back to tell him to fasten his seat belt for landing. Ryan had flown in the Mandretti corporate jet before and had previously succeeded in sleeping in its comfortable seats, but sleep eluded him now. Whenever he closed his eyes, he saw the red wine spilling across the white carpet. The image seemed to have burned itself into the inside of his eyelids. He was happy to replace it with a view of the white-sand beaches and turquoise seas of his home state.

"Did you call ahead like I asked?" Mandretti asked the attendant.

She nodded her elegant blond head. "Yes, Mr. Mandretti."

"And she's expecting us?"

"I think so," said the attendant, "but she sounded a little confused. I reminded her again that she had provided services to your brother and that you called her last night. She asked me why you had to come so early in the morning. She said she needed more time to prepare."

"She's had all night to prepare," said Mandretti. "Either she knows where the sword is, or she don't know."

"Perhaps she has to get a chicken," said Ryan.

"Chicken?" said Mandretti. "We don't want no chicken dinner."

"For the voodoo," said Ryan.

Mandretti shot him a dark, angry glance. "This is serious business. Don't you be making fun of her. If my brother says she's okay, then she's okay."

"Of course," said Ryan, hating himself for the fact that he had become no more than Mandretti's hired lackey.

Mandretti smoothed his short hair and ran his hand across his stubbly chin. "They got a shower in the terminal?" he asked.

The blond nodded her head again. "For the pilots," she said.

"Good."

Mandretti looked at Ryan. Ryan smoothed his hair.

"You look like a bum," Mandretti said.

"I had a rough night."

"We gonna shower," Mandretti said, "and you can put on that jacket I told you to bring, and we're gonna make a good impression on this dame."

The plane made a smooth landing and taxied toward the private aviation hangar.

"So you've never met her?" Ryan asked.

"If my brother says she's good, she's good," Mandretti replied.

"I just wondered what her name was," Ryan said mildly. "I'm from the Keys myself, so I thought I might have heard of her."

"Violet Chambray."

Ryan shuffled through his memories of Key West. "No, I've never heard of her. Of course, that might not be her real name. It sounds like a made-up name."

"Leave it alone," said Mandretti. "She might not be no Harvard professor, TV star, but we're gonna give this a try. If she can find Excaliver I don't care what her name is." He unfastened his seat belt and pulled himself to his feet. He looked at Ryan with a cold, calculating expression. "We gonna keep her waiting a few more minutes," he said, "but we ain't gonna let her know that. We're gonna keep her guessing; let her know the show."

Ryan and Mandretti made their way into the terminal. They showered quickly, and Mandretti emerged looking immaculate in an off-white seersucker suit and a pastel tie. Ryan wore gray slacks and his old network blazer as instructed. A taxi idled outside the terminal waiting to take them downtown.

Ryan rode through the familiar streets of the old town and noted how the gentle breeze from the southeast lifted the leaves of the palm trees and ruffled the waters of the harbor. A cruise ship hovered on the horizon, waiting for the tide to turn so it could come into port and discharge its cargo of shop-happy tourists. On Duval Street the vendors and shopkeepers were coming sleepily to life, and a garbage truck clattered along removing the evidence of the previous night's revels. He breathed deeply. He was home.

Three blocks from Duval Street, within sight of the Havana Dock, the cab came to a halt in front of a turn-of-the-century house. The building was one of the few remaining jewels of Conch architecture, and Ryan knew it must have cost a fortune. Although the house was virtually hidden from the street by a mass of tropical foliage, he caught glimpses of three screened porches, one facing the Gulf, one facing the Atlantic, and the other one overlooking the town, all painted in bright Bahamian blue.

Mandretti paid off the driver, and they entered along a narrow path through a jungle of bougainvillea and hibiscus. Three shallow steps led them to a front door flanked by Tiffany glass windows. Ryan automatically assessed the condition of the windows; obviously genuine, but in need of cleaning and restoration. The whole house spoke to him of neglect, an architectural jewel rotting in the Florida sun.

"Nice change from Vegas," Mandretti said, ringing the doorbell and looking around at the gardens, "but too damned hot."

The sun had burned through the clouds, and the air was beginning to steam. They were heading into an average Florida day.

"It'll be cool inside," Ryan said. "These old houses were designed to catch the trade winds."

"No air conditioning?" Mandretti asked.

"I doubt it. Real Conchs don't need air conditioning."

A dark-haired young maid in a black-and-white uniform opened the door.

"We're here to see Miss Chambray," Mandretti said, shouldering his way forward.

The maid held her place in the doorway. "She is not here," she said in halting English.

"Yes, she is," said Mandretti.

"No," said the maid. "She is not in the house. She will see you in the garden. You come, I will show you."

Ryan looked longingly into the cool interior of the house. He could see a black-and-white tile floor, a ceiling fan, and a series of louvered doors leading off the central hallway. Why, he wondered, would Violet Chambray be in the garden when she could be in the breezy interior of her house?

"You come," said the maid, stepping off the porch and leading them along a graveled walkway between massive stands of fountain grass and bamboo.

They emerged onto a tiny space of recently mowed lawn. Ryan breathed in the aroma of freshly cut grass. A screened gazebo trimmed in gleaming white latticework stood in the center of the lawn. The maid indicated that they should go into the gazebo and seat themselves on the white wicker patio furniture.

"She will join you shortly," the maid said, placing the emphasis on "she" as though it was a royal title. She bent her knees in a small curtsey and departed.

Mandretti dropped down into one of the chairs. His face was red beneath the Vegas tan, and sweat stains were appearing on his seersucker suit. "How can anyone live here?" he asked.

"You get used to it," Ryan said.

"Yeah, well, give me the desert any day."

And that's what she's counting on, Ryan thought. Violet Chambray, whoever she was, had managed to turn the tables on Mandretti. He had kept her waiting, and now she was keeping him waiting, and doing so in the heat and humidity of a Florida garden. Obviously, she was a force to be reckoned with.

"So, how did your brother know about her?" Ryan asked. "She doesn't exactly have a sign on the door?"

"He asked around," said Mandretti. "It was a personal thing. He'd been out on the town, taken off his wedding ring, you know how it is …"

"Sure," said Ryan, imagining Mandretti's brother enjoying some extracurricular activity in the nightclubs on Duval Street, his wedding ring tucked into his pocket.

"So she found it," Mandretti said. "Saved his marriage. Sit down, Doc, you gotta learn to relax."

Ryan looked toward the house and saw that someone was approaching. He allowed his hand to rest on the lattice for a moment and then snatched it away.

"Wet paint," he said.

"What?" said Mandretti.

"So sorry about that," said a husky voice behind Ryan's right shoulder.

He turned his head and found himself looking at a slightly built, handsome man in his late twenties or early thirties. He was dressed in pressed white pants, a crisp blue blazer, a white shirt, and a striped Ascot. The man inclined his head in a gracious half bow. "I'm Todd," he said. "I choose not to use my last name. Miss Chambray will join you in a moment. Please be careful of the paint."

Todd retreated toward the house and then stopped by the French windows, his hand placed on his hip. "She is coming now," he said with a sweeping gesture toward the house.

Ryan felt as though they were playing a scene from a Noel Coward play. In fact, everything he had seen so far had an air of theatricality; the stereotypical Hispanic maid, the strange posturing of Todd-who-chose-not-to-use-his-last-name, the wet paint on the gazebo, even the tiny expanse of newly mown lawn. And why, he wondered, were they being kept in the heat of the gazebo rather than the cool of the house?

The doors opened and Violet Chambray emerged. Ryan studied her as she crossed the lawn to greet them. He didn't know what he had expected, but certainly he had not expected this. For years, he had been dividing his time between television stations and high-visibility treasure locations. In both these areas, the women were lean and tanned and quite muscular, and they were nothing like the woman who was now approaching.

Violet Chambray's skin was so pale as to be almost white, and she was very far from being lean and muscular. The blue suit she wore was obviously expensive and designed to flatter a figure that was not now, and probably never had been, svelte. Her wrists and ankles were small and slender, the wrists accented by a series of gold bracelets, the ankles flattered by very high-heeled blue pumps. Her knees and elbows, both displayed by the cut of the suit, were round and dimpled. Her breasts appeared to be more than ample, and her hips were definitely what could be described as generous. When she smiled, dimples appeared on her cheeks. She was younger than he had expected, maybe no more than thirty or thirty-five. He had been mentally prepared to debunk and dismiss a withered crone or a voodoo priestess with a crown of dusty dreadlocks, but he was not ready to face the vibrant young woman, whose curvaceous figure and creamy complexion were causing him to rethink his long-held attraction to sun-bronzed athletic woman.

She made a beeline for Mandretti, who had risen to his feet with a look of astonishment on his face. However she had been described by Mandretti's brother, apparently the description had been inadequate. She was definitely not what Mandretti had been expecting.

"Mr. Mandretti, Doctor Ryan," she said. "Delighted to meet you. Sit down, please."

She turned back toward the house where the maid was approaching, staggering under the weight of a loaded tray. "Don't just stand there," she said to Todd. "Give Maria a hand."

Todd reluctantly took his hand off his hip and relieved Maria of the tray. Together they began to set out an array of utensils and delicacies on the coffee table. A polished silver coffee pot, delicate cups, a plate overloaded with chocolate croissants.

"Todd," said Violet, "would you bring the sherbet?"

"Don't eat all the croissants while I'm gone," Todd said. "Save some for someone else."

Violet raised her penciled eyebrows, and Todd turned away, sauntering back across the lawn toward the house, followed by Maria.

Violet poured the coffee and handed the cups around. Ryan realized that, beyond her first greeting, she had said nothing to them. She had not even looked at them. All of her attention had been on the food, which possibly accounted for her ample curves and dimples.

She sat forward in her chair, her face suddenly serious. "So, Michael, shall we get down to business?"

Mandretti stared at her. Ryan had never seen his boss at a loss for words, but that definitely seemed to be the case.

"I understood that you were in a hurry," Violet said. "We can waste time on the niceties if you wish, but I thought you might like to get down to business."

"Sure," said Mandretti. "That's why we're here."

She sipped her coffee. "Was the victim a friend of yours? Should I offer condolences?"

"No," said Mandretti. "Friend of the doc's."

She turned her eyes on Ryan. They were large and violet. "I'm so sorry," she said in a unique accent that he struggled to identify. American, quite definitely American, but quite unlike anything he had heard before.

She turned back to Mandretti, and her eyes were hard and businesslike. "But I'm doing business with you, Michael, is that correct?"

"Sure," Mandretti said. He had overcome his initial shock and was back to his normal self. "Same rate as my brother?" he asked.

Violet shook her head, and her dark curls swung easily on her shoulders. She smiled, displaying even white teeth. "From what little you told me on the phone, I think I would prefer a percentage. Fifteen percent."

Mandretti looked up at her from under his hooded eyelids. She looked straight back at him. He opened his mouth to speak, and she silenced him with a wave of her plump little hand.

"Michael, Michael, please don't bother with any of your mafioso haggling. If you want my services, you'll pay for them. You're free to find someone else, if you think you can."

Mandretti shrugged his shoulders. "If you find it, I'll pay," he said, "and if you don't, then you don't get nothing."

"Good."

Violet turned to Ryan. "I understand your friend's name was Taras Quentin Peacock, Professor of Medieval History, Oxford, occasionally Harvard, and most recently Visiting Professor at the University of the Witwatersrand in South Africa."

"I didn't know that," Ryan said. "I didn't know he'd been teaching in South Africa. I thought he'd retired."

"That was before he retired," Violet said. "Todd ferreted around. He's very good on the internet. The professor had a fine reputation. Do you have any theories, Doctor, as to who has done this, and why?"

"No, of course I don't," Ryan said. "I hadn't spoken to him in years, and he really didn't tell me anything in the time we had. If I knew anything, I would have told the police."

"He knows more than he's telling," Mandretti interrupted. "And he ain't told the police everything. He's frightened they'd think he was a loony. Just get on with it, Doc. I don't really care who done it, I just want what he found."

Violet sat back in her chair and smiled somewhat patronizingly at Mandretti. "Oh, Michael," she said, "you're so direct. No beating about the bush, no pretense that you even care who poisoned Doctor Ryan's friend."

"I want the sword," said Mandretti. "Find me the sword, and you get your fifteen percent."

"There is no sword," Ryan said. "Let's put an end to this right now. There is no sword. There has never been a sword. The whole thing is a fairy tale."

"Oh no," Violet said. "It's not a fairy tale. Make no mistake about it, there is a ring of truth to all of this."

Ryan set his coffee down and looked her in the eye. He was momentarily distracted by the luminous violet coloring of her eyes, and the passing thought that her astonishing eyes, along with her excellent presentation of her other assets, could go a long way toward ensnaring an unwary man.

He looked away from her hypnotic gaze. "Bullshit," he said.

"Now that's no way to speak to a lady," said Todd, who was ascending the steps of the gazebo, clasping a sheaf of papers and an iPad to his chest. He was followed by Maria the maid, carrying a tray of Key lime sherbets. The maid set the tray down, bobbed a curtsey, and departed.

Todd sat beside Ryan on the wicker sofa, patted Ryan's knee, and said,

"She never talks bullshit."

Violet reached forward eagerly for the sherbet and settled back into her chair, clasping a crystal bowl and a silver spoon. "Help yourselves," she said. She slid a spoonful of sherbet between her red lips and sighed contentedly. "Heavenly," she said. She waved the spoon in Ryan's direction. "So according to Michael, your friend thought he'd found King Arthur's sword?"

"That's what he said," Ryan replied.

Violet gestured to Todd. "Tell him what we found out, darling."

Todd flipped through the sheaf of papers and rose to his feet.

"Restrain yourself, dear," Violet said, "and don't dramatize. Save that for the theatre." She smiled and turned to Ryan. "He's appearing in Blithe Spirit at the Rep," she said, "and he's going to knock them dead, aren't you, dear?"

"Quite dead," Todd agreed.

He sat down again and patted Ryan's knee again. Ryan promised himself that if Todd touched him one more time, he would choke him with his own cute little striped Ascot.

"The sword Excalibur," Todd said, reading from a printout, "has two possible origins. The first possibility is that it was set in a stone by Merlin the wizard, and by pulling it out, Arthur became king of England. The second possibility is that it was given to Arthur at a later date by the Lady of the Lake, and it had magic properties that preserved Arthur's life."

"Yeah, that's right," Mandretti said. "This big arm comes up out of a lake, holding the sword, and Arthur grabs it and—"

"No," Ryan said. "No, no, no."

"Don't excite yourself," Violet said, pausing in her rapid demolition of the lime sherbet.

"Listen to yourselves," Ryan said. "I know you want this to be true, but it can't be. How can you believe that a wizard set a sword in a stone? How can you believe it had a spell put on it by a woman who lives under a lake? Think about it. It's all nonsense. It's a folktale. Look, I don't want to blind you with science, but—"

"Oh, please," Violet said, "blind us. Dazzle us with your knowledge."

"There is no possibility that Arthur existed," Ryan said. "There are no early writings to support any of the stories. He appears nowhere in the accounts of even the earliest British kings. The stories we know today didn't even surface until the middle of the twelfth century, written by an obscure scribe named Geoffrey of Monmouth, and those stories were just retellings of a great melting pot of French and Celtic legends, with references to Greek myths, Scandinavian folktales, and some heavy-handed Christian analogies."

"So you don't believe none of it?" Mandretti asked.

"No, I don't. No one has ever come up with a definitive location for Camelot, and believe me, an entire medieval city and castle of the size they describe cannot just disappear without any trace at all. Not one piece of concrete evidence has ever been found that points to the existence of the Round Table or the Isle of Avalon or any other elements of the legend. It's a fairy story, Mr. Mandretti. I don't know what Peacock found, but it wasn't Excalibur."

Violet rattled the silver spoon around in the empty sherbet bowl, scraping up the last possible morsel of sherbet, and then set the bowl back on the table. She sighed deeply and gave Ryan a look of long suffering patience.

"What about the Romans?" she asked. "Go ahead, Todd."

Todd consulted another paper. "Most scholars believe," he said, "that Arthur was a Roman, a remnant of the occupying forces. You are aware, of course, Doctor Ryan, of the Roman occupation of Britain."

"Of course I am," said Ryan.

"Four hundred years of occupation," Todd continued. "Most scholars"—he emphasized the word scholars, as if to imply that Ryan was not a scholar—"agree that many of the Romans remained in Britain. They didn't go back to Rome. So maybe Arthur was a Roman governor with an army, and for a while he held back the incoming barbarians and kept together the remnants of Roman civilization. Maybe he established his own kingdom and kept his small area of Britain at peace. Most scholars think that is possible."

"It's possible," Ryan conceded, "but we have no record of a King Arthur."

"Well, he wouldn't be a king," Violet said, "but he might have appeared that way to his people, don't you think?"

"Possibly," Ryan agreed, grudgingly.

"And if he was such a hero," Violet continued, "then isn't it possible that his sword would have been preserved? And isn't it possible that after many years ignorant peasants might have begun to imagine that the sword had magical properties?"

"Well," Ryan said, "if we discount Merlin, the Lady of the Lake, the Round Table, and the entire city of Camelot, then I suppose we are just looking at a very ordinary Roman sword with no real value."

"No value?" Mandretti interrupted.

"Just a minute," Violet said. "Let's not be hasty about this. Todd's research has led us to a sword that would have great value if it could be found."

"There is no magic sword," Ryan insisted.

"Perhaps not magic," Todd said, "but ancient and valuable and with a history lost in the mists of time."

"Don't be poetic, dear," Violet said. "Doctor Ryan is not looking for poetry."

"Oh, very well," said Todd. "There are a number of contemporary drawings of early English rulers, and also there are written accounts of coronations, and in all those drawings and accounts, there are references to a sword that is said to be the Great Sword of England. It's a primitive weapon, possibly Roman. The best description would be a warrior's broadsword of no obvious value."

He flicked through the sheaf of papers and passed them on to Ryan. "I printed this out, but the resolution was very low. It's a contemporary drawing of the coronation of King Alfred the Great."

"871," Ryan interrupted, determined to look as though he knew something.

"Note the sword," said Todd.

Ryan looked at the engraving and noted the sword.

Todd handed him another sheet. "William the Conqueror," he said.

"1066," Ryan informed him.

"Note the sword," Todd repeated.

Ryan noted the sword.

"A description of the coronation of King Ethelred the Unready," Todd said.

Ryan opened his mouth to speak.

"Don't bother telling us the dates," Violet said. "We're all sufficiently impressed with your knowledge."

No, you're not, Ryan thought. Despite her soft and attractive appearance, this woman's mind was sharp-edged, and she seemed determined to cut him down at every opportunity.

"There is little doubt," Todd said, "that the Great Sword of England formed part of the Crown Jewels up until the reign of King John in 1199. There is no record of it after that date."

Mandretti turned to Violet. "So what happened to it?" he asked.

"She doesn't know," Ryan said. "No one knows."

Mandretti looked admiringly at Violet. "She'll find out."

"How?" Ryan asked. He turned to Violet. "What is it," he asked angrily, "voodoo or psychic waves or just plain guesswork?"

"I'm not going to dignify that with an answer," Violet said. She turned her attention to Mandretti. "Did you bring me something Peacock had touched?"

"Yeah," said Mandretti. He opened the small duffel bag he had carried from the plane and produced the goblet that had so captured the professor's attention that he had used his dying breath to identify it.

Ryan thought about once again protesting the fact that Mandretti was flying around the countryside with important items of police evidence, but then thought better of it. Everything he knew about Mandretti told him that he would not be interested in Ryan's protests. He held the goblet in its plastic evidence bag and then gave Ryan a calculating glance. "So you don't trust her?" he asked.

Ryan shrugged his shoulders. "I don't know how much you told her in advance."

Violet sighed deeply. "I really don't like having to prove myself," she said, "but if you and I are going to work together, Doctor Ryan, then I will do something I don't normally do, and give you a small display of my abilities, although I don't know why I should bother. Michael trusts me, don't you, Michael?"

"I do," said Mandretti.

"Doctor Ryan," said Violet, "you have something in your pocket that was given to you by the professor. Give it to me." She held out a small, imperious hand.

Baffled by her request, Ryan dug deep into his pocket and felt the shape of the little stone that had fallen from the pin. He hesitated. How did she know? Was it a lucky guess? He had told no one that he had it, and he wanted to keep things that way. He wasn't sure why, but he wasn't yet ready to reveal what he held.

"You have something," she repeated.

Keeping his hand deep in his pocket, he unwrapped the pin and brought out the piece of paper that had been wrapped around it. He smoothed it out. It was a scrap of heavy parchment paper, the corner of some larger sheet of paper, with pen strokes scrawled on it. He handed it across to her.

She took it in her fingertips and stared at it for a long time. "What is this?" she said softly. "Where did you get it?"

"It's something Peacock touched," Ryan said. "That's what you asked for."

She stared down at the paper, rubbing it between her fingers, and then held it up to the light to examine the few visible pen strokes. She was breathing heavily, obviously agitated.

Todd looked at her in concern. "Violet?" he asked. "Are you alright?"

"No," she said softly. "I am not alright. I've never held anything like that before."

"It's just a piece of paper," Ryan said.

"It has no history," she said. "It's old but it has no history. I sense the touch of your friend, Peacock, but before that, nothing. There is a barrier. A barrier!" Her voice trailed away. They all sat in silence. "A gate," she said at last. "It's come through a gate, and time stands still."

Ryan looked around at Mandretti and Todd, who continued to stare at her in concern. He had to assume that she was either a great performer or she was genuinely baffled by that little scrap of paper, which she continued to grip in her fingertips.

"A portal," she said, "from another place. This paper has no history here." She shook her head again. "No, I'm wrong. It has history, but I can't read it, because I've never been through the gate."

"What gate?" Ryan asked.

"I don't know." She thrust the paper back into his hand. "I can't tell you anything."

"What gate?" Ryan asked again.

Violet glared at him. "Not now. Not yet."

"You saw something," Mandretti said.

"Yes," said Violet, "but what I saw is impossible. It speaks of something outside of this world, outside of time. Something that cannot be."

She lowered her head, and her blue-black curls fell across her face, hiding her expression. Ryan listened to the rustling of the breeze through the bushes and the distant lonely calling of seabirds. Time seemed to stand still.

Mandretti broke the long silence. "I guess you ain't gonna find it," he said.

"She'll find it," Todd said determinedly. "She needs the money."

"Todd," Violet hissed angrily.

"I'm just speaking the truth," said Todd.

Violet lifted her head and flung back her curls. "He's right, of course. Maintaining this lifestyle does take a great deal of money."

"Forget about the paper," said Todd, who seemed to be stepping far outside his employee status. "Give her the goblet."

Mandretti set the goblet in Violet's lap. Just as she had done with the paper, she touched it with the fingertips of her right hand. This time she smiled and nodded. "This one I understand," she said.

She closed her eyes, and her long dark lashes fanned out against her pale skin. Ryan had time to ponder whether or not they were fake lashes, before she finally leaned back in her chair and sighed.

"Is it coming?" Mandretti asked.

Todd motioned him into silence. Violet sighed again. Ryan raised his cynical eyebrows to the heavens and waited.

CHAPTER THREE

"A cold wind sweeps across the bleak marshes that border the North Sea," said Violet. "The short winter afternoon draws to an end. The sun sets behind leafless stunted trees. It will be dark soon, and there will be no light of human habitation. Not even the lowest peasant would dare to build a hut on the shifting sands of the Wash."

"Where are you, Violet?" Todd asked.

"With the King's baggage train," she said. "This object was with King John's baggage train; with his treasures."

"King John," Ryan said. "1199."

"King John has stolen his brother's crown," Violet said. She opened her eyes and looked around. "I can tell you the story now. King John is the most unpopular king the English have ever known. He is pursued by enemies on all sides. His subjects hover on the brink of starvation, and his rebellious barons have invited the French king to cross the Channel and rid them of their hated ruler."

"You can find this in any history book," Ryan said.

"I see the King," Violet declared. "He has ridden ahead of the baggage train, and he waits at the far end of the marsh. He is impatient. There is a road across the marsh, a causeway of rough-hewn logs skirting the deepest of the sinkholes. The King is anxious. The tide is rising. The sea is lapping at the edges of the road. Why doesn't he ride on? Why doesn't he ride to safety? His enemies are close by. Why is he waiting?"

"Why?" asked Mandretti.

Ryan said nothing although he knew the answer. He was taking Violet's words and filling in the scene for himself as though he was once again making a TV special.

King John was without a stronghold to call his own. He was fleeing across the country, accompanied by all of his personal possessions. Wherever he went on his desperate journeys, he was followed by a long lumbering train of baggage wagons dragged through dust and mud by teams of sweating carthorses. Wagon after wagon would be loaded down with gold and silver plate, tapestries, fine linens, armor, jewelry, and gold to pay the soldiers. Without the gold, the soldiers would desert. The baggage train was the King's only security, and he would never let it out of his sight.

"The sun is setting," Violet said, "in a sullen red ball. The King peers through the gathering gloom. He can barely make out the shape of the wagons, but he can hear the shrieking of the carthorses and the cracking of the drovers' whips, the plunging hooves and the rattle of the harnesses. Torches flare here and there along the causeway, and the King sees the rising water lapping at the logs and reaching for the wagon wheels. He is searching for one wagon, just one wagon from the whole train; the wagon containing the Crown Jewels of England. He sees it far back in the marsh."

Ryan listened to Violet's voice, and his mind continued to fill in the dramatic details. He set the King in motion, fuming and cursing as he rides down to the water's edge and threatens death to any man who abandons his wagon. The men aren't listening. They ignore him. Some of them take pity on the horses and cut the traces. Some of them abandon the horses and run for dry land. The sea sweeps in. The wagons roll onto their sides and sink into the mud. He clothed the King with the dark beard and moustache that he had seen in portraits, and translated John's curses into Norman French, the language of the kings in those times.

"The moon rises over a calm sea," Violet said. "The Wash has recaptured the causeway, and there is no trace of the King's baggage train. It is all gone. Beneath the dark waves, the Crown Jewels sink slowly down into the mud."

She returned the goblet to Mandretti. "This was under the mud," she said. "This was part of the treasure. This was with the sword."

For a moment, Ryan was lost in his own emotions. Despite himself he had been deeply affected by Violet's voice. As she spoke, he had felt himself carried back through time as though he had been there himself on that causeway as the tide rolled in. He felt as though he had personally witnessed the loss of the treasure. He had seen what happened to the Great Sword of England.

"Is that it?" Mandretti asked. "Is that what happened to Excaliver?"

"Excalibur," Ryan corrected automatically.

Violet reached weakly for another bowl of sherbet.

"Is that what happened?" Mandretti asked again. "Is it, Violet? Is it?"

"I think so," Violet said. "My visions are rarely wrong. Sometimes they are hard to understand, but they are never totally wrong."

"So the sword's gone," Mandretti said. "That's what you said, wasn't it? The tide came in and buried everything."

"I assume so," Violet said, "but obviously something else has happened. That goblet was part of the treasure, and it's certainly not under the mud now, is it?"

"No, it isn't," said Mandretti. "What do you think, Doctor?"

Ryan had nothing to say. He was deeply suspicious of Violet Chambray and everything she stood for, but in the hour that they had been at her house, she had provided more mental stimulation than he had felt in years. She had awakened his intellectual curiosity and his old treasure-hunter instincts. Whatever else Violet was, she was the tonic he needed. Against all the odds, he wanted to believe that she could lead him to Professor Peacock's killer. He had no idea how she would do that, but he believed that she would.

"So what will you do next?" he asked her.

Violet sat back in her chair. "I need to think," she said.

"But you've seen something?" Mandretti said. "I mean, all that stuff you just told us about the king and the horses and the mud and the waves. I didn't understand it all, but Doc Ryan did, didn't you, Doc?"

"I recognized the period of history," Ryan said, unwilling to admit how much Violet's description had moved him.

Violet leaned forward to Mandretti. "Michael," she said, "you need to understand that even if we find the Great Sword of England, it's not Excalibur. Excalibur doesn't exist, it has never existed."

"That's not what Peacock said," Mandretti protested.

Violet was silent for a moment. "No, it's not," she said, "and I don't understand it. He was a respected academic. I can't help wondering what he really found."

"Something worth killing for," Ryan said.

"Yes," she agreed. "And then there's the paper."

"Do you want to see it again?" he asked.

She flinched. "No, I can't touch it, not yet. I have never felt anything so alien. I have no way of processing that paper, Doctor. I need time."

Mandretti rose abruptly to his feet. "Well, if you're not going to do it, I guess I have to send Doc Ryan to England on his own."

"What?" said Ryan.

"Yeah," said Mandretti. "The doc here is a famous treasure hunter, and you've given him the start he needed. We can take it from here, Violet. We'll be on our way; just send me a bill for your time."

"Wait a minute," said Todd.

"No, no." Mandretti waved Todd away with his hand. "I understand. She don't want to do it. That's okay, we'll manage."

Ryan eyed his boss. Mandretti's ploy was so obvious that he couldn't believe Violet would fall for it. How greedy was she? How badly did she need the money?

"I have a friend in London who might be able to help us," said Violet.

"So you'll do it?" Mandretti asked.

"I'll take the next step," said Violet. She looked at Ryan. "Do you know Sir Carlton Lewis?"

"I know of him," Ryan said.

"Sounds as though you don't like him."

"He's queried some of my finds," Ryan said.

"Oh, I think he's done more than that. I think you two have been quite bitter rivals; him on the BBC, you on NBC."

"He's the one with the knighthood," said Ryan. "It opens doors."

"Oh yes," she agreed. "Well, we shall see what he has to say about all of this. He's a very well-respected author, historical novels and all that sort of thing, so I imagine that he has a more open mind than some people."

Ryan allowed the insult to pass without comment.

"He's also a member of the Society of Arthurian Scholars," she said. "It's a scholarly society and very well respected. Their main emphasis is on cataloging and preserving the writings on the Arthurian legends."

Ryan did not admit that he had never heard of this well-respected scholarly society and that he was amazed that Violet knew of their existence.

"Todd, dear," Violet said, "will you send Carlton one of those e-mail thingies. What time is it in London?"

Todd flicked back his shirt cuff and looked at his watch. "Ten o'clock here, so, 3 p.m. in London. Do you really want to—?"

"Yes, I do," said Violet.

"Should I remind him where you—?"

"He won't need to be reminded," said Violet. "Really, Todd, don't be so silly. Carlton and I have a very close relationship. Very close indeed. Of course, he may be at lunch, so we may have to wait for a reply. Carlton doesn't like to be disturbed at lunch. Ask him if there's been any unusual activity or if he's heard any rumors. He may be able to tell us what Professor Peacock was involved with before he came to see Michael. You know what to say, don't you?"

Todd sauntered out of the gazebo, and Violet stood up and smoothed down her skirt. "I'm really quite tired," she said. "I think I'll go and lie down. Make yourselves at home." She moved languidly to the steps, trailing clouds of expensive perfume. "Maria will make sure you have everything you need." She turned at the top of the steps. "If you would like to visit your wife in Marathon, Doctor Ryan, you are welcome to call a taxi from here."

"Ex-wife," Ryan said.

"Oh yes," she said. "She's remarried, hasn't she?"

"I don't think that's any of your—"

Mandretti silenced him with one intense look from his hooded eyes. Violet drifted away across the lawn and into the house, and Ryan stood staring at her, hating her and admiring her all at the same time.

Todd sauntered back across the lawn. "I'll show you to the library," he said, "and you can call your ex-wife from there. We don't get a good signal out here in the garden. This way. I understand you have daughters," he added conversationally as they crossed the lawn, "and one of them is getting married."

"What?" It was the first time Ryan had heard of this proposed marriage. Had he really lost track of so much time? Leanne, his elder daughter, was … He paused to work it out and realized that Leanne was nineteen already, and her sister was eighteen. How long was it since he'd seen them? He didn't really know.

Todd led them through the French windows into the cool interior of the house, where he flung open the door of an adjacent room. As soon as Ryan stepped into the room, his cell phone beeped. He looked at the message. Veronica had called. In fact, she had called five times in the last ten minutes. This was not, he thought, going to be a fun visit.

The library was a small room flooded with light. Instead of the dark paneling and leather-bound chairs of most libraries, this room was lined with limed oak shelving, and the library table was glass, as was the desk that housed a computer and printer as well as a telephone.

"Make yourself at home," Todd said, "but we would appreciate you staying in this room. Violet doesn't like to be disturbed when she's working."

He left the room, closing the door firmly behind him as if to emphasize his last instruction.

Mandretti settled down in one of the chintz-covered library chairs. "You don't believe her, do you?" he said.

"I don't believe in visions," Ryan replied. "I believe in things I can touch and feel. Everything I've brought you so far has been genuine, hasn't it? Everything has a provenance. I'm protecting your reputation, Mr. Mandretti. I can't authenticate dreams and visions and fairy tales."

"She's done pretty well out of dreams and visions and fairy tales," Mandretti said, looking around the room.

"I don't know," said Ryan. "There's something strange about this house. What's with the wet paint and telling us not to leave this room?"

"She seems to know more than you do," said Mandretti. "She managed to make you look like a fool."

Before Ryan could reply, his phone buzzed again. Veronica. As soon as he answered, she lit into him.

"What the hell have you got us into?"

"I'm coming," said Ryan. "I'm a tad later than I said, but I'm coming."

"Don't come near here. Don't you dare."

"What?"

"Don't come near us," she repeated. "Whatever trouble you're in, don't bring it to this house."

"I'm not in trouble," he protested.

"Yeah, well," she said. "What's all this about a goblet?"

His stomach seemed to be doing backflips while his heart rose in his throat. He was unable to speak.

"A thug." Veronica's voice came to him from great distance. "He looks like a hired thug. Hardly speaks any English. All he can say is he wants the goblet, whatever that is."

Ryan was stunned into silence.

"A goblet, Marcus. A man's been here looking for a goblet; says he's been sent by the one-eyed man, whatever that means."

Ryan struggled to find words. "Veronica," he managed to stutter, "I'm sorry."

"Oh, don't be sorry," she hissed. "Just do something about it before I call the police. I'm assuming you don't want me to call the police. What did you do? Did you steal the darned thing?"

"No," he said. "I don't steal. You know better than that."

"I don't know anything about you. You haven't shown your face here in the last five years. The girls have forgotten you even exist."

"Is Leanne getting married?" Ryan asked.

"No. It's Abby."

"But she's—"

"Old enough to get married. They're grown up, Marcus, and Erik is their father now. So don't come here. Stay where you are, and find a way to do something about that man. I swear that if he hurts my daughters, Erik will hunt him down and—"

"No," Ryan said. "Don't involve Erik in this. You don't know what you're getting into. Can you hold on just for a minute? Hold on, please."

"Just for a minute," she said.

He turned to Mandretti.

"Wife trouble?" Mandretti asked.

"A man hanging around her house and asking her to give him the goblet; says he's been sent by the one-eyed man."

"Ah." Mandretti pulled out his cell phone. "Give me the address."

Ryan gave him the address and turned back to speak into his own phone.

"Veronica, are you still there?"

"I'm here. Where else do you expect me to be?"

"I'm getting you some protection."

"What's that supposed to mean?"

He thought about it for a moment. "Large men in black cars," he said eventually.

"What?"

Mandretti looked up from his mumbled phone conversation. "Ten minutes," he said.

"They'll be with you in ten minutes," Ryan told her. "And believe me, they'll look after you."

"Is that what it's come to?" she asked. "Is that what Vegas has done to you? Large men in black cars?"

"Veronica," he said, "I'm serious about this. I have something that they want, but it's me they want, not you, but they could use you or the girls to get at me. If you don't believe anything else I'm saying, please believe that these men I'm sending will protect you."

He looked at Mandretti. "They're on their way," Mandretti said. "They'll take care of it. Does your wife speak Spanish?"

"I thought it would be Italian."

"It's Florida," Mandretti said with an eloquent shrug of his shoulders.

"Large Spanish-speaking men," Ryan said to Veronica.

She was silent for a moment.

"Veronica?"

"I'm scared," she said in a small voice.

"Do you want me to come there?" he asked. "I have what they want. I'll give it to them."

He heard and ignored Mandretti's hiss of disapproval.

"No," she said vehemently. "Don't come near us again."

The phone was dead in his hands.

"Are your men any good?" he asked Mandretti.

"Oh yeah," Mandretti said with supreme confidence. "No problemo. But I think I'd better get some protection for this house as well. If they don't find you or the goblet in Marathon, they're gonna come here."

Todd appeared in the doorway, or perhaps, Ryan thought, he had been standing there all the time.

"We have our own protection," Todd said. "We try to avoid large men in black cars." He looked at Mandretti. "I have printed out a contract. You and I should agree on the terms while Violet makes her final decision."

Mandretti rose from the chair.

"Mr. Mandretti," Ryan said, "will you—?"

He nodded his head. "If I hear anything, I'll let you know. Now quit worrying. My people are good. Nothing's gonna happen to your kids, and they ain't gonna let anyone hurt your ex. Unless you want them to," he added.

"No. God, no!"

"Just joking with you," he said, and he followed Todd out of the room.

The weight of the night before hung heavily on Ryan's shoulders. He sat in the library chair and tried to clear his mind, but all he could see was the goblet falling from Peacock's fingers and coming to rest in the midst of the red-wine stain on the carpet. He thought about his children; not children any longer; young women about whom he knew nothing. He thought about Veronica and her righteous anger. She was right to be angry with him. She had married Erik, and Ryan had reacted by giving up responsibility for his own kids. Erik didn't need Ryan's money to raise them, so Ryan stopped paying child support. The girls had been awkward and uncommunicative on the phone, so he had stopped phoning them. He had been traveling to the far corners of the world, and he had forgotten birthdays and Christmases. He had, in fact, abandoned them and allowed them to become Erik's children. And now his latest gift to them was a hired killer and a car full of Spanish mafiosi.

CHAPTER FOUR

The One-Eyed Man
London

The one-eyed man sprinted across the platform at Victoria station and flung himself aboard the London to Brighton commuter train. As the train rattled past the row houses of London's inner city and out into the leafy suburbs of Surrey, he made his way along the swaying train corridors, looking into every compartment. He was late. He should have identified his quarry before the man had boarded the train, but he had taken time on the telephone, talking to his contact in Florida. Now they were in the middle of rush hour. The traffic had been heavy around the airport, and there were no gates to use, just a taxi with an unflappable driver who would not be hurried.

"You should have taken the tube, mate," the driver informed him when he complained yet again about their slow progress through the choking traffic. When the taxi finally came to a halt outside Victoria station, the one-eyed man was tempted to use his dagger. Ending the driver's miserable existence would take but a moment, and he would be inside the station before anyone would know what had happened. He slipped his hand into his coat pocket, enjoying the feel of the metal and the possibility of a small, secret personal revenge. He glanced around and saw them, just as he had been warned, cameras; cameras everywhere, and one aimed directly at him. Things had changed since he was a boy here. How could the people of Britain live that way, he wondered, with cameras watching their every movement? He would have to be careful. His mission was not yet accomplished. He released the dagger and thrust a handful of paper money at the driver, and then he hurried to join the crowds pushing their way into the echoing vastness of the train station.

On board the train, he reached the end of the last corridor without finding his quarry. He had traveled almost the entire length of the train and found no sign of the man. The way ahead was blocked by a locked door separating the everyday commuter from the first-class compartments. Of course, he should have thought of that, the man he was looking for would surely be in first class.

He felt the train slowing for its first stop. A muffled voice announced its arrival, and weary commuters pushed past him, briefcases and umbrellas in hand. He stepped down from the train and moved along the platform and pulled open the door to the first-class compartments. Yes, this was where he would find him, in the cool quietness of padded seats and burnished woodwork.

The train pulled out of the station. The leafy suburbs gave way to open countryside, rolling hills, and a vast sky that held the promise of a cold ocean somewhere just ahead.

Maybe his quarry would give him useful information, and maybe he would not, but he would most certainly die. The one-eyed man reached into his pocket. No, not this dagger, the other one, the one he was going to leave behind just for fun. He wanted to set them a puzzle that could not be solved in their miserable little world of cameras and commuters.

Violet Chambray

Violet flung herself down among the tie-dyed cotton pillows on her bed. She closed her eyes, opened them, closed them again, opened them again, and stared at the familiar damp stains on the ceiling. She tried to concentrate on the idea of using Michael Mandretti's money to fix the roof, and perhaps there would be enough to hire the exterminator they so badly needed.

Last night she had told Todd and Maria that they might be able to pull it off. With a mixture of intuition, careful research, and a good deal of showmanship, she might lead Mandretti to discover an old, long-buried sword. Of course, it would not be Excalibur, because Excalibur had never existed, but it might be something sufficiently ancient and mysterious to satisfy Mandretti's inner romantic. When Todd brought up the possibility of linking together a series of Wikipedia illustrations of early English kings to create the possibility that the Great Sword of England had been in King John's baggage, she knew she had found the bait to catch a big fish.

The search for the sword was not what was troubling her. It was not because of the sword that she was now shut away in her room, frightened to close her eyes in case the feeling swept over her again. The fragment of paper, the one that Ryan had handed to her, terrified her. She had always had the gift, the ability to sense an object's history simply by holding it in her hand and allowing her mind to interpret the shifting shapes of the past. The goblet had spoken to her, or maybe holding it had helped her to recall something she had read. The paper was different. She recalled how it had felt in her fingers, not dead, and not like a newly made object without a history, but like a barrier. The paper was alive but alien, the inked characters deliberately resistant to her probing. She had spoken words without knowing what they meant. She had talked about a gate, a portal, time standing still. The words were not her own; they had come from some other place.

The bedroom door crashed open and Todd strode into the room, with Maria behind him.

"Nicely done," said Todd. "You really got him going. What are you going to do for an encore?"

"What are you doing?" Violet asked. "You can't come in here. They'll see you, and then what will they think? You're supposed to be my secretary, or assistant, or whatever."

"Well, at least he doesn't have to be the maid," said Maria, plopping herself down on the corner of the bed and kicking off her shoes. "This uniform is hot; it's nylon, it doesn't breathe. I don't know how real maids manage. And as for carrying that heavy tray around …"

"It's better than poncing around looking like I just stepped out of a Fred Astaire movie," said Todd, scrabbling to unknot his striped Ascot.

Violet pulled at the spandex girdle that was allowing her to squeeze into the blue suit. "Do you think all this spandex is comfortable?"

"Well, you're not exactly stock size," said Todd, "and that's all we had in wardrobe. Any more of those chocolate croissants, and that whole suit would have exploded." He dropped down on the bed and sat companionably close to Maria. "But you did good," he said. "How much of it was real?"

"All of it," said Violet.

Todd patted her hand. "If you say so, but I don't think that doctor was buying it, cynical bastard. You really went over the top, and you know what Mom used to say, less is more."

"Mom's not here any longer," said Violet, "and it's up to me. We can't keep this place going on your very occasional stage gigs—"

"I try," Todd interrupted.

"I know you do," said Violet, "which is more than I can say for Maria."

"You want me to be a waitress for real?" said Maria, who had entirely lost her Spanish accent.

"No," said Violet. "We're going to make this work. We're going to find this damned sword and make a pile of money, and Todd can buy himself a theatre, and Maria can do whatever she likes."

"I want to paint," said Maria.

"Speaking of paint," said Todd, "Ryan put his hand in the wet paint on the gazebo."

"Oh God," said Violet, "what did you say?"

"Something appropriately flaky," said Todd. "Mind the paint, or sorry about the paint, or something like that. I really had no idea what to say. It should have been dry. I finished it at midnight."

"It looked really good," Maria said encouragingly. "Did you like what I did to the library?"

"I haven't seen it yet," said Violet. She pulled herself upright against the pillows. "You'd both better get out of here. What if someone sees you?"

"The doctor has gone downtown," said Maria, "and the Mafia boss is making threatening phone calls on his cell."

"Okay," said Violet, "so we have a little time. Did you get on to Carlton Lewis?"

"That," said Todd, "was a stroke of genius."

"Well, thank you," said Violet in surprise.

"Not your genius," Todd said, "my genius. How long ago was it that you met him?"

"I don't know," said Violet. "Five years, six years."

"So there you are, perched on your little barstool, and in comes this Englishman from a private yacht, and he happens to be looking for this sunken treasure, and he has a map."

"He'd been looking in the wrong place for years," said Violet.

"But you found it for him."

Violet shrugged her shoulders. "All I had to do was touch the map, and I knew."

"You do know," said Todd, looking her in the eye, "that not everyone can do what you do? You do know that it's fricking amazing the way you know these things?"

"I suppose so," said Violet.

"I'm just worried he won't remember you," said Todd. "I mean, it's great that we looked him up and you could throw his name around like that, but I don't know if it was a good idea to promise that you'd actually consult with him."

"He'll remember me," said Violet firmly.

"Oh," said Maria, "another one of your conquests."

"I suppose some men like women with a little meat on their bones," Violet admitted.

"That's what I keep telling you," said Maria. "If I had boobs like yours, I would—"

"Never mind about her boobs," said Todd.

"I'm just saying that she should relax and appreciate what nature has given her. That gangster was really into her, and the doctor was all eyes. He didn't even know where to look first."

"But he didn't believe me," said Violet.

"One thing at a time," said Maria. "First the boobs and then the brain."

"So," said Todd, "if this Carlton Lewis guy remembers you, and if he comes up with something, are you really planning to go to England?"

"What?" said Violet.

"England," Todd repeated. "Mandretti's expecting you to go to England. Do you even have a passport?"

"Yes," said Violet, "I have a passport. I went up to Canada on that lost-child thing with the Montreal police."

"Do you know where it is?" Maria asked, looking around the cluttered bedroom.

"I'll find it," said Violet. "It's what I do."

She closed her eyes and leaned back against the pillows. "Do you think you could both go away and leave me alone? Go back into the library and see if Mandretti wants anything. Keep him busy and don't let him see the rest of the house."

"I have lines to learn," said Todd. "We have dress rehearsal tonight, and they're not in my head; they are simply not there. That's what happens when you have to spend all night mowing the lawn and painting the damned gazebo."

"It'll all be worth it in the end," said Violet. "Go away."

"We're going," said Todd. He leaned forward and touched Violet's hand. "You done good. Have a little nap and get your strength back; there's a lot more for you to do."

Violet tried to relax and enjoy the gentle warmth of the sun as it filtered through the louvered windows. The ceiling fan hummed softly, moving the cool breeze from the ocean. Birds chirped and called in the bougainvillea bushes. The house was quiet and, even with the knowledge that the Mafia boss was conducting his business from the library, she felt safe. She was confident that despite their teasing, neither Todd nor Maria would allow anyone to disturb her.

She tried to put her brother and sister out of her mind. When Alice and Nicholas Chambray had rescued her from life in a French convent, she had expected to be an only child, and she had been bitterly disappointed to find that her new mother had already adopted two younger children, and she would have a brother and sister. Young as she was, she had realized that one day she would be responsible for them, and now she was. Todd had a burning desire to be an actor but no talent to match his desire, and Maria dreamed of a career in dress design. It was Maria who had squeezed her into the constriction of the blue suit she was wearing and the high-heeled blue pumps that had made it impossible for her to walk with her usual relaxed stride.

She closed her eyes again, and for a fleeting moment, she saw a stone chamber and a nun in gray robes. It was nothing, she told herself. She was probably dreaming of the convent of her childhood, although the nuns at St. Philomena's wore black not gray. She drifted into sleep, the vision of the stone chamber slipping away and seeming to melt in the warmth of the sun and the gentle humming of the ceiling fan.

Maria's loud tapping on the door startled her into wakefulness. As if the banging was not enough, Maria had resurrected her Spanish accent, calling for Miss Violet loudly enough to wake the dead.

Violet's mouth felt dry, and she struggled to open her eyes because her liberal application of mascara had glued her eyelids to her cheeks. Maria flung the door open and regarded her sister with an expression of disgust.

"What you need is waterproof mascara," she said.

"What I need is for you to stop banging around," Violet replied. "How long have I been asleep?"

"Several hours," said Maria.

Violet sat up and rubbed her eyes.

"No," said Maria. "You're making a mess."

"I know. I'll have to redo my whole face. Where is everyone?"

"Mandretti is in the garden, and the other one, the doctor, who, by the way, is not bad looking—"

"If you like the tall, supercilious type," said Violet.

"He's gone shopping," Maria said.

Violet swung her legs over the side of the bed. "I fell asleep with my shoes on."

"And also your girdle," said Maria.

Violet tugged at the firm elastic encasing her stomach. "Mon dieu," she said, lapsing into the French of her childhood, "this thing is torture."

"There is a reply from your boyfriend in England," said Maria.

"Carlton? He actually replied?"

"He sent an e-mail and I printed it out for you, being that you're so utterly useless with computers. It's in the library."

"Where's Todd?" Violet asked. "He's supposed to be the secretary. You're supposed to be the maid."

"He's practicing his makeup for his dress rehearsal. Don't worry, no one saw me. Do you want me to go and get the printout for you?"

Violet swung her feet out of the bed and onto the floor. "No," she said. "I'll come with you. I have to try and wake myself up. Are you sure they're not in there?"

"I told you," said Maria, "the tall, dishy one went into town, and the short, scary one is in the gazebo having a snooze. He hasn't complained, so

I guess the paint is now dry."

Violet adjusted her girdle as best she could, smoothed down her skirt, and followed Maria down the hall and into the library. The e-mail was lying on the desk, printed on heavy-bond cream-colored paper.

"That's the expensive paper," Violet complained. "Why are you using that? Don't you understand, we have to cut corners or we won't have any money at all?"

"If you plan to show the e-mail to anyone," said Maria, "don't you think it should be on good paper? You have to look successful if you plan to be successful."

"Good point," said Violet.

"Apparently," said Maria, "your English boyfriend is as useless as you are with computers. He seems to have written his letter by hand, and I suppose his secretary scanned it and sent it. You two would suit each other just fine."

"He has a wife," said Violet.

As she picked up the paper, the vision hit her hard and fast with the force of a physical blow. She felt herself falling backward and heard Maria screaming for help as Violet's grasping hands dragged her down to the floor.

For a brief moment, Violet was unable to breathe. She felt as though someone had stabbed her in the heart. The library, with its lime-washed desk and open sunlit windows, faded from sight, replaced by a railway carriage with tufted blue upholstery, an overhead luggage rack, deep dark wooden paneling, and reverse lettering on the windows. First Class Only. The floor of the carriage was grimy, sticky, perhaps it had not been cleaned properly, although one would expect special attention to be given to first class. No, not dirt, blood. Whose blood? Her blood? No, his blood. Who was he?

Maria's loud scream shattered the illusion.

"Get off me," Maria shouted. "Get up, Violet. What's the matter with you?"

Violet drew in a deep, shuddering breath and realized that she was lying on the floor of her own library and Maria was staggering to her feet and calling for Todd.

"He's dead," said Violet, filled with certain knowledge.

"Shut up," said Maria, "You almost broke my arm. What kind of crazy stunt was that? No one's dead. What's the matter with you?"

"Carlton's dead," said Violet.

"No, he's not."

Violet heard Todd's voice coming from somewhere far away. "Let me handle this," he said. "She's having a vision."

"You mean, for real?" said Maria.

"I think so." He was kneeling beside her now, inexplicably wearing lipstick and eye shadow. He eased the paper from her hand. "What is this?"

"It's from that guy in London," said Maria.

"Wow," said Todd, "he actually remembered her."

"He's dead," said Violet. "In a railway carriage."

"Are you sure?" said Todd. He looked at the paper. "He just sent this message. Look, here's the time stamp. He's fine."

"No, he's not." Violet staggered clumsily to her feet and made her way to an armchair, where she collapsed in an ungainly sprawl.

Someone spoke from the doorway. "What's going on?"

"It's alright," said Todd, "nothing to worry about, Mr. Mandretti."

"Sure looks like something to me," said Mandretti, advancing into the room. "What's the matter, Violet?"

"He's dead," said Violet.

"She's had a vision," said Todd. "She's very shaken up."

"Yeah." This was another voice from the doorway. "She looks quite convincingly shaken."

Violet managed to focus on the tall figure of Marcus Ryan lounging against the doorframe with a cynical expression on his suntanned face.

"He's dead," she repeated. She seemed to have nothing else to say. The vision had robbed her of her ability to communicate.

"Who's dead?" asked Ryan.

"Carlton Lewis," said Todd. Violet noticed that he had slipped easily back into the role of secretary. Perhaps his acting skills were stronger than she had thought.

"Oh, really?" said Ryan. "And how do we know that?"

Violet managed a few more words. "I saw him in a railway carriage. Phone him, Todd. Phone his office. I know what I saw." She tried to rise to her feet, but Maria pushed her back into the armchair.

"Madam," Maria said softly, her Spanish accent back in place, "let me fix your skirt."

"What?"

Violet looked down at herself. Her girdle seemed to have given up its efforts at control, and her skirt had ridden up above her knees exposing her dimpled thighs. She pushed Maria away. "I don't care," she said. "Phone him, Todd."

"I will get you a glass of water," said Maria.

"Why is no one listening to me?" Violet asked.

"Because you're not making any sense," said Ryan. "Oh, by the way, I found out something about your friend Carlton Lewis."

"He's dead," Violet wailed.

"Yeah, well, before he was dead—" said Ryan.

"Hey," said Mandretti, "can it, Doc. Show the lady some respect." He took the sheet of paper from Todd's hand and passed it to Ryan. "Why don't you read what it says? Then perhaps we can get to the bottom of this."

Ryan studied the paper. "An office in Chelsea," he said. "That must be costing him a few bucks."

"Just read the letter," said Mandretti.

Ryan sighed and began to read aloud in a monotone.

"'My dear Violet, I was delighted to hear from you after all this time, and I have hastened to follow up on your request. I hope I will soon have the pleasure of seeing you personally to let you know all that I have discovered. I am sure that we can come to some amicable arrangement regarding Mr. Mandretti's fee.'"

Ryan stopped reading and looked at Mandretti. "So it's all about money," he said.

"Just read it, Doc," said Mandretti.

"Okay, okay."

Ryan continued to read in a monotone that took all of the life and spirit from the words.

"'I was surprised to learn that Taras Peacock's last commission was to catalog the artifacts of a regimental museum somewhere in the west of England. I thought it rather a mundane commission for a man of his talents. I will endeavor to find out which regiment was involved.

"'I did hear, through the archaeological grapevine, that Peacock had recently unearthed a document in the library of his family home in Shropshire. Apparently, he sent it to the Society of Arthurian Scholars for translation. I must say that I would not have expected him to need a translator. I always thought that Peacock was very well versed in ancient languages.'"

Ryan paused. "He was. He had a gift for ancient languages." He returned to his reading but with a slightly less cynical tone.

"'We in academia,'" he read, "'wondered why he would send anything to the Society of Arthurian Scholars. He was not known for his interest in the Arthurian myth.'"

Ryan paused again.

"Just read it," said Mandretti.

"'As for the sketch of the goblet,'" Ryan read, "'it bears a resemblance to a chalice that was stolen from a church in Norfolk, although I can't be certain without seeing it. The police circulated a bulletin with a description of a stolen chalice to antiquarians, but I'm afraid it did not arouse any great interest; thefts from churches are quite common.'"

Ryan stopped reading and looked across at Violet. "The rest is just expressions of … affection," he said.

Violet felt a blush creeping across her cheeks.

"Never mind about that," said Todd, snatching the paper from Ryan's hand.

Violet pulled herself to her feet and tried to take control of the situation. Now was not the time to fall apart. She accepted the glass of water that Maria offered her, took a quick sip, and then turned to Todd.

"Phone him for me," she said.

"It's evening over there," Todd protested. "He won't be in the office."

Violet glared at him. "Then phone his home."

Todd turned and picked up the telephone receiver.

"She doesn't see things," Ryan said to Mandretti. He spoke softly but Violet could hear him. "She reads them in books and then regurgitates them. She's a fraud."

"No, she ain't," Mandretti hissed. "You just watch yourself, Doc. I didn't bring you down here to insult her. My brother trusted her and so do I."

"I'll prove it to you," Ryan said, "just as soon as we're finished with this little scene."

Violet's panic gave way to anger. Maybe Todd wasn't her secretary. Maybe Maria wasn't her Spanish maid. Maybe the house wasn't falling down around their heads. Maybe all these things were lies, but what she had seen was not a lie. Ryan may have thought that she had been playacting for the benefit of her client, but she knew that it was no act. She knew beyond a shadow of a doubt that Carlton Lewis had been stabbed in the heart and left for dead on the grimy floor of a first-class railway carriage. Rarely had she received such a clear vision.

"When she had her last vision," said Mandretti "the one about the king and—"

"Oh yes," Ryan interrupted, "let me tell you about that one."

Mandretti glared at his employee. "When she had her last vision," he repeated, "she said that the goblet had been under the mud somewhere."

"Norfolk," said Ryan. "It's on the east coast of England, very flat country, mostly salt marshes, just as Violet described it and just as Carlton Lewis himself described it. "

Violet's heart skipped a beat. Although she was concentrating her attention on Todd as he dialed an international call, she was still concerned about what Ryan might say next. However, Mandretti was not willing to give Ryan a chance to say whatever damning thing he was longing to say.

"So, Doc," Mandretti said, "this document the prof found, was that from this Norfolk place?"

Ryan shook his head. "No," he said, "that was from Shropshire, a totally different place; hundreds of miles away."

"Oh," said Mandretti. "I thought maybe we was on to something."

"I'm willing to believe that the goblet might just possibly have come from King John's baggage train," Ryan said, "but as for the rest of it—"

Todd gasped and turned to look at Violet. The room fell silent. Violet held her breath until Todd replaced the receiver. "Dead," he said softly. ☐

CHAPTER FIVE

Violet stared at Todd. She knew what he was going to say next.

"His body was found in a first-class carriage of the London to Brighton train. He had been knifed. I'm sorry, Violet."

"It's alright," said Violet, because there was nothing else to say. She knew what she had seen and felt. Todd was only confirming something that had already happened.

"They left the knife behind," Todd said. "It was a dagger, pre-Saxon, possibly Roman."

Mandretti interrupted the silence with the certainty of his New York accent. "They're sending us a message," he said.

"Not necessarily," Ryan said quickly.

Mandretti looked at him scornfully. "You might be the expert on old stuff," he said, "but this kind of stuff is what I know. They wanted us to see the dagger. They want us to pay attention."

"They want you over there," Violet said.

"Yeah," said Mandretti. "It's a challenge."

Violet knew that she had to pull herself together. She wiped her eyes, tugged her clothes into place, and picked up the e-mail from the late Sir Carlton. The feelings of horror returned, and she dropped it rapidly onto the desk and took several deep breaths to clear her mind. She turned her attention to Ryan, who stood in the doorway with a shocked expression on his face. "Mr. Ryan," she said, "Maria will take you to the sitting room and bring you coffee."

Maria frowned, and Violet quieted her with a ferocious glare.

"Maria will bring you coffee," she repeated. "I need to talk to Mr. Mandretti for a few minutes."

"Just wait a minute," Ryan protested. "I need to know how—"

"You don't need to know anything," Violet snapped. The best defense being a good offense, she had already decided to set aside the fact that Marcus Ryan was a tall, slim, educated somebody, while she was a short, fat nobody with smeared makeup and an out-of-control girdle. So far as Ryan was concerned, she was about to become the chief negotiator, and he was not going to have any say in what would happen next.

"I need to talk to Mr. Mandretti alone," Violet said.

Maria squeezed through the doorway beside Ryan and caught hold of his elbow. "Come this way," she said, and Ryan followed her.

"So …?" said Mandretti.

"I will take the case," said Violet.

"You'll go to England?"

"Of course. As soon as possible. I would like to go to Carlton's funeral."

"Yeah, sure," said Mandretti, "but this ain't about your friend, sorry for your loss, of course, but it ain't about him. It's about—"

"I know what it's about," said Violet.

"I want the sword," said Mandretti. "All the rest of it, that's personal. "

"People have been killed," Todd protested.

Mandretti shrugged his broad shoulders. "That tells me that this sword exists and it ain't just some myth. People don't get killed over myths. There's something real at the bottom of all this. There's blood in the water, big sharks swimming around."

Violet did not care for Mandretti's analogy. She had never liked swimming, or perhaps she had never liked the sight of herself in a bathing suit. Whatever the reason, the thought of dark shapes slipping through deep water made her shiver.

She felt the pressure of Todd's hand against her back. What was he trying to say to her? She had never felt close to Maria, but sometimes she felt as though Todd really was her brother. He wouldn't want to see her get hurt, not even if the payoff was enough money to restore the Chambray family home and keep them all in luxury for years. Todd was trying to tell her that she didn't really have to do this, but he was wrong. This time she had to follow through and find the truth behind her visions. Who was the nun in the stone chamber? What was the source of the scrap of paper Marcus Ryan carried in his pocket? Why was she able to sense these things while those around her remained blind? Somehow the answer to these questions was linked to the mysterious sword, the sword that could not possibly be Excalibur.

"I'll get you three first-class tickets to London," Mandretti said. "I can fly you up to Miami in my Gulfstream."

"Three?" said Violet, tearing her mind away from her own personal questions. "Why three?"

"You, the doc, and fancy boy here," said Mandretti.

"Not Ryan," said Violet, horrified at the idea of Ryan trailing her around England in a cloud of cynicism.

"I'm not going," said Todd.

"What?"

"I'm not going," Todd repeated. "I have commitments."

"I don't need Doctor Ryan," said Violet.

"Wait a minute," said Mandretti. He looked at Todd. "What do you mean, you're not going?"

"I'm not going," said Todd. "I'm opening in Blithe Spirit tomorrow night; I'm not leaving the Keys."

"Todd, really!" Violet protested.

"I'm not going," Todd repeated, setting his penciled eyebrows in a firm line. "I'm committed to the company and we open tomorrow."

"Oh, come on," Mandretti said, "some rinky-dink little theater. They won't miss you. I'll send someone to replace you. I'll get them a real actor from Vegas. They'll love it."

"What do you mean, real actor?" said Todd, his outrage momentarily blocking out Violet's thoughts of how very much she did not want to be accompanied by Doctor Ryan.

"Well, you know what I mean," said Mandretti. "Someone with sex appeal. I mean, what are you supposed to be? You ain't exactly leading-man material."

"Don't typecast me," said Todd. "You don't know what I am until you see me on stage. I am not going."

"He's not going," said Violet, masking her own disappointment, "and I have no wish to take your tame treasure hunter with me. I'll do perfectly well on my own."

"Ryan's going," said Mandretti.

"No," said Violet.

"I'm paying the bill," said Mandretti, "and Ryan's going. No offense, Violet, but Ryan's the one with the degrees."

"I'm the one who finds things," said Violet.

"So does Ryan," said Mandretti, "and he finds them on TV."

"He's a has-been," Todd interjected.

"He goes," said Mandretti. "He has the reputation. He's a doctor, and he's the one who works for me. Fancy Pants can stay behind if he wants to, but Ryan goes."

"Fancy Pants," said Todd under his breath.

Violet shot him a glance to advise him not to push things any further. Mandretti seemed to be in a good mood. Perhaps his sympathy for Violet in the loss of her friend was holding back his more violent side, but it wouldn't be held back forever. He could be pushed so far and no farther.

"Todd," said Violet, "you'll need to find some clothes for Ryan."

"He has clothes," said Mandretti.

"You mean the old network blazer that was supposed to impress me?" said Violet. "I mean real clothes so he won't stand out like a sore thumb in England."

"London Fog and Harris Tweed," said Todd.

"Absolutely," said Violet. "A raincoat, tweed jacket, and some kind of sweater. You must have something at the theatre with all the Coward and Christie you do."

"Forty-two long," said Todd. "I'll run down and see what we have."

"Let's go tell Ryan," said Mandretti. "Where is he?"

"In the sitting room," said Violet. She gave her girdle one last determined tug, patted her hair into place, and led the way to the sitting room.

Ryan was talking on his cell phone.

"I'll let you know," Ryan said, ending his call and slipping his phone into his pocket.

"Veronica?" asked Mandretti.

"No," said Ryan, "that was Crispin Peacock, heir to the Peacock estate."

"They sure do have fancy names," said Mandretti. "What kind of family are they?"

"Old and full of history."

"So what did he want?"

"He was returning my call. I left him a message about Taras, and he called the Las Vegas police, and then he called me."

"So what is he, son, brother, what?"

"Distant relative," said Ryan, "but there being no one else, he's the heir. He'd never even met him." He paused for a moment. "He was offering to meet me in London. I told him I wasn't going to London, but he seemed to know more than I do."

"How could he know that?" Violet asked. "We only just decided …"

Ryan pulled the phone out of his pocket and held it out to her. His face was set in an angry glare. "Here," he said, "why don't you touch it and see if it talks to you. Perhaps it'll tell you the whole conversation. Might even tell you why he's offering to go with me to Norfolk."

Violet stepped back, genuinely puzzled. She knew that Ryan had been skeptical from the first moment they had met, but now he was downright antagonistic. Something had happened between the time she had left him in the summer house and the moment he had returned from his shopping trip on Duval Street. What could he possibly have seen or heard in the shops and bars of the tourist district that would make him so angry and so determined to prove her wrong?

"He also knows about the sword," said Ryan. "Someone's been talking."

"Not I," said Todd. "I am the soul of discretion."

"I'm sure you do whatever you're paid to do," said Ryan, "including making a couple of phone calls."

"Okay, enough," said Mandretti. "You two gonna work together, and that's all there is to it, so you'd better start talking civil. You and Violet are on the next flight to London, so get your stuff together, Doc. Do whatever you need to do. You got your passport?"

Ryan looked as though he would like to deny having his passport. It was quite clear to Violet that he had no wish to go with her to England, just as she had no wish to go with him.

"I have it," said Ryan.

"Right," said Mandretti, "so first thing we have to find out is how this Crispie fellow found out you was going to London."

"Crispin," said Ryan.

"Whatever," said Mandretti.

"He must have access to passenger reservation information," said Todd, and then he stopped. "No," he said. "Violet doesn't even have a reservation yet."

"He must be yet another psychic," said Ryan. "The world is full of them."

"I told you to can it," said Mandretti. "Obviously, I'm not the only person who wants the sword, and we got two dead bodies to prove it, so you'd better watch your backs, both of you, or you're gonna end up with some fancy antique blade in your gut. Capisce?"

"Capisce," said Ryan.

At 5 p.m., with the bright Florida sun still baking the tarmac, Violet and Ryan wheeled their carry-on bags into the first-class cabin of the Miami to Heathrow flight. The flight attendant relieved Violet of the lightweight Burberry raincoat that she rarely had occasion to use in Key West, and also took the somewhat rumpled London Fog trench coat that Todd had provided for Ryan. Violet allowed herself a small spiteful moment of satisfaction knowing that the clothes Todd had provided for the doctor were well used and not quite clean. Todd had taken the opportunity to dress Ryan as a tall, thin Inspector Clouseau, or perhaps Colombo, not that Ryan seemed to care, or perhaps he had not yet noticed.

They were seated together. Ryan was next to the window, with Violet on the aisle beside him. The seats, as befitted first class, were wide and well padded, but Violet already felt uncomfortable, and as the aircraft reached altitude and the seats could be reclined, she became even more uncomfortable. Because her legs were too short for the seat, she had to sprawl in order to reach the footrest, and sprawling was not the most flattering of positions for her. She looked across the generous mound of her stomach and wished that she had followed her own instincts, and worn pants instead of allowing Maria to squeeze her into yet another restricting skirt that rode up every time she moved.

The flight attendant brought champagne, and Violet took the glass with relief. Perhaps a couple of glasses of bubbly would relax her and allow her to set aside her feeling of impending doom, or at least help her to overcome her rapidly growing dislike of the partner that Mandretti had forced upon her.

Ryan asked for a beer. There we go, Violet thought, we're as different as chalk and cheese. There was no way this partnership was going to last or produce fruit.

Ryan reached down under his seat and brought out his briefcase. He smiled at Violet as he opened the case and produced a paper shopping bag from a store on Duval Street. "For you," he said.

"Me?"

"Yes," said Ryan, "I purchased this item for you although I assume you have, in fact, already read it."

The tone of his voice was sufficient to make Violet wary as she held the bag on her lap and took a measured sip of champagne. She thought over the things that Todd had discovered about Doctor Marcus Ryan. He had been a TV star at an early age, a handsome young academic with an Indiana Jones vibe, striding around exotic locations and introducing viewers to the forgotten treasures of ancient history. His star had waned with the coming of edgier reality shows where everything was a competition, and clothes were mostly optional. At forty-five he was a has-been with only Michael Mandretti's personal lust for treasure to keep him solvent. His ex-wife had remarried, he was estranged from his children, and his bank account was as precarious as her own.

Violet knew that any investigation Ryan might make into her own circumstances would come up empty. Todd had spent a considerable amount of time making sure that Violet Chambray existed in cyberspace only as a finder of lost items, with a hint that she might be of European origin, and a nod to a possibly Romany background. Her age, place of birth, even her current address were hidden from the general public, and all clients were sworn to secrecy on the theory that the best way to generate publicity was to create a cult of secrecy. Violet had recently come to the conclusion that Todd's secrecy gambit was not working, but so far she had not come up with any alternative.

"Open it," said Ryan.

Violet took another sip of champagne and then peeked inside the bag. It contained a thin paperback book. No, she thought, not a book, a journal or a calendar. She brought the book out into the light of the reading lamp above her head. The cover, garishly colored, showed a knight in dark armor, trampling on a dragon-emblazoned banner. Behind him flames engulfed a medieval castle, and dark thunder clouds gathered around his head.

"What on earth …?" she said.

"A Villain a Day," said Ryan. "I found it on the sale table at that new bookstore on Duval. Clever idea really, an evil deed for every day of the year, but apparently, it didn't sell well. It's written by your friend Carlton."

"Oh," said Violet, "well, that was thoughtful of you."

"Yes, it was," said Ryan. "I thought you would be especially interested in the entry for Bad King John and how he lost his treasure."

"I already know how he lost his treasure," said Violet.

Ryan took the book from her hand and flipped through the pages. "Ah, here it is," he said. "Allow me to read it for you."

"I can read it for myself," she said.

"No, I'll read it," said Ryan. He cleared his throat theatrically. "'A cold wind sweeps across the bleak marshes that border the North Sea. The short winter afternoon draws to an end. The sun sets behind leafless stunted trees. It will be dark soon, and there will be no light of human habitation. Not even the lowest peasant would dare to build a hut on the shifting sands of the Wash." Ryan paused. "Does it sound familiar?"

Violet shifted in her seat. Of course it sounded familiar; they were the very words she had used to describe King John's journey across the marsh.

"Same story, same words," said Ryan, "exactly the same words, right down to the part about the sun setting behind leafless stunted trees." He jabbed his finger at the offending words.

Violet grabbed the book from his hand. Had she read this book before? No, she would have remembered.

She read quickly, taking in the words and their sickening familiarity. The text was familiar, and yet she was certain that she had never read the book.

"That's amazing," she said. "I don't always remember everything I say in a trance, but I do remember seeing the scene exactly as he describes it. I even remember the shrieking of the carthorses and the cracking of the whips; just as he says."

"Oh, balls, "said Ryan loudly. "You're no psychic. You read this book before we arrived, and then you played it all back for Mandretti. You must really want this job."

So, Violet thought, that was why Ryan had become so antagonistic.

"It's possible that I was not actually channeling the goblet," she said, "even though it was in my hands at the time. After all, we had been talking about Carlton, and I had been in touch with him, so possibly I was channeling his thoughts and his—"

"Nice try," said Ryan.

"It's quite obvious now that I think about it," Violet said. She kept her voice steady and tried not to betray any of the doubt that was threatening to overcome her.

"Nice try," said Ryan again, "but don't expect me to believe it."

He reached down beside the seat and pulled out the airline-issue headphones. Without saying another word, he unwound the cord and planted the headphones on his head. He pulled up his personal video screen, pressed the power button, and turned his head away from her as the screen brightened with the entertainment menu.

Violet stared ahead, not seeing the cabin, not hearing the muffled roar of the engines or the discreet movements of the cabin attendants. How had this happened? Had she read Carlton's King John account in some other book? Had anything come to her through the goblet?

The plane droned on eastward across the Atlantic, toward the dawn. Ryan watched a movie and ate a steak dinner, all the time, ignoring Violet. She, in turn, pecked at the food she was offered and ignored the entertainment offerings. The cabin lights were dimmed, and beyond the window was nothing but darkness. The flight attendants ceased their comings and goings. Even the sound of crying babies in economy class came to an end. Ryan slept. Everyone slept.

Except Violet.

She was still awake when a sinking feeling in her stomach told her that the plane was beginning its long descent into Heathrow. The window blinds were closed, but she imagined they were somewhere over Ireland, and the sun had already risen across Western Europe. She had spent the long hours of the night grappling with her feelings of inadequacy and insecurity. Ryan's scorn and his accusation that she was merely a parrot repeating what she had read in a book had hit her hard.

The flight attendant slipped through the cabin and gently raised the shades. Sunlight streamed through the windows. Of course, Violet thought, that was no indication that the sun was actually shining on England. She wanted to lean across Ryan and look out of the window to see if land was visible or if the British Isles were wrapped in the blanket of cloud that had figured prominently in every book she had read about the United Kingdom.

The clinking of china in the galley disturbed Ryan, and he stirred in his seat, blinked blearily out of the window, and then stretched his long arms and legs without regard to the fact that he was invading Violet's personal space. Just as she was about to protest, he surprised her by smiling and wishing her a good morning.

"Oh, good morning. You slept well?"

"I did," said Ryan, stretching his limbs again. "How about you?"

"Nothing," said Violet. "I don't sleep on planes."

"Shame," said Ryan.

"Yes, it is," said Violet.

She waited. What would he say next? Would he return to the subject of Carlton Lewis and his description of King John?

"So," said Ryan, "we'll be landing in a couple of hours."

"Less than that."

"Okay, if you say so."

The flight attendant appeared with trays of breakfast foods, and Violet concentrated on pulling out her tray table and arranging herself into a more upright position.

"Crispin Peacock is meeting me at Heathrow," Ryan said.

"I didn't know," said Violet. She felt as though she was walking on eggshells. At any moment, Ryan's scorn might rear its ugly head.

"We're going to Norfolk," said Ryan. He took a long gulp of the coffee on his tray. "Do you want to come?"

"No." The word was out of Violet's mouth before she had time to think.

"Why not?"

Because you are rude and hostile, she wanted to say, but instead she said, "Because we don't even know what we're looking for yet. What do you expect to find in Norfolk?"

"Leafless stunted trees," said Ryan. "The sun setting in a sullen red ball."

Violet forced herself to smile. Somehow or another she had to work with this man if she intended to produce results.

"Very funny," she said. "What do you really expect to find?"

"I don't know, but we have to start somewhere. We'll ask around."

"It was eight hundred years ago," she protested.

"I'm a treasure hunter; that's what I do. I follow clues, old writings, rumors, legends. Haven't you ever watched my television program?"

"I watched a couple of episodes," she admitted, "but in the ones I saw, you were mostly underwater."

"Bingo," Ryan replied. "The tide came in, remember that? They'll be underwater."

"And the tide went out," she said. "They'll be under mud; if they're under anything at all."

"It's what I do," said Ryan.

"Well," said Violet, determined to achieve the upper hand before it was too late, "it's not what I do. I have absolutely no intention of going on some wild-goose chase in the marshes. Todd told me that Mr. Mandretti has made reservations at the Dorchester Hotel in London, which I understand is an excellent establishment. I don't intend to do anything until I have taken a long bath."

Ryan stared at her. "Really? You're not going to start work, you're just going to take a bath?"

"Yes," said Violet, although it was not so much the idea of a bath that interested her, as the desire to be rid of the constraint of her traveling clothes. "I'm going to take a bath," she repeated, "and then I'm going to call on Carlton's wife, or I should say widow, and see what she knows."

"But we have a lead," Ryan protested, "and I'm not talking about your vision or hallucination or whatever it was. The fact is that your friend Carlton thought the goblet had been stolen from a church in Norfolk."

"Do you have any idea how many churches there are in Norfolk?" Violet asked.

Ryan remained silent.

"You're wasting your time," said Violet, set now on her stubborn path. "I'm going to the Dorchester. I'm going to take a bath, and then I'm going to have a nap."

"That's all very well for you," Ryan said. "You may regard this as an all-expense-paid jaunt, but I have a living to earn, and like it or not, Michael Mandretti is my living. I don't have time to lie around in hotels, taking baths and naps—"

"You'll regret it," Violet said, "when jet lag catches up with you."

"So I should go to Norfolk on my own?"

Violet shrugged her shoulders. "If you want to. I can't stop you."

She began to pick up her possessions. The paperback journal lay on the padded divider between the seats. She thought about returning it to Ryan as though it was of no importance to her, as though it had not utterly destroyed her self-confidence. She looked at the cover and the lurid picture of the knight. Surely Carlton could have found a better illustrator. Who was this supposed to be? She flipped open the first page. Mordred, son of Arthur, and the destruction of Camelot. Hastily she closed the book and stuffed it into the magazine pocket beside her seat, where it could be picked up by the cleaners. She should not have looked. Now the image was emblazoned on her mind, ready to be dredged up by her subconscious and presented as a vision.

The pilot's voice crackled over the intercom. "We are beginning our descent to London Heathrow. The temperature on the ground is a balmy ten degrees Celsius, that's forty-eight degrees Fahrenheit for those who prefer to think that way, and the time is 7 a.m."

The plane descended rapidly with rainwater streaming past the windows and settled onto the tarmac with a couple of bouncing thuds.

They ran the usual gamut of deplaning, immigration, waiting for their baggage, and passing through customs, and emerged eventually into the crowded arrival concourse. Although Violet had not admitted it to Ryan or Mandretti, this was her first visit to England.

So far as she knew, she had been born in France, although she knew nothing of her parents. She had gone from France to the US with her adoptive parents and never set foot in Europe again. However, she had traveled the Caribbean and liked to think of herself as an international traveler. She approached the arrivals area with confidence and immediately spotted a uniformed flunky holding a Dorchester Hotel sign with her name scrawled on it. He came forward to relieve her of her luggage.

"It's my ride to the Dorchester," she said to Ryan. "Are you sure you're not coming?"

"No," he said. "I'm certain Crispin Peacock is here somewhere."

Violet searched the sea of faces. "Do you know what he looks like?"

"No," said Ryan, "but he says he'll recognize me."

The driver from the Dorchester began to move toward the exit.

"I have to go," said Violet. As she turned away from Ryan, she came face to face with a young woman who seemed to be trying to reach Ryan.

"Excuse me," said Violet.

The girl gasped. "What are you doing here?" she asked, staring into Violet's face. "You're not allowed here."

Violet stepped back and looked at her accuser. She was a frail, waiflike girl enveloped in a long black trench coat. A wide-brimmed black hat was pulled down low on her forehead. Strands of unkempt blond hair escaped from the hat and were tangled in the pale chiffon shawl that lay across her shoulders. Her eyes were huge and blue, and met Violet's with a desperate panicked stare that Violet thought might be attributable to illegal substances of some sort.

"Who are your sisters?" the girl asked. "How have you been allowed here? Why are you so fat?"

Violet pushed the girl aside. "I don't know what you're talking about. Leave me alone."

"You shouldn't be here," the girl said. "You'll spoil everything. This is my quest. He's mine."

She pushed past Violet and approached Ryan. Violet doubted that Ryan had heard any of the interchange. He was standing still, head and shoulders above most of the people in the crowd, waiting to be recognized.

The girl tugged at Ryan's arm. He looked down at her. Violet could see that he appreciated her waiflike beauty.

"Do you have it in your pocket?" the girl asked.

"What?" said Ryan

"The pin," she said. "Do you have a piece of the pin in your pocket?"

"She's high," said Violet.

"Go away," said the girl.

"Are you my driver?" Ryan asked.

"I hope not," said Violet. "You'd better come with me."

The girl tugged at Ryan with her pale, elegant hand. "Just hold the pin," she said.

A masculine voice called through the crowd. "Doctor Ryan?"

The girl looked around, panic showing on her delicate features, and then she melted back into the crowd as Ryan turned to greet a smiling young man with a mass of dark curly hair.

"This is my ride," said Ryan, "but it looks like yours is disappearing with your luggage."

Violet saw that the driver from the Dorchester was waiting impatiently at the edge of the crowd. She hurried to catch up with him and followed him out into the chilly, rain-soaked morning. As she was being ushered into the sleek black limousine, she saw the girl again, standing with the rain pouring down onto her hat and soaking into her hair, watching as Ryan and Peacock crossed the road. She was not the only observer. As the limousine pulled away from the curb, she saw another watcher standing in the shadows, a tall man with a patch over one eye.

CHAPTER SIX

Marcus Ryan

Ryan yawned, rubbed his eyes, and stared despondently at the cement surface of an elementary school yard in a small Norfolk village. A wire mesh fence was blocking his access to the yard itself, but even from a distance, he could tell that the surface was solid, unyielding cement. Lights shone from the windows of the little school, and he could see children moving about inside.

He saw a teacher looking out of the window. No doubt she would be making a report to the authorities that two strange men were lurking outside the fence and staring fixedly at the schoolyard.

"Oh well," said Crispin in his cultured British voice. "Not much good standing here, old man. This won't get us anywhere."

He patted Ryan's shoulder in a gesture of sympathy and turned back toward the warm interior of his Mercedes. Ryan followed obediently.

Crispin bore very little resemblance to Taras, but he had already told Ryan that he was only a distant relative. They shared the same great-grandfather, and that fact, coupled with the inability of most members of the family to produce offspring, had made him the heir to Taras's estate. He was tall and thin where Taras had been short and quite definitely not thin. They did share the same mop of curly hair and bright blue eyes. Ryan guessed that Crispin was somewhere in his early thirties. He also guessed from Peacock's accent and his tendency to call Ryan "old boy" and "old man," and sometimes "old chap," that he was the product of an upper-crust British education. His black leather coat looked expensive, as did his car, but his feet were adorned with battered old tennis shoes. Ryan was not sufficiently up on the subject of fashion footwear to know whether or not they were a ridiculously expensive brand. He only knew that they looked old and worn.

Crispin had wasted no time in leaving the airport, navigating a maze of junctions and roundabouts with speed and confidence, and giving the Mercedes its head as they headed out of London. They slowed only once when they encountered a roadblock created by a group of ill-clad, noisy protesters.

"It's our national pastime," Crispin confided. "We protest progress in any form. Doesn't really matter what it is."

"What are they protesting?" Ryan asked.

Crispin surveyed the array of banners. "A dam in North Wales," he said. "I've heard about this one. It's more than just a dam and the destruction of a village. There's a herd of wild horses living in the valley, and that's why everybody's upset. We're a nation of animal lovers, you know. Nothing like a bit of animal cruelty to rile up the population."

"Can't they move the horses?" Ryan asked.

"Of course they can," said Peacock, "although any horse with any sense would move itself. They have plenty of room to roam up there in the middle of nowhere. I doubt if they'll just let themselves drown."

"So all this protesting is a waste of time?" said Ryan.

"Rite of passage, old boy," said Peacock. "We all have to join in. One cannot be a bona fide student unless one has been in a protest. I personally lived in an oak tree for three months."

"Why?"

"So they couldn't cut it down," he said. "In the end, the police got me down with a crane, and the oak tree went the way of all flesh." He shrugged his shoulders. "But I did my bit," he said. "I earned my stripes, you know."

Ryan had the impression that Crispin Peacock would be the life and soul of any party he attended, and looked forward to spending more time with him. He was a refreshing change from Violet Chambray and her prickly pretentiousness, and quite definitely better company than Michael Mandretti.

Once they were through the protesters, they picked up speed and continued northeast with no regard for the posted speed limits, until they came to a standstill at the schoolyard.

"This is where legend has always placed King John's unfortunate encounter with the North Sea," Crispin said.

Eight hundred years had left their mark, and in the intervening centuries, the sea had receded, leaving acres and acres of flat new land. Man had moved onto the new acreage with houses, farms, roads, and railways, and a cement schoolyard. Ryan could smell the sea salt in the air, and way off in the distance, he could sense the gray waters of the North Sea rising and falling beneath the sodden sky, but it had been many, many years since this particular spot had been beneath the waves. The only evidence of the past in the whole featureless landscape was the spire of an old church breaking the line of the distant horizon.

"Oh well, back to London," said Crispin. "There's nothing to see here."

Crispin settled himself behind the wheel, and Ryan sank back into the passenger seat and stared out of the window at the damp countryside. Although it was no longer actually raining, a brisk wind was sending black clouds scudding across the sky and ruffling the emerging green shoots on the trees and hedgerows. The road unfolded ahead of them in an arrow-straight line aimed at the distant church spire. Ryan watched the spire grow closer and made out the church to which it was attached. He tried to put a date on it. Eight hundred years? Nine hundred years? In such an ancient countryside, centuries simply piled on top of each other, marked only by the slowly receding ocean and the ever-increasing farmland while the church remained unchanged.

"Just a minute," he said to Crispin as they hurtled down the narrow road.

Crispin applied the brakes and turned to look at Ryan.

"I want to see the church," Ryan said. "How old would you say it is?"

"No idea," said Crispin. "You're the expert."

"From the look of the tower, I would say it definitely predates the Norman invasion," said Ryan.

"If you say so," said Crispin.

"Which means," said Ryan, "that it was already here and already old when King John passed this way."

"Ah," said Crispin, "interesting thought, old boy."

"I suppose it was on the edge of the marsh at one time," said Ryan. "This place might even have been a port."

"High and dry now," said Crispin.

Ryan felt his spirits lift. His instincts were aroused. On that fateful evening when King John had fled in desperation across the marsh, this stone tower was standing there. From this tower, some medieval priest could have looked down and seen that long train of wagons struggling across the marsh. He would have seen the sun setting and heard the shrieking of the carthorses and the cracking of whips. Ryan pulled himself out of his reverie, ashamed to find that he had been mentally quoting Violet; actually quoting Violet's regurgitated mumbo jumbo.

"I'd like to stop here," Ryan said. "The letter from Carlton Lewis said that the goblet might possibly have come from a church in Norfolk."

"A church?" said Crispin. "He actually said it came from a church?"

"Yes."

"But he didn't say which church," said Crispin, "and there are hundreds of churches in Norfolk, so what makes you think—?"

"It's just a hunch."

Crispin brought the car to a halt in front of the church gates, and Ryan climbed out leaving Crispin alone in the warm interior.

"You're not coming?" he asked.

Crispin reclined the driver's seat and closed his eyes. "Just going to get a few minutes' shut-eye. It's a long drive back."

Not so long, Ryan thought. They had only been on the road for three hours. He was surprised that Crispin would be too tired to take an interest.

The church was quite small, built of gray stones and surrounded by a churchyard where gravestones of immense antiquity huddled amongst towering weeds. A weathered signboard announced that this was the Church of St. Mary, Lower Malden, and that the Rev. Barry Marshall was the vicar. A few cottages faced the church across the main road, and a shabby Victorian house stood alongside the back wall of the graveyard.

Ryan went through the gate and up to the oak door. Locked. He tried not to be disappointed. What else should he expect at three on a Thursday afternoon? He made a circuit of the building and discovered a small outbuilding, possibly a place to store a lawnmower and some tools for grave digging, although there was little evidence of anyone using a lawnmower recently and no obviously new graves; they all seemed equally ancient.

A sudden gust of wind reminded him that the temperature had still not exceeded forty-eight degrees Fahrenheit. He shoved his hands into his coat pocket, feeling the uneven shape of the jeweled remnant. He wondered how he had managed to make his way through the various airport metal detectors without being asked about it. Was it made of a metal that could not be detected? Taras Peacock had said that its structure was crystalline and not metallic, but how could that be?

He looked back at the car. He could see Crispin Peacock standing beside the vehicle, talking on his cell phone. His voice was carried on the damp air, not the words but the tone. Obviously, Peacock was involved in an argument in which he seemed to be doing most of the talking. Ryan hesitated, not wanting to interrupt. Disappointed girlfriend? Angry wife? A business deal gone wrong? His banker?

He turned aside and stepped off the path. Suddenly a thick gray mist boiled up from the ground among the graves, wrapping him in a dense shroud of fog. He blinked his eyes and took another step forward.

The mist cleared. He stopped in astonishment. If he could believe the evidence of his own eyes, he was no longer in the churchyard. He was no longer anywhere that he could possibly be. He was standing on a stone jetty looking out into a sheltered harbor. The sea was calm and gray, and boats rocked gently at anchor; not modern boats, Viking long ships.

The vision seemed real enough. A cold breeze ruffled his hair, and he heard the screeching of the seagulls that were swooping and diving above his head. He shuffled his feet and felt the surface firm beneath them. He turned to look at the land behind him. He was at the estuary of a great river where a series of stone jetties jutted out from the marshes into deep water. A seawall protected a huddle of cottages.

Two women stood on the seawall, one swathed in a fur cloak and the other ... He blinked again. The other person was the girl who had accosted him at the airport. She was still dressed in a long black coat, but now she was holding her hat at her side, and her blond hair was being ruffled by the wind. The fringing of her chiffon shawl rose and fell in the passing breeze.

He knew she wasn't real. Maybe she had never been real. Maybe this was all in his imagination, and he had only imagined an encounter with a girl at the airport. He was very tired, and obviously sleep-deprived. This hallucination was probably some kind of clinical psychosis that went along with being hurtled around the world from one time zone to another. Well, he would soon find out. He took a step toward her. Someone, or something, rushed at him, pushing him from the jetty into the water ...

He was not in the water. He was not even wet. He was lying on the ground, staring up at a small boy dressed in a dark green windbreaker, blue jeans, and mud-caked sneakers.

"You alright, mister?" he asked. "I didn't see you."

Ryan gathered his scattered wits and shook his head to clear the vision.

"I'm okay," he said. "I must have tripped."

Yes, that was it. Undoubtedly, he had tripped himself. No one had tripped him, and surely he could not possibly have seen what he thought he had seen.

The boy was still staring at him. "You weren't there and then suddenly you were," he said. "I didn't mean to trip you."

Ryan smiled at the boy. By his clothing he could have been an American boy, but there was an apple brightness to his cheeks and a mop-head haircut that seemed the ultimate in Englishness.

"Are you looking for something?" the boy asked.

"I'm looking for treasure," Ryan replied with complete honesty.

"Really?" The boy's eyes lit up. Obviously, Ryan had broken the monotony of a boring afternoon among the gravestones; probably the graves of the boy's ancestors.

"That your car?" he asked. "That's a Mercedes, ain't it?"

"Yes, it's a Mercedes," Ryan said, "but it's not my car."

They stared at each other.

"Have you seen anyone else here?" Ryan asked. He couldn't bring himself to actually ask, "Have you seen a medieval village, a clutch of Viking longships, and a blond-haired woman?"

"There was a girl," the boy said, "but she's not here now."

A hand shot out from behind a gravestone and pulled at the boy's coat.

"What?" the boy hissed. Keeping his eyes on Ryan, he edged sideways to speak to his hidden companion. "Ask him yourself," he said.

Another child emerged from the hiding place. This one was a girl in a navy-blue raincoat and bright red rubber boots. She appeared to be about six years old, which would make her a couple of years younger than the boy. There was a family resemblance in their apple cheeks and bright brown hair. Brother and sister, Ryan thought.

"What treasure are you looking for?" asked the girl.

"Well," Ryan said, "I'm looking for a treasure that might have been left here a long time ago."

"Oh, that," said the boy. "King John's treasure; you won't find that."

"Really?" Ryan said. "What do you know about it?"

"We learn about it at school. Local history. Jenny doesn't know about it yet; she's too young."

"Am not," said Jenny.

"Are too," the boy replied, and Ryan suspected that the exchange would continue that way unless he intervened.

"What exactly do they teach you," he asked, "in local history?"

"About how King John lost his jewels in the Wash," the boy said with strained patience. He looked at Ryan intently, and recognition dawned on his face. "You're him, aren't you?" he said. "The bloke on the telly what does those old Treasure Hunt programs. You're him. Cor, no wonder you got a flash car. Hey, Jenny, it's him. "

Jenny was unimpressed. "Who?" she asked.

"That man what's on that program that Dad watches on Sundays, the one about looking for treasure."

"I don't watch it," Jenny declared, but she looked at Ryan with something akin to respect. "You famous?" she asked.

"I was, once," he said, "famous enough for my shows to be in syndication."

Jenny stared at him blankly, obviously unaware of the importance of syndication.

"You gonna do a program here?" the boy asked. "You gonna look for King John's treasure?"

"Do you think I'll find it?" Ryan asked.

The boy shook his head.

"Do you know anything about it?" Ryan continued, although he knew it was ridiculous to think that, eight hundred years after the fact, the secret of the treasure would lie with this scruffy little boy.

"The sea used to come all the way up to here," Jenny volunteered. "My class went on a logical dig."

"She means archeological," her brother said loftily. "The whole school went, not just her class. We had to dig up bits of the seawall that used to be out there."

"And there were ships," Jenny said. "Long time ago. There's nothing left now."

Viking ships, Ryan thought, and a seawall. What had happened? Why had he seen what he had seen? Had he even really seen it? Maybe he had just spent too much time with Violet Chambray.

"No one's going to find it," the boy declared. "You're wasting your time, mister. Come on, Jenny, we're supposed to go home."

Ryan wondered what exactly they had been taught in their local history lesson and on their dig. Was there anything hidden away in local knowledge that had never appeared in a written history? He had found that to be the case in other places, so he made one last attempt to snare their interest.

"What I'm really trying to do," he said, "is to find clues to help me solve a murder."

The boy whistled softly, and his sister's eyes grew wide with wonder.

"So," Ryan continued, "if you know anything about King John's jewels, anything at all; local legends, superstitions—"

"The dagger," said Jenny, tugging at her brother's coat. "Michael, tell him about the dagger."

"I dunno," said Michael. "I'd have to ask Dad. He says we're not supposed to talk to strangers."

"Very good advice," Ryan assured him, "but you've already talked to me, haven't you?"

"I ain't saying no more," Michael announced. "You'll have to talk to my Dad."

"He's working in his office," Jenny said. "He told us to go out and stop bothering him, but he won't mind if we come back now."

"With someone famous," Michael added.

The children spoke together in a rush.

"He's the vicar."

"We'll go and get him."

"He's got the keys."

"'Cause he's the vicar."

Ryan watched them race off across the churchyard in the direction of the gloomy Victorian mansion. He heard the creaking of a rusted hinge, and saw Crispin enter through the lych-gate. He strolled languidly toward Ryan along the church path, pausing to read the inscriptions on the tombstones. Ryan looked back at the little toolshed. There was no sign of the mist. Perhaps he had simply given in to his imagination. This was a strange place and he was very tired.

He waited for Crispin in the shelter of the church porch. As soon as Crispin arrived, Ryan told him what he had discovered, which wasn't very much, except for the fact that there was, or had been, a dagger.

Crispin was impressed. "Well done, old boy. You're quite the expert."

"I know a thing or two about daggers," said Ryan, basking in the other man's approval.

The vicar turned out to be a serious, round-faced young man wearing blue jeans and an old overcoat opened at the neck to show his clerical collar. He unlocked the church door with a massive key and led them inside. They paused in the gloom just inside the doorway as the vicar went forward to turn on the light.

The inside of the building was cold, colder even than the air outside. The lights, when they finally came on, threw only faint rays down onto the cold stone floor and upward into the gloomy darkness of a vaulted ceiling. A sea of empty pews stretched before them, gleaming dully with the sheen of hundreds of years of beeswax. At the far end of the church, a red light glowed above the distant altar. The dusty silence of the ages seemed to envelope them. Even the vicar spoke in a whisper, and the two children reined in their boundless energy.

"Come into the vestry." The vicar withdrew another key from his pocket and opened a small door in the side wall. They climbed a couple of steps into a red-carpeted room where the last rays of the afternoon light shone jewel-like through tiny stained-glass windows. The room was furnished with a desk, some battered armchairs, and a couple of glass-fronted display cases; empty display cases.

The vicar extended his hand. "Barry Marshall."

"Marcus Ryan."

"I know," said Marshall. "My son and I watch your program."

He raised an inquiring eyebrow at Crispin. Ryan supplied the introduction.

"Tell him about the dagger," Michael said. "He's looking for the treasure."

"Tell him about your treasure," Jenny begged. "Go on, Dad."

"You're my treasure," Marshall said, ruffling her bright brown hair.

She giggled. "You know what I mean, Dad."

"It's not my treasure," said Marshall. "It was never my treasure." He smiled at Ryan apologetically. "But as vicar of St. Mary's, it was entrusted to my keeping. I'm afraid I didn't do a very good job."

"It wasn't your fault, Dad," said Michael.

"There was no money, you see, for burglar alarms," the vicar explained, "or a proper safe, and we liked to keep it on display. I'm afraid we were too trusting. The world is just not what it was."

Ryan wondered cynically whether the world had ever been what the Reverend Marshall would like it to be. Neither one of them was old enough to remember a world where treasures could be kept in unlocked cases in an unlocked church.

"I'm sure the Lord has his reasons," Marshall said with a kind of desperate resignation. He led them across to the empty display cases, where yellowing cardboard display cards marked the absent treasure.

"What exactly was in here?" Crispin asked.

"Some gold coins, a chain, an ornate drinking goblet, and a very unusual dagger," said the vicar.

Ryan pricked up his ears. A goblet and a dagger!

"Do you really think these were part of King John's treasure?" Crispin asked.

Marshall shook his head. "No. I think that's highly unlikely. If anyone seriously thought they were part of King John's treasure, they wouldn't have been left here. They would have been surrendered to the Crown."

"Of course," said Crispin.

"So how did you get them?" Ryan asked.

"I'm the one who lost them," he said apologetically, "not the one who found them. I've only been here for three years. One of my predecessors acquired them. That would have been 1952, the year of the bomb."

"What bomb?"

"A leftover from the war. We came in for some very heavy bombing around here. Lots of Americans stationed here in '44. The Germans were after their airfields. In 1952, when excavations began for the new primary school, an old bomb exploded and blew an enormous great crater in the schoolyard. Killed a couple of construction workers."

"It happened a lot," Crispin said. "Thanks to Hitler, the whole country was full of unexploded bombs."

"They found the treasures in the bottom of the bomb crater," said Marshall. "That's what started the rumors. You probably know that this was all marsh at one time, so of course, everybody started speculating about King John's treasure that was lost in the Wash. Every kid in the country knows the story. They had quite a little gold rush here for a while, with people digging around in the bomb crater and digging up the schoolyard. They never found anything else, and there was nothing to tie the few little pieces that were found to any historical records. For all anyone knew, they could have been someone's personal possessions buried a few years earlier to keep them safe. They're not really very valuable. The stones on the goblet weren't real. They were some kind of crystals, maybe garnets."

He looked at Ryan. "Are you alright, Doctor Ryan?" he asked.

Ryan knew that his face had betrayed him. He managed a tight smile. "I'm fine, just a little tired." His mind was racing. Rubies, garnets, some kind of crystals? He slipped his hand into his pocket and felt the sharp edges of the remnant of jewelry. In 1952, when the goblet had been uncovered, there were no scientific instruments to measure the molecular structure of the red stones, so they'd settled for calling them garnets.

"The treasure was handed over to the church for safekeeping and put in the display cases here," Marshall concluded.

"And when were they stolen?" asked Crispin.

"Six months or so ago," Marshall said. "Nice clean job. No fingerprints. I'm sorry Doctor Ryan, but if you were hoping to include them in your program, you're too late."

"That's okay" Ryan said, feeling the weight of disappointment adding to his jet lag.

"He doesn't want them for his program," Michael said. "He's trying to solve a murder."

Marshall gave Ryan a puzzled stare.

"He is, Dad," said Michael. "Tell him, mister."

"Michael—" said Marshall in an ominous tone.

Ryan interrupted before Michael could be accused of lying. "That's what I told him. I'm looking into it for a friend."

"And it has something to do with our treasures?" asked Marshall.

"Probably not," Ryan said, trying to sound dismissive, "but as a matter of interest, did the local police investigate?"

Marshall shook his head sadly. He seemed to be a rather despondent kind of man. "They don't care. It's petty theft from church property. Most of them think the church is a waste of time, and stealing from the poor box is pretty common. I know, I know, this wasn't the poor box, but they really don't care. If I could convince them that someone had stolen the communion wafers and was practicing satanic rites in the village hall, they might sit up and take notice, or maybe they'd join in."

"So you're not on good terms with the local police?" Crispin asked.

"My fault really," said Marshall. "I mean, I couldn't give them anything to go on. I didn't even know when the stuff had disappeared. It could have been gone for weeks without me noticing."

Michael tugged Ryan's sleeve. "Just before it happened," he said, "there was a girl hanging around and acting suspicious. She talked to me."

"I saw her too," Jenny said.

"You did not," said Michael. "You're just copying me."

"Did too," said Jenny.

"Be quiet, both of you," Marshall said, rubbing a weary hand across his eyes. Ryan wondered where their mother was. So far, she had not been mentioned by any of them.

"I don't think she was a thief," said Michael. "She didn't look like a thief. She was blond and pretty. She asked me what time my Dad was coming to open the church."

"But he wasn't coming," said Jenny, determined to stay in the conversation, "because it was his day off." She looked sideways at her brother. "Girls can be thieves," she said.

"She gave me fifty pence for ice cream," said Michael, offering the final proof that the blond, pretty girl could not be a thief.

"Why would she do that?" Ryan asked.

"'Cause the ice cream truck was on the green," said Michael. "She gave me fifty pence to go and get an ice cream."

"Did you see this girl, Vicar?" Crispin asked.

He shook his head. "It was my day off. I was at home."

"She was here again today," Michael said.

"Was not," said Jenny.

"She was," Michael insisted. "I was going to talk to her, but then she sort of vanished."

"People don't vanish," Jenny said.

"Well, she did," Michael replied.

Crispin took hold of Ryan's arm. "You look exhausted, old boy," he said. "Let's get you back to London and a comfortable bed at the Dorchester. Everything will look better tomorrow. Obviously, there's nothing to see here."

"I guess Violet was right," Ryan said. "She told me I needed a hot bath and long nap."

"Then let's take care of that," said Crispin.

The vicar reached into his desk drawer and handed Ryan a small printed pamphlet. "It's our church guide," he said. "There are a couple of photos of the treasures; black-and-white, I'm afraid, but they may be some use to you. The dagger and the goblet were the most interesting pieces; especially the dagger."

"Really?"

"It was made of Welsh gold, quite a rare commodity these days. It's what the royals use for their wedding rings, or so I'm told."

Crispin reached into his pocket. Coins clinked, and Michael and Jenny Marshall looked at him with interested anticipation.

"So," said Crispin, "I think the price of ice cream has gone up considerably, don't you?"

They nodded their heads in unison.

Crispin handed each child a small brass coin. "Here's a pound each," he said. "I know what it feels like when you don't have any money."

The remark pierced through the mental fog in Ryan's brain. Obviously, Crispin Peacock had been born with a silver spoon in his mouth; what would he know about being a child with no money? Ryan filed the question away with all the other questions that still needed answers; the most important being who was the blond-haired girl; what had she wanted to say to him at Heathrow; had Michael really seen her in the graveyard, and what had happened when the mist rose up on the path, and the world vanished?

They drove back to London in silence. Crispin seemed to be deep in thought, and Ryan had given up thinking. What he needed was sleep.

Crispin dropped Ryan off in front of the Dorchester. "Get a good night's sleep, old chap," he said. "I'm tied up tomorrow, but I'd like it if you'd get yourself down to Griffinwood the day after. There's a train from Euston. You can take a look around and see if I've missed anything. I'm sure you have a better nose than I do for that sort of thing. Bring your partner if you want to."

Not if I can help it, Ryan thought, as he hurried through the front door of the hotel, hoping that Violet Chambray would be nowhere in sight. Tomorrow would be soon enough to tell her that he had a solid lead. Tomorrow would be soon enough to say, "I told you so."

The One-Eyed Man
The Little Chef Restaurant, Ipswich, Norfolk

The one-eyed man was enjoying a cup of tea. Tea was not an available commodity in the world of his birth, but he had come to enjoy it while he was at boarding school. He had especially enjoyed Sunday afternoon at the school, when the tea was accompanied by ham or salmon sandwiches and scones with jam. Of course, that was before he lost his eye, at a time when he had been a more pleasant being. In those days, he had been quite popular with the other boys, and his wild streak had only revealed itself on the rugby field and in the boxing ring.

He reflected on the joy of winning a well-matched contest. Tonight would probably not be much of a match.

He poured some more tea from the white china pot. He would have a few miles to travel before his mission could be accomplished. He planned to ditch the car he'd stolen in Brighton and get himself something different; something inconspicuous. He was under strict instructions with this one. Don't make a mess. Don't harm the children. Don't take any souvenirs. Most importantly, make sure that the priest tells you everything he knows. Don't let him hold back.

CHAPTER SEVEN

Marcus Ryan

A ringing telephone woke him. Ryan reached out an arm and groped around the nightstand. The telephone continued to ring. He couldn't find it. He forced his eyes to open and saw the gloomy shadows of a strange bedroom. Heavy drapes covered the windows, admitting almost no light. He looked at the clock on the nightstand. Eleven o'clock, middle of the night.

He remembered falling into bed within minutes of Crispin dropping him off at the front entrance of the Dorchester Hotel in the heart of London. That would have been at about six o'clock. He'd been asleep only five hours. The telephone was still ringing. Who on earth, he wondered, was calling him at this time of night? He finally managed to locate both the reading lamp and the telephone, and then proceeded to knock the telephone onto the floor.

He could hear a tinny voice, far away but quite angry. "Hello, hello, Marcus?"

He picked up the phone and grunted, "Uh-huh."

"This is Violet."

"I know."

"Time to get up."

"Go away."

"Get up, Marcus."

"Go to bed, Violet."

A long pause followed. Finally Violet said, "Open the drapes, Marcus."

"Why?"

"Just do it, please."

He responded to the "please" and opened the drapes. He was greeted by bright daylight and the view of a watery sun shining down on the rooftops of London.

"It's eleven in the morning," he said with sudden comprehension. "Why did you let me sleep so long? I have things to do."

"I'm not your mother," Violet said. "You could have asked for a wake-up call."

He sat down on the edge of the bed and tried to collect his thoughts. However, even collected in one place, his thoughts were not worth sharing with Violet, especially his thoughts about a mysterious disappearing and reappearing young woman and a walk-through mist into another world.

"What did you find out yesterday?" Violet asked.

"A few things," he said.

"Tell me over coffee," Violet said. "I'll meet you in the lobby at noon."

"Noon?" he queried. "I don't need an hour to dress."

"I do," she replied.

He started to laugh. "You only just woke up, didn't you?"

She laughed with him. Her laugh was attractive, full and rich with nothing held back, a generous laugh that matched her generous figure. He reminded himself once again that she was not what she appeared. She was a fraud who had been forced upon him by his boss. He would have to work with her, but it didn't mean he had to like her. He replaced the receiver and went to take a shower.

He found Violet seated in a quiet corner of the lobby, nursing a cup of coffee and a plate of cookies. She stood up and brushed crumbs from her black skirt.

"You look better," she said.

Ryan looked her up and down. "So do you." It was the truth. She looked rested and considerably less frantic than she had been on the plane. Ryan could see how some men might even find Violet attractive, although he was determined not to be one of them.

Violet waved a manicured hand, and a waiter appeared with another coffee cup. "Well," she said, "did you find anything?"

Ryan nodded his head and sipped his coffee.

"Really? You're not just saying that to annoy me, are you?"

"No, I really found something. Did you?"

"No, nothing. That's ten points for you."

"Are we keeping score?" he asked.

"We don't have to," she replied.

She had made the first move. With the image of an impatient Mandretti lurking in the back of his mind, Ryan knew that he would have to respond. If Mandretti wanted him to work with this woman, that was what he would have to do. He extended his hand. "Partners," he said.

"Okay."

They shook hands. Her hand was very small and very soft.

"So?" she asked.

He gave her an edited version of his adventures at the Church of St. Mary, with no mention of the mist or the seawall or the Viking longships. "We got lucky," he said, "by stopping at the church. I don't know what made me do it, but I'm pretty certain that's where the dagger and the goblet came from."

"It wasn't luck," Violet said. "You had a hunch."

"Let's not go into that," said Ryan. "We agreed to start again, so let's forget all the other stuff. I think we're on the trail of something here. We don't need any more hunches, just solid research."

He hesitated, not wishing to do anything to upset Violet's newfound calm, but he had to ask. "Did you bring the message with you, the one from Carlton Lewis?"

"Yes." She was completely calm.

"We should try to find out—" he started to say.

She interrupted him. "I've been thinking about that. There are two leads in that message. One is the mention of Professor Peacock cataloging the contents of a regimental museum, and the other one was something about a document found at his estate in Shropshire. Do you think his next of kin could help us with that?"

"Crispin Peacock," Ryan said.

She chuckled. "That's quite a name. I assume that Crispin Peacock has inherited the house."

"I don't think the document is at the house," Ryan said. "Didn't the letter say that they had sent the document to be translated?"

"I think you're right," said Violet. "I believe it was sent to the Society of Arthurian Scholars for translation."

"We need to reread the message and be sure," Ryan told her.

Violet paled. "I know you don't understand this, Marcus, but I don't want to touch that document again."

"Then just give it to me and I'll read it. Or better still, have Todd e-mail it to me. I can get it on my Android."

"Android?"

"Yes," said Ryan. "I have it with me. I assume it will work."

"I don't do computers," Violet declared, "or Androids or whatever you're talking about."

"Well," said Ryan, "it's about time you started. It'll be a whole new world for you."

Violet glanced at her watch. "I've made arrangements to go to Carlton's funeral. It will be at his house in Surrey. I think it will be a good opportunity to talk to his widow. She may know something. I find talking far more effective than e-mailing, or androiding, or anything like that."

"Most people do both," Ryan told her.

"I have a limo and a driver," she said. "You should come with me."

Ryan smiled. The woman was a Luddite, but she had her own way of getting things done. He slipped his hand into the pocket of the tweed jacket that Todd had supplied him, and produced the pamphlet from the Reverend Barry Marshall.

"I got this from the vicar at St. Mary's. It's a description of the treasure they found in the bomb crater."

Violet took the pamphlet with her little white hand, smiled, opened it, and seemed to stop breathing. She set her coffee cup down very carefully. Ryan could see that she was struggling to control herself. Her face had turned pale, and she was pursing her lips as though fighting the urge to speak.

"What?" he asked. "Spit it out."

"You won't like it."

"Just say it before you pass out."

She took a deep breath. "Something has happened to the vicar," she said softly.

"He's a bit of a sad sack," said Ryan, "but he's perfectly fine. Come on, pull yourself together. Just walk with me to the elevator, and we'll go upstairs and get our things, and then we'll go to the funeral for Carlton Lewis. Something has most definitely happened to him, but nothing has happened to the vicar. Just stop doing this, Violet. We are trying to conduct an investigation based on facts, not your wild imagining."

"I'm trying," she said in a small strangled voice. "I'm really trying not to feel it."

The elevator arrived and Violet stepped in beside Ryan. The doors closed. She stared down at the pamphlet for a long time. "Something happened at ten minutes past eleven last night," she said in a carefully controlled voice. "He was in the church."

Ryan followed her out of the elevator and into her room. He tried to relieve his frustration by slamming the door, but the door, as befitted a door in an expensive hotel, closed with nothing but a soft swishing sound.

"We're putting an end to this nonsense," Ryan said, picking up the phone receiver. He consulted the phone number on the pamphlet. "I'll call him, and you can speak to him yourself."

Violet watched him as he dialed. He let the phone ring for a long, long time. There was no reply.

He knew that Violet was the kind of woman who would sulk. Her crimsoned lips set themselves into a tremendous pout and stayed that way as they departed the Dorchester in a chauffeur-driven car.

"He didn't answer," said Ryan. "What do you expect me to do? Do you want me to drive up there, or do you want me to come to this funeral with you?"

"I don't think you understand," said Violet. "This isn't about me."

"It's always about you."

"I would expect you to be more upset," she continued. "I haven't even met the man and I'm upset."

"I'm not upset," said Ryan, "because there is nothing to be upset about. The fact that he didn't answer his phone is neither here nor there. He's a busy man, and he has two children to look after."

Really, he thought, it was like talking to a sullen child.

Violet looked at the dainty gold watch stretched around her plump little arm. "We're going to be late," she said.

"Carlton's not going anywhere," said Ryan.

"Thanks for pointing it out," said Violet, shifting even further away from him on the soft leather seat.

Ryan turned away from her to look out of the window. Before long they had crossed the Thames, leaving the great city behind and heading out into the leafy Surrey countryside.

Violet broke the silence by leaning forward to ask the driver. "Are we nearly there?"

"Just a couple of miles."

She looked at her watch again. "We're going to be late," she said. It was a general complaint spoken to no one in particular, but Ryan felt that he was somehow being blamed.

The driver brought the car to a sudden halt.

"Are we there?" Ryan asked.

The driver shook his head. "Road block."

Violet looked at her watch again. The driver turned around and looked at them with an expression of strained patience on his Caribbean face. When he spoke, his accent was pure London. "Protesters. Nothing I can do about it. The police are directing traffic, and that just makes it worse."

Ryan leaned out of the car window. He could see flashing lights ahead, and a mob of people carrying banners and placards. The mob was heading in their direction.

Violet broke her sullen silence. "What is it? What do they want?"

"Well, if it's the same ones I saw yesterday, they're protesting building a dam in Wales," said Ryan, "but this is not where they were yesterday."

"It can't be the same group," said Violet. "We're nowhere near Wales. Why would you think it's the same group?"

"I didn't say it was the same group," said Ryan, realizing that his conversation with Violet was beginning to resemble the kind of conversations he used to have with Veronica before the divorce. "Maybe it's not the same group," he snapped. "Maybe they're protesting something else. I don't know who the hell they are. Why would you expect me to know who they are?"

"I don't expect you to know," Violet snapped back. She glared at the back of the driver's head. "They're making us late," she complained.

"I can't go ahead," the driver said. "I'm not allowed to run them down, and they won't get out of the way."

"What do they want?" Violet asked.

The driver wound down his window and looked ahead at the crowd, and then he turned back. "The gentleman is correct," he said. "They are protesting the building of a dam in North Wales."

"But why are they here?" Violet whined.

"They're everywhere," the driver said. "This has been a huge protest. The dam will flood a valley and drown several historic villages. The people have been compensated, but still we have protesters. That's just Britain. We don't like change, and we don't like it when old things are destroyed. And to make matters worse, there are wild horses in the valley. We are a nation of animal lovers, so you can imagine that doesn't go down well."

The mob came closer and flowed around the car in a sea of denim jeans, down jackets, and creative headgear. Ryan wound up the window and sat back. With cars piling up ahead and behind, they were going nowhere until somebody got the protestors off the road, or until they had all passed by, heading for whatever destination they had in mind. So far as Ryan knew, they were far from Wales, so maybe the protesters were marching on London.

Someone thumped on the car roof. "Oh really," said Violet, "as if we care about their protest."

The thumping ended, but someone was now tapping on the car window right next to Ryan's head. He turned to look and saw a face pressed against the window, a face he recognized. Somehow he was not surprised to find her there. She was part of the story, part of the mystery. She had been at the airport, she had been in Norfolk, and now she was here. Her hair was flowing free around her shoulders, and she was wearing a dark jacket. The chiffon scarf was tied around her neck.

"You," he mouthed. "What do you want?"

She made winding motions with her hands, and he lowered the window. "Open the door," she said. "I need to talk to you."

"Are you following me?" he asked.

"Yes, of course I am," she said.

"Why?"

"Just let me in, please, before this crowd knocks me down."

Ryan opened the door, and she squeezed inside, pushing him up against Violet. The driver turned and looked at Ryan disapprovingly.

The girl breathed a sigh of relief. "I've been waiting for you for hours," she said. "I knew you'd have to come this way."

"I take it you're not one of the protesters," said Ryan.

"They have enough people already," she replied, "but their protest will do no good. The dam will be built because no one can stop progress, not in this world. Of course, it's quite different at home."

"Home?"

"Where I come from," she said.

"And where is that?" Ryan asked, impatient with this waiflike girl and her circuitous rambling speech. Time to speak plainly, put aside cryptic remarks and get to the point of whatever it was that she wanted. He was quite certain that whatever it was, and whoever she was, she was part of the riddle of the sword.

"I saw you," he said, "you were standing on the seawall."

Her face lit up with delight. "You came through," she exclaimed.

"There were ships," Ryan said.

"Yes, I know, but I didn't see you. Why didn't you say something?"

"Say what? Where the hell was I?"

"We can go again and you can see for yourself," the girl said. "Do you have the pin in your pocket?"

"No," said Ryan. "I'm not wearing my coat. What's so special about the pin?"

Panic spread across the girl's face. "Where is it? Is it in a safe place? You have to go back and get it."

Violet had so far ignored their visitor. Ryan thought that she had probably not even noticed her. She had rolled down the window on her side of the limousine and was peering impatiently at the crowd of protestors. Now she turned back.

"We're going to be so late," she said, and then she saw the intruder. "You?" she said. "What are you doing here?"

"I could ask you the same thing," said the girl.

"That," said Violet turning her attention to Ryan, "is the rudest person I have ever met. She just outright called me fat. I've never even met her before, and she walked right up to me and called me fat. Is that what passes for manners in this country? And then she tried to steal your luggage. I saw her. Get her out of here before she steals something else."

The girl pointedly ignored Violet. "There is so much you need to know if you're going to help us," she said to Ryan. "We need the sword, and you are really our last hope."

Violet leaned forward across Ryan. "No way, sister," she said. "No way are you getting your hands on that sword. Mr. Mandretti has a lot of money invested in this—"

The car suddenly lurched forward, throwing Violet off balance.

"Be careful," she said to the driver.

"You want me to move or not?" he asked over his shoulder.

"Yes, I want you to move. We're already late," said Violet. She turned back to Ryan. "Will you please get your strange skinny friend out of here."

The girl leaned forward and glared at Violet. "This," she said, "is none of your business. You and your sisters have done nothing to help, and now … now that we are so close to an answer, you come here and you insert yourself into this situation. Go back; go and tell them that we are doing everything we can, and sending people like you will only make matters worse."

"What sisters?" said Violet. "I don't have any sisters. Do you mean Maria? She's not really my sister. Well, she is but she's adopted."

The car lurched forward again. Violet, caught off balance, reached out to steady herself against the intruder's shoulder. Ryan heard a gasp from each of them as they sprang apart. The car began to move again.

"I have to go," said the blond-haired girl. "I can't come with you; I have to go back. I have to tell someone about her."

"What are you talking about?" Ryan asked. "What's going on here, Violet?"

Violet ignored him, staring at the intruder. "Back where?" she asked. "Please tell me, back where?"

The girl opened the car door.

"Slow down," said Ryan to the driver.

The driver applied the brakes. Behind them a line of vehicles began to sound their horns.

The girl turned to Marcus. "Tomorrow," she said, "you will go to Griffinwood."

"How did you know?" he asked.

"I have no time to explain," she said. "Bring the token and the pin, and then you will see."

She sprang from her seat and slipped out of the door, closing it hastily behind her. Ryan watched as she was swallowed up by the noisy mob of protesters.

He turned angrily on Violet. "She was going to tell us something," he said, "and then you—"

He was unable to continue. Violet had shrunk back into a corner. Somehow, despite her more than ample curves, she seemed to be diminished, as though she was being swallowed by the upholstery. Tears were streaming from her eyes, mingling with her mascara and inscribing black streaks across her pale cheeks.

"Now what?" said Ryan. "Don't start crying; that won't get us anywhere. Do you know who she is?"

"No."

"Well, she seemed to know something about you," Ryan said.

"Apparently, she knows your sisters."

"I don't have any sisters," Violet replied in a small choked voice.

"Are you sure?"

"No." She spat the words at him. "No, I am not sure. Perhaps I have dozens of sisters. I don't know, because I don't know who my parents are."

"You don't?" Ryan said.

When he had first encountered Violet in her backyard gazebo, he had seen her as a woman who was obnoxiously sure of herself; a diva who drew all the energy in the room toward herself, leaving no room for other people. In the last forty-eight hours, he had watched as her confidence had been shaken, and he had done some of the shaking himself. He suspected that a very different woman would soon emerge from beneath the outer shell of expensive cosmetics and designer clothing.

"You don't know who your parents are?" he repeated, feeling that this might be the breakthrough moment.

"No," Violet said, taking a deep breath, "I'm an orphan, Marcus; a foundling. I was placed in a basket at the door of the Convent of St. Philomena in Vannes in Brittany. I know nothing about myself and neither do the nuns. I had no telltale locket or bracelet, no note pinned to my blanket. I understand it was a very ordinary blanket. I know nothing except that I was adopted by an American couple who took me to the States. I know nothing." Her voice rose to a fever pitch. "Nothing, Marcus, nothing," she said. "But this girl, this strange, rude girl, knows something. She knows who I am."

"She didn't say that," said Marcus.

"She told me to go back where I came from, and I don't think she meant America, and I don't think she meant Brittany. What did she mean, Marcus?"

"I have no idea," said Ryan.

"Are we going to Griffinwood tomorrow?" Violet asked abruptly.

"I am," said Ryan.

"We are," said Violet emphatically, "and you'd better bring that thing with you, the pin, or token, or whatever it is. "

She sat up straight in the seat and produced a tissue and a mirror from her purse. As she repaired the damage to her face, she looked at Ryan. "I don't work for you," she said, "I work for Michael Mandretti. Mr. Mandretti likes to get his own way."

"I know," said Ryan.

"He wants that sword."

"We'll get it for him."

"We'd better," said Violet

CHAPTER EIGHT

The One-Eyed Man
The Chapel, Griffinwood Manor, Shropshire

The one-eyed man made his way through the weeds and undergrowth surrounding the ruined chapel, trying to follow the path that had been beaten down by the one other person who used the chapel gate. He was leaving his mission unaccomplished; two bodies and still no answers. However, he had acted on his own initiative, and he had not physically harmed the children.

As he stepped forward into the clearing in front of the ruined chapel, it occurred to him that the clearing was wider than it should be; the undergrowth beaten down by the passage of more than one person. Who else, he wondered, had come through the gate? Had someone been sent to check on him and to make sure he was doing what he was told? No, he didn't think that would be the case. He was trusted; he was the right-hand man. So someone else was using the gate; no doubt one of the women. Killing one of them would feel good, really good, but legend said they could not be killed by the likes of him. He grinned and fingered the sharp blade of the dagger concealed in his pocket. It would be fun to try. Maybe he couldn't hurt them, but they couldn't hurt him either; that was the way it was.

He approached the gate cautiously. The women could not hurt him, but the creature could still kill. It did not usually move in daylight, but one could never be sure. He drew the dagger from his pocket and stepped through into the mist. His cell phone died and his watch stopped working.

Violet Chambray
Glebe Cottage, Oxted, Surrey

They were late for the funeral, and Violet hated to be late. No sooner had they cleared the traffic-clogging protesters than they encountered road works, and then a traffic accident. The narrow lanes of the Surrey countryside were proving virtually unpassable on this sunny spring morning, and Violet's mounting impatience made no difference to the driver or to Ryan, who stared out of the window, obviously trying to ignore her.

She was embarrassed by her outburst and her tears. In one violent sweep of emotion, she had destroyed the illusion that she had worked so hard to create, and revealed the pathetic little orphan girl who still lived beneath the sophisticated exterior.

She made an effort to pull herself together before they reached the church. The church doors were closed, and the mourners had apparently departed having laid Carlton Lewis to rest amid the daffodils and bluebells of an English country graveyard. She stood for a moment, looking at the freshly turned earth. The sun had appeared, and the sky was a brilliant rain-washed blue. Birds with unfamiliar songs chirped in the trees, and a cool breeze ruffled the new green leaves. She decided that if there was a perfect place to bury an Englishman, this was it.

A young man approached them, walking respectfully among the graves. "Doctor Ryan and Miss Chambray?" he asked. Ryan answered for both of them.

"Lady Clemma would like you to come to Glebe Cottage," the young man said. "The mourners have all departed. Now is a good time for her to talk to you. You can have your driver follow me."

They climbed back into the limousine with the ever-patient driver, told him which car to follow, and set off again down the leafy English lanes.

"Have you ever met the widow?" Ryan asked Violet.

She shook her head.

"So you only knew her husband?" Ryan asked.

"And what exactly do you mean by that?" she snapped back.

He shrugged his shoulders. "Nothing," he said.

Oh sure, nothing at all, she thought to herself. She was really trying to like Mandretti's tame academic, but it wasn't easy. Granted he had not said anything too stupid after her confession that she was an orphan with no idea of her own background, but how could he take her seriously now that he knew who she really was? How galling it must be for him to see that she could command a high price for conjuring up visions and dreams. Ryan had probably spent a fortune on his education, hours upon hours of study and research, and probably many uncomfortable weeks in primitive countries, and he had very little to show for it beyond his PhD and a failed television career, while she had the house in Key West and the illusion of wealth.

Glebe Cottage turned out to be a great deal larger than any cottage ever painted by the English romantics, but it did have a cottage garden crammed with crocuses and daffodils, and a very cottage-like front door with green bottle-glass windows and a massive door knocker. Their guide waited until they had parked and then pulled away. The driver settled down to wait.

"Why don't you go and have some lunch," Ryan said to him.

"Thanks," he said, "very thoughtful of you."

It occurred to Violet that she had really allowed herself to become thoughtless and selfish. She would never have worried about whether a limo driver was able to get lunch. Well, points to Marcus Ryan for thinking of it. She made an extra effort to try to like him.

Lady Clemma Lewis opened the door herself. She greeted them by saying, "They've all had their glasses of sherry and gone, thank heaven."

She ushered them into a parlor where a coal fire blazed in the grate and a large woman with wild gray hair stood with her back to the fire, warming her more than ample backside. Clemma herself was a tall, thin woman. She wore a sensible black suit, and her iron-gray hair straggled out from under a sensible black hat. Her pale blue eyes were rimmed in red, and she wore the stunned expression of the suddenly bereaved. She looked Violet up and down and then said, "Miss Chambray, are you even half as good as Carlton said you were?"

Violet felt herself blushing, but Clemma Lewis waved her hand dismissively. "Not that," she said. "I don't want to talk about that. I know what happened with you and my husband."

"I'm really sorry," Violet said. "It was nothing serious."

"No need to be sorry," said Clemma. "You weren't his only fling, my dear, although you may have been one of the more interesting ones. I was used to it. That's not what I want to see you about."

Violet felt suddenly small and worthless, just another fling among a great many flings.

The woman by the fire spoke in a rich, deep voice. "This, I assume, is Doctor Ryan?"

Ryan nodded.

The woman stepped away from the fire and extended her hand to Ryan. "Margaret Walker," she said. "Call me Molly. Have you eaten lunch?"

Violet looked around and saw that the room was littered with the remains of the funeral luncheon, with sherry glasses and tea plates spread around on side tables. A black-and-white cat sat comfortably on the buffet table, licking crumbs from a sandwich plate.

"Get down, Toby," Clemma said halfheartedly. Toby looked at her disdainfully and moved to another plate.

"Oh, leave him alone," said Molly. "He's had too much excitement for one day."

"Well, there won't be much of that from now on," Clemma said. "I don't suppose I'll be doing much entertaining in the future."

"Don't be morbid," said Molly. She turned to Ryan. "I've seen you on television," she said. "You seem to know your stuff."

Ryan nodded again.

Molly indicated that Ryan and Violet should sit on the sagging floral sofa. Ryan plopped himself down, and Violet lowered herself onto the cushion beside him, aware of the effect her weight might have on the furniture. As Violet expected, they rolled together with their thighs touching. Ryan appeared not to notice. He looked at Violet hopefully. It occurred to her that she had put the fear of God into him by invoking Mandretti's name and reminding him of the consequences of not getting Mandretti the item he was seeking. Now, apparently, Ryan was hoping that Violet would take charge of this meeting and ask all the right questions. Perhaps he was no longer quite as sure of himself as he had appeared to be.

Molly resumed her place in front of the fire. "Fire away, Clemmy," she said.

"Oh, yes, well …" Clemma cleared her throat and tried again. "I, uh …"

"Clemmy," said Molly, "I know you've had a bad day …"

Bad day, Violet thought, the woman had just buried her husband; that was more than just a bad day.

"But," Molly continued, "you must try to take yourself in hand. If you start crying now, you'll be crying forever. I've been there, Clemmy; I do understand. Now, let's get on with the business at hand. We have to find out what happened to Carlton, don't we?"

"Yes," said Clemma. "Yes, we do." She picked up the cat and sat down in an armchair, with Toby on her lap. As she talked, she stroked the cat's head, and the big old tom started to purr.

"Miss Chambray," she said.

"Yes."

"Have you … er … have you … seen … anything? My husband said that you used to … er … see … things?"

Violet thought about her sure and certain knowledge that some as yet unknown harm had come to the Reverend Barry Marshall. She was just as certain of this as she had been of Carlton's death, but she had no explanation for either. The grief in Lady Clemma's eyes was raw and real. How could she be comforted by Violet's hazy visions and hunches?

"Please," said Clemma.

"I don't really know anything but—"

Molly interrupted Violet impatiently. "Let me handle this, Clemmy. Miss Chambray, Doctor Ryan, we need you to get to the bottom of this matter. This is not an idle request, and we are not just a couple of useless old biddies."

"Oh, I never suggested you were," Violet said.

"It was written all over the doctor's face," Molly said. "I know who you are, Doctor Ryan, and I know that you're more than just a semi-famous treasure hunter, but you're out of your depth here, aren't you?"

"I'm here to help him," Violet said.

"I know all about you," Molly said, "and I don't doubt that you have had your fair share of success and made yourself wealthy in the process. As I understand it, Michael Mandretti has hired you both to find Excalibur."

"To find a sword," Ryan said. "I don't for one moment suppose the sword is Excalibur."

"Of course it's not," said Molly. She drew herself up to her full height, which was quite impressive. "We English don't like to boast," she said, "but if no one will blow my trumpet for me, I'll have to do it for myself. You may not have heard of me, Doctor Ryan, but within my own sphere, I am a very well-respected medievalist."

Ryan opened his mouth to speak, and she interrupted him. "Yes, I have been published," she said, "and no, you have never read any of my work, because the subject doesn't interest you, does it?"

"Molly is president of the Society of Arthurian Scholars," Clemma said.

"I know what you're thinking," Molly said, addressing Ryan, who had the grace to look a little shamefaced.

Violet realized that she was witnessing an all-out academic pissing contest.

"You're wrong," Molly continued. "We do not, and I emphasize the word not, we do not believe that the Arthurian legend is based in historical fact. As an organization, we have been in existence for some hundred and fifty years. We are serious scholars dedicated to preserving the body of literature and scholarship that has grown up around the myth of King Arthur and the Knights of the Round Table in order to better understand the medieval mind. Our hope is that one day we will uncover our own personal holy grail; the source document; what academics would call the ur-document; which is to say, the earliest ever mention of Arthur or an Arthur archetype. That will allow us to date the origin of the story and put the rest of the legends to rest."

"Oh, I see," said Ryan.

"Good," said Molly. "So now that we have that out of the way, maybe you'll allow us to help ourselves by helping you."

Violet tried to put physical distance between herself and Ryan. Sitting on the sagging sofa with their thighs pressed against each other gave the impression of a partnership and a relationship that certainly did not exist.

"We'd be delighted to help you," Violet said. "Take no notice of Doctor Ryan. He thinks this whole search is a little beneath him. "

"Of course he does," Molly said, "and he's quite right. For any serious scholar to look for Excalibur is a ridiculous waste of time. To ask me or Carlton or Doctor Ryan to find Arthur's sword is the same as asking us to look for Aladdin's lamp."

"So what is going on?" Violet asked. "Because something is most definitely going on."

"Someone killed my husband," Clemma said. She had stopped stroking the cat, and her eyes were filled with tears. "What did he do that he deserved to be killed?"

Molly went to sit on the arm of Clemma's chair. She patted her friend's arm. "Chin up," she said. "Tears won't get you anywhere." She lumbered to her feet and went back to stand in front of the fireplace. "After Carlton sent you the e-mail telling you what little he knew about Professor Peacock's recent activities, he came to see me," she said.

"Oh, so you know about the e-mail," Violet said. She wondered if Molly knew the effect the message had on Violet. Did she know it had resulted in Violet's certain knowledge of Carlton's death? Was Molly the kind of person who would understand Violet's unique gift? She certainly looked far too sensible and down-to-earth to be a believer in visions and premonitions.

"Carlton was upset," Molly said, "because he felt his reply hadn't been very helpful. Of course, he knew Peacock; we all knew Peacock, and we were all very upset to hear of his death, in Las Vegas of all places. Anyway, Carlton came to see me to find out if I had any background information. I think it was the information that I gave him that got him killed."

Clemma rose to her feet, and the cat landed on the floor with a thud. "Don't talk like that," she said. "Don't talk about blame." She looked wildly around the room. "Would anyone like tea?" she said distractedly.

Violet shook her head.

"Cake?" Clemma asked.

"Yes," said Violet, always a slave to her appetite, "I'll take some cake."

She took the opportunity to heave herself off the sofa and away from the heat of Ryan's leg. She joined Clemma at the buffet table. The cat wandered across the room, gave Ryan a supercilious glance, and took Violet's place on the sofa.

"What did you tell him?" Violet asked Molly.

"A year or so ago," she said, "Taras acquired enough money to reopen his family's ancestral home in Shropshire. It had been shut up for years because no one could afford to run the place, and he'd never lived there himself. He inherited it from a great uncle or some such relative. It's a manor house with some ancient ruins attached."

Clemma handed Violet a slice of lemon sponge cake. Violet tried not to let the excellence of the cake distract her from what Molly was saying. She could see that Ryan was hanging on Molly's every word.

"Griffinwood Manor," Ryan said.

"Yes," said Molly. "Apparently, there's a library; not an important collection, but a few interesting bits and pieces came to light. Taras found an interesting old manuscript in a language he didn't recognize."

Ryan leaned forward. "Taras was fluent in a number of ancient languages," he said, "and he had a passing acquaintance with quite a few others. Are you saying that he didn't recognize the language at all?"

"No," said Molly, "not at all. That's why he brought the manuscript to us."

"Why you?" Ryan asked. "Why not the British Museum?"

"Oh dear," said Molly, "you really don't have any respect for us, do you? He brought it to us because it was illustrated and there were a couple of drawings of what looked like knights sitting at a round table. He thought we might find it interesting and that we might have someone to translate it."

"And did you?"

"Not exactly. We are certain that it is earlier than the fourteenth century, but we don't know how much earlier. We thought we had found someone, but—"

Violet was seized with a sudden desire to take hold of Molly's hand. The sensation was new and unexpected. Her gift had never expressed itself this way before.

"There was a girl—" Molly said.

Violet set the cake plate on the table and gave way to her impulse. She reached out for Molly's hand. Molly looked at her in astonishment.

"Oh, don't do this," Ryan said.

"Leave her alone," Clemma hissed.

Violet grasped Molly's hand and closed her eyes. A new world opened in front of her. She saw a room with stone walls and candles in sconces. It was the same room that she had glimpsed in her restless dreams two days ago in Key West. A young woman, a novice in a gray robe and brief white veil, sat at a table. In front of her were sheets of parchment, a quill pen, and a pot of ink. Violet sensed that the young woman was there against her will; that she had been brought from some other place and that the clothes she wore offended her in some way. Someone else stepped into the pool of light thrown by the guttering candles; a tall woman in a black robe, her face framed by a white wimple beneath a black veil. She wore a large jewel-encrusted gold cross around her neck.

"Write," said the nun to the novice.

The novice hesitated. Violet could feel the young woman's fear and her sense of outrage. "What should I write, Majesty?" she asked, looking up at the nun.

The nun smiled, more of a grimace than a signal of joy. "You know where he is," she said.

The novice nodded her head although the remark had been more of a statement than a question. "Yes, Majesty, I know."

"Generations will forget," said the nun. "You must write for future generations."

The novice hesitatingly selected a sheet of parchment. She looked up at the other woman. The tall nun had turned away. With a quick gesture, the novice pulled another sheet of parchment toward herself, tucking it under the first one. She picked up the pen and dipped it into the ink.

Just as suddenly as it had come, the vision departed. Violet released Molly's hand. "It's gone, "she said.

"That's alright, dear," Clemma said. "Sit down. Here, sit in the armchair. Give it a few minutes. Maybe something else will come to you."

"Did I speak?" Violet asked.

"Yeah," said Ryan. "You spoke. Novice, nun, candlelight."

Violet's strange behavior didn't seem to have disturbed Molly at all. She looked at Violet inquiringly and then asked, as though nothing unusual had occurred, "Shall I continue?"

"Yes, please go on," Violet said.

"Of course," said Molly, "when Carlton came to me I told him about the manuscript. We hadn't managed to translate it; in fact, we had not even managed to identify the root of the language. We had given the document as much attention as we could, and then we locked it away for safe keeping until we could find another expert. Naturally, Carlton asked to see it. We both thought it was more than a coincidence that Taras would find this document, which was obviously something to do with Arthur, and then he would announce to you that he had found Excalibur. So I went to the safe to get the document, and it wasn't there. Gone. Stolen!"

Words formed themselves in Violet's head and came out of her mouth, very much against her will. "The novice is afraid," she said. "Her loyalties are divided, but the other woman will not be denied."

Ryan looked at Violet angrily, obviously resenting the interruption.

"What do you mean by 'gone'?" he asked Molly.

"Oh for goodness' sake, be quiet," Clemma hissed to him. "Let Violet speak."

The cat rose slowly to his feet, slithered from the sofa, and crossed the room to stand at Violet's feet. His ears were back and his tail was lashing furiously. His head was up, and he stared at Violet with ferocious intensity.

The cottage room faded again, and Violet was back in the nun's small room.

"I have no skill in the language of this world," the novice protested.

"Write in your own language," said the nun. "Show me where he sleeps."

The novice began to write. Violet saw the letters forming on the page in some ancient runic language. The nun watched for a few moments, staring down at the bent head of the novice. Then she turned away to look at the small fire smoldering on the hearth.

"Will we ever be warm again?" she asked. "Why do these Christian sisters of ours believe that lack of heat will lead us to their promised salvation?"

The novice glanced up, and, seeing that the nun's attention was concentrated on poking peevishly at the smoldering logs, she lifted the first sheet of parchment and began to write rapidly on the second sheet.

"Hah," said the nun as the logs burst into flames, "we shall be warm now if only for a few minutes."

She sat on a low stool by the fire, extending her hands to the flames. "Keep writing," she said.

"Yes, Majesty," said the novice. Her pen moved ever more rapidly, and Violet could sense the urgency in the young woman. This second document must be completed in secret.

The nun rose to her feet. Before she had reached the table, the novice had concealed the secret writing and returned to her laborious penmanship on the first document.

Violet tried to memorize the shapes as they were formed, but the vision was fading rapidly, and then she was back in Glebe Cottage with Toby the cat rubbing himself against her legs and purring.

"Astonishing," said Clemma. "Violet, my dear, you are quite astonishing."

"Oh yes," said Ryan, "she is definitely astonishing. Can we get back to the question of the missing document?"

"We called it the Griffinwood Document because it was found at Griffinwood Manor," said Molly.

"Two sheets of parchment," said Violet.

"No," said Molly, "only one."

"Whatever," said Ryan impatiently, "one sheet, two sheets, that's not important. Do you have any idea who took it? Did you call the police?"

"Well," said Molly, "we think it's more than a coincidence that a young woman who was working as a temporary in our office also vanished just before we found the document was missing. We were so pleased with her work. She was quick and she was quiet."

"And light-fingered," Ryan said.

Molly nodded. "Apparently so," she said. "She was a pretty little thing in a rather underfed way. Big blue eyes, a whole lot of blond hair. I suppose you might describe her as somewhat Bohemian, you know, droopy skirts and lots of scarves."

Ryan looked at Violet. They both knew who she was describing.

"One day she didn't show up for work," Molly said. "We phoned the number she had given us, but it was out of service. Of course, we didn't know the document had also gone missing; that never occurred to us. We just wanted to know what had happened to her. Everyone liked her. We wanted to know if she was okay."

"And when did you open the safe?" Ryan asked.

"Just a few days ago when Carlton came to see me."

"So it could have been missing for a while."

"Not too long," said Molly. "Taras gave it to us just before Christmas. It's not as though it's been lying around our office for years and years."

"What do you think the Griffinwood Document was?" Violet asked, still thinking of the runic characters that the nun had been writing.

"We don't know," Molly said. "We had made no progress with the translations. All we had to go on were the illustrations."

Something in her tone told Violet that Molly wasn't telling her everything. "Do you have a theory?" she asked.

"We all had theories," Molly said. She hesitated and looked around the room as though she suspected someone might be eavesdropping, and then she seemed to make up her mind. She lumbered over to the sofa and sat down heavily next to Ryan. He moved over to accommodate her bulk. "It's just a wild theory," she said, "and it wouldn't stand up under academic scrutiny."

"I won't give it academic scrutiny," Ryan assured her.

"I have my reputation to consider," Molly said.

"Oh for God's sake, Molly," Clemma said suddenly, tears welling in her eyes again. "Just tell us what you think; anything, anything at all. We're not getting anywhere like this."

"All right," said Molly, "but it's just a theory."

"We've got that," said Ryan.

"Well," said Molly, "I think that the drawings indicated Arthur's burial site."

"I thought you said he wasn't real," Violet said.

Molly continued as if Violet had not spoken. "I think that the manuscript describes the place where Arthur was taken by the Lady of the Lake and where he now lies sleeping."

"Sleeping?" Ryan repeated.

"According to most versions of the legend," Molly said, "Arthur did not die. He was taken to the Isle of Avalon to be healed of his wounds. He's sleeping now, and when Britain needs him again, he'll wake from his sleep."

Violet heard Molly's words, and somewhere deep inside her brain, or maybe her soul, a bell chimed. She knew without a shadow of a doubt that whatever disclaimers she might make later, at that moment, Molly wanted to believe that King Arthur was not dead and that he would return. Molly wanted to believe it, and so did Violet.

"That's nonsense," said Ryan, who obviously had not heard any bell chiming in his soul, but nonetheless, he looked distracted, as though maybe he knew something that he hadn't told anyone else in the room.

"The theme of Arthur's return appears in most of the earliest versions of the story," Molly said. "Mallory used it in Le Morte d'Arthur."

"Then why hasn't he come back already?" Clemma asked. "I can think of dozens of times when we've needed him. What about the Blitz? If Arthur was going to help us, he could have helped us with Hitler, couldn't he?"

"He doesn't have his sword," Violet said with sudden intuition.

Molly looked at her and nodded. "You know something," she said.

Violet shook her head. "No, I don't know anything."

"But you feel something," said Clemma.

"Maybe," Violet said. "I really don't know."

She had no idea where the words had come from or why she felt them to be true. Her heart was pounding, her mind was racing. She had to get out of the room. She had to leave Glebe Cottage. The heat of the fire, the patterned chintz, the knowing green eyes of the cat, the dirty dishes all seemed to be screaming at her to leave. She felt overheated, overdressed, overstimulated.

"I have to get out of here and clear my head," she said abruptly. "I have to go back to London."

"The answer's not in London," said Molly. "The answer's in your head."

Violet ignored her. "Doctor Ryan," she said, "we have to go."

Ryan rose to his feet. Violet thought that he was as eager as she was to be away from the cluttered room and the two demanding women.

"You'll keep in touch, won't you?" Clemma pleaded, looking so stricken that Violet wished she could bring herself to stay.

"Oh, yes, as soon as we know anything," Violet said. "I'm sorry, I'm so sorry."

Molly extended her hand, but Violet was afraid to take it in case the room disappeared again. She could not cope with any more visions.

Molly turned her attention to Ryan. "I don't really believe it," she said. "I don't even know why I said it. I know it's a myth."

Ryan nodded. "It's a myth," he agreed.

Violet saw a look pass between them. She assumed that they had now established academic equilibrium, with each of them having said something wildly speculative, and each of them having then denied their belief in myths and legends.

They walked outside to the car and the ever-patient driver. Violet was surprised to find that night had fallen and the flowers in the cottage garden were dark shadows under a starry sky and a quarter moon.

They rode in silence for some miles, and then Ryan said, "What happened in there?"

"I don't know," Violet said. "I've never experienced it like that before. It's been different since that girl touched me."

"Yes," said Ryan. "Blond hair, blue eyes, floaty scarves."

"It has to be something to do with her," said Violet.

"But what?"

She didn't want to answer. She did not even want to think. She especially did not want to think about an ancient king in full armor sleeping through the ages in a cave; not dead, only sleeping.

They left the dark Surrey lanes and headed toward London on brightly lit streets whose lamps blotted out the starry sky and the magic moon under which Violet's dreams and Molly's speculation had seemed possible.

"We're not really getting anywhere," Ryan said, "unless we believe that girl knows something and that your visions are true."

"So what do we tell Michael?"

"Oh shit," said Ryan. "I wasn't thinking about Mandretti."

"Well, start thinking about him," said Violet.

The driver pulled up under the portico at the Dorchester.

"I could use a drink," said Ryan. "You want to join me?"

What Violet really wanted was to go to her room and think, but she realized that Ryan was making a gesture of friendship. "Sure," she said. "I'll have a drink. I just have to freshen up a little."

Ryan headed for the bar, and Violet went to get her key. As she stood at the desk, she saw that the hotel had printed a news bulletin for the benefit of their guests. How kind of them, she thought, to realize that some people still like to read the printed word. She glanced down at the headlines, financial news, foreign news, gossip about the royal family. Now that would be interesting, just the diversion that her overheated brain needed. She would like to know more about the shenanigans of the staff at Buckingham Palace as told by a dismissed housemaid, or about the scandalous lifestyle of a certain young royal prince. She flipped the page, and another headline caught and held her eye. Two children missing from Norfolk village.

Frantically reading the small print, she learned that an all-out search was being conducted for the children of the Reverend Barry Marshall, Vicar of St. Mary's, Upper Malden, Norfolk, who had been taken from their bedrooms at the vicarage.

"Miss Chambray." The desk clerk was trying to give her the room key. "Miss Chambray, your key."

She saw Ryan making his way toward the bar. She should go to him. She should say, "Look, I told you so," but her feet would not move her in that direction.

"Miss Chambray."

She took the key and hurried to the elevator. She needed to be alone. She needed to be in the quiet solitude of her room. Images were already forming. A cord was tightening around her throat. She was already gasping for breath as she flung herself down on her bed and closed her eyes.

She had no idea how much time had passed when she was dragged back into the present by the ringing of the phone. She picked up the receiver and managed a subdued hello.

"Where are you?" Ryan said. "I'm waiting down here."

Oh God, Violet thought, I was supposed to meet him at the bar. What have I been doing? Was I asleep? No, not asleep, not dreaming; seeing. She had been with Barry Marshall in the church while the children were taken from the vicarage.

"Marcus," she said, "go to the front desk and pick up the printout of the news headlines."

"Why?" he asked. "I can get headlines on my Android."

"Then get them on your damned Android," she hissed, "or get the printout or go out on the street and buy the evening paper. Just do it."

She slammed down the receiver. The room was in darkness. She barely remembered riding up in the elevator or opening the door or flinging herself down on the bed, but apparently, she had done all of those things before the vision had overtaken her. Now she went through the room, turning on all the lights. She wanted the room to be bright as possible and not filled with shadows. Marshall's church had been filled with shadows, and his attacker had come out of the shadows. How many attackers? He had been aware of at least two shadows flitting along the side walls.

She paced the room, waiting for the phone to ring and Ryan to say … What would he say? What could he say? This time there could be no denial.

Instead of calling her on the phone, he came to the door, knocking softly, almost apologetically.

"How the hell do you do it?" he asked as he stepped in through the doorway.

"I don't know," she said.

"But you knew something had happened?" Ryan said.

"I know what happened to the vicar, but I don't know where the children are."

"What can you tell me?"

She sat on the edge of the bed. She knew that Ryan had seated himself beside her, and she felt him take her hand, but there was no comfort to be found in the brightness of the hotel room or the touch of a human hand, because there had been no comfort in the cold stones of the ancient church; no comfort for the frantic father whose thoughts and feelings filled her mind.

Barry Marshall unlocks the door of the church, his church, the church that is his responsibility. He stands for a moment, savoring the darkness and the stillness and the ineffable sense of centuries of prayer. Moonlight filters through the stained-glass windows, and he sees the outline of the carved pews gleaming dully under their coating of beeswax polish. Up ahead the red votive lamp above the altar beckons him, and he strides forward, his footsteps echoing on the flagstones.

He is concerned for his children, but they are asleep in their beds and he will only be a minute. He only needs to refill the sanctuary lamp, and then he can go home again. The lamp must never be allowed to go out. Of course, no one would know, no one would see, but he would know and it would be on his conscience.

He wishes that his wife were home, but she has gone on a journey, a parent's death in a faraway place. He's lost without her. She's his anchor, the one who helps him with his skittish, unreliable memory, who keeps the confusion at bay. She is the one who makes it possible to remain as vicar despite the progress of his illness, despite the tumor growing so slowly in his brain. They have told no one, not even the bishop.

As he approaches the altar, his everyday thoughts become prayers, and he drops to his knees on the stone steps. The steps are hard and uncomfortable, but he doesn't care. He looks at the window above the altar; the Savior with his hands spread and welcoming. He remains kneeling for a long time, accepting comfort from the stained-glass Jesus, praying that he will be healed, that the tumor will shrink.

He rises to his feet. It's time to go back to the vicarage. The children will be fine; he has been gone no more than ten minutes and they were sleeping.

Even as he turns to leave, he hears a door slam with a sound that echoes through the church.

His heart begins to pound. He's afraid now. Bad things have been happening in other parishes. Even in front of the altar, he feels unsafe. He should have locked the door behind him. He should have turned on the lights. He peers into the gloom. He hears the rustling sound of feet shuffling across the flagstones. Someone is slipping toward him along the side aisle. He creeps closer to the altar and presses himself into the shadows. An image comes into his mind, Thomas Becket, Archbishop of Canterbury, murdered on the altar steps by order of Henry II.

He is still thinking of Thomas, saint and martyr, when he sees shadows flit along the side walls, among the burnished brass memorial plaques. He hears voices whispering. He thinks there are two attackers. Thomas Becket had been brought down by three, but here there are only two. The soft light of the votive lamp illuminates a pair of red shoes, or perhaps they are not red; perhaps it is the light of the lamp that turns them red.

He wants to defend himself. He tries to reach up for the heavy candlesticks on the altar. He thinks about the consecrated host kept in a safe behind the altar; he plans to defend it from the satanists. He pauses and tries to feel concern for the troubled souls in front of him.

"Let me help you," he says. "We can talk."

"Not interested in talking," says the intruder. "Just give me the sword."

"I don't have it," says Marshall.

"Then who does?" asks the intruder.

"I don't know. No one knows. You need to leave now before I call the police."

"Oh, you won't be doing that," says the intruder.

A sudden, fierce blow knocks Marshall to the floor.

"Where is the sword?"

"I don't know," says Marshall, frantically searching through his unreliable memory for something, anything, to say.

"Take the children," says the second voice. "Perhaps that will jog his memory."

"That's all I know," Violet said. She was still clasping Ryan's hand, clinging to it as her only link to reality, trusting him to be the anchor that would hold her in safety in the brightly lit hotel room.

She could see that he was shaken by her story. He had scoffed at her description of the night that King John's treasure had been lost, and he had dismissed her knowledge of Carlton Lewis's death as a lucky hunch, but how was he going to get around this? Would he put this down to imagination?

"I can't see the children," she said. "I've tried, but I can't see the children."

"You will," said Ryan. "Give it time."

He was still holding her hand.

"You really think so?"

"I don't know what to think, but your visions are all we have to go on."

"It's not enough," said Violet. "We have to tell someone. The police?"

"They won't believe you."

"No," said Violet, "I suppose not, and I don't really know anything."

"There's something else," said Ryan. "I haven't been totally honest with you."

"Really?"

"I haven't told you everything."

"Oh?" She waited. She didn't want him to let go of her hand.

"The girl we met, the blond—"

Now she tried to pull away from him. What was he going to do? Was he going to confess that she was someone he knew? Was she an old girlfriend? Did he think she would be jealous?

He would not release her hand. "Violet," he said, "listen to me. I didn't want to say anything, because it was just so strange, really, really strange, but now … well, it's not any stranger than anything else, I suppose."

"What do you mean?"

"When I was in Norfolk, at Marshall's church, something happened. I still don't know really what it was, but it happened."

He was staring into her eyes now, begging to be believed.

"Go on," she said.

"I was in the graveyard at the end of a path, and suddenly there was a mist. I stepped through the mist, and …"

"And?" she said encouragingly. She remembered how she had felt the first time she had told someone of a vision. She had been young, barely old enough to talk, but she knew she had seen something that she couldn't possibly have seen, and she had not known how to tell anyone. Now, so many years later, she could not even remember who she had told or whether she had been believed.

"Go on," she said.

"I was somewhere else," said Ryan. "I was on a dock, a stone dock, in a harbor. The sea used to come right up to the church at one time, but that was centuries ago. I saw the water and boats, like Viking longships, and one other thing …"

Violet waited.

"That girl was there on the seawall, talking to another woman. I saw her. I know it was her, but I don't know how it could have been her, and I don't know how I could have been where I was, but I was. What on earth have we gotten ourselves into, Violet?" he asked. "Do you have any idea?"

"No," she said, "but it's way bigger than Michael Mandretti looking for an old sword."

He patted her hand. "He's not going to like it," he said.

"And which one of us is going to tell him?" Violet asked.

"I don't know," Ryan said. "Let's sleep on it. The police are already looking for the children, and we can't do anything more tonight. It's been a hell of a day. I'll see you in the morning. Perhaps it will all make more sense in the daylight."

"I doubt it," said Violet.

"So do I," he agreed. "But what choice do we have?"

She followed him to the door.

"Good night," he said. "Thanks for listening."

"Sure," she said. "No problem."

He hesitated with his hand on the doorknob. "Will you be alright on your own?"

"I don't—"

"I could stay with you," he offered. "Sleep in the chair, just in case you have any more …"

"No," she said hastily.

"Of course not," said Ryan, and he sounded offended.

"I didn't mean …"

"I know what you meant," he said. "Good night, Violet."

"Good night, Marcus."

She closed the door behind him and turned the lock. She reached up to turn off the lights and changed her mind. She couldn't bear the thought of the darkness. With the lights on, she could just about bring herself to think about the day's events and wonder what it was that Ryan had seen through the mist. If she turned off the lights, she would be back in the darkness, watching Barry Marshall's assailant slipping through the shadows in his red shoes.

CHAPTER NINE

Once again it was the sound of the phone that dragged Violet from her sleep. She opened her eyes and blinked against the brightness of the room. She had slept with all the lights blazing, but, blessedly, she had not dreamed.

Ryan was on the phone. "Get downstairs," he said. "We have a visitor."

"What?"

"There's someone here to see us."

Violet remembered him sitting on her bed and holding her hand while she poured out her fears. And he had told her his secret, the unfathomable thing that had happened to him; how he had seen what he could not possibly have seen. They were friends now, she thought, and no longer competitors in the scramble for Mandretti's money.

"Hurry up," said Ryan. "He can't stay long."

Violet rubbed her eyes. "I need a shower."

"Not now," said Ryan. "This is important. I don't care what you look like."

"I care," she said.

"Violet," said Ryan, "I'm in the lobby. I have someone with me, and I need you to come down now, so just get over yourself and get down here."

She heard the click as he hung up the phone, giving her no time to argue with him.

She sat for a startled moment and then untangled herself from the bedclothes. Get over herself? What was that supposed to mean? No one had ever said that to her before. The sting of the words propelled her from the bed. She looked at herself in the mirror, assessing her own pale, frightened face and tangled hair. It would take hours to restore the image she had worked so hard to portray, to smooth out her complexion, restore luster to her dark hair, and replace the mask of cosmetics that gave her age and sophistication.

She squared her shoulders and faced up to the fact that she didn't have time to spend on herself. While she obsessed about her appearance, a murderer was approaching ever closer, kidnapping children and silencing the people who might give her answers. Right now Ryan was in the lobby with someone who might help untangle the mystery. He was right. It was time to get over herself.

Not daring to look in the mirror again, she threw on a pair of pants and a sweater, ran a comb through her hair, and hurried down to the lobby.

Ryan, dressed in the ill-fitting tweed jacket that Todd had given him, was seated in a quiet corner at a conversational grouping of sofas and armchairs. He was deep in conversation with a man who wore dark glasses and had a baseball cap pulled down low on his forehead. In the elegance of the Dorchester's lobby, he stood out like a sore thumb.

She hurried over to them. The man remained seated, his head down as though he was hiding from the world.

"Violet," said Ryan, "this is Reverend Barry Marshall."

"Oh," said Violet.

She dropped down into the chair next to the vicar. "I know what happened to you," she said. "I felt it."

"The children?" he asked.

"I'm sorry, but I don't know about anything them. I only know about you."

"They want the sword," said Ryan.

"Who does?" Violet asked.

"I don't know," said Marshall. "They said they will contact me and I should tell them everything I remember." He took off his dark glasses and swiped a hand across his red, swollen eyes. "They have my children," he said softly. "My children."

"Just tell them where the sword is," said Violet impulsively, forgetting about Mandretti, her paycheck, her house in the Keys, and everything else. "If you know something, just tell them."

"I didn't know anything," Marshall stammered, "or at least I didn't think I knew anything. I panicked. I couldn't think straight. I have this thing in my brain …"

"A tumor," said Violet. "It's benign."

"How did you—?"

"I just know," said Violet.

"I've been awake all night, and this morning my mind cleared. That's the way it's been lately. I can't remember things and then suddenly I remember. My wife has always helped me, but—"

"She's away," said Violet.

"New Zealand," said Marshall. "Her mother died. I haven't even phoned her yet about the children."

"You should call her," said Ryan. "It's in the newspapers. You don't want her to read it online, do you?"

"I thought that if I could give her good news; if I could say I remember where the sword is ..."

"Do you remember?" Ryan asked.

The vicar shook his head. "Not exactly, but there is something. I couldn't even think of it last night, but this morning I remembered something. That's why I came to see you. The police don't even know I'm here. It's something, a start, a beginning, and I'm hoping you could follow up. It's what you both do, isn't it?"

"Yes," said Ryan. He looked at Violet. "We'll work on this together. What do you have?"

"Well," said Marshall, "when you came to see me, I told you I didn't know anything about the sword."

"Yes," said Ryan.

"That wasn't completely true. It was true that I don't know where the sword is, but I do know how it was found. I didn't want to say anything, because it reflects badly on one of my predecessors. At the time, that seemed important, but now I don't give a damn. I just wish I'd remembered it last night, and then maybe they wouldn't have taken the children."

"They would have killed you," Violet said with certainty. "If you had told them what you knew, they would have killed you; that's what they do."

"But the children would be safe," said Marshall.

"They're still safe," said Violet. "Nothing is going to happen to them if we can help it. Tell us what you know."

Marshall reached into the pocket of his raincoat and produced a large sealed envelope and a little notebook. "It's all in here," he said. "I wrote it down on the train while I still remembered."

He flipped the notebook open. "God forgive me," he said, "it really makes the man look bad, but I don't think he was."

"What man?"

"My predecessor," said Marshall, "or rather my predecessor's predecessor. You see, I was appointed vicar after William Trevelyan retired. He was much loved by his congregants. They don't seem to feel the same way about me."

"Please," said Ryan, "just stick to the subject."

"I'm sorry." Marshall cleared his throat and looked at the notebook again. "Trevelyan took over from Clive Wilshire, who had been at the church since 1952. Wilshire died quite unexpectedly in 1962. He wasn't all that old, and I don't know what he died of, but when he passed away, his widow just upped and left the parish as fast as she could. I don't think she was well received by the parishioners, although I don't know why."

"It doesn't matter why," said Ryan.

"It might," said Violet.

"Just get on with it," said Ryan.

"Well," said Marshall, "Wilshire left all of his personal papers behind, a whole box of them. Trevelyan didn't even look at them, he just put them up in the attic, and I suppose he forgot about them. A couple of years ago when I was putting some of my own stuff up there, I saw the box, and I thought that maybe somebody should see what was in it. I didn't want my children to be poking around up there and finding something unsuitable, if you know what I mean. Just because a person is in ministry, it doesn't mean …"

He fell silent, staring at the notebook.

"So," said Violet expectantly.

"Oh, yes, well, it turned out that he had left his personal journal behind, or at least his wife had left it behind. I'm sure he never intended that anyone else should read what he had written. It was personal and honest, and it didn't show him in a good light, especially when it came to the treasure."

"What did he say about the treasure?" Ryan asked impatiently.

"It's all in the journal," said Marshall.

"Just tell us," said Ryan.

"It seems," said Marshall, "that Wilshire was first on the scene in 1952 when that World War Two bomb exploded. It was early morning and very few people were around, just Wilshire heading home on his bicycle from early morning devotions at the church."

Violet pictured the scene with Wilshire in a long black cassock, riding an old bicycle through the early morning mist, and then the sudden explosion of the bomb. The blast would have sent the birds calling and shrieking into the cold air while clods of earth rose up into the sky and then rained down on the surrounding fields. Probably knocked the vicar off his bicycle, she thought.

"He ran to see if he could help," said Marshall, "but the two men who had been digging were already dead. I'm sure he prayed for their souls."

"Of course," said Ryan.

"Then," said Marshall, and it was obvious that he was coming to the climax of his narrative, "he looked around at the bomb crater, and he could see a glint of gold. He dug with his fingernails; that's what he says in his journal, he dug in the ground with his fingernails, and he found a sword."

Violet realized that she was holding her breath.

"Keep going," said Ryan.

"Wilshire says that he thought someone might steal it," said Marshall. "He knew that people would be arriving at any minute, and he thought that it might be taken, so he took it and hid it in a bed of stinging nettles. You know how that is, no one's going to poke around in a bed of stinging nettles."

"He actually found the sword," Ryan whispered. "There really is a sword."

"He hid the sword and went back to the bomb crater," said Marshall. "By that time the fire brigade had arrived, and there were people everywhere, and of course, they found the rest of the treasure." He closed the notebook. "I am sure he had good intentions."

"Who cares about his intentions?" said Ryan. "It exists! The sword actually exists!"

Violet could hardly breathe. If the sword existed, what else existed? If this was the Great Sword of England, was it also Excalibur? No, that was impossible.

Ryan took the envelope from Marshall's hand and pulled out an old leather-bound journal. He flipped through the yellowed pages. "What did Wilshire do with the sword after that?" he asked.

"I don't know," said Marshall. "I read the whole thing, and I don't think he mentioned it again."

Ryan continued to flip through the pages.

"I don't think that will help," said Violet. "I'm sure Reverend Marshall would tell us if he had found anything. It's a dead end."

"No," said Ryan, "don't give up so easily. This is what I do, Violet. This is how I find things."

"There really is a sword," said Marshall, "and all we have to do is find it. God only knows what's happening to my children while I'm standing here."

Violet could see the man's anguish. She had no idea if what she was about to do would make things better or worse. "Do you have anything with you that belongs to your children?" she asked.

"I don't know," said Marshall. He dug around in the pockets of his raincoat. "I have Jenny's hair clip," he said, holding out a scrap of red plastic shaped like a row of hearts.

Violet held out her hand. "Do you want me to try?" she asked.

"Is it witchcraft?" said Marshall.

"I don't know," said Violet. "I have no idea what it is, but it's what I do." She cast a sideways glance at Ryan. He had his clues and his meticulous research, but she had this. From the moment she had stepped off the plane onto English soil, her abilities had been growing. Previously she had only been able to read faint emanations from objects, vague clues and hints, and occasional flashes of brilliance. Seeing King John and his baggage train crossing the Wash had been a moment of brilliance, or maybe not. Maybe she had only regurgitated something she had already read.

She held the little red clip in her hand, tracing the pattern of hearts.

"Anything?" said Marshall.

She closed her eyes, concentrating on the sharpness of the little hair clip as it pressed into the palm of her hand. For a brief moment, she became a little girl sitting up in her bed, her heart pounding because she heard footsteps on the stairs; footsteps that did not belong to her daddy. She tried to extend her vision. Where was she now? Where was the frightened child? Nothing. No pain, no fear, nothing, and nothing to tell the anxious father.

She handed the clip back to Marshall. "Sorry, I'm not getting anything, but don't give up hope. Doctor Ryan is very good. He knows how to find things. We'll find them."

"I have to call my wife," said Marshall.

"Yes, you do," said Ryan. "If she finds out from someone else …"

"I know, I know," said Marshall. "I'm going now."

"Back to Norfolk?" Violet asked.

"I'll call her from the train," said Marshall. "I want to be home in case I hear anything. So they know where to find me."

Violet watched him leave, a sad figure with slumped shoulders. Ryan was still leafing through the journal. He looked up at her. "So, you didn't feel anything?"

Violet sat down and leaned forward to look at Ryan. "I felt something."

"Why didn't you tell him?"

"Because it was the same thing I felt with that piece of paper you gave me in Key West. The children are not here. They're somewhere far away, behind a barrier. I don't know how else to describe it. They're beyond reach."

"Dead?" he asked.

Violet looked down at her hand, where the hairpin had left a row of heart-shaped impressions. She shook her head. "No, I don't think so. Not dead, just gone."

Ryan contemplated the journal. "I feel responsible," he said. "If I hadn't gone up there—"

"We had a job to do," Violet said, "and you couldn't know."

"No, I suppose not," he said, "but somehow you knew."

"No, I didn't know. I just didn't want to go to Norfolk with you. I was tired and I wanted to take a bath."

Ryan was silent.

"Well, at least we know there actually is a sword," Violet said encouragingly.

"Yeah," said Ryan abstractedly, still paging his way through the journal.

Violet watched him for a few minutes, realizing that he was now in a world of his own.

"I have to go and get dressed," she said at last. "We're supposed to go to Peacock's house. You can read it on the train."

Ryan glanced at her sharply. "How do you know we were supposed to go to Peacock's house?" he asked.

Violet thought about it for a moment. "I don't know," she said eventually, "but that girl said she would meet you at Griffinwood Manor. Considering what you told me last night, I have to assume that she knows something."

"I think she's been following me," said Ryan. He set the journal down on the table and looked at Violet. "This journal is the only thing I understand," he said. "All the rest is smoke and mirrors and mumbo jumbo, and people knowing things they couldn't possibly know, and people being where they can't possibly be. I don't work like this."

"Neither do I," said Violet. "I have dreams and hunches, but nothing like this. All I know for sure is that people are being killed all around us and we could be next. So is this journal worth killing for? Is it worth taking children away from their father to God knows where?"

"I suppose it could be," said Ryan. "Fortunately, no one else knows we have it. Let's just keep it that way." He slipped the journal back into the envelope. "I guess we'd better go and see what Peacock has to say. We're getting nowhere sitting here. This isn't going to bring those children back, and maybe we'll find something at Griffinwood. I'll put the journal in the hotel safe while we're gone."

Violet looked around the lobby, making certain that no one was watching them. She saw a flurry of activity around the entryway. A porter wheeled in a cart loaded with expensive luggage. He was followed by a slight, raincoated figure directing activities with graceful hand gestures. She recognized him instantly. Todd. Todd was here in London, and following close behind, dressed in stylish tweeds, came Michael Mandretti.

Mandretti strode toward them with Todd at his heels.

"So," said Mandretti, "did you find it yet?"

The White-Haired Woman
Snowdonia, North Wales

The white-haired woman stepped easily from the frail craft onto the pebbled beach of the high mountain lake. A group of wild horses who had been drinking along the shoreline scattered as her feet crunched on the pebbles.

"You will not wait," she said to the girl who sat in the stern. "I will call for you if I need you. You may prepare the barge."

"Will he come?" asked the girl.

The white-haired woman offered her companion a cautious smile. "Our hope is greater than it has been for centuries," she said. "We now know where he sleeps."

"But the sword …" said the girl.

"The one-eyed man has returned empty-handed," said the older woman. "He has no gift of finding, but there is a woman, a daughter of Avilion, although she does not know this about herself, and she possesses the gift. If this is to be done, it must be done now and it must be done by her, or it will not be done at all."

"And what will happen to us if it is not done?" asked the girl.

"If he is allowed to truly die, the gates will close," said the white-haired woman, "and neither world will see us again. We will return to the mists. Now go."

She stood on the beach and watched as the frail craft made of cunningly knotted reeds moved without the benefit of sail or oar out across the cold depths of the lake. She watched until the mists parted to reveal a heavily forested island. The girl in the stern turned her head to look back at the beach, and then the mists closed in around her. She and the island were gone from sight.

"Will I ever see them again?" the white-haired woman wondered. She turned away from the beach and set her sights on the distant hillside preparing herself for a long, lonely walk. She glanced at the cheap plastic watch that she wore on her wrist. Useless. Time was not measured here as it was measured on the other side. The watch would not work until she passed through the gate.

She grasped her ornate staff, the insignia of her office, and set her face resolutely toward the east, where the sun was appearing above the mountains. She would not look back at the lake and the mists that concealed her island home. To move the island would take all of the power she possessed, and she would not survive, but the island would be safe and forever hidden. By what great plan, she wondered angrily, was it decreed that so much should depend on an orphaned daughter of Avilion who did not yet know her destiny? Perhaps there was no plan; perhaps there was no solution; perhaps there was only chaos and war from now until eternity.

Violet Chambray

Violet was overcome by a wave of anxiety at the sight of Mandretti. Her heart actually seemed to skip a couple of beats as he approached her.

"Did you find it?" he demanded.

Although he was dressed like an illustration from English Country Life, he still managed to look dangerous with his black hair slicked back and his dark, hooded eyes glancing from side to side, always on the alert for trouble. He still looked like a man who could handle any trouble that came his way with money or influence, or brute force if necessary.

Ryan sprang to his feet, towering above Mandretti in height.

"Did you find it?" Mandretti asked again.

"We're getting closer," Ryan said.

"Close don't count," Mandretti replied as he dropped down into an armchair next to Violet. Todd continued to hover in the background. He looked tired and angry.

"What are you doing here?" Violet asked Todd, looking away from Mandretti's determined stare. "What about the play?"

"Ah, well," said Todd dryly, "it seems that someone bought out the whole entire run and then closed the show, thus making me available to come here and help you."

"Oh, I'm so sorry," Violet said. "I know you were looking forward to it."

"He was playing a dame," Mandretti said.

"I was playing Madame Arcati and it was a concept," said Todd, "the idea of the feminine within the masculine. We were emphasizing the spiritual side of masculinity."

"He was in drag," Mandretti said. "Running around being some kind of crazy gypsy fortune-teller."

"Blithe Spirit," said Todd. "We were reinterpreting Noel Coward."

"You weren't getting no audiences," Mandretti said.

"So you bought him out?" Violet asked.

"Well, first I was just going to buy the property, it's not much more than a flea pit, but then I talked to the director, and he said I could just buy out all the tickets. He was happy. It gave him a few bucks for his next production."

"And now I'm not even there to audition," Todd complained.

Michael leaned forward, lifted Violet's hand, and carried it to his lips.

"So?" he said.

She had a little trouble breathing. Hand-kissing was a new and unwelcome approach, and she was not sure what it said about their relationship or Mandretti's expectations of her.

"We're working on it," she said.

"Yeah, well, I thought you'd work better with your brother around."

She looked at Todd. "He knows?" she said.

"He had to have my real name for the reservation."

"Don't make no difference to me," Mandretti declared. "Brother, uncle, he might even be your sister for all I care. Just so long as he gets the job done."

Violet looked at her brother. "Thank you for coming," she said. "I really do need you."

Todd flounced over to the sofa and sat down. "I am utterly exhausted. This whole experience has been emotionally draining. Traveling with that man is just …"

"Just what?" asked Mandretti.

"Oh, nothing. There's nothing I like more than hanging out with gangsters," Todd said. He turned his back on Mandretti. "So, fill us in, Violet. What do we need to do?"

Violet tried to assemble her thoughts. Where would she begin? Should she start with the kidnapping of Marshall's children, or should she start with the mysterious blond woman who knew things she should not know, or should she start with the Griffinwood Document?

Ryan held out Wilshire's leather-bound journal. "Read that from cover to cover," he said to Todd, "and see if you can find anything Marshall missed."

"Marshall?" said Todd. "Who is Marshall, and why do I need to read that book, or journal, or whatever it is?" He looked at his sister. "I can't just pick up in the middle. I can't read minds, not like some people I know. You have to use your words, Violet. You have to fill me in."

"Yeah, what's happening, doll?" said Mandretti.

Remembering the hand-kissing, Violet decided to settle her relationship with Michael Mandretti once and for all. She had slept with his brother, but she had no intention of sleeping with him. "I'm not your doll," she hissed.

"Sorry."

"Violet and I are going out," Ryan said. "We have a train to catch."

"But we've just arrived," said Todd. "Do you really need us to go with you?"

"No," said Ryan. "That's the last thing in the world we need." He leaned forward, suddenly looking more like the charismatic young TV star he had once been. "Here's what we'll do," he said. "Violet, you go upstairs and get changed."

"Changed?" said Violet.

"Are you going like that?" Ryan asked.

Violet suddenly remembered what she looked like in baggy slacks and a loose sweater, with her hair barely combed. Oh God, she couldn't believe that she'd allowed Mandretti to see her like that.

"Go and get changed," Ryan said again, "and while you are making yourself beautiful, I'll bring Mr. Mandretti up to date."

"What will you tell him?"

"Everything that's relevant."

Violet left Ryan to do the talking and hurried across to the elevator, glad to take her mind off the children and occupy it with planning how she could repair her appearance, and what she should wear for the train trip to the manor. Being very careful not to slip back into thinking of the little girl's fear or the dense barrier that now cut off all contact with the child, she made a mental inventory of the contents of her suitcase. She decided the occasion called for her new suede jacket, and perhaps her earth-toned peasant skirt. Casual but not too casual, and boots definitely, but not heels.

By the time Violet returned to the lobby, freshly showered and appropriately attired for visiting an English country manor, Todd had stopped sulking and had become his usual efficient self. The cartload of luggage had been whisked away. He had somehow acquired cell phones for himself and Mandretti, his laptop was open on the table beside him, and Mandretti was nursing a Jack Daniel's on the rocks.

Ryan was standing a little aside talking on his phone. As Violet approached, he slipped the phone into his pocket.

"Just talking to Professor Molly," he said.

"Really?" Violet was surprised. "I got the impression you didn't like each other."

"We're fine," said Ryan. "We just had to give each other a little respect."

"So it's a professor thing," Violet said caustically.

"Academic courtesy. I called her and gave her my number in case she had anything to tell me, which, of course, she doesn't."

"Did she say how Lady Clemma was doing?" Violet queried.

"Didn't ask. You can do that later, if you like." He looked at her impatiently. "Can we go now? Your … er … brother seems to have everything under control."

"Do we know how to get there?" Violet asked.

Todd passed her a slip of paper. "Euston to Shrewsbury," he said. "Change at Shrewsbury. Take the twelve fifteen stopping train to Littlehaven and get out at Griffinwood Halt. "

"They have their own train station?"

"No, but Todd has discovered that it's just a short walk," Ryan said.

Oh goody, Violet thought, a short walk. Well, at least she had chosen not to wear heels.

"Taxi's waiting outside," said Todd. "You have to get going."

Violet and Ryan departed, and Violet looked back to see Todd obediently leafing through the journal while Mandretti shouted impatient instructions down the cell phone. She felt a hard knot of anxiety in her stomach just knowing that Mandretti was no longer far away across the Atlantic.

They climbed out of the train several hours later when it came to a stop at the tiniest railway station Violet had ever seen. The size of the station was appropriate because they were also riding on the shortest train she had ever ridden. When they changed at Shrewsbury, they had boarded a train with only two carriages, and the little train had stopped again and again at tiny villages nestled among rounded hills. Griffinwood was the smallest village of all and consisted of a pub, a post office, and an unmanned railway station. Violet could see the manor itself in the distance, silhouetted against the skyline on a grassy hill behind the pub. It was, she thought, more than a short walk away, more like a short hike, uphill.

A sweeping tree-lined driveway led up toward the impressive front entrance. The manor itself was redbrick, with tall chimneys and lattice windows. Beside the manor was a far older construction, the stone remains of a castle with crumbled battlements and mullioned window arches indicating that there had once been a chapel. The lawn around the manor was neatly mown, but the castle ruins stood amongst tall weeds, with stunted trees growing up through the stonework. The sun was high in the sky, the air smelled of rain-washed grass, and Violet could see clearly to the far western horizon, where clouds piled on top of each other above shadowy purple mountains.

"I know he's expecting us," Violet said. "Do you think he'll send a car?"

"Oh, come on," said Ryan, "it's just a short walk."

"I don't do much walking," she complained.

"So now's the time to start. The fresh air will wake you up,"

I'm already awake, Violet thought. Barry Marshall took care of that.

Ryan strode ahead on his long legs. The day was mild, verging on warm, and he carried his raincoat over his arm. Violet tottered along behind him, regretting the weight of the fashionable but large purse that she had elected to carry.

They passed through the wrought iron gates of the manor, and she began to notice signs of neglect. The gates hung open on rusted hinges, and the windows in the gatehouse were broken, the door sadly in need of a coat of paint. The driveway was cracked and pitted with weeds. Apparently, all was not well financially at Griffinwood Manor.

The driveway dipped into a valley, and they lost sight of the house.

"Slow down," Violet said to Ryan, who was now well ahead of her, but he was like a hound following a scent, never even looking back. She moved her purse from one shoulder to another and paused to unbutton her coat. She stopped abruptly as someone stepped out from behind one of the chestnut trees that lined the driveway.

"Oh, it's you," Violet said. She was not surprised. She had been expecting to see the blue-eyed blond, and here she was, just as expected. This time the girl was wearing a sky-blue ankle-length dress that clung closely to her slim body. Her hair fell in a long flaxen braid down her back. The effect was distinctly medieval.

"I'm supposed to take you," the girl said, sounding not at all happy at the prospect.

"I'm going to the manor," Violet said.

The girl shook her golden head. "No," she said, "not the manor. You'll find nothing there. I've already looked."

"Violet?" Ryan had turned to look back.

"Get back here," said Violet.

Ryan hurriedly retraced his footsteps and loomed angrily over the slender girl, forcing her to step back so that she could look up into his face.

"Who the hell are you?" Ryan asked.

"I'm called Elaine," she said. "I'm really sorry about this. I was going to take you and show you—"

"Show me what?" said Ryan.

"The other side of the mist," Elaine said. "I was going to take you through the portal so you would understand everything. But now I can't. I have to take her."

"Me?" said Violet.

"Yes," said the girl angrily. "They want to know who you are."

Ryan looked up toward the manor house and then back at Violet.

"It might be time to split our forces," he said.

Violet was again reminded of a hound dog being pulled in two different directions by two conflicting scents.

"I'm not going with her," Violet said. "You go with her; you're the historian."

"I'm not permitted to take him," said Elaine.

Ryan shrugged his shoulders. "It's out of my hands," he said.

"I would prefer to take him," Elaine said wistfully.

"Then take him," said Violet.

Ryan managed to look both apologetic and impatient at the same time.

"I think the search of Griffinwood would be a much better use of my time and skills," he said.

"I thought we were partners," said Violet.

"Yes," said Ryan. "We're doing this together. I'll go to the manor, and you go to … wherever it is that she wants to take you, and then we'll meet up and swap notes."

Now, Violet thought, he was positively straining at the leash.

Elaine looked sideways at Violet. "What do you have in that bag?" she asked. "Do you really have to bring that large bag with you?"

Violet clutched her purse for reassurance. "I'm not going anywhere with you," she said. "You're going to tell me what you know, and then you're going to leave."

"No, you're coming with me," said Elaine. "You are to meet your sisters."

Violet's heart skipped a beat and she forgot about everything else. "Sisters? Do I really have sisters?" she asked incredulously.

"That is what I am told, although I see no family resemblance."

"So you're going with her?" asked Ryan.

Violet made a snap decision. Despite the fact that Todd and Maria were legally her siblings, having been adopted into the same family, they were not blood relatives. She could only imagine what it would be like to meet actual sisters. Perhaps they would have her violet eyes, or her problem with weight. "Yes," she said, "I'll go with her. I even have my passport with me."

"Our border is not crossed with a passport," said Elaine.

"Stop being so mysterious," Violet snapped. "Just say what you mean."

Elaine turned back to Ryan. "Did you bring the jewel?" she asked.

"What jewel?" Violet said.

"He knows," said Elaine. "It is the passport into our realm." She held out her hand to Ryan. "I will take you as soon as I can, but I must take her now. Time is short. The dam is almost complete."

"What dam?" Ryan asked.

"The one we've been protesting. The protesters will never win. The valley will be flooded and all will be lost. This matter is urgent. I need the jewel. Some have said she can pass through without the jewel, but we are not certain. I will use the jewel."

Violet glared at Ryan. "I thought we told each other everything," she said.

"Almost everything," he said.

Ryan put his hand into the pocket of his jacket and produced a fragment of gold set with a dull red stone. "Is this what allowed me to go through?" he asked.

Elaine nodded. "Give it to me, please."

"I'm holding it in my hand now," Ryan said, "so why isn't anything happening?"

"You're not at a gate."

"Where is the gate?" he asked.

Elaine's glance shifted to the ruined chapel and then shifted back again. "This one is of no use to us," she said.

"Oh, just give her whatever it is she wants," Violet said impatiently. "Obviously, I'm the one who has to go with her, and I'm not going to stand out here all day. Do I have to remind you that there are two children waiting for us to find them, or has Miss Blue Eyes made you forget about everything else?"

"No," said Ryan, his face suddenly serious. "I have not forgotten. You misjudge me, Violet."

With a look of deep hurt, he placed the fragment of jewelry in the palm of Elaine's hand.

"Now what?" he said to Elaine.

"Now we go," she said, grabbing Violet's hand in a painful grip and leading her off the driveway and into the trees.

"I expect it back," she heard Ryan shout, and then she turned her attention to following Elaine through the woods.

They came out from among the trees onto a side road where a small blue car was parked with one of its wheels in a ditch. Elaine unlocked the doors and indicated that Violet should get into the passenger seat.

"Wait a minute," said Violet. "What was all that talk of gates and mists and portals or whatever, and now we're going by car? Just where are my sisters?" Disappointment welled up in her chest. "You've been lying, haven't you? I don't have any sisters. What do you really want?"

"We're going west," said Elaine, bunching up her skirts and climbing into the driver's seat. "We could have gone through the Griffinwood gate, but travel on the other side of that gate is difficult. We don't have cars or trains or buses, only horses, and I can't imagine you on a horse. So we're going by road to the next gate, which will bring you where we need to go, and then you will see your sisters, if they are your sisters. Get in."

Violet struggled along the ditch between the hedge and the car, and squeezed herself through the passenger door. Elaine stamped on the accelerator. The little car rocketed out of the ditch and onto the road, and they set off in the general direction of the mountains that Violet had seen, purple against the rain-washed blue sky.

Violet struggled to find the seatbelt.

"What's your relationship with the doctor?" Elaine asked suddenly.

"We've been hired to work together," Violet replied, reaching down beside the seat to find the other end of the belt.

"But that's all?" Elaine asked. "It's nothing personal?"

"No, it's nothing personal," Violet replied.

A small smile lit up Elaine's face.

"Oh, wait a minute," said Violet. "Are you …?"

"Maybe just a little," said Elaine.

"For goodness' sake," said Violet caustically, "don't tell me you have some kind of pathetic crush on my partner."

"It's not pathetic," Elaine said. "We're encouraged to bring back the right kind of men. It's just that I've never found one before, and I am—"

Violet's anger came upon her quite suddenly. She was angrier than she had ever been before, so angry that she had no room in her brain to think rational thoughts. She could only think that she was being used as a means for Elaine to make her mark on Ryan, or perhaps the girl saw Violet as a rival and intended to get rid of her. Obviously, she was getting Violet away from Griffinwood as fast as the little blue car would carry them. People were dying, children were being kidnapped, women were losing their husbands, and this girl, this waiflike child, was setting it aside in order to chase a man.

Violet abandoned her attempt to fasten the seat belt and abruptly flung open the passenger door. Elaine brought the car to a screeching halt as the door slammed against the hedge at the side of the road.

"What on earth?" she asked.

"That's exactly what I want to know," said Violet, climbing shakily out of the car. "I am going to stand here by the side of the road, and I'm going to refuse to move until you tell me what's going on. You lured me into this car with hints that you know something about my birth mother, but quite obviously you don't. If you're abducting me, or kidnapping me, or whatever it is you think you're doing, just to get me away from Marcus Ryan, then you're crazy. I'm sick to death of hints and half-truths and mysterious jewels and disappearing swords and promises that I have a pack of sisters. You are going to tell me everything you know, or I will simply refuse to get back into this car; and don't try to make me. I'm considerably stronger than I look."

Elaine leaned forward and rested her head on the steering wheel. For a moment, they were both speechless, with nothing but the sound of Violet's heavy breathing to break the silence.

After a few moments, the birds, who had stopped singing when the car screeched to a halt, began to chirp again with a first few hesitant notes and then with full song. Insects hummed and buzzed. Violet could hear the sound of vehicles on a distant motorway, and, somewhat closer, the clattering of a tractor engine. She considered reaching into the car, taking her purse, and simply walking away. She would retrace the route to the manor, walk up the driveway, find Marcus Ryan, and tell him that it was over. The case was finished. They had fallen into the hands of lunatics.

Elaine drew in a shuddering breath and turned to look up at Violet. She spoke in a small pleading voice. "Please come with me," she said. "This is more important than you could possibly imagine."

"No," said Violet. "No more mysteries."

"Your mother was one of us," Elaine said. "We don't know who she was. In every generation, we send women into your world to learn your ways and to listen for any word that might be said about the King, or the sword."

"What king?"

Elaine appeared not to hear. "Some of them never return," she said. "Perhaps it was your mother or perhaps it was your grandmother. Our elders think they will be able to tell if they meet you. Don't you want to know how you came here?"

"I suppose so," said Violet. She was growing uncomfortable standing in the ditch, with the sun blazing down on her head. "But that's not what this is about, is it? What I want to know is where you came from."

"It's another place," said Elaine. "Please come back into the car. I'll tell you everything, but we have to hurry. Time is running out."

Violet hesitated.

"Please," said Elaine again. "I'm sorry about Marcus ... Doctor Ryan. I was being silly. My feelings were totally inappropriate for the situation."

"Well," said Violet, thinking of the many times she had lost control of her own emotions, "we can't choose our feelings."

She clambered out of the ditch and back into the car. Elaine put the car in gear, and they started off again, heading toward the mountains.

"Well?" asked Violet.

"Our kingdom is called Albion," said Elaine. "It exists in another reality."

"Oh please," said Violet. "Do you really expect me to believe that?"

"I expect you to listen," said Elaine, "because you have asked me to tell you the truth. You may reserve judgment until we arrive at our destination. All you have to do until then is to open your mind to hear things you have never thought possible, and when I am finished, I will show you the proof."

Violet sighed. "Very well," she said, "but Albion isn't new to me. Britain used to be called Albion, didn't it?"

"Yes," said Elaine, "but our Albion was never your Albion. Our Albion exists in another world, a world that lies close to your reality, but is not your reality. Our Albion has followed a different destiny, and it has never become Britain. There has been no British Empire, no Industrial Revolution, but we have had our Dark Age. We are still in our Dark Age."

"What do you mean?"

"You'll understand in a minute," said Elaine, "and the story will be very familiar. You may not realize it, but your world has been aware of us for a long time. Let me continue. Albion is placed just as Britain is. It's an island in a northern sea. The northern and western territories are wild and mountainous, and the south is a fertile land of rolling hills where great rivers water the land. Our summers are gentle and fruitful, and our winters bring deep snow and soft rains. The people of Albion were once united under one great warrior king. The King taught them to build stone castles for the defense of the realm. Nobles learned the skills of war and that led to the wearing of armor and the practice of knighthood."

Elaine pulled up at a crossroads. For a moment, she seemed to be getting her bearings, and then she started forward again. They were drawing closer to the mountains.

"That's what Albion was once," she said to Violet. "What I'm telling you is history. It was a peaceful and idyllic land until the High King, Uther Pendragon, coveted Ygraine, the wife of the king of Cornwall. When Merlin, Uther Pendragon's magician, wove an enchantment that allowed Uther to possess Ygraine, the peace of the land was ended."

"Wait a minute," said Violet. "You're telling me the Arthurian legend."

"Yes," said Elaine. "Does that surprise you?"

"Does it surprise me?" Violet repeated. "Of course it surprises me. In fact, I'm way more than surprised. I'm ... well, I don't even have a word to describe how I feel. I don't even know if I believe you. Why should I believe you?"

"Have you ever wondered where the legend came from?" Elaine asked.

"Well, certainly not from some alternate reality," Violet declared.

"I will prove it to you," Elaine said, gesturing forward through the windshield, "as soon as we reach those mountains."

"I've seen movies, quite a few of them," said Violet. "Are you trying to tell me they're true?"

"No," said Elaine, "the movies you speak of are very imaginative, but not the truth."

Violet's memory flashed back to images from books and movies. Uther Pendragon with the dragon crest on his shield. Merlin the magician lurking furtively in the background in his long black scholar's robe. Ygraine, blond and beautiful, seduced by a magic spell, giving birth to Arthur the secret heir, carried away to be kept until he was old enough to claim the throne. She remembered epic poems about the deeds of the Knights of the Round Table and the sword Excalibur, which Arthur accepted from the Lady of the Lake. And there had been the sordid side to the story; Arthur being deceived into conceiving a son with his half-sister, a son who grew to become Arthur's enemy; and, of course, Guinevere committing adultery with Lancelot.

"So you're saying that there's no truth in the legend," said Violet, "or at least not true in this reality that you supposedly come from?"

"I am telling you our history," said Elaine. "You can decide for yourself when we reach the mountains."

"And what's so damned convincing in the mountains?" Violet said impatiently.

"You'll see," said Elaine. "Let me tell you where history differs from romance. You have to understand that King Arthur was not seated firmly on the throne of Albion. He lacked a legitimate heir, and there were knights and nobles who looked for the boy Mordred, Arthur's illegitimate son, to be the next king. For some years, the land was at peace, and the knights grew bored. They'd been trained for war, and when they found no wars to fight at home, they invented quests and rode the length and breadth of Albion looking for ways to prove their worth either to the King or to Mordred. So far as the peasants were concerned, the knights were a nuisance, crashing around and fighting everything and everyone they came across.

"But then, just as matters were reaching a head, with the peasants threatening to revolt, the King growing older, and Mordred becoming more demanding, a rumor reached Camelot of a great quest that could be made. Merlin, equally bored with life at court, had expanded his powers and had opened a gate into another world. Your world."

"You mean Britain?" said Violet.

"Yes," said Elaine. "Merlin had discovered another reality; your reality. He went through the gate himself and found an island identical in all respects to Albion, except it was ruled by a different king, and a different religion. Christianity."

"You don't have Christianity?" Violet asked.

"We didn't," said Elaine. "We had magic."

"Oh."

"The first person to pass through the gate was Sir Percival," Elaine said, "and he was very much affected by the Christian religion. Apparently, he received a vision of a golden chalice, which he said was the cup used by the Christian God-Man to create a mystic communion between man and God. With Merlin's encouragement, Percival returned to the court at Camelot to raise a brotherhood to ride in quest of the cup that he called the Holy Grail. The truth was that Arthur was desperate for any activity that would occupy the knights and delay civil war, so he ordered Merlin to open yet more gates, and the Knights of the Round Table, resplendent in shining armor and filled with chivalrous and religious zeal, rode into another world."

"The Dark Ages of Britain," said Violet.

"History and legend," said Elaine.

Violet tried to absorb what Elaine was telling her. Some of it made sense, or at least enough sense that she was forced to consider it might be plausible. Elaine's story explained why no source could be found for the Arthurian legends. Of course Arthur couldn't be placed among the English kings, and Camelot couldn't be found, because neither of them had ever existed in British history. They had come through Merlin's gates from another place, another time, a parallel world. No wonder the legend appeared to have sprung up suddenly with no foundation. There was no foundation. The Knights of the Round Table had ridden through the misty portals and descended on the population of Britain even as Britain sank into the abyss of the Dark Ages, when scholarship was forgotten and ignorance reigned, and they had been remembered as figures of legend and bringers of hope.

"While the knights were away questing, Mordred rose up in rebellion," Elaine said.

"Smart move," said Violet.

"What do you mean?"

"If all the King's most loyal knights were away in this alternate reality, or whatever you want to call it, obviously, that's the time for the enemy to make his move."

"So you think our king was stupid?"

"No," said Violet. "I was just pointing out—"

She was interrupted by Elaine jamming on the brakes and bringing the small car to a shuddering halt. They had rounded a curve and come upon a line of stationary vehicles.

"Traffic jam," Violet said. "Where on earth are they all going? We're in the middle of nowhere."

Elaine muttered to herself under her breath in a language that Violet could not identify.

"What are you saying?" Violet asked. "Is that some kind of spell?"

"No," said Elaine. "I am simply expressing my frustration in my own language. What makes you think I can cast spells?"

"I don't know," said Violet. "That just sort of slipped out. No, of course I don't think you can cast spells. So far, you haven't proved to me that you can do anything."

"Oh, I will," said Elaine. "I'll prove it. I'll prove what I've said is true."

Elaine backed up and made a U-turn, narrowly avoiding the car that was pulling up behind them, and headed back in the direction they had come.

"I don't do magic," Elaine said angrily. "You're the one with the magic."

"No, I'm not," said Violet. "Where are we going?"

"There's a place just down the road here," Elaine said. "It's supposed to be abandoned, but I think we can get some help there."

She reached into the pocket in the car door and handed Violet a cell phone. "Call the number in there for Gavin," she said, thrusting the phone into Violet's hands.

"What do you mean?"

"Call the number," Elaine said. "It's under G for Gavin. It's illegal for drivers to talk on the phone, and the last thing we need is to draw attention to ourselves. Just get Gavin on the phone for me, and I'll tell you what to say."

Violet stared at the phone. "I don't know how," she said helplessly.

"He's under my contacts."

"I'm sorry," said Violet. "I don't know how to use this phone. I don't know what you're talking about."

"You don't know how to use a phone?"

"Not a cell phone."

Elaine pulled over at the side of the road. "What's the matter with you?" she demanded, taking back the phone and bringing it to life.

"I don't do electronics," Violet said.

"Are you stupid?"

"No, of course not."

"You sound stupid," Elaine said. "Why don't you know how to use a phone?"

"I have people to do that for me," said Violet.

"Well," said Elaine, "your people aren't here, are they? Do you know how ridiculous you sound? I've had to learn everything, your language, your culture, how to drive a car, how to use a computer, how to live in your modern world, and you, well, you can't even use a phone."

Violet watched Elaine's fingers dancing over the phone's tiny keyboard. Why don't I know how to do that? she asked herself. When had she decided that she didn't need to know how things worked? She thought back over the past few years. She remembered her first encounter with a computer, and her impatience when the screen had suddenly gone blank. She remembered a supercilious technician who came to her house and talked to her unintelligibly about firewalls and viruses, rams and gigs, and asked her if she wanted to sync her desktop to her laptop, whatever that meant. Fortunately, Todd had returned from a tour with a black-box fly-by-night theatre company, put the teenaged computer nerd in his place, and offered to take over the technical aspects of Violet's business.

And then Maria came home, having flunked out of design school for being too creative. "As if," Maria had said by way of explanation. Suddenly Violet had an unpaid staff to relieve her of the burden of electronics. From then on, it had just been easier to let Todd and Maria take care of everything high-tech. She never discussed technical details with clients, preferring that they know only that Violet Chambray was possessed of certain mystical powers of deduction that rose far above internet searches and e-mails. So far, it had worked well for her, but not today.

Elaine spoke softly into the phone, ended the call, and pulled back onto the road. "They've done it," she said. "They've closed the valley. That's why the traffic is backed up. No one can get through."

"What valley?"

"It's just over that last hill, but we won't get there that way," Elaine said, hunched over the wheel and driving fast. "The police are all over it. Everyone's being evacuated. No more protests."

"You're talking about the dam," Violet said.

"Yes, I am. We knew it would happen, but we've been trying to hold it off as long as possible because we really believed that you and Doctor Ryan would find the sword."

Elaine threw the car into a sharp turn and onto a small side road. They were climbing a steep hillside with open moorland on either side. They paused at the top of the hill. Before them lay a wide valley nestled among hills that rose to become the purple mountains that Violet had seen in the distance. Sunlight sparkled on a series of waterfalls that cascaded down the hillside and formed a river that snaked across the wide bottomlands. At the narrowest part of the valley, the hillside was scarred with signs of construction, the grass ripped away and the land laid bare. Huge yellow construction vehicles crawled across the hillside, and the concrete dam was immediately visible closing off the valley.

"That's the dam you're talking about?" Violet queried.

"It will flood this whole valley," said Elaine. "Water for the suburbs."

"What?"

"A reservoir," Elaine said. "They've already demolished the houses in the valley and moved the people out. But that's not the end of it. Look, do you see what's down there?"

"No," said Violet.

"You don't see those large animals running around?" queried Elaine, pointing out the windscreen.

"Are they cows?" said Violet, taking note of the shapes moving along the valley floor.

"Horses," said Elaine, "the last wild horses in Britain."

"Ponies," said Violet. "Do you mean wild ponies? Why don't they just get out of the way?"

"They're not ponies," said Elaine. "They are an ancient breed of horse. They've been in that valley for centuries, and they're protected by law. The government says they'll be fine. They say there's plenty of grazing land left and the reservoir won't make any difference, but they're wrong. Those horses are not going to move. The horses are waiting."

"What are they waiting for?" Violet asked.

Elaine left the question unanswered. "At least they haven't demolished Taliesin Farm yet," she said.

She pulled the car into a gravel driveway and then through an open gate into the walled yard of an old slate-roofed farmhouse. The house looked abandoned with no glass in the windows, slates missing from the roof, and the door hanging open on rusted hinges, but a dark green jeep-like vehicle was parked in the yard. Two young men and a rough-haired hound dog came running as Elaine stopped the car.

"We were just leaving," said the taller of the young men, a gangly youth with a patchy beard and pale watery eyes.

"It's alright, Gavin," Elaine said. "You did your best."

"We couldn't hold them off," said the other young man. He was smaller and much darker than his companion, with brown eyes and dark curly hair. "Everyone just left us. They said they couldn't bear to watch. The horses won't move. They're going to drown and no one wants to watch that. I heard they're going to try to frighten them away with helicopters, but I know they won't move. They've never left this valley. No one remembers them ever leaving this valley."

"I told the guys we need to stay here," said Gavin, "but Justin had heard about some oak trees in Wiltshire, and they all just took off."

"Bloody Druids," said the other boy. "Like trees are more important than animals. Justin didn't even take the dog."

"I told you," said Gavin, "it's not Justin's dog. I don't even know where it came from. You'll have to take it home with you, Robby."

"What about the horses?" Robby asked. "Are we just going to leave them here to drown? They won't leave. They'll just stay here and drown."

Elaine closed her eyes and took a deep breath. "They might," she said.

"Yeah, well," said Gavin, "no one's gonna want to see that on the six o'clock news."

"But by then it will be too late, and they'll just go on about how we're idiots who worship oak trees," said Robby.

"Is that what these people do?" Violet whispered, completely out of her depth in the discussion of drowning horses and endangered oak trees.

"No," Elaine whispered back. "Druids worship oak trees, but these are not Druids, they're followers of Arthur."

"They believe in him?"

"They believe they are his descendants," Elaine whispered back.

"How can they be?"

"They might possibly be descendants of some of the questing knights," Elaine said, "and it's interesting that they feel a kinship with the horses of this valley. The important thing is that they believe that I have spiritual powers. That's all we need them to know. Now get out of the car and act mysterious."

"How about mystified?" Violet asked. "I can do mystified."

"This is nothing to joke about," Elaine said sternly. She climbed out of the car and revealed herself to the young men, who were obviously impressed by her clinging blue dress and the commanding way she carried herself.

"You look different," said Gavin.

"This is an important occasion," Elaine said. "I have brought another of my people. This is the Lady Violet."

She gestured to Violet to leave the car. Violet climbed out feeling more overheated than dignified in her suede jacket and uncomfortable boots. The dog, a large brown-and-white creature with soulful eyes, wandered over, sniffed her boots, and inserted his cold wet nose under the hem of her skirt.

"Get away," Violet hissed. The hound retreated a few feet and stared at her as though she alone was responsible for his abandonment.

"We need to go into the valley," Elaine said. "Can we get there in the Land Rover?" She indicated the battered green open-top vehicle that stood by the farm gate.

"Oh yeah," said the dark youth. "We do it all the time. It's a bumpy ride."

"Can we get to the waterfall?" Elaine asked.

"Not all the way there," Gavin said. "We can get you down to Dai Gwynn's pasture."

"Used to be Dai Gwynn's pasture," said the other youth. "He's gone."

"Yes, Robby, I know," said Elaine. "He really didn't have any choice."

"He should have held out," said Robby.

"I always thought he was one of us," said Gavin.

"Loyalty is a rare commodity," Elaine said, "and it brings its own reward. But let's not talk about that now. We don't have much time."

Gavin jumped into the driver's seat of the Land Rover, and Robby waved an inviting arm toward the back of the vehicle. Despite her encumbering skirts, Elaine somehow managed to vault lightly into the back seat behind the driver, but Violet was immobile. She could not imagine any combination of moves that would allow her to levitate high enough off the ground to clear the side of the vehicle and land next to Elaine.

With an impatient sigh, Robby tilted the front passenger seat forward, and Violet climbed clumsily into the back. The dog looked at her for a moment as though considering joining her, and then he retreated, nose to the ground, snuffling energetically.

"Sorry there's no seat belt," said Robby. "Just hang on tight."

Violet sought desperately for a handhold as the Land Rover careened down a barely discernible road into the valley.

"We have to make this quick," Gavin yelled as he held onto the bucking steering wheel. "The helicopters will be here soon."

Halfway down the hillside, the graveled track joined a smoother, wider road and passed through a sad collection of partially demolished houses, roofless, with stone walls and gaping windows. They left the road again and shot off across the floor of the valley, paralleling the river. As they bounced across the rough, dry grass, Violet caught glimpses of the wild horses, brown, black, and white, racing away from them, with their manes and tails streaming in the wind.

The Land Rover eventually screeched to a halt at the base of a steep, stony hillside at the point where the waterfall crashed down to form the river.

"Can't go no further," Gavin declared.

Violet breathed a sigh of relief and released her death grip on the back of passenger seat.

Robby climbed out and lifted up the front seat. Elaine made a swift exit. "Hurry," she said to Violet.

"I'm trying," Violet said, heaving herself across the back seat and trying to untangle her legs from the various items of junk strewn across the foot well.

Elaine held out an impatient hand. "Come on," she said.

Violet more or less fell out of the vehicle and staggered across the stony ground, gasping for breath but maintaining a firm grasp on her purse.

"Leave that behind," Elaine said.

Violet shook her head. "I never leave this behind," she declared.

Elaine turned to the two young men. "You have to wait for us," she said, "and I don't know how long we'll be. Can you hide the vehicle?"

"Sure," said Robby. "We'll get in behind Dai Gwynn's shed. They didn't knock that down."

"Go then," said Elaine. "Go quickly."

The Land Rover bumped off across the field, leaving Violet alone with Elaine.

"This way," said Elaine.

Violet hesitated, looking at the narrow track up the steep and stony hillside. "Why are you dragging me up here?"

"To give you the proof you need, and because we need your help."

"You have a strange way of asking for it," Violet commented.

Elaine sighed. "I'm sorry. I know you don't understand me and you don't believe me, but please believe that this is urgent, and if you will just come with me, I will show you something that will convince you that I'm telling the truth."

Violet slung her heavy purse across her shoulder. "Lead on. I can't wait to be convinced."

They had walked only a few yards along the path when Elaine stopped again, at a thicket of bushes clinging to life on the edges of a rocky outcrop. She pushed her way through the bushes, and Violet followed her. Deep within the thicket, Violet almost stumbled across a low stone wall.

"This is all that's left," Elaine said. "Centuries ago this was a chapel. This is the door."

"It doesn't look like a door," Violet commented.

"The portals exist outside of time and space," said Elaine. "The condition of the wall has no significance. Here, take this and hold onto it."

Elaine pressed something sharp into Violet's palm. Violet looked down and saw the fragment of jewelry that Elaine had retrieved from Ryan.

"Don't lose it," said Elaine.

Violet closed her hand around the sharp edges of the fragment. Elaine stepped forward and Violet followed her. A mist rose up in front of her; the outline of the bushes shimmered and wavered, and Violet had a sense of something beyond; a hillside and a distant castle, and a roughly clad peasant following plough horses as they labored.

A shadowy figure came toward her, forcing her to step back. She tripped on the low stone wall. As she fell to the ground, she heard Elaine gasp in surprise. She released her hold on the stone and the mist vanished.

CHAPTER TEN

Todd Chambray

Todd was surprised to find that he could admire Michael Mandretti. In fact, although he would never admit it to him, he was actually grateful to Mandretti for closing down the show in Key West. Dressing in drag and performing Noel Coward to an empty theater had turned out to be, well, a drag. As soon as he was off the stage and onto an airplane, the lure of the greasepaint had dissipated, and he knew how ridiculous it had been to think that tourists from the cruise ships would flock into a grimy little backstreet theater to see a cut-rate production of Blithe Spirit. For goodness' sake, he thought, they have Broadway dancers on those ships, high-priced crooners, top-of-the-line comedians, why would they want to see Todd exploring the feminine within the masculine in a new interpretation of a play that wasn't even funny when it was written seventy years earlier?

He also appreciated the fact that, unlike Violet, Michael Mandretti actually understood and valued Todd's skills as a researcher. Violet took him for granted with her demands that he should send "one of those e-mail thingies" or just "look it up on your little computer, dear." He could see it clearly now; Violet's disdain for all things electronic made him feel undervalued. Violet did not value computers, and therefore, she didn't value Todd. On the other hand, Mandretti had offered him nothing but compliments, thanking him over and again for the information he'd been able to come up with after just a quick search.

He glanced sideways at the man riding beside him in the back seat of the black limo, a small limo by Vegas standards but large enough to allow Mandretti to sit with his legs spread, hands on knees, in a position of controlled power.

"Okay," said Mandretti, "let's get this straight. We're going to see this old French broad because she's gonna tell us what her husband did with the sword."

"I don't know that's she's French," Todd said, "but Claudette is normally a French name."

"So maybe she's French, maybe she's not, but she's old, right?"

"Oh yes, quite definitely. If she's the widow of Reverend Wilshire, then she's probably in her nineties, but the people at the home say she's quite capable of carrying on a conversation most of the time."

"Most of the time," Mandretti repeated. "Well, let's hope today is one of those times." He paused. "You sure it's her?" he asked.

"No, not really," said Todd, "but it's my best guess. Her name is Wilshire, and she's living in a home for clergy widows. It's the best lead I could come up with."

Mandretti patted Todd's knee. "You done good," he said. "So how far is it?"

"Not far," said Todd, "but you should ask the driver. He knows where he's going."

"Nah," said Mandretti, "don't get the driver involved in this. Freddie's been paid to drive, not to answer questions. In fact, Freddie's usually paid not to answer questions."

"Okay," said Todd, looking at the back of the driver's thick neck and bullet-shaped head.

"Oh, don't worry," said Mandretti, "Freddie is also paid not to listen. He comes recommended."

Best not to ask who did the recommending, Todd thought.

He'd performed his internet research quickly and efficiently, and come up with the name of Claudette Wilshire living in a retirement home just south of London, but it was Mandretti who had come up with what looked suspiciously like a bulletproof limo and a driver as wide as he was tall, with the face of a failed prize fighter. Now they were on their way to visit Claudette Wilshire in the hope that she was the Reverend Clive Wilshire's widow, and that she would know what her husband had done with the sword he had found in the bomb crater.

"Did you bring the journal?" Mandretti asked. "Maybe we'll have to show it to the old girl to show her we're for real."

Todd patted his pocket where the thick journal was totally destroying the fit of his gray tweed sport coat.

"Did you read the whole thing?" Mandretti asked.

"I read enough," Todd said. "Reverend Wilshire definitely had a sword, presumably the sword we're looking for, and he'd taken it from the bomb crater up there in Norfolk where the rest of the stuff was found."

"And he didn't tell no one," Mandretti said thoughtfully.

"I doubt he even told his wife," Todd said, "but I'm hoping that she found the sword after he died."

"What I don't understand," said Mandretti, "is the connection between old Professor Peacock working in some regimental museum and finding the sword he said was Excalibur, and this old coot stealing a sword from a bomb crater fifty years ago."

"It's a very loose thread," Todd said. "I was hoping we could just find out what regiment Wilshire was in and go from there, but I can't find any reference to him having been in the army, although he was the right age for World War Two."

"And there's the French wife," said Mandretti. "She could be a war bride."

"We don't know that she's French," Todd reminded him.

Mandretti lapsed into silence as the black car purred through a depressing urban sprawl lit by a watery afternoon sun. Eventually, they pulled through the gates of a redbrick building, obviously a converted Victorian mansion.

"This is it," the driver said over his shoulder. "The Laurels."

The driver pulled into a graveled parking space and remained stoically in his seat. Todd heard the click of the back doors being unlocked. Apparently, they had been locked in on their ride from London. He was glad that he had not been aware of that fact. He couldn't think that there would be anything comforting about being locked into a car with Freddie.

"You want me to wait, mate?" Freddie asked.

"Yeah," said Mandretti. No please. No thank you. Obviously, Mandretti and Freddie's employers had an understanding of Freddie's role in Mandretti's business in London.

"You speak any French?" Mandretti asked as he climbed out of the car and adjusted his jacket. He was impeccably dressed in a light-brown tweed jacket, cavalry twill trousers, and a turtleneck sweater. His Vegas tan positively glowed in the pale rays of the sun.

"Just theatre French," said Todd, following him up the red-tile steps. The front door stood open, and they entered a gloomy hallway imbued with the institutional smell of cabbage and cleaning fluid, overlaid with pine.

Mandretti marched up to the tiny reception desk that occupied a corner of the dim space. The woman behind the desk stepped back as he shouldered his way forward.

"We called," said Mandretti. "Come to see Mrs. Wilshire. Mrs. Claudette Wilshire."

The receptionist said nothing. She was an elderly woman dressed in a high-buttoned blouse, her flyaway gray hair caught in a careless topknot.

Todd moved quietly forward and slipped between Mandretti and the hapless woman. "Good afternoon," he said quietly.

She nodded.

"So sorry to disturb you," he continued. He found his stride. This called for the Noel Coward approach. No, he corrected himself. This was more Agatha Christie. Yes, he would be a nice young gentleman from an Agatha Christie story.

He smiled. "We rang you earlier this afternoon," he said. "Did I speak to you, or did I speak to someone else?"

"Oh yes, I remember," the woman said, fixing her smile on Todd and shying away from Mandretti. "You spoke to me. I'm Mrs. Laurel."

"Of course," said Todd. "Mrs. Laurel of the Laurels."

"It was in my husband's family," Mrs. Laurel said. "I wanted to put the house to the best use."

"Very wise, very wise," said Todd unctuously.

"Did you both want to see Mrs. Wilshire?" said Mrs. Laurel. "She's not very good with visitors, and I didn't tell her there would be two of you."

Todd looked at Mandretti. "Perhaps I should go in alone," he suggested.

Mandretti narrowed his gaze, and there was no mistaking his reaction to Todd's suggestion. "I'll come with you," he said.

"But if she's—"

"I'll come with you."

Mrs. Laurel came out from behind the counter and skittered past Mandretti. "This way," she said, taking Todd's arm and leading him up the stairs.

Mandretti followed closely behind.

"Mrs. Wilshire is rather an unusual resident," Mrs. Laurel confided to Todd.

"Is she French?" Todd asked.

"Oh, it's not that," said Mrs. Laurel. "There's nothing wrong with being French. It's a lovely language."

"Lovely," Todd agreed.

"But it's somewhat unexpected for the wife of a clergy person to be Jewish," said Mrs. Laurel.

"Yes, that is unusual," said Todd.

"We didn't know, of course," said Mrs. Laurel, "not that it would make any difference; she certainly qualifies for help. Poor old dear doesn't have a penny. It's just that when we heard that she was French and that she was married to Reverend Wilshire in 1945, well, we just assumed she was a war bride. But apparently, that wasn't the case. She was a refugee. Oh, that man Hitler! It's wrong to hate, I know, but sometimes I can't help myself."

"Hate's not the answer," Mandretti said unexpectedly.

Todd turned around and looked at him.

"Revenge," he said. "I believe in revenge."

I bet you do, Todd said to himself, hoping that he would never ever get on the wrong side of Michael Mandretti.

Mrs. Laurel stopped outside an open door. She looked at Mandretti.

"Are you sure you won't upset her?" she said. "She's very frail."

Mandretti bowed from the waist. "I will be charm itself," he said, and sailed into the room.

"Oh dear," said Mrs. Laurel.

Todd patted her hand. "We'll just ask her a few questions," he said. "We won't take a minute. We're just clearing up a little inheritance matter."

"She has nothing to leave," Mrs. Laurel said. "She doesn't have a penny."

Mandretti popped his head around the bedroom door. "Perhaps we can fix that," he said.

Todd followed Mandretti into the room. "We'll be fine," he said to Mrs. Laurel. She hovered in the doorway. "Really," Todd said, "it won't take a minute."

Mrs. Laurel retreated, and Todd crossed the room to find Mandretti kneeling beside a frail figure in a wheelchair. He saw Mandretti raise the old lady's pale hand to his lips and heard him murmuring soothing phrases in Italian. It was the same gesture that Todd had seen him use with Violet earlier in the day, and the effect was roughly similar. The old lady sat up straighter in her chair, and her brown eyes became birdlike in their attentive stare at Mandretti's face.

"Carlo?" queried Claudette Wilshire, in a small cracked voice.

Mandretti said nothing but continued to hold the old lady's hand.

Mrs. Wilshire looked again at Mandretti's face. "Non," she said, "no, you are not Carlo." Her French accent was slight but still noticeable.

Mandretti remained silent.

"My sister married an Italian," Mrs. Wilshire said. "Carlo Bergonzi. He was a lovely man. He played the saxophone."

Mandretti still said nothing. Todd moved quietly across the room and sat down on the bed. It was evident that Mandretti had everything under control. If Mandretti continued to clasp Claudette Wilshire's hand and murmur the occasional agreement, she would be putty in his hands.

"They went to Rome," said Mrs. Wilshire.

"Ah, Roma," Mandretti sighed.

"It should have been me." Mrs. Wilshire shifted in her wheelchair, and a sour expression crossed her face. "I was the pretty one," she said. "It should have been me. She stole him. And all I had was Clive."

"Clive was a good man," Mandretti said.

"Clive was a bore," Mrs. Wilshire snapped.

"Ah."

"I had to marry someone."

"Oh, I see," said Mandretti.

Mrs. Wilshire pulled her hand away sharply. "No, you don't see," she said. "It's nothing like that. That was the trick my sister used. That wouldn't work on Clive. He was too good, too Christian."

Mandretti made a faint murmur of sympathy.

"I had to marry," Claudette Wilshire said again, "to stay in England. Where else could I go? We had no country. There was nothing for me in France. Everyone was gone. So I married Clive and I told him I would be a Christian."

"About Clive ..." Mandretti said.

"Dull," said Mrs. Wilshire.

"I'm sure he wanted to make you happy," said Mandretti.

"We had no money," said Mrs. Wilshire, "and all those church ladies staring."

Mandretti looked up at Todd and winked. Todd imagined that he was trying to convey the fact that if they would just be patient, Mrs. Wilshire would tell him everything they needed to know.

"They didn't understand you," Mandretti said. "How could they understand someone like you? They were dull like your husband."

Interesting, Todd thought. When Mandretti wanted to, he could put entire sentences together with the subject and the object in the right order and without using double negatives.

"All I wanted was a new hat," Mrs. Wilshire said. "But no money; always the same thing, no money."

Mandretti cocked his head sideways, looking at Mrs. Wilshire from beneath his dark lashes. "Did your husband try to get money?" he asked. "Did he do something to get money?"

She threw her hands up in the air in an animated Gallic gesture. "He said he had this thing; he was going to sell it and we would have money. But then he changed his mind, and no more money."

"No new hat," said Mandretti sympathetically.

"It was red," said Mrs. Wilshire. "Ah, those church ladies, what would they say about a red hat?"

"I can only imagine," said Mandretti. He gestured behind his back to Todd. Todd took that to mean that it was time to produce Wilshire's journal. He handed it across to Mandretti.

"Claudette," said Mandretti, "do you recognize this?"

For a moment, Todd thought that Mandretti had overplayed his hand. The old lady was no longer looking at him. It seemed that she was still thinking about the red hat. He imagined her as a young woman, dark haired, dark eyed, struggling to speak English and pretend Christianity under the scrutiny of her husband's stiff-necked parish ladies. He understood the lure of a shocking red hat displayed in a shop window challenging the young Claudette to wear it as a badge of differentness. And in the end it had come to this, a tired, dusty room in a tired, dusty house, surrounded as ever by well-meaning Christian ladies. Todd knew what it meant to be different, to be the outcast, smart but different, yearning for a life on the stage but without the talent to back up his yearnings. He made a vow to himself that somehow he was going to get a red hat for Claudette Wilshire, a spectacular red hat with a veil and a feather.

"It's your husband's journal," Mandretti said.

Claudette Wilshire looked at the book with scant interest. "Always scribbling," she said.

"He wrote about a sword," said Mandretti.

"Always scribbling," she repeated. "Scribble, scribble, scribble."

"Do you remember a sword?" Mandretti persisted.

"Sword?" Mrs. Wilshire said. "What about the sword?" Her glance slid away from Mandretti, and her face took on a wary look.

"Do you remember it?" Mandretti asked.

Todd realized that Mandretti was losing her. He was misreading her mood. Mrs. Wilshire wasn't suffering from memory loss, she was suffering from guilt.

"Tell her it's okay," he hissed to Mandretti. "Tell her you understand why she did it."

Mandretti turned his head and looked at Todd.

"Did what?"

"I don't know," said Todd, "but she did something with the sword."

Mandretti nodded his head and turned back to Mrs. Wilshire. "Claudette …"

"I don't want to talk anymore. Who are you? I don't know who you are."

"You can tell us all about it," Todd said suddenly.

Claudette Wilshire turned her head and saw him sitting on her bed. Todd rose to his feet and came to stand next to her. "We're not blaming you," he said. "We just want to find the sword."

"I don't know where it is," Mrs. Wilshire said. "It could be anywhere now."

"But you did see it?" Todd persisted.

Mrs. Wilshire shied away from him, pushing herself back in her wheelchair. "It was mine to sell," she said.

"Of course it was," Todd said with a sinking heart. She had sold it. Now what?

"He collected swords," said Mrs. Wilshire. "He kept them in a big room. He said he would hang it on the wall. Old. He said it was really old."

"Yes it was," said Todd.

"I don't know where it came from," said Mrs. Wilshire. "Clive never said."

"He wrote in his journal," said Todd.

"Scribble, scribble," said Mrs. Wilshire.

Mandretti looked at Todd. "No need to explain," he said softly. "She doesn't care. Ask her who she sold it to."

"Mrs. Wilshire," said Todd.

"You can call me Claudette," she said. "You look like a nice young man." Her eyes were suddenly bright again, and Todd could see the shadow of the flirtatious young woman she had been, flirtatious or desperate, a refugee selling herself to find a country.

"Claudette," said Todd, "who bought the sword?"

"He put it on the wall."

"Yes, I know he did. What was his name?"

"Oh," she said, "it was Colonel Peacock."

CHAPTER ELEVEN

Todd hunched over the tiny screen of his cell phone with Mandretti breathing down his neck. He longed to tell the big man to back off but somehow lacked the courage, so he contented himself with saying, "It's loading but it's very slow."

Mandretti looked around as though he could detect the errant signal and speed it on its way. The limo, with Freddie at the wheel, pulled up at a red light. Todd steadied the phone and finally saw information scrolling down the screen.

"Okay, this is what we have," he said. "Peacock, Hubert Reginald, Colonel, Shropshire Light Infantry. Born 1895, died 1984. No issue."

"What's that mean?" Mandretti asked. "What's no issue?"

"No children," said Todd.

"No heirs?"

"Oh, I'm sure he had heirs; they just weren't his own children. That family seems to have trouble reproducing. The professor also had no children, so I'm guessing that Hubert's heir was from some distant and more fertile branch of the family."

"And what else does it say?" asked Mandretti.

"We don't need anything else," Todd said. "Now we know his regiment, we can find out if they have a museum."

"And how long is that gonna take?" Mandretti asked.

The light turned green and the car pulled forward. They were approaching the center of London in the fading evening light. Traffic streamed past them; workers heading home for the evening.

"If we could just wait till I have my laptop …" Todd said.

"You snooze, you lose," Mandretti announced.

Todd shrugged his shoulders and began another painfully slow web search. Mandretti fidgeted restlessly. "So, you think the Colonel lived at this Griffinwood Manor place?" he asked.

"It doesn't say," said Todd. "I can look it up."

"Yeah, yeah," said Mandretti. "Look up the museum first." He patted Todd's shoulder. "You're good at this stuff, kid. You should come and work for me. You'd love Vegas."

Todd let the remark pass, unable to imagine leaving the Keys, leaving Violet and Maria, leaving his tight circle of theatrical friends.

The regimental website opened slowly, very slowly. Todd watched the information filter onto the screen.

"Well?" said Mandretti, still breathing down Todd's neck.

Todd read aloud, "'King's Shropshire Light Infantry were based at Copthorne Barracks (built 1877–81) in Shrewsbury: this is now the HQ of the 5th Division and 143rd West Midlands Brigade, along with Territorial Army, cadet and support units. Its regimental museum has been located in Shrewsbury Castle since 1985 and combines the collections of the 53rd, the 85th, the KSLI to 1968, the local Militia, Rifle Volunteers and Territorials, as well as those of other county regiments – the Shropshire Yeomanry and the Shropshire Artillery. The museum was attacked by the IRA in 1992, and extensive damage to the collection and to some of the castle resulted. It reopened in 1995.'"

"So where is this place?" Mandretti asked.

"I don't know," said Todd, adding with strained patience, "I can look it up."

"Nah, don't bother," said Mandretti. He leaned forward and spoke to the back of Freddie's thick neck.

"Where's Shrewsbury Castle?"

"Dunno, mate," came the reply. "Shrewsbury, I suppose. It's out of my bailiwick."

"What does that mean?" said Mandretti. "What's a bailiwick?"

Freddie turned his head slightly sideways, offering a view of his dented and battered profile. "I ain't never been to Shrewsbury, Mr. Mandretti, but I suppose I could take you there if that's what you want. I'll have to phone it in. I wasn't supposed to take the car out of London. We'll be at the Dorchester in five minutes. I'll give the boss a bell when we get there."

Mandretti was silent.

Freddie turned his head again, looking just slightly nervous. "Is that okay, Mr. Mandretti?"

So, Todd thought, Freddie's been told to keep Mandretti happy, which means that Freddie's boss wants to keep Mandretti happy. Given Freddie's terrifying appearance, Todd didn't care to speculate on what kind of person employed him or what hold Mandretti might have over such a person. The offer of employment with Mandretti in Vegas was becoming increasingly unattractive.

Freddie brought the limo to a halt under the portico of the Dorchester, where a doorman sprang forward to open the door. Mandretti tapped Freddie on the shoulder.

"Wait," he said.

Freddie nodded. Mandretti and Todd proceeded into the Dorchester's art deco lobby.

"Go get your computer," Mandretti said to Todd.

Todd headed for the elevators but was waylaid by a large gray-haired woman in a voluminous cape. Todd, an Agatha Christie fanatic who had seen every filmed characterization of Miss Marple, was immediately reminded of Margaret Rutherford in Murder Most Foul.

"Are you Violet Chambray's person?" asked the Miss Marple look-alike.

"Well, I suppose you could say that," Todd replied.

"Are you or aren't you?" the woman asked imperiously.

"I am."

"Where is she?"

Todd hesitated. The large woman looked at him impatiently and then thrust out her hand.

"Professor Molly Walker," she said, "Medievalist. I met your employer at Carlton Lewis's funeral. We agreed to collaborate. I've been waiting here all afternoon. Where have you been?"

"Was she expecting you?"

"No, not exactly. I wouldn't have come except for the fact that Doctor Ryan is not answering his phone and I have important information. The person at the reception pointed you out to me; you and the other rather untrustworthy-looking gentleman."

Todd followed her gaze back to Michael Mandretti, who had dropped down into one of the gilded armchairs and was fixing Todd with an impatient glare.

"That's Mr. Mandretti," said Todd.

"I assumed as much," said Molly Walker. "And you are …?"

"Todd."

Todd realized that he would either have to invent a last name or reveal the fact that he was a member of Violet's family. "Todd Chambray," he said.

The large woman raised her bushy eyebrows but refrained from comment. "Well, Mr. Chambray, we have a problem."

"I'm sorry Doctor Ryan isn't answering his phone," Todd said, "but I don't think I can help you. Violet is with him but she never uses a cell phone. Perhaps they're on their way back. Maybe they can't get a signal."

"I've been trying all afternoon," Molly said. "Where did they go?"

Todd hesitated.

"Oh for goodness' sake," Molly said. "You can tell me. I told you, we're collaborating on this."

"We only arrived today," Todd said, "and I haven't had time to talk to Violet, so—"

Molly interrupted him in a loud voice; loud enough to disturb the expensive calm of the marbled lobby. "Where did she go?"

"She went to Griffinwood Manor."

"Damn," said Molly. "Damn, damn, and double damn. Look here, young man. That Mr. Mandretti, is he as dangerous as he looks?"

"Possibly," said Todd.

"And is he the man who hired Violet to find the sword?"

Todd nodded his head.

"Good," said Molly. "Let's go and talk to him."

"We're in a bit of a hurry," Todd said. "We think we have a lead, and we need to go to—"

"You think you have a lead?" said Molly. "Well, I have something much more than a lead."

She marched across the lobby with her cape swirling around her. Todd followed behind. Mandretti rose to his feet. For a moment, Todd thought that Mandretti might try his charm on the professor, but apparently, Mandretti was a quick judge of character. He stood completely still, allowing the force of Molly Walker's personality to crash like waves around his feet.

"This is Professor Walker," Todd said, dodging around the professor to stand beside Mandretti.

"Yeah," said Mandretti. It was neither a query nor an exclamation. It was simply a word.

"I'm holding you responsible for this," Molly said.

Mandretti spread his hands. "What have I done?"

"Nothing, nothing at all," Molly said. She collapsed into a chair, and Mandretti sat down again, watching her under hooded eyelids. Molly wiped a hand across her forehead, scraping back her untidy gray hair. "Sorry," she said. "It's not your fault. It's just that I've been waiting all afternoon. Do you have any idea where Violet and Doctor Ryan are?"

"None at all," said Mandretti. "I ain't seen them since this morning when Todd sent them off to get the train. They'll be back."

"Oh, I hope so," said Molly.

"Todd," said Mandretti, "go order a brandy for the lady."

Todd looked at Molly. She nodded her head and again ran her fingers through her hair. Todd raised a hand, and a waiter was immediately by his side. He placed the order and dragged up another chair.

"You're from here, ain't you?" said Mandretti.

"Yes," said Molly.

"So you can tell me where this castle place is. What's it called, Todd?"

"Shrewsbury Castle," Todd said.

"Yeah," said Mandretti. "How far is it?"

"Shrewsbury Castle," said Molly. "Eleventh century, but not much of the original left. Besieged by King Steven, that would have been 1138, and I think the Welsh held it for a while. It had a commanding position over the River Severn. I did a couple of digs there; didn't find much, too much modernization. I don't know why they can't leave things alone. I suppose you could drive it in four hours." She paused and looked at Mandretti suspiciously. "Why do you want to go to Shrewsbury?" she asked. "Have you found something?"

"Maybe."

"Now, wait a minute," said Molly, springing impulsively to her feet. "The Shropshire Regiment Museum. That's it, isn't it? That's why you want to go there. Taras was cataloging a regimental museum when he found the sword. Oh, that makes perfect sense. Griffinwood is practically next door."

"I didn't know that," said Todd.

"Oh, it's very close," said Molly. "Obviously, there's a family connection of some kind." She hesitated. "I've been in that museum. It's all recent regimental equipment. There's no medieval sword. Believe me, I would have noticed something like that."

"Professor Walker is a medievalist," said Todd to Mandretti.

The waiter appeared and set a glass of brandy on the small table beside Molly. She looked at it in surprise. Apparently, she had forgotten her initial upset and was trying to get her mind around the idea of the missing sword being in Shrewsbury Castle. Her face was flushed red with excitement.

"It'll be closed at this hour," she said, "and the traffic out of London is ridiculous this time of night. We should plan on leaving very early tomorrow morning. If we leave at six, we'll be there by ten. Don't worry about opening hours; my academic pass will get us in. We'll get a private tour."

She dragged her hand through her hair yet again, causing it to stand out like a gray crown around her head. "It's all eighteenth-century stuff," she said. "Regimental Honors, battle flags, light armament, and that kind of thing. I don't know what Peacock could have seen there."

She stopped abruptly, a shocked expression on her face. She looked at the brandy as though she had suddenly remembered why it was there.

"Peacock," she said. "Oh, no wonder Ryan thought we were a pair of useless old biddies. "

Mandretti looked at Todd and raised his eyebrows. Todd shrugged, indicating that he, too, had failed to follow Molly Walker's train of thought.

Molly picked up the brandy and swallowed a hearty mouthful. "Peacock," she said, "Crispin Peacock."

"He's at Griffinwood," said Todd.

She shook her head. "No, he's not," she said. "He's dead on his living-room floor in his Kensington flat."

"What?" said Mandretti.

Molly took another hearty swig of brandy. "It was in the paper this morning. Apparently, his housekeeper found him. He's been dead for a couple of days. Foul play, of course."

"Wait," said Mandretti, "is this the same Crispin Peacock?"

"Well, obviously not," said Molly impatiently. "This is the Crispin Peacock who is second cousin to Taras Peacock, and this is the Crispin Peacock who stood to inherit Griffinwood Manor, but it's not the Crispin Peacock who took Doctor Ryan to Norfolk. The real Crispin was already dead by the time Violet and Doctor Ryan landed at Heathrow."

She swallowed the last of the brandy. "That's what I came to tell you," she said, "before you distracted me by talking about Shrewsbury Castle."

"We didn't distract—" Todd started to say, but Mandretti was already in motion, grabbing Todd by the arm and dragging him toward the door.

"Violet's at Griffinwood," he said.

"Yes."

"And Ryan?"

"Yes."

"And they're with this man, whoever he is."

"Yes," said Todd.

"Well then, let's go," said Mandretti, marching Todd across the lobby to the front doors.

"Where?"

"To Griffinwood. We ain't gonna find nothing standing around here. I expect people who work for me to take care of themselves, but those two don't got no clue. We're gonna lose them and the sword if we don't get a move on."

Freddie was still parked outside with the engine running on the black limousine. Mandretti yanked open the driver's door and leaned in. "Get going," he said.

"Where to?"

Mandretti looked at Todd. "You tell him," he said.

Todd realized that Mandretti was pale under his tan, and with no one available to shoot or bully, his mind was racing so hard that he could not frame his thoughts.

"Well," said Todd, "I think he wants you to drive us to—"

Molly shouldered Todd aside. "Shrewsbury," she said. "M1 to the M6."

"That's a long way," Freddie protested. "I'll have to phone it in."

"I'll phone it in for you," said Mandretti as he ran around to the other side of the car and dropped into the front passenger seat. "Get going."

"Whatever you say, mate, so long as you clear it with the governor."

"I'll clear it. I'll clear it," said Mandretti.

Todd stood indecisively on the sidewalk. Molly gave him a shove. "Get in the car," she hissed, "or he'll go without us."

Todd scrambled into the back seat and then moved quickly across to the opposite side as Molly Walker heaved her bulk in beside him. The doorman, who had come forward to assist them, stepped back in a hurry as Molly slammed the door and Freddie eased the big car forward and into the flow of traffic.

"You got a gun?" Mandretti asked.

"No guns, mate," said Freddie.

"Knife?" Mandretti asked.

"Yeah, we got knives," said Freddie.

CHAPTER TWELVE

Violet Chambray

Violet put her hand up to the back of her head, and it came away sticky with blood. She sat up and looked around. She was still beside the ancient stone wall. The mist had cleared, but nothing else seemed to have changed. She pushed aside the branches obscuring her view of the valley and saw the scene exactly as it had been before she tripped. The yellow construction equipment still crawled across the raw scraped earth, and the cement wall of the dam still spanned the valley. No magic, no alternative reality, no magical kingdom of Albion. What a fool she had been to believe any of Elaine's nonsense.

"Just a surface wound," said a woman's voice close by. "Scalps always bleed."

The opinion of the wound on her head was being given by an elderly woman who stood beside her. She was leaning on an intricately carved wooden staff and wore a dress in the same style and same sky blue as Elaine. Her white hair was plaited into an elaborate pattern of braids piled on top of her head. The impression she gave of dignity and authority was somewhat lessened by the fact that she was wearing white high-top sneakers decorated with red flashing LED lights.

Elaine came into Violet's line of vision carrying a large green leaf, which she handed to Violet with instructions that she should place it over the wound on her scalp.

"Go away," said Violet. "I'm not putting that on my head."

"Oh, just do it," said Elaine.

"I'm not putting a leaf on my head," Violet said. "It's not sanitary, and you're a lunatic."

The elderly lady poked Violet with her staff, and then smacked the

142

staff none too gently across Elaine's posterior. "Is this what has delayed you?" she asked. "Is this why I have had to come to you? Have you squabbled and argued every point?"

"No," said Elaine and Violet together.

The older woman glared at Elaine and then turned her attention to Violet. "You have your mother's eyes," she said.

Violet gasped. Could there be a grain of truth at the bottom of this pile of fantasy? Hope returned. "You knew my mother?"

"I think so. I think you are the daughter of Ariana. I have been informed of your gifts, and they are the same gifts that were given to your mother. We sent her into your world as we have sent so many others, to find the sword. She never returned. One day, my dear, we will discover her story and learn why she abandoned you to the care of strangers, but now is not the time."

The white-haired woman looked across at the construction equipment on the hillside. The silence of the valley was suddenly ruptured by the wailing of a siren.

"They're closing the sluice gates," said Elaine.

The older woman nodded her head. "We are out of time," she said. "Within the next day, it will be too late, and this valley will be a lake." She looked at Elaine. "What have you told her?" she asked.

"There has not been time," Elaine said.

"You have wasted time on your own affairs," her companion replied, "and now I have no time to prepare her properly. It's too late now to go through the portal and show her what lies beyond."

She took the leaf from Elaine's hand and held it out to Violet. "My name is Rowan," she said, "and I am in the habit of being obeyed. It may be that you doubt things told you by this silly girl, but do not make the mistake of doubting what I tell you. We have very little time, and because of your mother, and because of the gifts you have received, I believe that you can help us. Now take the leaf that Elaine has brought you and apply it to the wound on your head. It will stop the bleeding. Elaine is foolish at times, and she's been very much distracted by her infatuation with your traveling companion, but her knowledge of herbs is without equal."

Violet obediently applied the large green leaf to the throbbing wound on her scalp and felt immediate relief.

"Come," said Rowan.

Violet struggled to her feet, straightened her clothing, and retrieved her purse. Rowan led the way out of the thicket and began to climb a narrow rocky path that bordered the waterfall, stepping energetically in her high-top sneakers. Elaine trod gracefully behind her, and Violet climbed as best she could.

Rowan paused halfway up the path and waited for Violet to catch up.

The sound of the water was loud, and Violet strained to hear Rowan's words.

"You will not get wet," Rowan said.

Violet shrugged her shoulders. So far, she had been in no danger of getting wet although they were walking close beside the waterfall. Rowan turned a corner in the path and stepped into a dark shadow beside the rushing water. Then she disappeared. Elaine stepped aside and urged Violet forward. "Go," she said.

"Go where?"

"Behind the water," said Elaine.

Violet edged hesitantly into the darkness and found herself in a cave behind the waterfall. A wall of water cut off the view of the valley and admitted only a small amount of daylight, but the cave was dry. Rowan had spoken the truth, Violet was not getting wet. The rushing water muffled the urgent wailing of the siren. Ahead she could see the flashing red lights of Rowan's sneakers. So that's why she wears them, she thought.

Violet followed the lights, and within moments she was standing beside Rowan, with Elaine close behind her. Elaine produced a flashlight from somewhere within her clothing, and Violet could see that the small cave was at the entrance to a network of caves. Elaine moved the flashlight, and Violet saw the dark entrances to numerous tunnels, some wide and welcoming, some small and narrow.

"This way," said Rowan, setting off along one of the smaller tunnels, where Violet had to stoop to enter. A few feet further in, and the tunnel opened into another cave. The sound of the waterfall was muted and distant now, and the siren could not penetrate. Violet found that she could hear Rowan even though she spoke in hushed whispers.

"Light the torches," Rowan said.

Elaine's right hand moved in graceful gestures, and the light of the flashlight was replaced by the flickering light of flaming torches set in sconces on the walls of the cave. Magic, Violet thought, true magic. If Elaine could bring forth fire with a wave of her hand, what else could she do?

The dancing flames showed Violet that this cave was larger than the one before, and that entrances to even more caves lurked in the shadows. She was already confused and doubting that she could find her way back to the waterfall without a guide.

"I am going to tell you a story that you have already heard," said Rowan. "All of the people of this island have heard the story, and they have carried it with them throughout your world. Few have believed its truth, and many have perverted the facts for the entertainment of the masses, but the story has never been forgotten."

The old woman looked around for a moment and then located a rock where she was able to sit.

"There is such a thing as racial memory," Rowan said, "and this story is in the racial memory of the people of this land. That's why young people seek so desperately for meaning in ancient rituals, in worshipping oak trees and making pilgrimages to Stonehenge, and why so many ancient inns have the names of romance." She nodded her head. "It is part of the racial memory of this island."

She sighed deeply. "I have no time to tell you all of it, and there are many things that I don't know; those are the things that you will tell me."

"I can't tell you anything," Violet protested.

"You will," said Rowan, "if you are, in fact, Ariana's daughter. Now listen carefully, for this is what you must know before we go any further. I will tell you of Arthur's son Mordred and the great rebellion."

Violet heard Elaine give a little sigh of impatience.

"I will be brief," Rowan said.

"The valley is filling with water," Elaine protested.

"There is nothing we can do about that," Rowan said. "All I can do now is to tell Ariana's daughter the story of her people."

She looked up at Violet and continued her story. "Arthur, the King, grew older," she said, "and the Queen produced no heir. The Knights of the Round Table roamed across the island of Britain, searching for their Holy Grail, and the old powers were weakened by the new beliefs. The people turned from the ancient magic and embraced the creed of the new God-Man, the Carpenter, the one who died on a cross and returned to life. Merlin was forgotten, and some say that he left Albion. Only the gates he had created into your world remained. And then Mordred rose up in rebellion against his father. Better, he said, for the kingdom to be in the hands of a bastard than to be in the hands of an old man and a barren woman.

"When word of the rebellion reached the questing knights, they returned to Albion through the portals Merlin had created, and they took up arms, some on the side of the King, but many on the side of Mordred the usurper. Even then it might well have been possible to avert war, because Mordred was lacking in charm and not well liked, but a terrible sin came to light; the relationship of the Queen Guinevere and Lancelot her champion."

"Was it true?" Violet interrupted.

"Yes," said Rowan, "much to their shame, it was the truth. Guinevere had cuckolded the King. All hope was gone that she could provide Arthur with a legitimate heir, and many feared that she might try to pass off a child of Lancelot's as a child of Arthur's. The Queen was banished through the gate to the island of Britain, where she was to spend the rest of her days among the holy women of the new religion."

"A nun," Violet said. "I saw a nun, a tall woman with a gold cross. She was making someone write. She wanted a map, a description, something like that."

"The Griffinwood Document," said Elaine.

"Is that what it was?" Violet asked.

"Yes," said Rowan, "but who wrote it and why it was written is what we don't know. "

"It was a novice," Violet said. "I don't know anything else."

"It's no longer important," said Rowan. "Let me complete my story."

Violet subsided into silence, but her mind was filled with the memory of the room she had glimpsed, the young novice in terror of the tall demanding nun; the nun she had called Majesty.

"Albion was thrown into civil war," said Rowan, "with Arthur and his remaining loyal knights set against Mordred and all those who had failed to profit from Arthur's long and peaceful reign. The land was ravaged by war, crops were destroyed, and villages were torched, whole towns destroyed. The Knights of the Round Table were defeated one by one until Arthur, gravely wounded, and with just a few knights to support him, was forced to retreat to the west. Strange as it may seem, Lancelot returned then to stand by the King. His love for Guinevere was never as great as his loyalty to Arthur."

"The woman had bewitched him," Elaine said.

"Possibly," said Rowan, "but even without magic, a woman can bewitch a man."

"Merlin could not be found in Albion," Rowan continued. "He had not been seen since the new religion of the Holy Grail had been carried back by the knights. The portals to Britain remained open, but they were the only evidence that Merlin's magic had ever existed. The knights, even the Knights of the Holy Grail, knew that magic would be needed to heal the King, and so they carried Arthur westward into the highest mountains, searching for the last refuge of the old magic.

"After a long journey in which the King grew weaker by the hour, they came to their final destination, the lake from which Arthur had obtained Excalibur. The island of Avilion could still be glimpsed through the eternal mists although it was slowly receding from human sight. They lay the dying king on a stony beach, and Sir Percival raised Excalibur high, calling on the same power that had forged Excalibur in the depths of the lake to come now and save the King."

Rowan stopped speaking for a moment and rose to her feet. "I am not asking you to believe," she said. "I am not even asking you to comment. I ask only that you come with me now."

Violet obediently bit back the thousand questions that had come to her mind. The old woman's tale had been strangely compelling, a mixture of Mallory, Tennyson, and Disney, told in a voice of absolute certainty.

Elaine took a lit torch from the wall sconce and handed it to Rowan.

"I am the only one who knows the way," Rowan said.

Leaning on her cane, she crossed the cavern, selecting one of the many cave entrances that Violet had seen as dark shadows. She ducked her head and led the way. The floor of the cave sloped sharply downward. After some hundred yards, the slope turned to steps, and the light of the torch that Rowan carried ahead of them showed her that they were no longer walking through a natural tunnel. Stone walls rose on either side and formed an arch above them.

"More light," said Rowan.

Elaine gestured again, and torches and wall sconces gave a flickering light to the tunnel ahead. The floor and walls of the tunnel were green with the moss of ages, but the steps were firm and straight.

"When the reservoir is full, this will be underwater," Elaine said.

"We cannot prevent it," Rowan said, "and therefore, we will not waste our time discussing it."

Violet felt the first prickling fingers of panic. Despite the amazing events of the day and the incredible tale told by the old woman, she had not so far been truly afraid, but now she faced something she knew to be reality. The valley was filling with water. She had seen it with her own eyes. She could imagine the water seeping into the cave and slowly making its way down the various tunnels until the whole system was flooded. How long would it take? Would she still be here in the thrall of the old woman's story when the water rose and cut off their exit? If she turned around now, could she even find her own way out?

Rowan continued to make her way down the long flight of stone steps. With a pounding heart, Violet followed her until they came to the bottom of the steps, where a heavy iron grill barred their way.

Rowan turned and looked at Violet. "More than nine hundred years have passed since this gate was opened," she said. "Our sisters came only once and saw what had been done, and then they knew why Arthur had not returned. They sealed the gate with more than iron bars. It is sealed with enchantment, but if you are Ariana's daughter, you may open the gate."

"And if I'm not Ariana's daughter?" asked Violet.

"You will not survive," said Rowan.

"Why don't you just open the gate yourself?" Violet asked.

Rowan nodded her head. "I could do that, but then we would not be certain of who you are or how you came by your gifts. We would not know if we could trust you."

"I don't want you to trust me," Violet said, uncomfortably aware of the long, dark corridor behind her, and the rising water in the valley. How long did she have before she would hear the sound of water trickling down the steps? "So you want me to risk my life by touching the gate? Why should I do that? What's in there?"

"We answered Percival's call and we came for the King," Rowan said, taking up the tale she had been telling, and that Violet was trying to keep straight through the many distractions of their journey deep underground.

"We?" Violet queried. "Who is we?"

"The people of the Magic Isle," said Rowan. "We are the people of Avilion. We were the guardians of the sword Excalibur. We gave Arthur his power."

"The Lady of the Lake—"

"Was one of us," said Rowan, "although much of her legend is without any basis. Your poets have lent a great deal of romance to the event. But it is true that when Percival raised Excalibur and called to us, we came. The King was gravely wounded and beyond the help of any of our medicines. The only magic that remained to us was the bond between Arthur and Excalibur, and such magic takes time. There was no safety for Arthur in his own kingdom. We could not hide him on Avilion. The isle is wrapped in mists, but it is not hidden from the sight of any determined seeker. Arthur could not remain there. So we brought him through the portal. We brought him here."

"Here?" Violet queried.

"Here," said Rowan. "He lies before you, beyond that gate that we long ago sealed with our magic."

"Do you really expect me to believe that?" Violet asked, looking at the ancient forged iron bars. Beyond was nothing but darkness.

"I expect you to see for yourself," Rowan replied.

"Open the gate," said Elaine.

"Oh, you'd like that, wouldn't you?" Violet hissed.

Rowan laid a hand on Violet's shoulder. "Forget your quarrel with this girl. Forget the rising water. Forget the absurdity of the story I have just told you. Forget everything you know of history and logic and common sense. Take a deep breath and think of your gifts. Where do they come from, Violet? Where do you come from?"

Violet closed her eyes and tried to calm her racing thoughts. She could not argue with the fact that she had a unique gift. Who else did she know who could touch an object and know its history? How did she know that Carlton Lewis had died? Why had she seen such a clear vision of the attack on Barry Marshall; seen and felt it so clearly that she had even experienced his fears as her own fears? And the piece of paper, the first one that Ryan had handed to her, why had it seemed so dead, so alien? How had she known that it came from a place outside of history? How had she known anything she had known? Was it possible for her to believe that she was the daughter of a woman named Ariana, a woman born outside of time and space on the mystical island of Avilion?

If this was true, then all she had to do was open the gate and see for herself. She reached out and touched the iron bars.

CHAPTER THIRTEEN

Marcus Ryan

"This," said Ryan, "is the most amazing library I have ever seen."

"Yes, I agree, it's quite impressive," Crispin Peacock said, with his typical British understatement.

Ryan stood in the center of the space and looked around. The library of Griffinwood Manor occupied an octagonal tower, a later addition to the mainly Tudor building. The tower rose three stories high to a stained-glass dome. Galleries circled the walls at each level, and books occupied every inch of wall space, rising in row upon row of bound volumes. A circular stairway hugged the wall leading from one level to the next, and a library stepladder ran on rails around the lower level.

"Who on earth …? " Ryan asked.

"Don't know," said Peacock. "I really don't know much about my relatives. I never really expected to inherit this place. I thought someone would produce a child, but we seem to be perennially short of heirs in this family, lots of old uncles and aunts unable to produce offspring. I don't think old Cousin Taras ever expected to inherit, and I know I didn't, but that's the way it worked out. Bit like Queen Victoria."

Ryan scoured his mind to find a reason why Queen Victoria and her multitude of children should in any way resemble the Peacock family and their inability to reproduce.

"She was only very distantly related to the royal family, you know," said Peacock. "All kinds of people had to die before she had any chance at the throne. Lots of old dukes and duchesses who couldn't produce legitimate heirs, a lot of bastards involved. If you ask me, she should never have been given the throne. Personally, I can't see any good reason why a bastard can't make a claim. After all, no one asks to be born a bastard, do they? Can't be blamed for having a father who plays for the away team, if you know what I mean."

"She seemed to be very popular," said Ryan.

"Manic depressive, if you ask me," said Peacock. He shrugged his shoulders. "Oh well, I suppose I shouldn't complain. All those infertile uncles have resulted in me inheriting this place. So what do you think?"

"It's magnificent," Ryan said, "truly magnificent. Where did it all come from?"

"No idea," said Peacock. "I can only assume that someone bought up entire collections. This whole library wing is quite a recent addition, but some of the books are ancient. I know this is where Taras was working, but quite frankly, I have no idea where to begin. Libraries are not my thing."

"I love libraries," Ryan said. "They bring out the treasure hunter in me. This room is full of information; it's just a matter of knowing where to look."

"I thought you were bringing your partner with you," Peacock said. "Isn't she supposed to be helping you?"

Ryan spared a guilty thought for sending Violet away in the company of the mysterious Elaine. Perhaps he had been wrong not to insist that he should accompany her, but he had been preoccupied with thoughts of the library at Griffinwood and the possibility of finding a real clue to the location of the sword. Just as his instincts had told him to go to Norfolk, so they were now telling him to go to Griffinwood library and follow the trail that Taras Peacock had most certainly left behind. He was pretty certain he knew where to begin, and now he had no wish to waste time talking about Violet, or mulling over the mystery of Elaine.

"Violet was delayed," Ryan said dismissively. "She might be along later."

"I'm sorry not to meet her," said Peacock.

"We'll be fine without her," Ryan said.

"So where do we start?" Peacock asked.

Ryan looked around the library. "I assume you've checked on all the books that are actually on the table," he said.

Peacock nodded. "Yes, I did that. I don't see any connection, but maybe you should look. You have a better idea of what you're looking for."

Ryan looked at the small pile of books that sat on the dark oak table. He picked them up one by one. "Sons and Lovers, 1916," he said, flipping open the flyleaf of the first book. He opened the next one. "Agatha Christie, 1933." He worked his way rapidly through the pile. "Well," he said, "I think you've inherited a small fortune here. These are all first editions. It looks as though Taras was planning on cashing in and getting himself some spending money."

Peacock fingered the books with very little interest. "Nothing about the sword?" he asked.

"Not in here."

"So where do we look now?"

"The card index." Ryan pointed to a row of index cabinets standing at the left side of the main entrance to the library.

"All of those?" Peacock asked. "There must be thousands of them."

"We'll go through and see if he left any markers among the cards," Ryan said. "That will give us a clue as to where he might have been looking. Of course, that's assuming that every book in here is cataloged, which I very much doubt."

Peacock thrust his hands into the pocket of his jeans and stared around at the vast array of books. "This is impossible, isn't it?" he said.

"No," said Ryan. "It might take a while, but it's not impossible."

Peacock shook his head. "There has to be an easier way."

If it was easy, everyone would have a TV program, Ryan said to himself, but he refrained from making the remark aloud.

"There's probably nothing here," said Peacock. "I was just hoping that he left some kind of note or record that would tell us why he went off to catalog the contents of a regimental museum. That sounds like pretty small potatoes for someone of his standing. If we could just find out about the museum …"

"It's not just about the sword," Ryan said. "It's about …" He hesitated. Peacock knew nothing about Barry Marshall's children, and perhaps it would be better to keep quiet for the time being.

"Obviously, we need to bring my cousin's murderers to justice," Peacock assured him, "but finding the sword would go a long way toward doing that."

"He also found the document here," Ryan said.

Peacock took his hands out of his pockets. "What document?" he asked quietly.

"The Griffinwood Document," Ryan said.

"The Griffinwood Document?" Peacock repeated, fixing Ryan with his pale blue eyes.

"Oh," said Ryan, "I forgot. I haven't seen you since Lewis's funeral."

"No, you haven't. Is there something you haven't told me?"

"Well, yes," Ryan said, thinking of the very many things he had not told Crispin Peacock, including the fact that he was being followed by a mysterious but beautiful woman named Elaine. He knew beyond a shadow of a doubt that Elaine was a secret he should share with no one, mainly because no one would believe him.

"So what haven't you told me?" Peacock asked. "I thought we were in this together. I thought we were helping each other. After all, Taras Peacock was my cousin."

"I don't really know what it is," Ryan said. "Violet and I went to Carlton Lewis's funeral, and Carlton's widow told us about a document that had been found by your cousin, here in this house. Apparently, he wasn't able to translate it, and he had given it to the Society of Arthurian Scholars for translation."

"Why would he do that?" Peacock asked, a scowl crossing his features.

"I don't know. Your cousin was fluent in a number of ancient languages, so I can't imagine why he was unable to translate that particular document."

"But why give it to that society?"

"It was illustrated," Ryan replied, "and the illustrations led them to believe that the document was something to do with Arthur, or Camelot, or the Knights of the Round Table. I don't know all the details."

"For goodness' sake," said Peacock, sounding not just peeved but distinctly angry, "why are we here messing around in this library when the document is with these people? Where are they? Are they in London?"

"They don't have it anymore," Ryan said. "It was stolen from them."

"Who stole it?"

"I don't know," Ryan lied, still hesitating to mention Elaine and the mystery surrounding her activities.

Peacock looked desperately around the library. "Are you sure Taras found it here?" he asked.

"That's what he said," Ryan replied.

Peacock's eyes roved around the room, looking up and down at the thousands of books. "And you've no idea who stole it?" he said.

"No."

"Or what it was about?"

"No idea at all," Ryan said, "although Violet—"

"Violet? Does she know something?"

"No," said Ryan, wishing he had never started into the whole subject of Violet. "Violet sometimes has sort of visions."

He expected Peacock to lose interest at the idea of obtaining serious information from the visions of a hysterical woman, but Peacock's reaction was not what he expected. His eyes snapped into focus, abandoning their wild search of the acres of bookshelves.

"What kind of visions?"

"Oh, it's nothing," said Ryan. "She said she saw a nun."

"Fancy a cup of coffee?" Peacock said, suddenly changing the subject. "Or would you prefer something stronger? I haven't stocked the cupboards yet, but I can probably come up with something from the wine cellar."

"Your cousin liked wine," said Ryan.

"All my forebears liked wine," Peacock said. "I have inherited quite a decent cellar. I'll go down and see what I can find."

"Don't go to any trouble on my account," Ryan said.

"No trouble, old boy," said Peacock airily. "I have to go outside anyway." He patted his shirt pocket, where Ryan could see the outline of a cell phone. "No signal in here; must be all the books. Don't understand the mechanics of it but can't imagine anything penetrating that wall of paper. I'll be right back."

Although he stuck his hands back in his pockets as he sauntered out of the room, Ryan could not help but believe that Crispin Peacock was in a hurry to do something, and that something was not a visit to the inherited wine cellar.

As Peacock left the room, he passed through the pools of light beamed down from the stained-glass dome, and his white tennis shoes appeared to change color; blue, green, red. Something tickled at the back of Ryan's mind. Red shoes, there was something about red shoes.

He pushed the thought away and allowed it to be replaced by a new idea, the library ladder. The ladder ran on a rail around the ground floor of the library and reached up to the top row of the ground-floor stacks, to the books that were stored just below the first-floor gallery. Theoretically, with the use of the ladder and the stairs to the galleries, every book was accessible. So if Taras Peacock had been using the ladder in his search for first editions, then maybe the search had also caused him to find the Griffinwood Document. If that was the case, perhaps the ladder was still in the same position. Well, it was worth a try. Ryan's pulse was racing as he climbed the ladder. He was back on track, doing what he did best, following a trail that no one else could see.

As he climbed past the first stack, he schooled himself to be patient. There was no reason to believe that Peacock had necessarily climbed all the way to the top of the ladder. He could have found what he was looking for at any level, and the ladder ran up four levels.

The ladder was a work of art made of polished oak to match the bookshelves, with wheels that ran on a track around the library. As he climbed, Ryan noticed that the ladder builder had incorporated a book container at every level, making it possible for a person standing on the ladder to pull a book off the shelf and place it in the box to be carried down later. It was not until he reached the third level that he found a box that contained what appeared to be books. Closer inspection revealed that the two volumes in the box were, in fact, storage boxes disguised as books. Ryan looked along the shelf of books that met him at eye level and realized with a thrill of excitement that none of the books were actual bound volumes. The entire shelf was occupied by storage boxes bound in leather with gold lettering on the spines. He could only imagine that one of Crispin Peacock's ancestors had nursed such a passion for this beautiful room that he could not bear to have the appearance destroyed by shelving mismatching document boxes.

Ryan could see the space left by the removal of the two volumes already at hand on the ladder. In fact, it would seem that more than two volumes had been removed. Apparently, there had once been a third volume. He carried the two volumes down the ladder and over to the library table. He judged the binding on the boxes to be Edwardian, early twentieth century, several generations removed from Taras Peacock's generation. He wondered what had caused Peacock to climb the ladder and select these two volumes. No, he corrected himself, make that three volumes. One volume had excited Peacock so much that he had abandoned his search and hurried down the ladder to look more closely at his treasure. It was no great stretch of the imagination to conclude that the missing box had contained the Griffinwood Document.

Ryan opened the first box and found a pile of accounting ledgers, row after row of expenses and receipts written in black ink that had faded to brown. Despite the luxury of their leather binding, the document boxes had not been designed for maximum preservation of the contents. The papers were spotted with mildew and rust marks, and held together with relatively modern paper clips. A quick glance was enough for him to know that the documents were not especially old, but without taking the time to read them, he would have no idea whether they were important. Accounting ledgers often revealed unexpected secrets. There was a lot to be said for following the money. He closed the box and looked at the lettering on the spine. Benedictine Hospice, Glastonbury.

Years of experience had taught Ryan not to jump to conclusions; nonetheless, his mind insisted on taking a shortcut. His excited thoughts ignored the sensible conclusions of a trained academic mind and jumped straight to the fact that the papers had come from Glastonbury, the home of the miraculous Glastonbury thorn, purported to have been brought to England by Joseph of Arimathea, along with the Holy Grail. Glastonbury had once been rumored to be the original site of Camelot, although no proof had ever been found.

He opened the box again as though, knowing now that it had come from Glastonbury, he might find some mystical insight into its contents. He scrutinized the neatly written accounts. Nothing had changed; the pages contained nothing but the daily accounting of the expenses of a small group of Benedictine nuns at the turn of the nineteenth century.

He picked up the second box and found another pile of papers, older than the first ones and in much worse condition. He shuffled through, treating the documents with scant respect and barely noticing that the papers were shredding under his fingers. This was nothing but death and burial records for the Sisters of St. John, showing the slow dwindling of the population of the motherhouse until its dissolution in 1901. Presumably, that was when the documents had been sent to Griffinwood Manor for safekeeping.

He worked his way to the bottom of the box until his fingers closed over a small package tucked under the mound of paper. He pulled the package out into the light. It was wrapped in brown paper, limp with age and tied with string that fell to dust beneath his fingers. He folded back the paper, and the light from the stained-glass library dome flashed down on the golden object inside, a cross some four inches in length and decorated with dull red stones. He took a shuddering breath. He knew those stones, he had seen them in Professor Peacock's hand in Vegas, and he had clutched just such a stone as he stepped through the mist in Norfolk. It was the same kind of red stone that he had handed to Elaine that very morning, the stone she said would allow Violet to step through the gate. He missed it, Ryan thought. Taras Peacock had been so excited by what he had found in the third box that he had not even looked into the other two boxes.

Ryan looked around the library. If Peacock had found the Griffinwood Document in one of these boxes, what had he done next? He knew it had ended up in the hands of the Society of Arthurian Scholars, but that would never have been Peacock's first thought. First he would have tried to translate it himself. He would have to swallow a great deal of academic pride before he could admit that the language was unknown to him. So what would he have used? A dictionary? So where were the dictionaries?

No, he thought. Peacock would not have kept his personal reference books in the library. He would have kept them in a study somewhere else in the house. Despite his penchant for sending handwritten notes, surely Peacock had a computer and an e-mail account and all of the other things that a serious researcher would need. Therefore, he must have had a study.

Ryan slipped the gold cross into his pocket and set off in search of the study. He stepped out of the library into the magnificent but sadly neglected grand entrance, which featured a black-and-white tiled floor, a sweeping staircase to the upper floors, and several suits of armor. He had noted the armor when he had first arrived at the manor and had already made the assessment that they were poor Victorian imitations of the real thing. However, they certainly lent a gothic atmosphere and drew the eye away from the peeling paint and chipped tiles.

He thought again about the Griffinwood Document, hidden away in a bound leather box. Two boxes sat on the library table, but where was the third box? Had Peacock delivered it to Molly Walker along with the document, or had he left the box somewhere in the house? For once, he was presented with a question that was easy to answer. Call Molly Walker and she would tell him. He checked his cell phone. No signal. So the library was not the only place without a signal. If he wanted to make a phone call, he would have to go outside.

A figure appeared out of the deep shadows behind the staircase, Crispin Peacock with a tray containing a dusty wine bottle and two glasses.

"I was just coming to find you, old boy," said Crispin. "What are you doing out here?"

"Looking for your cousin's study," said Ryan.

Crispin shook his head. "Already looked," he said, "nothing there; no computer, no nothing."

"Books," said Ryan. "Did he have reference books?"

Peacock shrugged his shoulders. "I suppose so," he said. "The place is a bit of a tip. Do you want to see it?"

"I certainly do," said Ryan, forgetting entirely about his need to phone Molly Walker.

"Follow me," Peacock commanded, turning on his heel and retreating into the gloomy shadows behind the stairs. Ryan followed, and Peacock led him past several formal living rooms, through an enormous dining room, and into a small room with a beamed ceiling, a brick fireplace, and a huge oak desk.

Peacock set the tray down on a corner of the desk while Ryan fumbled along the wall for a light switch. The light flickered for a moment as though the bulb was on its last legs, but eventually it steadied, and Ryan was able to see that the study did in fact contain a bookcase.

"What are we looking for?" Peacock asked.

Ryan spread his hands. "I'm not sure," he said. "Here's what I think might have happened. Your cousin found the document in the library—"

"You're sure of that?" Peacock asked.

"Yes, I'm sure of that," Ryan replied. "I'm also sure he would have tried to translate it himself, so it's possible he used one of the reference books in this room."

"I don't see how that helps us," said Peacock. "Apparently, he couldn't translate it, and that's why he took it to those people in London."

"Trust me," said Ryan. "There's method in my madness. I know what I would do, and I think most researchers would do the same thing. The document was old and probably fragile, so he wouldn't want to handle it very much, and he most certainly would not photocopy it. Photocopying would expose it to too much light. I think he probably hand-copied some of the major paragraphs or diagrams, or whatever they were, and he would have used that to try to find the language. I'm betting that somewhere in here we will find at least a few lines from the document."

"Well, it's worth a try," said Peacock, "although I don't know how that gets us to the sword."

"It's not just about the sword," said Ryan. "There's something much bigger than just the sword."

"Any idea what?" Peacock asked.

Ryan hesitated, thinking of all the things that he had not shared with Crispin Peacock, and ashamed that he had allowed himself to forget about Barry Marshall's children. The thought of where they might be and what might be happening to them dulled the excitement he felt as the pieces of the puzzle came together. Now, he thought, was not the time to mention the children.

"So what's behind it all?" Peacock asked.

"No idea," Ryan said, "but I plan to get to the bottom of it one way or another. You look through the papers on the desk. We're looking for something that looks like writing but isn't."

"Looks like writing but isn't?" Peacock repeated.

"Squiggles, hieroglyphics, pictograms, curlicues," said Ryan. "I'm going to check the dictionaries."

Peacock began to leaf through the papers on the desk, and Ryan checked Professor Peacock's reference shelf. He pulled the books out one by one, shaking them to see if any papers would fall out. He went through Norse languages, Sumerian, West Germanic, Tibetan, and Welsh without finding anything. No surprise there. Taras Peacock would have had no trouble recognizing any of those languages. He ran his finger along the shelf and came to rest on a slim volume with tattered binding. It was a book that had been much used, or much abused. He read the title; The Search for Our Ur-Language; Vincent Cornwellian, PhD. He knew the name, knew the man's reputation and understood the subject; the search for the original, the Ursprache, source of all written language. Ryan did not personally believe that such a language existed, but obviously Taras Peacock had found the book useful.

He flipped through the pages and found what he was looking for. A sheet of notepaper was folded in among the pages; Taras Peacock's copy of the Griffinwood Document.

"Got it," he declared.

Crispin Peacock looked up from his search of the papers on the desk. "What?"

"I have it. I've found his notes."

He spread the paper on the desk under the light, which had again begun to flicker. "Well, no wonder he was stumped. I've never seen anything like this."

The page was filled with sweeping runic-like characters transcribed by Taras Peacock in ballpoint pen. Nothing on the page was familiar to Ryan.

Peacock looked over Ryan's shoulder and then stretched out his hand and turned the paper sideways. His hand trembled slightly as he touched the paper.

"That doesn't help," Ryan said.

"No, probably not," said Peacock. "Still, well done, old chap, very well done. Good detective work. Shall we have that wine now?"

Ryan registered the abrupt change of subject and the sudden loss of interest. Peacock had done the same thing in the library when Ryan mentioned that Violet had a vision of a nun. Peacock had already uncorked the dusty old wine bottle, and now he poured red liquid into the two wine glasses. Ryan wished it had been white wine. The memory of the red wine in Las Vegas still haunted him, red wine spilling across the carpet. Red, he thought. Red light spilling across Crispin Peacock's white shoes, turning them red.

Ryan held the glass steady and concentrated on regulating his breathing. Red shoes. The man who took Barry Marshall's children wore red shoes, or maybe not; maybe he had simply crossed into a pool of red light, the red light of the sanctuary lamp. Could the shoes have belonged to Crispin Peacock? Why, he asked himself, would Crispin Peacock do such a thing?

"You okay, old man?" Peacock asked.

"I just need to make a phone call," he replied, needing to find an excuse to leave the room. He needed to be alone. He needed to think. He needed not to drink the wine. "I had an idea I wanted to run by Professor Walker."

"Professor Walker?" Peacock asked. "Do I know her?"

Ryan was alert now, wondering how Peacock knew that Professor Walker was a woman. He was certain that he had never mentioned her name, never referred to her as Molly Walker.

"She's with the Society of Arthurian Scholars," Ryan said. "I was wondering about what else your cousin took to them."

"Probably nothing," Peacock said airily. He sipped his wine, or maybe he only seemed to sip his wine. "I can usually find a signal in the corner of the dining room, up against the window," he said helpfully.

"Thanks." Ryan set down his wine glass and went out of the study and into the vast dining room with its yellowed wallpaper and mismatched chairs around a huge refectory table.

A dim light filtered through the veil of dust cloaking the French windows, and as he stepped into the light, his phone sprang into life, chirping and beeping the day's activity. He checked the screen. Molly Walker had called him at three o'clock, and again at four, and then about every half hour for the rest of the afternoon. Interspersed with her calls were missed calls from Todd and Michael Mandretti, and finally a voice mail. He dialed and waited for his message. As he waited, he looked out the window and saw Crispin Peacock hurrying across the lawn in the direction of the ruined chapel.

The voice mail was from Todd, speaking quickly but enunciating very clearly so that there could be no mistake. Crispin Peacock, a man in his fifties, had been found dead in his apartment. He had been dead for several days. Michael Mandretti was very concerned about their safety and unhappy that Ryan was not answering his phone, and they were all on their way now to Griffinwood Manor. And, by the way, they believed that the sword was in Shrewsbury Castle.

Ryan looked out of the window again. Peacock was already across the lawn and disappearing into the undergrowth around the ruins. He remembered that he had asked Elaine about the gate and that Elaine had glanced quickly at the ruins and then refused to answer him. Obviously, there was a gate right there on the other side of the lawn, and the man he knew as Crispin Peacock was about to go through it.

Thoughts began to line themselves up for Ryan to consider. When Peacock had looked at the rough notes of the Griffinwood Document, he had turned the page sideways, and his hand had trembled. If he knew how to read the ancient runes, then what else did he know? Ryan thrust his hand deep into his pocket and felt the shape of a little gold cross and the smooth outline of the red stones. Violet had taken the jeweled pin, but fate, or divine providence, or some other power, had provided him with an alternative key, and he made up his mind to use it.

He retraced his footsteps from the dining room, back through the cavernous front hall, and let himself out the front door and into the fading evening light. He tightened his hold of the talisman and sprinted across the lawn, through the undergrowth, and into the shadows of the ruined chapel. He walked around the crumbling interior walls on the theory that if he was looking for a gate, then the gate would probably be in a wall rather than in the middle of nowhere, although that had not been the case in Norfolk.

His phone beeped at him, and he pulled it out of his pocket. Michael Mandretti.

"Hello," he said.

"Finally," said Mandretti. "Where the hell have you been, Doctor?"

"I'm at Griffinwood Manor, but there's no signal in the house. What's been going on?"

"That's what I'd like to know," Mandretti snapped back. "Where's Violet? Does she know anything?"

"She's not here."

"Then where the hell is she?"

"She left with a woman who has been following us."

"What?" Mandretti bellowed. "What woman? Do you know where she went?"

"No, not really," said Ryan.

"We're on our way," Mandretti said. "I want that sword."

"Violet's not here," Ryan repeated, "and I'm just leaving."

"No, you ain't," said Mandretti. "You ain't going nowhere. We're on our way, and you'd better damned well wait for us."

"Sorry," said Ryan, "I can't do that. I'm going after Peacock, or whoever the hell he is."

"You wait," Mandretti repeated.

The stone wall in front of Ryan began to shimmer, and a mist rose around his feet. He tightened his hold on the gold cross.

"I'm following Peacock through the gate," he said.

Mandretti's voice rose to an angry crescendo. "What gate? You ain't going through no gate. Wait for us. Where the hell is Violet?"

"She's not here," Ryan said again.

He heard Mandretti's last angry growl, and then the phone went dead, and Ryan walked through to the other side of the mist.

CHAPTER FOURTEEN

The village on the other side was completely familiar to him. He could name the purpose of every building. Enough of the evening light remained for him to see the sagging outlines of a cluster of wattle-and-daub huts, all badly in need of repair. He recognized the fetid green waters of a neglected duck pond, and the muddy wasteland of an overgrazed village green. Then his other senses came into play, hearing the persistent bleating of a goat, the squawk of chickens settling in for the night, and absorbing the overwhelming smell of unwashed humans, animal waste, and the midden heap. Over it all was the scent of wood fires.

A little above the village stood the longhouse of a minor nobleman, larger than the other buildings, but still in a sad state of neglect. The dim glow from some of the huts told him that tanned leather had been stretched across window frames by the more prosperous villagers, and tallow candles were burning inside the huts. As he watched, a group of small boys in ragged tunics and bare feet drove a herd of skinny cattle through the village and into the safety of a wattle enclosure.

He had seen such villages before. He had walked their streets, identified their kitchen hearths, dug through their midden heaps, even exhumed their burial mounds, but in each case, the village had been a thousand-year-old ruin. He had never seen torches burning outside the long hut, women gathering their children into the safety of the family bed, mangy dogs fighting for scraps on the street. The historian in him examined the scene with excitement. He could see where archaeological deductions had been correct, and he could see where mistakes had been made.

One sweeping glance gave him enough material for an entire article in any professional journal, but who would believe him? If he wanted to be taken seriously, he would have to go down into the village and collect artifacts to take back with him.

He put a stop to his racing thoughts. He was aware that his brain had been attempting to bury itself under a pile of academic questions instead of dealing with the reality of where he was and what he was seeing. He was not here to collect evidence for a learned treatise on life in the Dark Ages. He was here to find the man who called himself Crispin Peacock. And, more to the point, he had no idea where here was, or how it could be that he had stepped from the twenty-first century into a living, breathing twelfth-century village. All he knew was that it had happened once before, when he had stepped through the mist in Norfolk and found himself looking at a fleet of ships that could not possibly exist.

This time the mist had brought him through to a forested hillside. The ruined chapel wall no longer existed, or perhaps that was the wrong way to look at it; perhaps the chapel was yet to be built. One more mystery in a week of mysteries. One more impossible anomaly.

He knew he must put aside his disbelief and apply his thought processes to this hunt as though it was any other treasure hunt. The treasure was the man who had gone through the gate ahead of him. Only a few minutes had elapsed between Peacock's disappearance into the ruined chapel and Ryan's own journey into the unknown. Did time move at the same pace in this alternate universe? If that was the case, then Peacock must be near, very near. Where was he likely to go?

Ryan studied the village. The villagers were bringing their livestock indoors and barricading themselves in for the night. Ryan knew it was not unusual for the poorer peasants to sleep alongside their animals for warmth and safety. He heard the howling of wolves from the wooded hillsides above the village, a reminder that he too was vulnerable. Whatever this place was, whatever reality it represented, it was quite possible that he could die here just as easily as he could die in his own world. His need to get himself indoors was just as great as the need of the peasants.

Well, if he wanted information, the best place to find it would be at the longhouse, the home of the minor nobleman who controlled the village. Visitors would be expected to make themselves known to the local chieftain and would be welcomed into the hall to sleep by the fire along with the dogs and servants. Custom would demand that if he knocked, he would be admitted. He doubted that he would be welcomed anywhere else. No peasant would open his door to a stranger who came knocking at sunset.

He scrambled down the hillside, uncomfortably aware of the darkness descending on the forest behind him and imagining the yellow eyes of timber wolves following his progress. The road that ran through the huddled village was better maintained than he expected. Tree trunks had been laid down in the mud to keep the road passable. So, he thought, this was not just an isolated settlement. Someone was expecting horsemen and wagons to pass this way. This village might not be the final destination, but this road led to a destination of sufficient importance that the road had to be maintained. Perhaps the villagers were not just wary of wolves in the night; maybe they were also afraid of whoever passed along the timber road.

As if in answer to his own thoughts he heard the jingle of harness and the thudding of hooves approaching along the road. He ducked behind a pile of hay, noting that it was fetid and moldy and would provide scant nutrition. A horseman passed by, clods of mud flying from the horse's hooves. The man rode bareheaded and lightly armored with nothing but a dented breastplate over a leather jerkin. His hair was brown with sun-bleached streaks catching the remaining light. He wore a patch over his right eye, and on his feet were white high-top tennis shoes. Ryan knew him immediately; the waiter who had poured the wine for Taras Peacock.

The horseman clattered through the village and up to the longhouse. His arrival was obviously expected. Torchlight flared in the darkness as he was admitted into the hall. The doors closed behind him. Ryan hesitated. Now what? He could hardly go up to the longhouse himself and demand entrance now that he knew who was in there. Anyway, he said to himself, what could he have been thinking? What had made him think that the local chieftain or nobleman who ruled the hall would have accepted him without question? Had he truly forgotten what impression he would make dressed as he was and carrying a pocket full of twenty-first-century gadgets? On the other hand, the horseman who had just passed by was wearing white sneakers, and he had been admitted without question.

"If I wanted you dead, you'd be dead by now," said a voice from the other side of the haystack.

Ryan sprang to his feet and found himself face to face with the man who had called himself Crispin Peacock.

"He likes to kill," the man said. "I really do try to discourage him, but he just likes doing it. Well, at least I persuaded him to leave the children alive. I don't think that poor old vicar can really tell us anything, but I had to let the kids be taken. Sometimes he's beyond my control."

Although Ryan opened and closed his mouth, he had no words; none at all. The man patted him on the back sympathetically.

"Bit of a shocker, isn't it, old chap?"

"Enough with the old chap," Ryan blurted out. "You're no English prep school boy."

"Public school, old bean," the man replied. "For some reason, what you Yanks would call a prep school, we call a public school, although heaven knows the public don't attend. Don't worry, I came by it quite legitimately. All the best schools, Cheam and Harrow."

"Where am I," Ryan asked, "and who the hell are you?"

"Ah yes, that's a much better question. My name, the name I was given at birth, is Mordred, but I've had various names since then. I could hardly be registered among the flower of English youth as Mordred Pendragon, could I? Don't worry about the other names, just call me Mordred. You are obviously aware that I am not Crispin Peacock, although it really is a good name."

"You killed him."

"Not I," said Mordred. "I told you, I have very little control over Bors, that's the name of my one-eyed friend. He kills. That's what he does. Don't worry about that now; I can explain it later. For the moment, I think we should be more concerned with getting indoors. There are things in the forest that you would not care to meet."

"Wolves?"

"Worse than wolves," said Mordred. "Come on, old chap, chop-chop. We'll go up to the hall. In another reality, of course, that would be Griffinwood Manor, but we're not in that reality, are we?"

"Aren't we?"

"Of course not. You're the expert, Doctor; where would you say we are?"

"Britain, twelfth century," said Ryan.

"Wrong on all counts," said Mordred, hurrying Ryan along the timber road toward the longhouse. "We are in Albion, and it is the twenty-first century."

"Another name for Britain," said Ryan.

"Not anymore. This is Albion, and in this reality, we are not fated to become Britain."

"How …?"

"Oh, it's really tedious," said Mordred. "Arthur, Camelot, Guinevere, what a bitch she was, and all the rest of us locked in eternal warfare. We can't win, we can't lose, and we can't modernize. We can't do a damn thing until Arthur either dies or comes back."

"Is he really …?"

"Really sleeping?" said Mordred, who seemed determined not to let Ryan complete a question. "Well, that's what we're going to find out thanks to the paper you found today."

"You could read it, couldn't you?" Ryan asked.

"Yes, I realized I gave myself away there," said Mordred. "I had a pretty good idea you would follow me. Still, this must be quite a shock for you. Don't doubt you could do with a stiff drink. Bors keeps a pretty good stock; primitive stuff, but it does the trick."

Ryan stopped in his tracks. "That longhouse belongs to Bors?"

"Yes, I'm afraid it does," said Mordred, "and I have to agree that he's a vile sort of person, but he's useful. I'll have to get rid of him after we've dealt with Arthur and we finally have some kind of peace and progress here."

Mordred rapped on the heavy oak door of the longhouse. The doors opened to reveal the torch-lit interior. Once again Ryan was met with a scene that he had only imagined in two dimensions. He knew that the floor of the longhouse would be strewn with rushes, but he had not realized that the rushes would be so damp and dirty and littered with filth of all kinds. A blazing cook fire occupied one end of the room, sending out clouds of choking smoke that hung low over the heads of the men at the table. The room smelled of rancid meat, unwashed bodies, and wet dogs.

The room fell silent when Mordred entered. The dozen or so men who had been seated at the table rose to their feet. At the head of the table, Bors lifted a wooden cup and said a few words in an unknown language.

"Oh, come on," said Mordred, "you can speak English."

"I can," said Bors, "but these men cannot."

"Better if they don't understand us," said Mordred. "You know Doctor Ryan, of course."

Bors nodded his head. "Do you want me to kill him?"

"No, I do not," said Mordred, "or at least, not yet."

Ryan stared at the man who had killed Taras Peacock and Carlton Lewis, and taken Barry Marshall's children. He felt a kind of hopeless anger; anger at what had been done, and hopelessness because he could see no way to right the wrong. He was out of time and out of place in a primitive thatched hall, surrounded by men who were armed with weapons that he recognized from his own archaeological digs; broadswords, heavy and blunt for hacking through flesh and bone, daggers, sharp and furtive, axes for fighting one on one. He had nothing but the gift of his own wits, which at that moment seemed to have deserted him, and the faint hope that the children were somewhere in the village. Violet had said that they were beyond her reach in a different place. Well, this was definitely different.

Mordred caught hold of his arm and led him to a corner of the hall where the air was a little clearer, motioning to Bors to stay back.

"Owe you an explanation, old boy," said Mordred. "I've been watching you for a while, and you strike me as an intelligent kind of chap, and you definitely know your history. Of course, you don't know this particular history, but I think you can make yourself at home here."

"Here?" said Ryan. "I'm not staying here."

"It's that or I give you to Bors," said Mordred.

Ryan looked over his shoulder to where Bors had shouldered his way onto one of the benches and was demolishing a chunk of meat. He appeared to be listening to the talk around the table, but his one eye remained focused on Ryan.

A small, ragged boy approached Mordred and offered two wooden mugs. Mordred handed one mug to Ryan. "Drink up. You'll feel better.

Going through the gate is a bit disconcerting, isn't it? No idea what the science is. It's Merlin's magic, but you and I have both been to school; we know there has to be a scientific explanation. I imagine it's something molecular." He paused. "Ah, maybe you think I've given you poison. I can't blame you; after all, your old friend Taras … Well, let's not talk about that." He took the mug from Ryan's hand, took a long swallow, and handed it back. "See, nothing. It's safe to drink. Try it."

Ryan sipped at the drink. The flavor was smoky and sweet with a hint of fruit, maybe apple. It was, in fact, delicious. He drank again.

"Feels better, doesn't it?" said Mordred. "So, let me tell you, old man, you're not in Kansas anymore." He laughed at his own joke. "Wizard of Oz," he said. "Oh, you have no idea how confusing it is to live in two worlds. Bors understands, but basically, despite his experience in your world, he's an oaf."

He indicated two rough wooden stools tucked into a secluded corner. "Come, sit," he said.

Ryan, still nursing the drink, dropped down onto one of the stools. Mordred scooted his seat closer to Ryan and dropped his voice to a whisper.

"I'm going to tell you quickly and quietly," he said. "The people in this hall probably wouldn't understand if I shouted it from the rooftops, but I don't want to take the risk. Believe it or not, they do actually speak a very early form of English, and they will recognize certain words. So we'll keep this quiet and just between us. We don't want the peasants to be revolting, do we?" He laughed again. "Sorry, I just can't resist a joke; it's the result of my ridiculous education."

Ryan drank again, feeling the calming fumes from the smoky liquid pacifying his angry thoughts and stilling the clamor of questions. He resolved to be quiet and to listen. When he had listened, then he would take action, if action was possible.

"So, in a nutshell," said Mordred, "this is Albion, an island very similar to the island of Britain, occupying a similar position in a similar world, but in a different reality. I read some science fiction when I was in your world, watched some TV, caught a few episodes of Star Trek, so I don't think you're going to be too shocked when I say that we are in a parallel world. For all I know, there could be millions of parallel worlds, but I can't speak from experience. I only know of two, yours and mine. Thanks to the work of Merlin, who the people here think of as a magician, a select few of us are actually able to travel between the worlds. Any questions?"

"Not yet," said Ryan. "Keep talking."

"Oh, I intend to," said Mordred. "Just remember that I'm giving you the basics. There are people here who could tell you the same story in epic poem form, and it would take hours, and you'd be none the wiser because of all the talk of magic. Anyway, let me continue."

"Please do," said Ryan.

"Some nine hundred years ago, we were ruled by a high king. His name was Uther Pendragon—no, don't interrupt me. I know you've heard of him, and that's the point of my story. Uther Pendragon, misusing his royal powers, raped the wife of the king of Cornwall, and she gave birth to a son."

"Arthur," said Ryan.

"I told you not to interrupt," Mordred said with a sudden flash of fierce anger that gave the lie to his cheerful schoolboy exuberance.

Ryan subsided into silence.

"Arthur raised in secret, blah blah blah," said Mordred, "brought out of hiding by Merlin, pulls the sword out of the stone, becomes the king. Well you know all that. He was a good king, brought peace and prosperity to Albion, brought the army under control, married a beautiful woman, and all the rest of it. Unfortunately, Arthur's knights soon got bored with peace and nothing to do but hunt dragons—yes, we had, and still have, a few dragons—so Merlin opened the gates to another reality and let them go through into your world, Britain in the Dark Ages, and that's why you have your Arthurian legends and why you have no historical source for King Arthur."

"Really?" asked Ryan.

"Yes," said Mordred. "If you think about it for a moment, it makes perfect sense."

"If I hadn't seen this with my own eyes …"

"But you have, haven't you?"

"Yes, I have," Ryan agreed, "but if it was nine hundred years ago, and—"

"Yes, well, that's the rub, as dear old Willie Shakespeare would say," said Mordred. "We are, for want of a better word, under an enchantment. Arthur, you see, only managed to father one child, and the Queen was not involved. Arthur and his half-sister produced a child who was double cursed, a bastard born of incest, my ancestor, Mordred."

"Your ancestor?"

"Of course. That's why I've had all the privileges of an education in your world. For centuries, the first born male child of Mordred's line has been educated to become king. We, along with some of our relatives, are educated in your world, where learning has flourished. We stand ready to assume the throne of Albion and usher in a new era, but we are still condemned to continue to live like pigs in darkness and ignorance."

"But if Arthur is dead," Ryan ventured to ask, "what's to stop you?"

"If!" Mordred bellowed. "If only. But he's not. Your poets, Tennyson, Mallory, Taliesin, they have the story straight. Arthur is not dead, he's sleeping."

"That's what Molly Walker believed," said Ryan, "or at least what she wanted to believe."

"Yes," said Mordred, still angry, still shouting. "It's a lovely story, isn't it? Righteous King Arthur sleeping until he's needed again. Does anyone stop to ask what's supposed to happen to the rest of us? We were at war, and we were winning. Mordred was Arthur's only true heir, bastard or not, but Arthur wouldn't give up the throne to a bastard, which is ironic because he was himself a bastard. So he's wounded, he's dying, and what happens? Well, I'll tell you what happens. The interfering old temple maidens from Avilion come and carry him away; that's what happens."

Ryan stared at Mordred, whose face was red with anger. Although he was telling a story that was nine centuries old, he was as angry as if it had happened yesterday. Perhaps in Albion's strange time warp, nine hundred years was the same as yesterday. When one reality could become another reality and molecules could shift between universes, who could say what would happen to the reality of time itself?

"Well," said Mordred, abruptly abandoning his anger, "thanks to your research, Doctor Ryan, we now know where Arthur is sleeping. It's as we suspected; he's not in our world, he's in yours, and it appears that he doesn't have his sword."

"Does that make a difference?" Ryan asked.

"None of us know how Merlin worked his magic," Mordred said. "For centuries, we believed that Arthur and Excalibur were somewhere together, and that Arthur would eventually be healed through the power of Excalibur and he'd be back to finish the fight. Well, it hasn't happened, so we have to assume something went wrong, and my best guess is that Arthur and Excalibur are separated. Arthur is neither dead nor alive, and while he waits in limbo, so do we."

"So what will you do," Ryan asked, "now that you know where he is?"

"We'll take him," said Mordred. "I haven't told Bors the good news yet, but I will as soon as I've finished here with you. Bors and I will go back through the gate, and we'll bring him here. Alive or dead, he's coming back here. That should be enough to bring Merlin out into the open."

"Merlin's still alive?" Ryan asked.

"He's somewhere," said Mordred. "He's in the wind or the trees or the water. He's still with us, still weaving his magic, and Arthur is our bargaining chip. He'll come out of hiding to rescue his precious Arthur, and the price will be a throne for me and the end of this war."

"You mean you're still at war?" Ryan asked.

"Yes, that's exactly what I mean," said Mordred. "We can't win and we can't lose, but we still fight. That's Merlin's curse for us, the result of his interfering magic. There is technology in your world that could end this war in a couple of days, a few rifles, a couple of bombs. It would take very little, but nothing like that can come through the gate. We just go on hacking at each with broadswords, hurling spears and shooting arrows. It's pathetic. Without Excalibur we can't end it ourselves, but if we have Arthur, then we'll have Merlin. Of course, it would be better to have Excalibur, but I think we've waited long enough."

"It's all very hard to believe," Ryan said, risking another outburst of anger from Mordred.

Mordred shrugged his shoulders. "You can hardly deny reality," he said, "unless you can come up with another explanation. Do you think you're dreaming or hallucinating?" He abruptly raised his hand and struck Ryan hard across the face. Ryan sprang to his feet, spilling the remains of his drink and knocking over the stool.

"See," said Mordred, "not a dream and not a hallucination. You're really here, Doctor. And it's time to choose sides, because I'm not letting you back through the gate. You're either with me or I let Bors take care of you. Which would you prefer?"

Ryan, still shaken by the sudden blow, struggled to form an answer. He looked at Bors, who stared back with undisguised menace in his one good eye. He looked around at the other roughhewn men. Although they appeared to be at rest, each had a sword at his side, and each wore a metal breastplate. Even the shaggy long-legged dogs nosing for scraps among the rushes looked at him with malevolence. How could he fit into such a world?

"Well?" said Mordred.

Any answer that Ryan might have made was cut off by a trumpet blast from outside. The men at the table sprang to their feet, swords in hands. The dogs growled. Bors rushed to Mordred's side and handed him a sword and a breastplate.

Mordred buckled on the armor and turned from a caricature of an English gentleman into a primitive warlord. "Stay out of this," he ordered. "Get yourself into a corner and keep quiet."

He bounded to the center of the room, raising the sword above his head and screeching a glorious wild war cry. The doors of the longhouse were flung open, and Ryan heard the sound of women screaming and saw the flicker of burning thatch. Mordred and Bors led the warriors out into the night, and a small boy closed the doors behind them. The boy looked at Ryan with dark eyes full of fear, dropped a crossbeam into place, and ran to bury himself among the reeds in a dark corner. □

CHAPTER FIFTEEN

Todd Chambray

Todd allowed himself the luxury of a loud yawn. The effect of the third cup of coffee was wearing off, and he could scarcely keep his eyes open. On the other hand, Molly Walker and Michael Mandretti seemed to have energy to burn. They were finally in among the display cases of the regimental museum at Shrewsbury Castle. They had spun out the hours between their arrival in Shrewsbury at three in the morning and now by slumping around a table in an all-night cafe, drinking coffee to keep themselves awake while Freddie took a nap outside in the limo.

They arrived at the redbrick castle not long after sunrise. The museum was not due to open until 10 a.m., but Molly had waved her credentials, and Mandretti had raised his voice, and they had finally persuaded a security officer to phone the assistant curator to come in and open the door.

Todd, generally a soft-spoken and non-confrontational soul, had distanced himself from his bullying companions, nursing his Styrofoam coffee cup and trying to remain invisible. Now he watched Molly Walker stalking through the exhibits with the museum official, a small man who had obviously dressed in a hurry and failed to shave, close on her heels. Michael Mandretti tagged along, waiting eagerly for her to pronounce sentence on the various weapons on display.

"Is this everything?" she asked the assistant curator.

He nodded his weary and rumpled head. "Everything, Professor," he said.

"They're all eighteenth century," Molly declared.

"Yes," he agreed. He stifled a yawn. "I told you on the phone," he said.

"What about the bomb damage?" Molly asked. "In 1992, the IRA bombed the castle. Did it destroy any of the exhibits?"

"No," he said. "Nothing was destroyed, and everything has been cleaned and put back on display."

"And this is what you showed to Professor Taras Peacock?" she confirmed.

"Yes, he cataloged the collection for us, and it was very kind of him. He said his family had a connection with the area, and he was happy to help out. I'm sure you know, Professor, the value of a well-curated exhibition."

"Yes, of course," said Molly, "and I also know the value of rotating the exhibits and bringing some out for special events. So do you have some items that are not currently on display?"

"No," said the assistant curator. "Professor Walker, if you could just tell me what you're looking for ..."

"A sword," said Mandretti. "A big sword."

The official looked wearily at Mandretti. "I've shown you the swords," he said. "I don't know what else to tell you. I've given you every courtesy here, Professor Walker, but I really don't see how I can be of any further assistance. So if you'll excuse me—"

"Did you put everything back on display?" Molly asked.

"Almost everything," he replied.

Todd pricked up his ears and stepped closer, sensing the first chink in the assistant curator's armor.

"Almost everything," said Mandretti. "Are you keeping something back?"

The official took a step backward. "No, I'm not keeping anything back. There's nothing else here."

"But you said almost everything," Mandretti insisted. "Perhaps you don't understand how serious we are about this sword. If it's a question of money?"

"Money?" said the assistant curator. "I don't know what you're implying. I'm sure I don't know what the custom is in your country, but let me tell you—"

Todd stepped forward before anyone could say anything else, and before the official took it into his head to call the security guard and have them ejected from his museum.

"If we can all calm down for a minute," he said, "I'm sure we can achieve an understanding."

"Understanding?" The assistant curator was red in the face. "What kind of understanding are you suggesting? You Americans think you can come over here and throw your money around and buy anything you want. Let me tell you, those days are long gone. The treasures of this regiment are not for sale, not to you or to anyone else."

Todd stepped back. Obviously, he was not helping the situation, and he could think of no way to calm the official's ruffled feathers. However, he could see that Molly Walker didn't give a damn about ruffled feathers. What a character! She would be magnificent on the stage. He filed her away in his mental catalog. One day, he was going to reproduce her, especially the way that she now thrust her chin forward as she loomed over the assistant curator.

"Don't be silly," she said. "No one is trying to take anything from you. Quite obviously, you don't have what we want in any of these showcases. We're looking for something much older and considerably more important than the items you have here, and our research suggests that it must be in this museum."

Somewhere in Todd's brain, the pattern shifted, and he saw what he had not seen before. "No, it doesn't," he said.

Molly Walker and Michael Mandretti turned to look at him.

"We don't know that," he reiterated. "We've jumped to a conclusion. We know that Peacock found … it, and we know that he was cataloging this museum, and we put two and two together, and perhaps we made five."

"What?" said Mandretti.

"You may be right," said Molly. "We just assumed that because he was working here, that's where he found it."

"No," said Mandretti. "That old French broad said that she gave it to Colonel Peacock."

"Sold it to Peacock," Todd corrected.

"And Peacock was in this regiment," Mandretti concluded.

"So we assumed he gave it to this museum," Todd said, "but we don't know it for a fact."

"Excuse me," said the assistant curator.

"Yes, but where else would it be?" Molly asked. "If it's not here, it could be just about anywhere."

"Excuse me," said the assistant curator again.

"So what are we supposed to do?" Todd said. "Without Violet and Doctor Ryan, we're screwed."

The assistant curator raised his voice. "Excuse me!"

Todd looked at him and tried to retrieve his normal good manners. "I'm sorry," he said. "Are you trying to say something?"

"Yes," the assistant curator replied. "I have no idea what's going on here, and quite frankly, I don't want to know. What I would like to do is go home and take a shower and eat my breakfast."

"I'm sorry," Todd said again.

The official ignored the apology. "You appear to be looking for an item donated by Colonel Hubert Peacock," he said.

"Yes," said Molly Walker. "Is it here?"

"No."

They waited. The rumpled little man seemed determined to enjoy his moment of triumph. He looked from one to the other of them, holding on to the moment. Todd knew what he wanted.

"We'd be most grateful if you would tell us what you know," he said.

"What I know," the assistant curator repeated. He paused. "Well," he said, "we did have a bequest from Colonel Peacock, before my time, of course, and long before the bombing. Apparently, he was a bit of a collector, with weapons from all over the place. Some of them are on display. We have some items from the Boer War, Armentières, Ypres. His collection really helped with our World War One display, but when we reassessed everything after the bombing, we had to tell the family that a lot of the items had no place in our collection. We're a regimental museum, and some of them were just not appropriate; much too early."

"Was there a sword?" Molly Walker asked.

"Oh, several, I think," said the assistant curator. "I wasn't here at the time, but I've been told there were swords, battle axes, that kind of thing, although nothing of any great value."

Todd could see that Michael Mandretti was doing his very best to exercise patience. "So," said Mandretti through gritted teeth, "what did you do with the swords?"

"I didn't do anything," the official replied.

Mandretti took a deep breath. Todd would not have been surprised to see smoke coming out of his ears.

"What did the museum do with the sword?" Todd asked.

"We gave them back."

"You gave them back to the family?"

"Yes. I expect they're all hanging on the wall at that old manor house they have."

"No," said Molly. "It can't possibly be that simple."

"It isn't," Todd said. "If the sword was hanging on the wall, Ryan would have seen it."

"Not to mention Crispin Peacock, or whoever is pretending to be Crispin Peacock," said Molly.

"Are we done here?" asked the assistant curator, heading for the door and looking hopefully to see if they were following him.

"Yeah, we're done," said Mandretti.

They filed out into the lobby. The day staff was beginning to check in. The lights were on in the gift shop, and a woman was taking her place behind the ticket counter.

Mandretti slapped a handful of paper money on the counter. "For our admission," he said.

The woman behind the counter looked at him doubtfully. "I haven't opened the register. I can't give you change."

"Keep the change," Mandretti said as he sailed out of the front doors and headed for Freddie and the waiting limousine.

Todd turned to thank the assistant curator, but he had already vanished from sight.

"Where to now?" he asked.

"Griffinwood," said Molly. "Maybe Ryan missed something."

[ ]

CHAPTER SIXTEEN

Violet Chambray

Violet opened the gate. Her first touch had been tentative. She was ready to step back at the sight of sparks, flames, waves of blue light, or any other kind of magical protection her mind could think of, but there had been nothing, and so she simply opened the gate and stepped inside.

Torches on wall sconces flamed into light at a graceful wave of Elaine's hand, and Violet saw what the gate had been protecting year after year, century upon century; unchanging and hidden from the changing world outside.

For a moment, she could only stand and breathe long slow breaths to calm her racing thoughts, for if what she saw was possible, then everything that she had been told was true. Everything.

At last she was able to grasp what she was seeing. Twelve knights lay at rest on wooden pallets. No, she corrected herself, only eleven knights, one pallet was empty. The armor the knights wore caught the light and sent blazing reflections from the flare of the torches. It was armor that she had only ever seen in fantastical drawings, shining in silver and gold. The knights were bareheaded; their helmets rested beside them on the floor. Each knight clasped a sword in his hands. No, not each knight, not the knight who rested on a higher, more ornate pallet. His armor shone brighter than the others, and his red surcoat was emblazoned with a golden dragon. His hands were empty.

Violet heard Rowan's sudden intake of breath and saw the light of the torches diminish as Elaine struggled to regain control of herself and reassert the power that kept the torches alight. So, Violet thought, they've never seen this before. They didn't know for certain what was in the cave. They were as overwhelmed as she was.

"Is it them?" Elaine asked.

"I don't know who else it would be," Violet said.

"Of course it's them," said Rowan.

She walked forward into the chamber, the red LED lights on her sneakers flashing incongruously on the shadowed floor. She looked at each knight and began to identify them by their emblems. Names from legend rolled off her tongue.

"Sir Ladinas of the Forest Savage, Sir Melion of the Mountain, Sir Gawain of Orkney, Sir Percival, Sir Lionel, Sir Bedivere, Sir Pelleas, Sir Edward of Carnarvon, Sir Dinadan."

She paused and looked down at the empty pallet and then moved on to a knight whose surcoat was white with a red cross. "Sir Galahad the Pure," she said.

She came to the last of the knights, the one who wore a red surcoat with a gold dragon emblem, the knight with no sword. "Arthur, the High King," she said.

"Are they dead?" Violet asked.

"No," said Rowan. "It is exactly as we were told; they are sleeping. If they were dead, they would be nothing but bones and dust, but Merlin's magic was strong; even their armor shines."

"I still can't believe it," said Violet. "Maybe they're statues or waxworks or something."

Rowan raised her eyebrows. "After everything you've seen today, do you really think that they are wax dummies?"

"I don't know what to believe," said Violet. "Perhaps I'm hallucinating. Maybe I'll wake up in bed at the Dorchester, and everything that's happened today will turn out to be a dream."

"Would you prefer that?" Rowan asked.

Violet looked at the row of sleeping knights. "Can you make that happen? Can you send me back to London?" she asked.

Rowan shook her head. "No, of course not. My powers are very limited and growing weaker all the time. I'll be honest with you, daughter of Ariana, I have also doubted the truth of the legend."

"No," said Elaine.

Rowan looked at the younger women. "Be honest, Elaine," she said. "We have all doubted. It's very hard to keep a belief alive for nine centuries. No one living today has ever seen what we're seeing now. I don't know that anyone other than Merlin has ever been in this cave, and Merlin lingers beyond our sight."

"Someone's been here," said Violet. "Someone took the sword."

"If there ever was a sword," said Rowan.

"How can you say that?" Elaine demanded.

"I say it because it has to be said," Rowan replied. "Violet lives in a world without magic. Her world requires rational thought, so I am offering her rational thoughts." She smiled at Violet. "But, my dear," she said, "I think that by now you are beyond rational thought."

"Way beyond it," Violet agreed.

"So what about your gift?" Elaine asked. "We brought you here because of your gift. Are you feeling anything? Do you have anything to tell us?"

Violet closed her eyes and allowed her mind to explore its own sensations, but there was nothing. Try as she might, she could find no thread to follow; her mind was a blank.

"I'm sorry," she said.

"Sorry," said Elaine. "The water's rising. This cave is going to be flooded. They'll all be washed away."

"Perhaps we could take just the King," Violet said. "We could carry him through the gate." She couldn't really imagine how that could be accomplished, but it was the best solution she could offer.

"He can't be moved," said Rowan. She stepped a little closer to the King on his bier and studied his face. "I believe that he's healed," she said. "I imagine he was healed a long time ago. If he's healed, then they are all healed, but without the sword, they can't be awakened."

"And who lay here?" Elaine asked, standing beside the empty bier.

"Sir Lancelot of the Lake," said Rowan.

"Are you sure?" Elaine asked.

"I have identified the others," Rowan said. "At the Battle of Camlan, Lancelot returned to fight beside the King. He should be here." She looked at Violet. "Come and touch this place, see if you can tell us anything."

"The room is dead," Violet said. "Not even a whisper."

"Come closer."

Violet walked around to the other side of the empty bier. As she approached, her foot struck something that rattled and moved. She took a hasty step backward.

"There's something down there," she said, hardly daring to look down.

Elaine crossed to her, carrying a lighted torch. "Probably a dead animal," she said. She held the torch high, and they both looked down at the pile of bones that Violet had disturbed.

"Oh," said Elaine, and the torchlight flickered.

"Control yourself," said Rowan, coming around the bier to stand beside them.

The torch trembled in Elaine's hand, but she was able to keep it alight.

"Human," said Rowan, "female and very old. Treat these bones gently, Violet, or they will turn to dust."

"I don't intend to treat them in any way at all," Violet declared, but even as she withdrew her foot from the huddled bones, she felt her mind awakening and entwining with the faint tendrils of another person's thoughts. A woman, she thought, a queen. Guinevere!

She said it aloud. "This is Guinevere."

Elaine shook her head. "No, she was exiled to the religious women in Glastonbury. She never came here."

"The trace is faint," said Violet," but it's her."

"She followed their religion," Elaine protested. "They gave her the symbols of their Carpenter God. Her soul has gone to their heaven."

"Or to their judgment," Rowan added bitterly, "the judgment of an adulterous traitor."

"Wherever her soul has gone," Violet said, listening to the harsh whisper flooding her senses, "the bones still want to speak to me."

She lowered herself cautiously to a sitting position on the stone floor and allowed her hand to rest on the white mound of the skull, and Guinevere began to tell her story.

Guinevere leaves the convent on a clear, cool spring night when the moon is no more than a fingernail in the sky. She wears men's clothes and rides astride. Her maidservant rides behind her, also dressed as a man. Guinevere carries a dagger at her waist and a sword strapped to the pommel of her saddle. She is confident that she will use them if the need arises, but she has less confidence in her maid. She has become so accustomed to calling the girl Sister Agnes that she has almost forgotten the maid's true name; the name she was given in Albion, Nareena. She smiles and calls to the girl by name just for the joy of using her name and abjuring the titles forced on them by the sisters.

How good it is to be free of the conventions of the convent and the endless regulation of the hours of the day. Matins, lauds, prime, terce, sext, none, vespers, compline, and the Great Silence. She feels the power of the horse beneath her and revels in the thunder of his hooves as they race away from Glastonbury, galloping beneath the spring stars to the place where she will find the man she loves.

They will ride by night and sleep by day, and no one will find them. How shocked the sisters will be when they find the Queen's convent weeds folded neatly on the wretched wooden shelf they call a bed.

They will look for Agnes to demand an explanation, but Agnes will be Nareena again, and nothing will remain of the two captives except the nugget of Albion gold that had been tortured into the cross symbol of the Carpenter God.

Soon, very soon, she will rid herself of Nareena; a regrettable necessity. The girl has spent too much time kneeling before the wooden cross, and she has changed. Her loyalties are divided. Guinevere no longer trusts her. The girl's magic has surely been weakened by her sojourn among the sisters of the other God, and she is mortal; she can die just as easily as anyone else. With the parchment in her possession, Guinevere will make her own way across the miles that separate her from her lover's resting place.

Guinevere slows the pace of her horse and allows Nareena to come alongside her. "Give me the document," she says, thrusting out an imperious hand.

"Majesty?" The girl's eyes are bright, and clear of any apparent deception.

"The document," says the Queen again. "I wish to read the directions, to be sure we are on the correct path."

"I know the path," says Nareena.

"Give it to me." Now the Queen is angry.

"I do not have it," says Nareena, and still her eyes reveal nothing but innocent confusion. "I left it in the convent."

"Fool," says the Queen, but the thought occurs to her that there is nothing foolish about this girl.

"I know the way," Nareena says, "and I will guide us."

"Ride ahead of me," says Guinevere.

She watches as Nareena urges her horse into a slow canter. No, the girl is no fool, but no harm has been done. The sisters of the convent will find a cross made of a metal that does not exist in their world, and a document written in a language that will defy their understanding.

When the sword had done its work, the gates would close and the people of Albion would never again talk with the people of Britain, and the cross and the document would remain as nothing but an ancient mystery. But in Albion the magic would be restored, and Lancelot will be king, with Guinevere as his queen, and the magic of the sisters of Avilion will make the barren queen fruitful.

Guinevere and Nareena arrive at the place where the great River Severn pours into the ocean and then turn north toward the river's source, seeking a place where they can cross into the land beyond. They are two women traveling alone at night under a waxing moon. Their eyes search the shadowed forest for signs of man or beast, and Guinevere's hand is constantly on her dagger.

At last they see that the river is growing shallow, and they find a ford protected by the fierce Eorle people. Guinevere approaches in fear, but the tribesmen who guard the ford seem not to notice the two riders as they splash their way across the ford and enter the Kingdom of Gwynedd.

Nareena turns her horse toward the distant mountains, but Guinevere refuses to move.

"Majesty," says Nareena, "we must move on."

Guinevere looks back at the ford, and the Eorle watchmen gathered around their fire pit.

"Have you enchanted those men at the ford?" Guinevere asks.

Nareena hangs her head in shame. "It is forbidden by the Christian law," she says.

Guinevere laughs to hide her concern. "We are no longer under Christian law," she says. "How long have you been practicing enchantments?"

"Since we left Glastonbury," says Nareena. "We are invisible to those who wish us harm."

"And yet you let me ride in fear," says Guinevere.

"I was not sure that you would allow me—"

"And I was not sure that the magic in you had survived the magic of the Christians," says Guinevere.

"I wished to be rid of it," Nareena says. "I wished to be Sister Agnes."

"You are a child of Avilion," says Guinevere. "How can you wish to be anything else?"

"The Christian magic is different," says Nareena, "and can be possessed by all."

"Well," says Guinevere, "if you wanted to keep the Christian magic, you could have refused to help me. You could have told my plans to our prison keepers."

"I was torn," says Nareena, "between my desire to serve the new God, and my desire to help you to rescue the Knight of the Lake."

"Sir Lancelot."

"Yes."

"He is mine," says Guinevere.

"Yes, Majesty," says Nareena, but Guinevere does not like the girl's secret smile.

"How much magic remains with you?" Guinevere asks.

"Very little," says Nareena.

Very well, says Guinevere to herself, she shall serve me until her magic is gone, and then we shall be rid of her.

"Ride on," she says to Nareena, "and keep the protection around us."

They ride on into the mountains, moving farther and farther away from human habitation, until they come to a wide valley and a stream fed by a waterfall. Nareena's magic is failing, for it seems that the few people they pass are becoming aware of their presence. Guinevere keeps her hand on her dagger and forces the tired horses forward.

They ride now without food. Nareena's magic had previously enchanted rabbits into the traps she set, and her hands had created fire for roasting, but now the rabbits scatter as they pass, and Nareena can conjure little more than tiny sparks.

"I will go alone into the cave," Guinevere says.

"But, Majesty" says Nareena, "the path is complex."

"My love will guide me," says Guinevere. "Stay here and mind the horses."

Guinevere begins to climb the path beside the waterfall. She looks down at the figure of the girl waiting beside the grazing horses. Two horses for three people. She shrugs her shoulders. Lancelot will ride. She enters the darkness of the cave system. Without Nareena beside her to kindle fire, she must carry her own flame, and she has carried a smoldering reed with which to light her torch. The torch flares into light, and Guinevere follows its light along the dark passageways and into the chamber where the knights lie sleeping. Here is Arthur, clasping the sword Excalibur. She holds the torch high and surveys her husband's face. He seems to be sleeping peacefully, and she can see no sign of the grievous wound he had supposedly sustained. She feels a sense of urgency. Is he already healed? Will he open his eyes and see what she is doing?

Slowly, gently, she removes the great sword from his grasp. She moves along the row of sleeping knights until she finds the face she seeks, Lancelot of the Lake.

His hands are crossed on his chest. She moves them aside and lays the sword across his breastplate. She fastens his hands back around the carved hilt. She waits. The flame in the torch burns low. At last he moves. He opens his eyes, bright blue in a pale, waxen face.

"Our time has come," she says.

He rises from his bed. Excalibur seems almost too heavy for him to hold. He is dragged down by its weight as he follows her from the cave. He'll grow stronger, she thinks. The longer he holds it, the stronger he will be.

They emerge into the daylight and look down into the valley. Lancelot closes his eyes against the glare of the sun and leans against the rock face, breathing heavily.

"We have horses," says Guinevere, "and the gate is very near. Albion will be ours."

"Arthur?" Lancelot asks. "Where is Arthur?"

"Killed at the Battle of Camlan."

"No. The maidens came for him."

"He could not be saved," she says. "Albion is yours now."

"Mordred?"

"We will defeat him," she says, "together."

Lancelot staggers under the weight of his armor, but he lifts Excalibur high. "For Arthur," he says.

"Yes," says Guinevere, "but Arthur is gone."

She leads him down the rocky path. His eyes are becoming accustomed to the daylight, and he sees the figure below in the valley.

"Nareena?" he asks.

Guinevere's heart twists in fear and jealousy. How can he recognize the girl at such a distance? How well does he know her?

"She's no one," says Guinevere, "just a local girl holding the horses for us."

She takes another step down the path and sees a band of horsemen riding along the floor of the valley. For a moment, she fears that Mordred's men have come through the gate, but then she sees that these men are dressed in hides and riding small, shaggy ponies. They are nothing but local tribesmen.

Lancelot is beginning to think like a fighting man. "They're after the horses," he says.

Guinevere can see that Nareena is desperately summoning the last of her magic. Her small figure fades in and out of view. A mist curls around her ankles and then dissipates. Surely she has used up the last of the enchantment of Avilion.

"Nareena," Lancelot says again.

"Leave her," says Guinevere. "We don't need her." But Lancelot is already stumbling down the path, raising Excalibur above his head.

"Leave her," Guinevere demands again.

Violet ran her hands gently across the skeletal remains, finding the place where the ribs were crushed.

"Traitorous whore," said Rowan suddenly.

Violet nodded. "She certainly seemed to be," she agreed.

"So what became of them?" Elaine asked.

Violet looked at the crushed ribs. "I don't know," she said. "Lancelot had no strength. He could barely lift the sword. I imagine that he died. Guinevere saw him taken away."

"And Nareena?" asked Rowan

"I don't know," said Violet. "She was wrapped in mist."

"She did not return to Avilion," said Rowan. "We have no more knowledge of her."

Violet touched the small bundle of bones. "There was nothing honorable about this queen," she said.

"It is as we suspected," said Elaine. "She betrayed her husband, her king, and her country."

"And Lancelot betrayed her by loving Nareena," said Violet. "What a sorry story."

"Such a waste," said Rowan. "Did she really think to give Excalibur to Lancelot and make him high king?"

"Yes," said Violet.

"All of this for a foolish dream," said Rowan. "Lancelot could never be king. Only Arthur can return Excalibur to Albion. It was Guinevere who condemned us all to this endless war that cannot be won or lost. If Arthur cannot freely give the sword to his heir, then it must be taken from him in battle; there is no other way. And now Excalibur is lost. Arthur is healed, his knights are healed, but Excalibur is not here."

"Is there anything here that tells you of the sword?" Elaine asked.

"It was taken from Lancelot; that's all I know," said Violet.

"But how did the Queen make her way here?" Rowan asked. "How did she die?"

"The memory is faint," Violet said. "When I search for her thoughts, I can see her scrambling down the cliff path and screaming Lancelot's name. She doesn't know if he is alive or dead, but she sees him tied across the saddle of a horse, and she sees that one of the attackers has taken Excalibur. They don't look back. They don't even see her."

"Then who wounded her?" Rowan asked.

Violet shrugged her shoulders. "I don't know," she said.

"Perhaps she fell and hit her head," Rowan said. "That would explain why the memory you are retrieving is so confused."

Violet touched the broken ribs and shook her head. "It's not clear. I know she was in terrible pain."

"Her pain is nothing compared to the pain she has inflicted on others," said Rowan sharply.

"I have a sense of her crawling through darkness on her hands and knees," Violet said. "She has no light but she knows the way. She's returning to the cave. She wants to die among the sleeping knights. Her mind is filled with thoughts of the glory days."

Guinevere is a queen again in the fullness of her youthful beauty. The King adores her, the people cheer as she passes by, and the most handsome knight in all of Albion is her champion. She is returning to lie by his side.

She comes quietly to his bedside. He has made the bed ready for her, piled high with a feather mattress and dressed in finest damask. She will slip in beside him and they will lie together, and no one will ever know.

Something is wrong. She is on her hands and knees beside the bed, straining to stand. Her hands clasp at the covers and come away empty. There is no bed, only an empty wooden bier. There is no fine fur rug beneath her feet, only a cold stone floor. There is no lordly bedchamber, only a dark cave. There is no handsome lover, only the still form of Arthur, the king she has betrayed. □

CHAPTER SEVENTEEN

Todd Chambray

"So are we going to do a bit of B and E?" Freddie asked as they turned into the driveway and saw the impressive bulk of Griffinwood Manor ahead of them.

Mandretti turned around from his seat beside Freddie and looked back at Todd as if he thought Todd would provide a translation of the question. Todd, already fractious from a night without sleep and a caffeine-loaded morning, not to mention the fact that they still had not found Violet, could only shrug his shoulders and wish himself anywhere except where he was.

"He's asking if you're planning on breaking into Griffinwood Manor," Molly said. "B and E, breaking and entering."

"You any good at that?" Mandretti asked Freddie.

"Been known to do a bit in my time," Freddie replied with equanimity.

"I don't think it will be necessary," Molly said as they rounded the final curve in the driveway, and the massive oak doors came into view. "It seems that someone left the door open."

The doors were indeed wide open. Lights were on inside the house, and a black Mercedes was parked in the gravel turnaround.

"Oh dear," said Todd. "Is anyone thinking what I'm thinking?"

"Depends on what you're thinking," said Molly.

"'Come into my parlor,' said the spider to the fly," Todd replied.

"Yes," said Molly, "it certainly does look that way."

Freddie brought the limo to a halt beside the Mercedes. "You going in?" he asked.

"I'm gonna knock," said Mandretti, "and see what happens."

He climbed out of the car and faced the open doors. Todd saw him squaring his broad shoulders and adjusting the set of his jacket; then he slipped his right hand into his pocket.

Well, it's not a gun, Todd thought, because Freddie already told him no guns, so I guess it's a knife.

Mandretti pounded on the open door, but no one appeared. He turned and looked back at the limo and gestured to Freddie. Freddie climbed out from the driver's seat and went through the same routine as Mandretti, squaring his shoulders, adjusting his jacket, and slipping his hand into his pocket. The two men disappeared through the front door.

"Go and get in the driver's seat," said Molly.

"Me?" said Todd.

"In case we need to get out of here in a hurry," she said.

"Not me," said Todd. "You all drive on the wrong side of the road."

With a deep sigh, Molly climbed out of the back of the car. She was opening the driver's door when Mandretti and Freddie reappeared.

"Ain't no one here," Mandretti called. "Come on in."

Todd approached the front doors with caution, hiding as much as possible behind Molly's bulky body. "They haven't searched the whole house," he complained under his breath. "They weren't in there long enough."

They passed through the front doors into the gloom of a cavernous foyer with a black-and-white tiled floor. Molly looked around and spotted two suits of armor. "Fake," she said dismissively.

Mandretti stood at the bottom of the stairs. "Freddie's searching downstairs; we'll take the upstairs. There's no sign of anyone."
He looked at Todd. "You been calling Ryan like I told you to?"

"I have," said Todd, "but he doesn't answer." He checked his phone. "No signal in here."

"So," said Mandretti, "Ryan could be here, but just not hearing his phone, and Violet don't have no phone. They could both be here."

"All night?" Todd queried.

Mandretti looked at him with raised eyebrows. "That supposed to mean something?" he asked.

"No, of course not," Todd said.

Mandretti started up the stairs, with Molly close behind him, and Todd bringing up the rear. They stopped and huddled together at the first landing, looking right and left along wood-floored corridors. All the doors were closed.

Downstairs a door slammed, and Todd gasped in surprise, moving closer to Mandretti. Mandretti pushed him away. "Go open some doors," he said. "You go right, the prof can go left, and I'll go on up to the next floor. Yell out if you find something."

As Todd approached the first door, he tried to hide himself behind a stage character. Who could he be? He had never actually played a door-busting hero, or really any kind of hero, and a hero was needed to open all the doors and look inside. They could be dead, both of them. Marcus Ryan and Violet could be behind any of the doors, lying dead, their sightless eyes still open and staring. On the other hand, they could both be alive and waiting desperately for rescue. They could be waiting for Todd to be a real-life hero.

He opened the first door, a bedroom, shabby and dusty, but empty. He continued along the corridor, opening doors with increasing confidence and finding only shabby bedrooms and even shabbier bathrooms with no sign of either Ryan or Violet.

As he reached the end of the corridor, he heard Mandretti calling from the landing. "Nothing here. *Una perdita di tempo.* Don't waste no more time looking. They ain't here." He raised his voice several more decibels. "Hey, Freddie, where you at?"

Freddie's voice drifted up from somewhere downstairs. "Come and have a butchers at this."

"What?" said Mandretti.

"He wants you to look at something," Molly said, appearing from the other corridor. "Butcher's hook, look."

Following the sound of Freddie's voice, they hurried down the broad staircase, past the suits of armor, and into a huge reception hall with beamed ceilings and stained-glass windows. A massive brick fireplace occupied one end of the hall, and above the fireplace hung a collection of weapons.

"Those must be the weapons that the museum returned," Molly said. "Find a light switch. Someone turn on the lights."

Freddie found a switch, and lights came on along the walls, with a spotlight focused on the fireplace and its collection of fearsome weapons. Todd could not name all the weapons he saw, but he recognized swords and sabers, spiked balls on the end of chains, vicious-looking axes, antique pikes, massive hammers, and short stabbing knives. The weapons were dusty, and some looked rusted, as though no one had cared for them in a long time.

Molly seemed to take no time at all in making up her mind. "Not here," she said.

"How do you know?" Mandretti demanded. "What about the swords?"

"No. Nothing there fits the description."

"You sure?"

Molly nodded. "Quite sure. It would be a brilliant hiding place. Just cover the sword in dust and stick it on the wall with all the others, but it's not there. If it was there, the guy who's pretending to be Crispin Peacock would have found it, not to mention the fact that Marcus would recognize it immediately."

"Perhaps he did," said Mandretti, glowering at Molly from beneath his lowered eyebrows. "Perhaps that's why we haven't heard from him."

"There's no empty space," Molly said. "Look at the way they've been displayed. They form a pattern and there's nothing missing."

Freddie scrutinized the wall. "No hooks," he said.

"What does that mean?" Mandretti asked. "I don't understand a word this guy says."

"It means exactly what it sounds like," said Molly. "There are no empty display hooks. The sword was never on this wall."

"Then where the hell is it?" Mandretti shouted. "And why are you all standing around?"

Because we don't know what else to do, Todd thought, but he didn't voice his opinion out loud. Mandretti's frustration was obviously building, and Todd kept thinking of the way Mandretti had slipped his hand into his coat pocket. He had something in there, something sharp and dangerous.

"Well," said Freddie, "I'm going to take a gander at that car outside."

Todd tried to sort out Freddie's strange goose reference, but it soon became obvious what Freddie had in mind because he once again went through the ritual of squaring his shoulders and straightening his jacket, and apparently fixing some little problem inside his trousers. Todd had never been in a brawl and had no idea what would need to be adjusted in the crotch area in a situation that involved a goose and a car.

"Good idea," said Molly. "Let's all go and look. Strength in numbers, you know."

Oh, Todd thought, we're going to check on the black Mercedes outside. Good idea.

They made their way back through the gloomy foyer and out through the front doors. Freddie was first to reach the Mercedes and peer in through the windows.

"Is it locked?" Mandretti asked.

Freddie turned his back on them, and a few moments later, he turned around and smiled. "Not anymore," he said, as he slid behind the wheel.

"Pop the trunk," said Mandretti.

"Open the boot," Molly translated.

The trunk opened with a faint hiss. Todd stood back. Once again, he feared what they might find. Given everything else that had happened, finding a body in the trunk seemed a distinct possibility.

Mandretti shook his head. "Clean," he shouted. "Anything on the seat?"

Before Freddie could answer, they were interrupted by the sound of a car coming up the long driveway. Todd caught a flash of blue before the approaching car disappeared from view, hidden by a curve in the driveway.

By the time it reappeared, Mandretti and Freddie were both out of the Mercedes. They were standing quite still but, nonetheless, giving off an air of aggression.

The car was small, a tiny blue hatchback dwarfed by the size of Freddie's limo. As it screeched to a halt, the passenger door was flung open, and Violet practically fell out onto the ground.

"Violet," Mandretti shouted, "where the hell have you been?"

Todd managed to bypass Mandretti in time to help Violet to her feet. She leaned heavily against him and stared at the faces around her.

"Did he find it?" she demanded. "Where's Ryan? Did he find it?"

"Do you have my sword?" Mandretti asked.

"Your sword?" said Violet. "Your sword? No, Michael, it's not your sword."

"What the hell?" said Mandretti.

Violet ignored him. She looked at Todd. "What are you doing here?" she asked, and then she saw Molly. "Molly? Oh God, wait till I tell you. You were so right, Molly, so right."

"About what?" Molly asked.

"About everything," said Violet.

Todd was taking in his sister's windblown appearance; dragged backward through a hedge came to his mind. "Where have you been?" he asked.

"Yeah," said Mandretti, "where the hell you been? What do you mean, it's not my sword?"

Before Violet could answer, Todd saw another woman climbing out of the car. She was a pretty blond with long, tangled hair and a figure-hugging blue dress. "Where's Doctor Ryan?" the blond demanded.

"We don't know," said Todd. "We don't know where anyone is. Where have you been, Violet?"

"I was … somewhere else," Violet said vaguely. "Doesn't Ryan have a phone?"

"He's not answering it," Todd said.

"Did you find the museum?" Violet asked.

"Yeah," said Mandretti, "we found the museum, but the sword ain't there, and what do you mean by saying it ain't my sword? What the hell do you think I'm paying you for?"

Violet ran a hand through her already tangled hair. "We don't have any time left," she said, "The water's rising."

"What water?" Todd asked.

"The water in the cave," said the blond girl. She turned to Violet. "I don't know what else to do," she said. "Without the sword, we have …"

"I know," said Violet. "But what about the children?"

"What children?" asked the blond girl.

Todd saw the confusion and frustration on his sister's face.

"Barry Marshall's children. If we get the sword, we have to give it to … Oh hell, I don't even know who to give it to. It's him or the children. The King or the children."

"There are swords inside," said Todd in an attempt to be helpful, "but Professor Walker says that they're not what we're looking for."

"They're not," Molly insisted. "I know what I'm doing."

"We have to look," said the blond, rushing ahead of them through the front door.

"Who is that?" Mandretti asked. "Where did she come from?"

"That's Elaine," Violet said, "and I've been with her and … Well, I can't really say anything else, not yet. Where are the swords you found?"

"On the wall above the fireplace," said Molly, "but I can tell you that—"

Violet was already gone, following Elaine through the front door. Todd had never seen her move so fast. As he turned to follow her, he heard a loud crash from just inside the door, followed by a penetrating female scream. Mandretti was halfway to the door when Violet reappeared holding a sword, with Elaine following close behind her. Both women were flushed and exultant.

"This is it," Violet shouted. "This is Excalibur!"

"No, I looked," said Molly. "It wasn't on the wall."

"The armor," said Elaine.

"Fake," said Molly. "Cheap imitation."

"The armor's fake," said Violet, "but not the sword. He hid it in plain sight."

"Where?" demanded Molly.

"In the scabbard."

"But we all walked past it," Molly complained. "How did you find it?"

"It's my gift," said Violet.

Todd observed that his sister did not look as smug as she usually did when she found a lost object or boasted of her gift. She looked overwhelmed.

"Well done," Todd said softly. "But is it really—?"

"Excalibur," said Violet. "Yes, oh yes, this is the real thing. I can hear its voice." She closed her eyes for a moment. "What shall I do?" she said. "How do I save them all?"

"Well," said Mandretti triumphantly, placing an arm around Violet's shoulders and ignoring her distress, "we don't have to wait for Ryan. We can go home without him. I ain't giving him no commission on this; you did all the finding while he disappeared."

Violet pulled away from him. "What are you talking about?" she said. "You can't take this to Vegas. The sword has to stay here."

"We had a deal," Mandretti said. "I've shelled out a lot of money to get you over here to find this, and it seems it don't belong to this Peacock fellow, because he's not really who he says he is, so that makes it mine."

"What do you mean? Who is not who he says he is?" Violet asked.

"Crispin Peacock," Molly replied, "is not really Crispin Peacock. We don't know who he is, but we do know that the real Crispin Peacock has been dead for several days, which doesn't look good for Doctor Ryan if he's been taken somewhere by whoever this person is."

"Ryan will have to look after himself," said Violet. "I have to decide what to do with the sword."

Mandretti's eyes had taken on a determined gleam. "Just give it to me, and I'll take care of everything."

Todd could see that the man's entire attention was centered on the sword. It had a plain-looking blade with a dull gold hilt ornamented with opaque red stones. It had nothing to really distinguish it from any other sword, but Mandretti wanted it. Mandretti had paid to have it found. He was a collector, and he was determined to add it to his collection.

"It's illegal," said Molly. "That's part of our heritage."

Violet looked at Molly. "There's more to it," she said. "You know what you told me, about the cave and the sleeping king—"

"I was being ridiculous," Molly interrupted. "I know that's not really Arthur's sword, but nonetheless—"

"It is Arthur's sword," the girl Elaine said.

"There's a cave," said Violet, "and they're sleeping."

Todd frowned. "Who's sleeping?" he asked.

"Arthur and his knights. Molly, you have to believe me."

"I'd very much like to," said Molly, "but really …"

Violet took another step away from Mandretti. "Michael," she said, "if you come with me now, I will show you something that is beyond anything you can imagine."

"This thing you're going to show me," said Mandretti, "can I take it home with me?"

"No," said Violet, sounding angry. "You can't take anything home with you."

Todd was pretty certain that this was not the answer that Mandretti wanted to hear.

"Oh, I'm taking something," said Mandretti. "It's all arranged with Freddie. We'll get it out of England and across the Channel." He reached out and grabbed the sword from Violet. He held the sword in both hands, his eyes alight with excitement. "Excalibur," he said.

He started to back up toward the limousine. From the corner of his eye, Todd saw Freddie adjusting his jacket and moving to stand beside the limo. Todd had seen the gesture before as Freddie prepared to enter the manor house. He assumed that Freddie was getting ready to pull a weapon, most likely a knife.

"You're not taking it," said Violet flatly.

Todd wanted to tell her to back off. No sword in the world was worth what Freddie could do to Violet with a couple of knife slashes; what he could do to all of them.

"Come on, doll," said Mandretti, "be reasonable. We had a deal."

"Deal's off." Violet held out her small, plump hand, which Todd noticed was considerably dirtier than usual. "Give me the sword, Michael."

Freddie shouldered his way forward and stood shoulder to shoulder with Mandretti. They made a formidable barrier.

"Get in the car," said Freddie.

□

CHAPTER EIGHTEEN

Jenny Marshall, Aged Six

Jenny was trying not to cry. She wanted to be a big girl. They were in trouble, terrible trouble, and her brother, Michael, had told her that she could not be a baby, not now.

"You have to be brave," he said.

When the horrible man was driving them through the night, she had seen the way that her brother's bottom lip had quivered and his eyes had turned red. Michael never cried. He was too big to cry, but Jenny was sure that he wanted to cry. He probably wanted to cry and scream just the way she had when the terrible one-eyed man had snatched them from their beds.

Michael had fought as hard as he could, and Jenny had cried out for her father, but no one had come to help them, and the horrible man had tied their hands behind their backs and thrown them into the back of his big black car. They drove for a long, long time, and Jenny really needed to tinkle. She told him. She told the horrid man what she needed to do, and he just turned in the seat and told her to pee in her pants.

She had peed her pants, just like a baby, and her Peter Rabbit pajama bottoms were wet and uncomfortable. The horrible man had complained when he dragged her out of the car and slung her across his shoulder. Daylight was dawning when the horrible man parked the car outside an enormous old house. Jenny thought it might be a haunted house. Perhaps the horrible man was going to turn them into ghosts, and they would be stuck in the house forever, and her father and mother would never know where to find her.

She was relieved when the one-eyed man turned away from the big old house. He had Jenny over one shoulder, and he dragged Michael with his free hand.

"Shut up, both of you," he said. "Be quiet and you won't get hurt."

Jenny tried to be quiet, swallowing her sobs and making eye contact with Michael, who stumbled through the long grass in his bare feet.

"You're wet," the man complained.

"You wouldn't let her stop and tinkle," said Michael.

"Shut up," said the man. "Put this in your hand. Don't drop it. If you drop it, I'll kill you."

Michael's eyes grew wide with fear as the man pressed something into his hand. Then Jenny felt the man pressing something into her hand. It was a small, sharp thing.

"Hold it," the man snarled.

Branches whipped against Jenny's face as he forced a path through the weeds and bushes. Suddenly a mist rose up around their feet. Jenny screamed and screamed and screamed, but she felt as though she was screaming into a blanket, as the fog muffled her voice and closed off her view.

That was hours and hours ago. So far as she could tell, a whole day had gone by since the man had locked them in the smelly little room where the floor was littered with scratchy straw. At first a little sparkle of light had filtered through the cracks in the wall, but now it was completely dark. She knew that there were people on the other side of the wall because she could hear them talking. No, not really talking, more like shouting. And they were laughing, and dogs were barking. They sounded like really big dogs. Jenny was afraid of big dogs. Her mother had promised that when she came back from Nana O'Keefe's funeral, she would allow Jenny to have a dog, a little one.

Jenny tried to think about the promised little dog. She didn't want to think about her nasty wet pajamas, or the fact that she was really, really thirsty, or the fact that Michael was being unusually comforting. They were sitting together, and he had his arm around her shoulders. He was her big brother but he wasn't big enough. What they needed was an adult; not the horrible man with the eye patch, but a good adult. She wasn't supposed to talk to strangers, but if a stranger came into the room now, and if it was someone who had both eyes and a nice face, she would most definitely talk. She had a feeling that the rules that applied when you were walking home from school, and someone came and offered you sweets, didn't apply when you'd been snatched from your bed in the middle of the night, tied up with string, forced to pee in your pants, dragged through bushes, choked by mist, and then thrown into a dark, smelly room. No, the rules were not the same.

She leaned her head against Michael's shoulder and felt him stiffen.

"What?" she said. "I'm not being a baby. I'm just afraid. I'm really afraid, Michael."

"I know," he said, but he didn't seem to be concentrating on her. Normally, he would complain that her hair was tickling his nose, and surely he wouldn't like her wet pajamas, but he didn't seem to notice.

"I can smell something," he said.

"What?" said Jenny.

"Smoke," said Michael.

"I think they were cooking something," Jenny said. "I could smell something like barbecue a little while ago. I'm really hungry."

"It's not barbecue," Michael said. "It smells like burning grass."

"They're making a lot of noise outside," Jenny said.

"Yeah," said Michael. "It sounds like fighting."

"Really?" said Jenny.

"Yeah," Michael repeated. "Listen to that; it sounds like horses and sword fighting."

"Why would they have horses?" Jenny asked. "The horrible man had a car. I didn't see any horses." She drew in a gulp of air and felt the tickle of smoke at the back of her throat. "It's smoke," she whispered.

Michael pulled her to her feet. He held her hand and looked desperately around the dark little room, but the room was not as dark as it had been. A dull red glow filtered through the chinks in the wall and flared orange in one of the corners.

Jenny pointed a shaking finger. "Michael, the roof's on fire."

As she spoke, a clump of burning thatch fell from the roof and landed at her feet. The straw on the floor began to smolder, and the room filled with smoke.

Marcus Ryan

Fire arrows, Ryan thought as he looked up at the smoldering thatch above his head. Remembering the small boy who had buried himself among the filthy rushes on the floor, he groped his way through the darkness and smoke to the corner where he had last seen the boy.

"Come on out," he said.

As he had expected, nothing happened. Mordred said that the people spoke an ancient form of English, and maybe it was a form he would have understood if it had been written down, but he had never heard it as a spoken language.

Despite the smoke and the imminent danger of the roof collapsing in a shower of sparks, the scholar in him thrilled to the moment. He was hearing and seeing something that no scholar in his world had ever heard or seen before. If only he had come at a different time and not in the middle of a raid, he might have sat for hours in the longhouse, just listening and observing; a witness to living history.

He kicked around in the reeds until he heard a groan, and he plunged his hands into the stinking pile and dragged out the small, wriggling boy.

"Fire," he said pointing up at the roof.

The boy wriggled in his grasp, but Ryan held onto the rough wool of the boy's tunic and dragged him toward the door.

"We're going outside," he said. "We'll be burned alive in here."

He eyed the crossbeam that was holding the doors closed. Could he lift it with one hand and still hold onto the boy? Did he really have to? What difference would it make if the boy was killed by fire inside the longhouse, or by an arrow or a sword outside?

The boy pulled away from the door. He was trying desperately to go in another direction. Where? Was there another door? Ryan tried to see through the rising smoke. The boy spun free and darted to the back of the hall where a crude tapestry hung behind the high table. He lifted a corner of the tapestry, holding it aloft and calling words that had no meaning.

Barn. The boy appeared to be shouting the word barn. Ryan could make no sense of the boy's frantic shouts. Barn? No. Bairn? Was the boy saying something about a bairn, the old Gaelic word for "child"? Perhaps some ancient Gaelic had found its way into the language of Albion.

The boy shouted again, his desperate voice rising above the sound of warfare outside, and the crackling of the flames in the rafters. He was screaming another word, something that sounded like "plentyn." The word had no meaning for Ryan, but obviously the boy was frantic to rescue something or someone hidden behind the tapestry, and he was not going to move until Ryan came to help him.

Ryan groped his way through the smoke to the place where the boy had disappeared behind the tapestry. He found that the heavy drape had been hung in front of a narrow door. The door was held shut by a heavy bar. The boy was struggling unsuccessfully to raise the bar while someone on the other side pounded and screamed in a high childish voice. The fact that the voice was screaming in English barely registered with Ryan. He didn't care about the language, he cared that the voice was the voice of a child. He pulled the boy out of the way. He had no need to hold the boy's ragged tunic; the kid was not going anywhere, refusing to even take his hands off the bar.

The bar moved easily in Ryan's hands. He lifted it, threw it aside, and pulled the door open. Two children tumbled out of the door and fell at his feet, choking and sobbing. Behind them the small chamber erupted into flames.

He grabbed the smallest child, a girl in brightly colored pajamas. She flung her arms around his neck and buried her head against his shoulder.

The boy stumbled to his feet and looked up at Ryan. The recognition was immediate. These were Barry Marshall's children. These were the hostages whose price was the sword Excalibur, but they had been left behind. A few more seconds, and they would have lost their lives.

The ragged local boy was still shouting and pointing to the main exit. Somehow he had known that the children were being held prisoner, and he, unlike everyone else in the longhouse, had cared about their plight. Now it was time to go. He danced impatiently from one foot to another.

The little girl pulled back for a moment, raising her head to look at Ryan's face.

"Michael," she gasped. "It's him. It's the Treasure Hunter."

In that moment, as the child identified him and the boy stared at him in wonder, Ryan became someone else. He took on the character his network had invented for him; strong, heroic, and incredibly charismatic. The awe in the boy's face imbued him with a strength that he thought he had lost and drove him to stride confidently forward through the smoke and smoldering rushes, with the little girl clasped in his arms and the two boys clinging to his side.

He set the girl on the floor as he lifted the bar holding shut the main doors. All three children tried to run outside, but Ryan managed to gather them together.

"Slowly," he said. "Take it easy. Maybe they won't see us."

Michael and Jenny understood him, and the other boy seemed willing to do anything they did. He pushed the children down onto their knees and indicated that they should crawl out on all fours.

"They won't be looking for us on the ground," he whispered. "Maybe we can get away into the woods."

He cracked the doors open and took in the hellish scene outside. The village was ablaze, and the night rang with the sound of steel on steel as armored knights on snorting steeds battled up and down through the ruins of the village.

The villagers were fleeing from the fight. He could see them running for the woods, but no one was following them. Apparently, the object of the raid was not to capture or kill the peasants. The fighting was only for the armored knights hacking and slashing at each other. The peasants were simply fading away into the darkness of the forest. Their village and their crops were destroyed, but the villagers themselves seemed to be in no danger from the knights, although Ryan wondered what danger might face them in the forest.

He could see Bors, bareheaded in the midst of the battle. He was off his horse and fighting fiercely in hand-to-hand combat. The flaring flames lit his face and showed not a trace of fear, but only savage delight. Ryan looked for Mordred but could see no sign of him. The other knights were all anonymous to him. They wore armor and colored surcoats, but Ryan knew nothing of their heraldry and had no way to distinguish them from each other, or even how to tell which men fought for Mordred and which for the raiders. Time to leave, Ryan thought.

He saw an occasional flare of light on the hillside, marking the escape route of the peasants. They were not straggling among the trees but moving together, so presumably a path existed, leading them to some place of refuge. He decided to follow them. They were climbing to the top of a ridge, and he suspected that they were escaping along a route that might take him to the gate where he had first entered the nightmare world of Albion.

His first task was to get the children away without being spotted. The raiders might not be interested in everyday peasants, but they would surely take notice of a visitor from beyond the gate. Did they even know the gate existed? he asked himself.

He looked at the progress of the battle. Bors was still fully occupied flailing at all comers with a two-handed grasp on his broadsword. He was not the only knight to abandon his horse. Most of the fighting had deteriorated into hand-to-hand combat with maces, swords, and axes. Riderless horses stamped and whinnied at the perimeter of the battlefield. At another time, Ryan would have been more than happy to stay and observe the way the weapons were used and to analyze the fierce taunts that the combatants hurled at each other, but he knew he had to leave while he could. For the moment at least, fate was on his side, and he stood a good chance of getting himself and the children away without being noticed.

Any lingering instinct he may have had for further delay was wiped out when the roof of the longhouse collapsed, showering them with sparks. Jenny cried and looked at him in mute terror as the embers stung her hands and face. The local boy, his duty done, slipped away into the darkness, leaving Ryan to fend for himself.

He hastily brushed the burning cinders from Jenny's clothes and then gathered her up in his arms again. With Michael clinging to his side, he hurried toward the hillside, skirting the blazing huts and dodging the riderless horses.

He breathed a sigh of relief when he reached the shelter of the trees and began to climb. Although he could see the flare of torches above him, he could find no trace of the path that the villagers had followed. Jenny tightened her grip on his neck into a stranglehold as he stumbled through thick undergrowth, tripping on rock and roots. Eventually, he had to put her down on the ground.

"We have to crawl," he said. "I can't see where I'm going, and I don't want to fall and drop you." He unwound her arms from their death grip around his neck and pointed upward. "Stay with me."

"Are you really him?" she asked in wide-eyed awe.

Poor kid, he thought, she's terrified. She's probably hoping this is a nightmare.

"It's really him," said Michael's voice from the darkness. "It's him, Jenny. He's going to look after us. Just do what he says."

"Good boy," said Ryan.

He turned one last time to look down into the valley. The fires were dying and sending out more smoke than flame. The combatants were no more than dark shadows moving through the choking fog.

He moved on up the hillside, encouraging the children with his voice, and reaching out to touch them to make sure they were with him. At long last his hands told him that he was on a smooth path. He rose hesitantly to his feet, remaining stooped over to make himself a smaller target. He groped for Jenny's hand and clasped it in his own. Then he found Michael's hand, and the three of them broke into a stumbling run. He knew they needed to be away before the fighting below had come to an end, and already the sounds of battle were diminishing. The battle cries faded into silence, replaced with groans and screams and the sound of horses' hooves beating a retreat.

So who had won, he asked himself. Were Bors and Mordred lying injured among the smoldering ruins of the village, or were they on horseback pursuing the raiders? We can't win and we can't lose, but we still fight. That's what Mordred had said to him. What did that mean? The fight he had just witnessed was no illusion. The fire and smoke were real. The cinders from the fire had burned when they touched his hands. The roof of the longhouse had collapsed, and surely he and the children would have been dead if he had stayed inside.

Perhaps Bors and Mordred would believe that they had indeed remained inside, in which case, no one would be looking for them. The thought comforted him as he continued to climb, gaining ground on the retreating villagers. If Mordred thought him dead, then maybe no one would come looking for him.

He reached the top of the ridge. Finding the gate was going to be tricky. He slipped his hand into his pocket and grasped his talisman, the red stone that acted as a key to open the door to his own world. In the daylight, he had been able to see the mist and the shifting of reality that marked the entrance, but what would he find in the dark? Would he have to wait for daylight? More importantly, how would he get the children through? He would have to break up the Glastonbury cross and give the children a piece each.

A shower of sparks shot up from the village as another roof collapsed. For a moment, the path was illuminated, and he could make out the shapes of the trees and the bushes, and one patch of total darkness. Was that it? he asked himself. Was that the gate? Could it be that simple? He needed to find a heavy rock. Something he could use to smash the talisman into smaller pieces. He stepped off the path.

Someone or something grasped and clawed at him from the shelter of the bushes. Michael's hand was snatched away and then Jenny's, and then he felt himself grasped by strong hands and pulled backward, away from the gate. He fought the grasping hands and kept his eyes fixed on the patch of darkness, determined not to lose sight of their escape route.

From the heart of the darkness came a low, rumbling growl, and the gate began to change shape. It was moving toward him. He was wrong. Whatever this was, it was not the gate into his own world.

He scrabbled backward, pulled by the unseen hands. A rough, work-worn hand closed over his own hand, and a voice hissed in his ear. "Shhh."

"What the—?" Ryan exclaimed, but his question was cut off by a hand over his mouth. The hand tasted of earth and dirt.

Again the whisper in his ear. "Shhh."

The darkness ahead of him was forming a shape, something tall that moved toward him on two legs, but not a man, most definitely not a man. He glanced behind him and saw that Jenny and Michael were being carried away through the bushes. The unseen hands continued to pull at him, and he gave way to their urging, turning and running blindly, following the children.

Behind him something crashed through the woods, snapping off branches as it moved, and the threatening growl grew closer. He felt hot breath on his neck. Suddenly lights appeared ahead of him, the dancing flames of dozens of torches. By the flickering light, he could see that the children were being carried in the arms of ragged peasants. As they retreated, other peasants ran beside them, brandishing torches.

The menacing darkness halted, revealing its shape by the light of the torches. It was a shape beyond Ryan's understanding, a creature that stood on two legs and spread its wings as though it were an enormous bird. The head that tossed and growled and challenged the flames was the head of a great beast with red eyes reflecting the firelight.

The creature moved forward again. Ahead of him Ryan saw a rectangle of brightness. Light streamed from the door of a building. The peasants danced backward, jabbing their torches at the approaching menace. He saw Jenny and Michael carried inside, and then rough hands grabbed him and hurried him forward. As he stumbled inside the building, the door slammed shut.

A great weight crashed into the door from outside, and the growling ceased, replaced by outraged shrieks. Instinctively he staggered backward, but the door held. The creature battered futilely against the barricade, slamming its weight repeatedly into the door. Inside the building, the peasants were silent, holding their torches aloft to illuminate the door as it shivered under the onslaught.

Ryan had no idea how many times the creature hurled itself against the door, but finally the attack was over. The creature gave one last howl of frustration, and the battering ceased.

"*Factum est.*"

Ryan turned away from the door. Someone had spoken to him in Latin.

"*Pax tibi. Sit laus Deo.*"

Yes, definitely Latin, the ecclesiastical Latin of the early church. Latin as it would have been spoken in the Dark Ages.

"*Venite.*"

The words were familiar. He had heard those words muttered in tiny incense-infused churches throughout Europe, where people clung to the old ways and prayed in the old language. The translation came easily. "Come and sit. It will be over soon, and they will come for you."

The man before him was lit by the flickering flames of a crude torch. He was a small man in a rough brown robe. His hair was shaved into a monk's tonsure and a plain wooden cross hung around his neck.

"Who are you?" The Latin words came easily to Ryan's tongue, but, uncertain of his pronunciation, he asked again, emphasizing different syllables.

"I understand you," said the monk, "but I am surprised that you understand me. Does the mother church still use our tongue?"

"The mother church uses … No, well, the Vatican …" Ryan stuttered and then, "Who the hell are you?"

"Brother Anselm," said the monk.

"What was that thing?" Ryan asked.

"A griffin," said Anselm. Apparently, the name was the same in English as in Latin.

"Really, truly, a griffin?" Ryan asked. "I didn't think they were real."

"Here they are real," said Anselm, "but perhaps not so in your world. Did you truly come through the gate?"

"Yes," said Ryan, still thinking about the reality of the huge winged beast. "The place I came from is called Griffinwood."

"The griffin guards this gate," said Anselm. "The name must have been given by a traveler long ago, one who passed from here into your world, perhaps one of the Knights of the Grail."

"So you know about our world?" Ryan asked.

"I am aware of the gate, but I have never passed through. At one time all of the gates were guarded by Merlin's creatures, but now only the griffin remains at this gate, and he is a creature of the night. We of common blood may not pass through the gate; only those of royal blood may come and go as they wish, although I have heard that the maidens from the lake once traveled into your world."

"Have you seen one of these … er … maidens of the lake today?" Ryan asked, thinking of Violet and Elaine.

The priest shook his head. "No," he said. "We saw Bors, the lord of this village, come through early in the morning with these two children you are now returning, and then you came just as the light was fading. You were fortunate that it was not yet dark."

Very fortunate, Ryan thought, remembering the hulking shape of the griffin. He had arrived at sunset. A few minutes later and he would have been food for the guardian beast. But if Violet and Elaine had not been seen entering this gate, where had they gone? Now that he was here, and Albion was a violent reality to him, he knew he should never have let Violet go alone with nothing but the waiflike Elaine for company. His lust for treasure had overcome even common decency. Violet was ill-equipped to cope with almost every aspect of daily life, and yet he had cast her adrift without a second thought.

"Is there another gate that the maidens could have used?" he asked.

"I know little of the maidens," said Anselm. "They practice the old religion and their magic is dying. I am of the order of Percival, who brought us the religion of the Christ. This is my chapel."

He lifted the torch higher, drawing Ryan's gaze away from the stout oak doors and toward the stone altar, where the peasants had now congregated. Some people were still standing, but many were on their knees, with their heads bowed before the carved wooden cross.

"This is a church?" said Ryan. "This is a Christian church?"

"Yes," said Brother Anselm. "I have the honor to be a missionary to these people. Our congregation is small, and we cannot grow until the King returns. Nothing can change until the King returns. When the war is over, we will grow, and the magic of Merlin will be nothing but a memory. Avilion will return to the mists, and Albion will be at peace." He paused, and then raised his eyes heavenward. "God willing," he added.

Jenny tugged at Ryan's hand.

"What was that monster?" she asked.

What, he wondered, was the matter with him? Had he lost every shred of humanity? First he had sent his partner into the unknown without a second thought, and now he had managed to forget that he was the de facto guardian of two very frightened children who regarded him as a hero.

Ryan knelt down so that he was on a level with Jenny's terrified face. "That thing was a griffin," he said, "but it's gone now, and it won't be coming back. We're perfectly safe now. We're in a church, and these people will look after us."

"It must be hard for the children to understand," said Brother Anselm.

"I was surprised that the lord of the village brought them here, but I see that you have come to take them home. It is a good thing. Our world is violent, but I imagine that your world is peaceful."

"No," said Ryan, "I wouldn't describe it as peaceful."

"But your world is Christian?" asked Brother Anselm.

"No, I wouldn't say that either."

"How can that be?" asked Anselm. "The Knights of the Grail brought the message of peace from your world. We are all waiting now for the King to return and for the war to end so that we may be at peace."

"What if he doesn't return?"

"He must; there is no other way."

Anselm turned his head toward the door. "You will not be able to leave here tonight; the creature still prowls, and the warriors still fight."

"Will Mordred win tonight's battle?" Ryan asked.

The little monk shrugged his shoulders. "It matters not," he said. "There is no winning or losing, only the endless war."

"But surely, if people are killed …"

"They are replaced by others. If this village is lost, another will be won."

"But that's pointless and terrible," said Ryan.

"We wait for the return of Arthur and the last great battle," said Anselm. "This should have been over many centuries ago. Arthur was grievously wounded, but because of Merlin, he did not die. Perhaps there are those who know why he has not returned, but it is not known to us." He sighed. "We are weary of waiting."

"I imagine you would be," said Ryan.

"The children look tired," said Anselm. "I will find a place for you all to rest until morning. At this time of year, the nights are short."

Ryan was struck by the fact that Anselm showed no curiosity as to why two little children should have been brought through the gate or why they were now being returned. Apparently, safety for the little missionary was secured by minding his own business and asking no questions.

Ryan glanced at his watch and saw that it had stopped working.

"Is that a device from your world?" Anselm asked.

"It tells me the time."

"It is of no use here," said Anselm. "I will wake you when it is safe to leave."

He led Ryan through the crowd around the altar and into a small, windowless room set off to the right of the altar. Ryan looked at the straw mattress and threadbare blanket spread on the bare floor. "This is your room," he said.

"I will not sleep tonight," said Anselm. "It is best you stay here. Do not go out among the people; they will ask too many questions, and you will have no answers."

Ryan glanced at his useless watch again. In this world it was no more than a piece of jewelry and not as valuable as his only other important possession, the Glastonbury cross that had brought him through the gate.

He settled Michael and Jenny together on the monk's lumpy straw pallet.

"Don't leave us," Jenny said.

"I won't," he promised.

"When are we going home?" Michael asked.

"In the morning," said Ryan.

"Will you come with us?"

"Of course."

He sat on the floor beside the children and watched as their eyelids drooped. Jenny opened her eyes one last time, checking to see if he was still there. He smiled at her. She closed her eyes again and moved closer to her brother.

Ryan looked at the sleeping children. He could not remember ever sitting that way with his own children. His quest for treasure had taken him to every corner of the globe except the place where his children lived. He had never sat this way, watching his own children sleep, and now he never would.

Sounds from the chapel became muted as the short night progressed toward dawn. Soon there was little to be heard except the murmur of a hundred sleeping people and the occasional wail of an infant, or the short, sharp exclamation of a person gripped by dreams. Ryan had no intention of sleeping, but as the darkness closed in around him, his eyelids started to droop. He renewed his hold on the golden cross, gripping it so tightly that the sharp edges of the stones dug into his fingers. The pain kept him awake, and in his wakefulness his mind turned to wondering where Violet was spending the night. If she had come through the same portal, then surely she was somewhere close. He had promised to take the children home, so how was he going to find Violet?

The monk shook him awake.

"I'm not asleep," he muttered, shaking his head and blinking his eyes to clear his vision. The cross had fallen onto the ground beside him. The little room was still in darkness, but through the open door, he could see faint slivers of light showing through the tanned hide tacked over the chapel's window openings.

The villagers were on their feet and moving quickly to open the doors in response to the sound coming from outside, a commanding knocking of a sword hilt wielded by someone with authority.

"*Aperi portum.*" The command to open the door was loud enough to be heard even through the stout oak.

"It is the Prince," said Anselm.

"The Prince?"

"Prince Mordred. He has come for you."

"Suppose I don't want to go with him?"

"I will not hide you," said Anselm. "You presence here is part of God's plan, and I will not stand in God's way."

"Will you hide the children?" Ryan asked.

"I will not tell the Prince they are here," Anselm said, looking down at the brother and sister who were beginning to stir in their sleep, "but when you leave, what shall I do with them?"

Before Ryan could think of an answer to the monk's question, the doors were flung open, and Mordred entered on horseback, followed by Bors and a contingent of armed horsemen. The peasants pressed back against the walls of the chapel as the horses crowded in with tossing manes, stamping hooves, and wild, battle-hungry eyes.

"Pax, pax," Anselm shouted, running out of the little room and in among the horses.

Ryan did not move from the doorway. Maybe Mordred knew he had the children, or maybe Mordred thought the children had died in the burning of the longhouse. He would have to think of a way to get them back through the gate and find a guardian to take them.

He stepped out into the chapel and closed the door behind him. He could see Mordred now, and he bore very little resemblance to the man he had known as Crispin Peacock. Mordred's dark curls were matted with sweat and blood, his face streaked with ash from the burning huts, and his pale blue eyes that had seemed so languid and harmless were now bloodshot and wild, roaming across the faces of the peasants even as his hand rested on the hilt of his sword.

"Well, old bean," he said, his eyes coming to rest on Ryan, "you certainly have caused me a lot of trouble."

The voice was still the same, redolent of English boarding schools and careless country weekends. "I was sure that the dear old griffin would get you and save me a lot of trouble and a lot of tedious explaining, but it seems you have a charmed life."

He nodded his head at the monk and switched to Latin. "Thank you, Brother Anselm, for saving this man. We will take him now."

He turned back to Ryan. "Bors has brought a horse for you," he said. "I assume you can ride."

"I can ride," said Ryan.

Bors' mount tossed his head wildly, setting his bridle and harness jingling as Bors forced his way through the throng, leading a riderless gray horse.

"Bors is grateful to you," said Mordred.

Ryan looked at the one-eyed man, trying to discern any gratitude or softening in his dirt-streaked face or malevolent single eye.

"Yes," said Bors, his English accent as startlingly out of place as that of Mordred. "The kid you saved is one of mine. So I owe you one."

"It's okay," said Ryan. He waited for Bors to mention the other two children. Surely he could not have simply forgotten that he had left two children in a locked room in a burning building.

"I don't like to owe," said Bors. "What do you want from me to make us equal?"

"I'll let you know," said Ryan.

"Now," said Bors.

"Carpe diem," said Mordred. "Seize the day, Doctor. You won't get another offer from Bors. He doesn't do well with long-term gratitude."

"Okay," said Ryan. "How about you agree not to kill any more people?"

Bors threw back his head and roared with laughter. "One person," he said. "Name just one person."

Ryan hesitated. He was formulating a plan for the children. It was already taking shape in his mind. The plan would depend on Bors having no knowledge that the children had been rescued. He dared not mention their names, but he had another person to worry about.

"Violet Chambray," he said. "Agree not to kill Violet under any circumstances, and we'll be even."

Mordred looked at him sideways. "Interesting," he said. "You would have been wiser to suggest that Bors should refrain from killing you. Oh well, the heart does strange things. You and Violet Chambray, well I never."

He turned back to Brother Anselm. "Great events are under way," he said. "Tell your people to light the beacon. Send up the smoke. The armies are massing at Camlan."

Anselm looked at him in wonder. "Can this be true?" he asked.

"Do you doubt me?" Mordred asked.

The monk shook his head. "No, of course not, my Prince. May God speed your footsteps."

"Well," said Mordred in English, "I'd rather have a couple of tanks and a Humvee, but I'll take the blessing. Ryan, you had better be telling the truth about being able to ride; we have a long road ahead of us."

"What about the griffin?" Ryan asked. "Is that thing still out there?"

"It's morning," said Mordred. "He's back in his lair, crunching on the bones of some poor chap who wasn't quick enough last night. Mount up; get on with it."

"Not before I pray," said Ryan.

"Pray?" said Bors. "Don't be ridiculous, old man. You're not the praying sort."

"You underestimate me," said Ryan. "I thought it was the custom of all of you to pray before a battle."

"Some men do," said Mordred, "and some don't. Bors is not one for prayers."

"I will pray with Brother Anselm," said Ryan, "alone in the room behind the altar."

"Make it quick," said Bors, "or I might forget my promise."

Ryan led Brother Anselm back into the little room and closed the door behind him. The monk gestured to Ryan that he should kneel, but Ryan shook his head.

"I need you to do something for me. You are the only one I trust."

He leaned down and placed a hand on Michael's shoulder. The boy awoke and looked at Ryan with wide, scared eyes. His sister turned in her sleep and continued her dreaming.

Ryan stumbled to find the Latin words to describe his plan, and he knew he would have to speak twice; once to explain to Brother Anselm and one more time to explain to Michael in English. He began with Brother Anselm.

"I want you to take these children home," he said.

"Me?"

"Yes, I want you to go through the gate with them."

"I cannot."

"Yes, you can. I will give you a talisman that will allow you to pass. You simply hold it in your hand."

He pressed the Glastonbury cross into the monk's hand and heard him gasp.

"What is this?"

"I don't know," said Ryan, "but it is the key to opening the gate. You must break it into three pieces."

"No," Brother Anselm protested. "It's a cross."

"It is a means of saving lives," said Ryan, retrieving the cross impatiently. He held it in both hands and applied pressure. The cross bent but did not break. He tried again and was rewarded by a snapping sound. Three large pieces and one small piece.

"Now listen carefully," he said. "As soon as the coast is clear, you will take the children through the gate. Once you are through the gate, Michael will use my phone to get in touch with his father."

"I don't understand."

Ryan took the phone from his pocket. The face was an inert black square, bereft of all information. "It is a device that will work on the other side of the gate, and the boy knows how to use it."

He turned to Michael. "You do know how to use a smartphone, don't you?"

Michael nodded his head.

"And you know your dad's phone number."

"Yes."

"Good. This man is going to take you through the gate. I know you don't understand what the gate is or what it does, but when you get to the other side, you will be back in your own world, and the phone will start to work again. Call your father and tell him that you are at Griffinwood Manor. He'll come and get you."

"Griffinwood," Michael repeated. His eyes were wide with fear and concentration, but Ryan felt that he could and would follow the instructions.

"If we can truly pass through the gate, what will I do with the children when we arrive in your realm?" Anselm asked in Latin. Ryan knew that the monk had not understood a word of the instructions that he was giving to Michael.

"The boy will call, make a signal, for his father," Ryan said. "His father is a priest of the church."

"A married priest," said Anselm in a shocked voice.

"You will find many things to shock you," said Ryan. "Don't be afraid, just stay with the children until their father comes."

"And then I must come back?" Anselm asked.

"Not if you don't want to," said Ryan.

"I have always dreamed that one day ..."

Ryan had no more time to hear about the little monk's dream. Mordred was calling his name. It was time to leave. He had given Brother Anselm all but a sliver of the jeweled cross. He had no idea if it would be enough to allow him to return through the gate. Perhaps he had marooned himself in Albion. It no longer mattered. He was already committed. He was not going home, he was going to war, and saving these two children was the only thing he could do now to make up for abandoning his own children so many times and for so long.

Ryan left Brother Anselm with the children and went out into the chapel. Bors flung him the reins of the gray mare. She tossed her head and rolled her eyes as he vaulted into the ornate saddle. The shape of the saddle was unfamiliar, and the stirrups were too long and not designed to accommodate a modern shoe.

"So you prayed?" asked Mordred.

"Yes, God and I arranged everything."

"I'm glad to hear it."

Mordred turned his mount and clomped noisily out of the confinement of the chapel. Ryan gave the mare her head, and she trotted out of the door and into sunlight of a bright, clear morning.

Mordred gestured him to come forward, leaving the other riders behind. He raised his hand and pointed. "The fires are lit."

Ryan followed his pointing finger. Ahead of them lay a range of hills, backed by purple mountains. Fires were burning on the hills, sending sparks and smoke up into the clear blue sky and passing a signal from hilltop to hilltop. Whose fires were these? he wondered. Did they summon the troops for Mordred or for Arthur?

Bors approached them on foot. He had removed his breastplate and wore a modern but very well-worn leather jacket. Even without his battered and bloodstained armor, he presented a fearsome figure. "I will not kill your woman," he said to Ryan.

"She's not my—"

"I will leave her alive," Bors said.

"Leave them all alive," said Mordred. "We may need them."

"Even the Italian?" Bors asked.

"Do what you like with him," said Mordred. "Maybe he'll give you a job if you get stuck there."

"Stuck where?" Ryan asked.

"Bors is going back through the gate," said Mordred, "to keep an eye on your friends."

"Are you saying that Violet is not on this side of the gate?"

"No, she's not," said Mordred.

Ryan breathed a sigh of relief. He could not imagine Violet being able to cope in the primitive world of Albion, but safely back in her own reality, she might be able to accomplish many things.

"Not to be too mysterious about this, old boy," said Mordred, "but something is happening; powerful forces are at work. Excalibur is rising."

"What? How can you know that?"

"I am of Arthur's blood," said Mordred. "I have a little of his connection to the sword, and I can tell you that the sword has been found. It has already been touched by someone from Albion, perhaps that wretched girl who has been following you around."

Or perhaps by Violet, Ryan thought. "Where is it?" he asked aloud.

"That is what Bors is going to discover," said Mordred. "I suspect that it's just the other side of the gate at Griffinwood."

Now Ryan actually prayed in earnest, short and sharp. Don't let Bors see the children. Make Brother Anselm wait until Bors is through the gate. Let him keep the children hidden.

"They'll never let Bors have the sword," said Ryan.

"Not without a fight," said Bors, apparently relishing the thought.

"I'm sending Bors to make sure that the sword ends up in the right hands," said Mordred, "and not in the hands of your grubby little gangster boss."

"But if Bors is going to fetch the sword, why are we leaving?" Ryan asked. "Why don't we just wait for him to get back with it?"

"Because no one except Arthur can bring Excalibur back to Albion," said Mordred. "Now that we know where Arthur has been hidden, Bors will take him the sword. Arthur and his knights will wake up, they'll come back through the gate, and I will be waiting for him. I will finish what my ancestor started, and the kingdom will be mine."

"You're just going to ... ambush him?" Ryan asked. "Is that honorable?"

"Was it honorable of him to run away and hide?" Mordred asked. "Was it honorable of him to abandon his kingdom? Was it even honorable to turn the whole kingdom into a battleground rather than cede the throne to his true heir just because he was ashamed of the way he was conceived? Arthur was an impotent old man whose barren wife had already left him for another. The Grail Knights had brought a new religion that robbed Merlin of his powers, and even the power of Excalibur couldn't bring Arthur a victory. He was already defeated."

Mordred spurred his horse forward, turning its head toward the mountains where the beacon fires sent their message into the clear blue sky. "It's time for the old man to die," he said.

CHAPTER NINETEEN

Freddie "Fingers" Fowler

Freddie felt the reassuring bulk of the Vegas mobster at his back. This was going to be a piece of cake. Nothing to fear from the angry old professor woman, the plump little American bird, the skinny girl in the blue dress, or the prissy little actor bloke, who already looked terrified. The American woman was distinctly pissed, and the skinny girl looked like she was going to cry, but what could they do? Really, what were they going to do?

Far more important was the fact that Pearlie White, Freddie's boss, had given him orders to keep on the right side of Mandretti. "Whatever he wants," was the word from Pearlie. "Give him whatever he wants, and get him off my patch as fast as you can."

Freddie was tired. He'd been driving the whole night, chasing all over the countryside looking for this damned sword, and now they had it, so now what were they fighting about? It was not like the sword was anything to write home about. Freddie had helped himself and his boss to articles of much greater value. He knew enough about jewelry and gemstones to know that those red stones were not rubies. He couldn't say what they were, but they weren't rubies; garnets maybe, or just red glass, but not rubies.

Well, rubies or not, all he had to do now was get Mandretti to Dover to meet up with the contacts who would take Mandretti and the sword across to the Continent. After that it was up to Mandretti to take it the rest of the way.

"Get in the car," said Freddie.

Mandretti sidled sideways, the sword still in his hand, and tried to open the rear door.

"Locked," he hissed to Freddie. "Why did you lock the damned door?"

"I didn't think we'd have to scarper like this," said Freddie. "I thought you was all in this together."

"Well we ain't," said Mandretti.

Freddie reached into his pocket to find the keys of the limousine.

"Hurry up," said Mandretti.

"You can't do this," said the American woman. Freddie knew her name because he had spent all night listening to them talking. This one was Violet.

He pulled the jangling bunch of keys from his pocket. As he glanced down to find the correct key, a figure burst from the bushes at the side of the driveway.

"Cor, struth," said Freddie, "who the hell is that?"

He shoved the keys back into his pocket and turned to face the new attack. The man was tall and broad shouldered, with a mane of unkempt sun-streaked hair caked with something that looked suspiciously like blood. He wore a tattered black leather jacket and a matching leather patch over one eye. The remaining eye was focused not on Freddie, but on Mandretti and the sword.

He heard the little man's squeal of fear. Todd, that was his name. Todd's voice had gone up an octave as he screamed. "It's the one-eyed man. It's him."

"Open the door," said Mandretti.

Violet hurled herself forward to stand between the attacker and Mandretti. Her sweat-streaked face was a mask of determination. "You're not taking it," she said, looking between Mandretti and the newcomer.

Freddie was unsure of his priorities. Was he to protect Mandretti or the sword? Was he also supposed to protect Violet? She was Mandretti's employee, so was she entitled to his protection? Freddie's boss protected his employees. Did Mandretti do the same thing? On the other hand, Mandretti and Violet seemed to be having their own disagreement about the sword.

Freddie made the kind of snap decision that had made him his boss's most valuable and trusted asset. Mandretti and Violet could sort out their disagreement later. The real danger came from the one-eyed madman rushing toward them, screaming an unintelligible battle cry and wielding something that looked like an antique battle ax, against which Freddie's switchblade would be no protection.

Freddie reached back and pulled the sword from Mandretti's hand.

"Hey, what the hell—?" said Mandretti.

"I'll give it back," said Freddie.

He wrapped two hands around the sword hilt and raised it above his head. Everything stopped.

He heard the music of the sword singing in his head, a shattering anthem of war, conquest, and magic. Time no longer had any meaning. He saw history unfolding before him. Knights in bright armor poured through a misty portal into a sundrenched land of green valleys and forested hills. Here was a dragon for the sword to slay. Here was a veiled lady to be rescued from a stone tower. Here were burning villages and kneeling peasants, and here was a white castle with its gates open and the drawbridge down to welcome the sword and the man who carried it at his side.

Here was a mystical golden chalice holding itself at a distance, beyond the reach of human hands. Here was love and betrayal.

The sword was held by hands that had no right to hold it, and it was used to attack the weak and defenseless. After that came the darkness, a long, long period of darkness, and then a shattering explosion, daylight, and ignorant hands, and minds that could not hear the song of the sword.

Freddie heard the man's voice coming to him from a great distance, drowning the music. "I'm taking it home." It was the voice of the one-eyed man.

"Yes," said Freddie, taking his first reluctant step away from the dream world. "It needs to go home."

"Get in the car." Mandretti had obviously felt nothing, but the girl in the blue dress was beside Freddie, her hand on his arm and her small white fingers entwined with his around the hilt of the sword.

"Is this Excalibur?" Freddie asked.

"Yes," she said.

"I told you, I told you," said Mandretti triumphantly. "Come on, we have to get it out of here."

Freddie shook his head. "The sword has to go home," he said dreamily.

"Home with me," declared Mandretti.

The one-eyed man stepped forward and dealt Mandretti a stunning blow to the side of his head. He dropped to the ground like a felled ox.

"Why can I feel it but he can't?" Freddie asked, looking down at the unconscious mobster and not even caring what the boss might have to say about Freddie's handling of the situation. Pearlie White and his East End gangsters were no longer of any interest to Freddie.

"I saw everything," said Freddie. "How?"

The girl smiled at him. "You have the blood of the Pendragons in your veins."

"Me?" said Freddie. "I'm just Freddie Fowler."

The girl gazed at him with her startling blue eyes. "Long ago," she said, "centuries ago, the knights of Albion came here and fathered children. Arthur, the High King, had only one child, but Uther Pendragon had many. They were half-brothers to Arthur, and they were Knights of the Grail.

They fathered children here, and you are their descendant. The sword has recognized you."

"No," said Freddie. "I'm just a bloke from the East End. I'm a Londoner."

The girl's gaze was becoming hypnotic. Her blue eyes were the only thing penetrating the fog in Freddie's mind.

"You are of Albion," she said, "and the sword has spoken to you."

"And now it's speaking to me," the one-eyed man said as he pulled Excalibur from Freddie's grasp. The sword seemed to leave Freddie's hand willingly, sliding smoothly from his grip.

The one-eyed man introduced himself in a cultured English accent that was completely at odds with his appearance. "Bors, sometimes known as Pendragon."

"You can't take it," said Violet.

Bors turned his one-eyed gaze upon her, and she stood her ground.

"Arthur needs it," she said.

"And he shall have it," said Bors. "I am here to return it to him."

"What about the children?" said Violet.

"I'll send them back," said Bors.

"I don't believe you."

"Believe whatever you like," said Bors, "but I can't see any of you stopping me. By the way, your boyfriend sends his regards. I've promised him that I won't kill you."

"What boyfriend?"

"Doctor Ryan."

"He's not my—"

"He said the same about you," said Bors.

"You don't know where Arthur is," said Violet defiantly.

"But you do," said Bors, "and from what I understand, we have very little time. How fast is the water rising?"

"I'll tell you nothing," said Violet.

"I am already regretting my promise not to kill you," said Bors. He turned to the girl in the blue dress. "Lady Elaine," he said, "you will tell me, won't you?"

She nodded her head.

"No," said Violet.

"We must," said Elaine. "Without the sword, Arthur can do nothing."

"Yes, but he's—"

"I know what he is," said Elaine, "but he is our only hope. If we delay, the cave will flood and there will be nothing we can do. Nothing. Ever."

Freddie felt a vast sadness flooding his brain, as though his mind was no longer his own but still the mind of the sword. The sword needed to be reunited with its owner; the centuries had been too long.

"I'll drive you," he said to Bors. "I don't know where you're going or what's going to happen, but I'll take you."

"Then you'll take us all," said Violet, "I want to see the children."

"Okay," said Freddie, "I'll take you all."

He looked down at the still-unconscious form of Mandretti. He poked him with the toe of his shoe and was answered with a groan.

"He ain't dead," he said.

"If I meant to kill him, he wouldn't be alive," said Bors, "but we have no need of him. Leave him here."

Freddie unlocked the limo. "Everybody in," he said. "Somebody tell me where to go."

Freddie's passengers tumbled through the doors. Before they could even arrange themselves on the seats, Freddie floored the accelerator, sending gravel flying as he roared down the long driveway. As they crested the last rise, with the battered iron gates already in sight, he brought the car to a screeching halt.

Despite the magical spell of the sword and the images dancing in his brain, his driver's instincts had kicked in and registered three people standing in the road. He jabbed his finger on the window button and lowered the dark glass.

"Get out of the road," he yelled.

The two children and the man in the brown robe scurried away into the bushes. The boy appeared to be talking on a cell phone and unaware of how close they had come to being run over.

"Idiots," said Freddie.

"How the hell did they get here?" said Bors.

Violet pounded on Freddie's back. "You have to stop. They're Barry Marshall's children."

Bors twisted in his seat and caught hold of Violet's wrist. Glancing in his rear view mirror, Freddie saw Violet grimace in pain.

"No stopping," said Bors. "I don't know how the hell they got here, but they're here, so just shut up about them. You understand me? Shut up."

Violet's face twisted in pain again.

"Your boyfriend owes me one for keeping you alive," Bors muttered as he released her wrist. Violet shrank back into her seat.

Soon Freddie was on unfamiliar roads, driving away from Griffinwood Manor and heading west toward the mountains. He was a Londoner, familiar with the alleys of the East End, and had a passing familiarity with the main roads between major cities, but he had to be guided by Elaine through every twist and turn of the narrow rural roads, where the bulky limousine could barely fit between the encroaching hedges and stone walls.

At first they encountered little traffic, but after a few miles, they began to see people, cars, and then construction equipment and TV news vehicles.

"What's going on?" he asked.

"The dam," said Elaine who was seated directly behind him.

"You mean the one with the horses?" said Freddie.

"Yes, that one."

"Hard to believe," said Freddie. "We're supposed to be a nation of animal lovers, but we don't mind drowning horses."

"They won't drown," said the old professor lady, who was crammed into the back alongside Violet. "They have plenty of room to get out of there."

"They won't move," said Elaine. "They're waiting."

"What the hell are they waiting for?" Freddie asked. "I always thought horses had sense, you know, horse sense."

"They're waiting for Arthur," said Elaine.

"What do you mean?" said Violet. "You said that before; you said they were waiting. How can they be waiting?"

Todd interrupted any answer Elaine was about to give. "We're being followed," he said.

"What?" Freddie looked in his mirror at the winding road behind them. "I don't see nothing."

"Blue car," said Todd, twisting to look out the rear window. "I get a glimpse of it every now and then."

"My car?" Elaine asked.

"I think so," said Todd.

"Mandretti," said Freddie, putting his foot down on the accelerator.

"I left the keys in it," Elaine wailed.

"Wouldn't make no difference," said Freddie, "not to Mandretti."

"Turn," Elaine screamed suddenly. "Turn here. Turn right."

Freddie could not see any side roads or any other place to turn, only an abandoned farmhouse perched on the edge of a steep hillside.

"Here," Elaine said. "Turn here."

He turned the big car, the brakes screaming and the wheels sliding on the gravel.

"Now what?" he said.

"They're not here," said Elaine. "Why aren't they here?"

"Who?" asked Todd.

"Gavin and Robby," said Elaine. "I told them to wait for me. Drive up to the edge."

"What edge?" said Freddie.

"The edge of the hill. Hurry up, and he won't know we've turned."

Freddie drove cautiously to the point where the ground dropped away into a vast blue nothingness. "Now what?" he asked. "Where do you want me to go?"

"They're not here," said Elaine. "We'll have to risk it. Go on down before he sees you."

"Down there?"

"Yes."

He hesitated on the precipitous brink. Far down below he could see abandoned farmhouses. On the opposite side of the valley, a waterfall poured down into a sluggish river. Bright yellow construction equipment crawled along a road that topped the towering dam that now closed the valley and stopped the flow of the river as it became a lake. A herd of panicked horses pounded along beside the ever-widening river as helicopters roared overhead.

"Down there?" he asked again.

"We did it," said Violet.

"Yes, we did," said Elaine encouragingly. "Go, before he sees us. There's a sort of path."

Freddie identified the rough outlines of an old gravel road that might once have been accessible by jeep. He had no idea what Pearlie White would say if he wrecked the boss's new limo, but it no longer mattered. The blue car was close behind, and the sword was still singing in his mind. Cautiously, and then with a rapidly growing fatalistic confidence, he guided the heavy vehicle between the ruined stone walls, through the rusted farm gate, and over the edge into the valley.

At first he was able to control their descent, but soon the weight of the limo began to work against him. The wheels slipped on the gravel, and the gravel gave way to grassy tussocks and rocks. The steering wheel shivered and bucked in his grasp. He jammed the engine into a lower gear, and for a moment, he had control. They were nearing the valley floor. The road seemed to be leading him toward some ruined stone buildings, and he caught sight of a green vehicle tucked behind one of the buildings. A Land Rover, he thought. Well, if they could do it …

His left front wheel climbed up onto a rock. He slammed on the brakes, but he was too late. He hung onto the steering wheel, feeling himself rising into the air as the car tipped over onto its side. As the car buried itself into the ground, with a scream of torn metal and shattering glass, Freddie saw something flying past them, rolling and bouncing. Elaine's blue car was turning cartwheels as the sun reflected off its bright paint. Then Freddie's view of the world was extinguished as the airbag slammed explosively into his face.

[]

CHAPTER TWENTY

Marcus Ryan

Ryan's horse was obstinately opposed to falling in line and following the other horses as Mordred led his war party north. She tossed her head, danced sideways, and tried to scrape Ryan from her back as she careened under the low hanging branches of the forested path. In pursuit of treasure, Ryan had crossed the rainbow-colored mountains of Bolivia on horseback, and ridden camels in the Sahara, and he knew he would prove more than a match for the willful gray mare. By the time they left the forest and moved out onto high heather-coated hillsides, they had reached an agreement. She would continue to toss her head and roll her eyes, but she would follow in the train of Mordred and his black stallion.

With the mare under control, Ryan had the freedom to listen to the conversation around him. The language was a mixture of Latin and early English, and the longer he listened, the more he understood.

The war party consisted of perhaps a hundred armored knights on horseback, accompanied by their squires and pack horses. Along the way, they met parties of peasants, some on foot and some riding short-legged shaggy ponies, all eager to respond to the call of the hilltop beacons.

The historian in Ryan's soul was absorbed in all of the details of their progress through the countryside. This, he thought, was how it had been in Britain in the twelfth century, when King Stephen fought the Empress Matilda for the throne. As darkness and anarchy spread across the land, the people of Britain, huddled in their mud and wattle huts, had watched the war parties passing by and declared that God and his angels were sleeping. And then, in the midst of darkness and despair, a gate from another world had been opened, and the knights of Albion had ridden into Britain and into legend, creating the myth that the beleaguered people so desperately needed.

Mordred and his war party traveled through a land of ruined castles and squalid villages. Here and there, Ryan could see where a castle wall had been hastily repaired with bright new stonework, but most of the buildings showed the ravages of fire and war and long drawn-out sieges.

He could see no sign of an opposing force. The peasants who marched beside the horsemen all seemed to be committed to Mordred and his cause. Where, he wondered, were Arthur's forces? Perhaps they were coming from another direction, making their way down from the high mountains in the far north. It seemed that Mordred controlled the lowland hills. Not that anyone really controlled anything, he thought, for Mordred had said that the war could not be won unless Arthur returned. Without Arthur and Excalibur to oppose them, the army Mordred had assembled could not win and could not lose. The only losers would be those who died a futile and pointless death. Either side could win the battle, but no one could win the war.

The mare, apparently aware that Ryan's thoughts were elsewhere, gave a warning toss of her head and danced sideways to scrape Ryan's right leg against a high stone wall. He jerked her head around to show her that he was still in control and leaned down to look at the long grazed wound on his leg.

"You'll never win," said a voice in Latin. "She's just waiting for the right moment."

A knight rode up beside him, his own brown gelding under perfect control. He was bareheaded, his black hair falling in curls to his shoulders. The green surcoat that he wore over his body armor was matched by the caparison on his horse.

"She is a mist horse," he said. "It was not kind of the Prince to put you on such a horse."

"I'm fine," Ryan declared, settling back into the saddle and deciding to ignore the sharp pain in his leg, and the blood oozing from the long scrape made by the rock. He was certain that his wound was minor compared to the wounds normally inflicted on the knights of Albion.

"You handle her well," said the knight, and he smiled a snaggle-toothed smile, his yellowed teeth standing out against the darkness of his beard and moustache.

Ryan thought of Mordred, who was obviously the beneficiary of modern dentistry. Apparently, some modern amenities could survive the journey through Merlin's portals, but not anything that could affect the balance between the warring parties.

"There's another mist horse behind us," said the knight, "with the baggage train. She's old and she usually gives no trouble, but she has been troublesome all day. No doubt this one is talking to her."

Ryan looked down at the mare's head. Her ears were twitching, but she was at least pointing forward and following in the general direction of the rest of the war party.

"How can they be talking?" he asked.

"They are a mystery," said the knight. "Who can say how they come and how they go?"

"I don't understand you," said Ryan.

"Ah, I was told you would understand the church language," said the knight.

"I understand your words," said Ryan, "but I don't know what you mean. What is a mist horse?"

"They come from a high valley north of Camlan, and we are nearing their home," said the knight. "Some say it is the valley of Avilion, where the sisters live on the island that cannot be seen."

Ryan set his face in a deliberately puzzled but neutral expression. Here were words that he wanted to hear. Here was information about Elaine. He decided not to ask questions, not to push for information. Too many questions, and the knight would realize that Ryan knew more than he was willing to admit. Better just to let the man talk.

Ryan smiled encouragingly at the knight. "Interesting," he said.

Obviously glad to have an audience for his speculations, the knight smiled back, again displaying the lack of dentistry that marred an otherwise handsome face.

"You have come from beyond the gate," he said.

"Yes, I have," said Ryan. "Have you ever been through the gate?"

The knight laughed derisively. "Only those with the blood of the Pendragons may pass through the gates, but we know of them. We also know," he added, "that many gates are now closed. The Prince gives us very little information, but I understand that even he cannot find the oldest of the gates. They are gone. Some say it is because Merlin has retreated into the mists."

"About the mists …" said Ryan, turning the knight's attention back to the mystery of the horses.

"We know that the horses move between worlds," said the knight. "Sometimes they are in the misty valley, and sometimes they are not visible. It is thought that they graze on the other side, but no one has found the gate through which they pass."

"Surely if someone just kept an eye on them …" said Ryan.

"The valley is a mystical place," said the knight.

Ryan's mare tossed her head and took a couple of steps off the path. He brought her back in line with a sharp tap of his heels. He mulled over his Latin vocabulary, aware that his conversational skills were limited and his speech was stilted, but he needed to keep his companion talking. He was receiving information that Mordred would never offer.

"Why do you use the mist horses?" he asked. "They're obviously not well suited. How do you even capture them?"

"Some were captured long ago," said the knight, "and we breed from them. They are fast and intelligent, but in every generation, we find some who are like the one you are riding. They are compelled to return to their home. The valley is close by; she can probably scent her home pastures. If you give that she-devil her head, she will throw you off and you will not see her again. Tie her tight when we make camp. As for the old one back there, I think this might be the last cart that she will pull; she will not see the morning. The baggage train is no place for a wild horse."

A blast from a trumpet interrupted the conversation. The green knight stood up in his stirrups and looked ahead. "We have arrived," he said.

"Arrived where?" asked Ryan.

"I cannot say. I have no knowledge of this place, but we are told that this is where we will win our final battle."

The line of men and horses had come to a restless halt, with harnesses jingling and hooves stomping. Mordred rode back along the column and stopped alongside Ryan.

"Well done," he said, and it was a relief for Ryan to hear modern English. "I guess you meant what you said about being able to ride."

"She's spirited," said Ryan, not wishing to reveal that he knew the source of his mount's high-spirited behavior.

"Ride with me," said Mordred, spurring his horse toward the head of the column.

Ryan rode close behind Mordred and observed the army setting up its encampment along a ridge that overlooked a wide valley. A waterfall fell from the hillside, pouring water into a river that meandered along the valley floor.

Mordred pointed down to the waterfall. "Arthur rests there behind that waterfall," he said.

"Really?"

"Yes. This is the information that I obtained from the Griffinwood Document. It was so good of you to find it for me, old bean. He's in a cave, but unfortunately, it's not on this side of the gate, not in this reality. The cave and everything in it is duplicated on the other side of the gate, and that's where Arthur is. The same river, the same waterfall, the same cave system. The only difference is that in your world, they've built a bloody great big dam, and they're about to flood the whole valley. If Arthur doesn't come out now, he'll never come, so we'd all better hope that your lady friend has the sword."

"I thought that was what you sent Bors to do," said Ryan.

"I did," said Mordred, "but he can't exactly phone me and tell me how he's getting along, can he?"

"No, I suppose not."

"You suppose correctly."

"So where's the gate?" Ryan asked.

"According to the map, it's about halfway down the hill," said Mordred. "I think it's hidden by a clump of bushes, but if anyone goes near enough, they'll see the mist."

"And you're just going to wait here?" Ryan asked.

"Right by the gate," said Mordred.

"I don't know why you would need an entire army just to ambush one man. You afraid he might fight back?"

Mordred made a derogatory snorting sound. "He won't fight back. I won't give him time."

"So why the army?"

"Arthur still has his supporters," Mordred admitted. "By bringing my army here, I'm setting a trap for them. They will have no idea that Arthur has returned and that we have Excalibur; they'll only know that my army is here and they'll attack. That will be the end of them. Don't look so disgusted, old chap; I told you, we have to end this thing. I know it's not cricket, or baseball, as you might like to call it, but it will get the job done, and I'll be the high king."

Mordred turned away from the ridge and sat for a moment, watching as his soldiers went about setting up their encampment.

"Lots to do, lots to do," he said. "No time to talk now, but play your cards right, and I'll give you a chance to come to court. No good thinking you'll get back through the gate; no good at all, old bean."

"You want me to stay here?" Ryan asked with a sudden onrush of disbelief. "You're not going to let me go back? I have a family—"

"You don't give a damn about your family," said Mordred. "You haven't cared about them in years. No, I'm not letting you go back. If I sent you back now, you'd probably warn your friends about what's going to happen, so I'm going to wait until Arthur is through the gate, then no one's going back. I thought I made it clear; when Excalibur and Arthur come back, everything closes. Everything."

"Bors?" said Ryan.

"I sincerely hope that he will stay on the other side. The man's an oaf and I won't need him." He clapped a gloved hand on Ryan's shoulder. "You're a historian," he said. "You will be here to observe history. Really, you should thank me for the opportunity."

Ryan looked at Mordred with a sinking heart. He was speaking the simple truth. The gate would close, and Ryan would be trapped in Albion, a silent observer of the history of another world.

"Don't think of going down there and trying to pass through the gate," said Mordred, indicating the waterfall with a nod of his head. "I've already set guards. You won't get off this ridge alive. Now, please, go and wait at the rear. You're no use to me in this fight."

"I wouldn't exactly call it a fair fight," said Ryan.

"Call it whatever you like," said Mordred, "but get the hell away from here."

He leaned from his saddle and slapped the rump of the gray mare, who responded with a startled toss of her head and a clatter of hooves as she bolted away from the ridgeline. By the time Ryan had her under control, he was at the rear of Mordred's encampment, in among the supply wagons.

The mare came to an unwilling standstill and complained of her treatment with a loud whinny. Ryan heard an answering whinny from the place where the cart horses had been released from their traces and hitched to various trees and bushes.

He looked around. It seemed that every member of Mordred's army was fully occupied with their tasks, and no one was taking any notice of him.

He considered his options. What he needed to do was get through the gate and warn Violet that Mordred was lying in wait for Arthur, although he had no idea what Arthur could do about the ambush, even if he was made aware. There was only one gate ... or was there? He was close to the home of the mist horses, and his companion, the green knight, had told him that they were rumored to come from Avilion, the secret island home of Violet's mother. They were known to be able to pass between the two worlds. So if another gate existed, might it be in Avilion?

He loosened his grip on the reins, giving the gray mare her head. "Go home," he said. He clutched the pommel of the saddle, ready for her to burst into action, but she was motionless. "Go home," he said again. "You've been trying to go all day, now just go already."

The gray stepped sideways, moving daintily and soundlessly, and he saw what he needed to do. The old horse, black with a grizzled muzzle, stood patiently among the other pack animals. She shivered slightly despite the warmth of the sun, and he could see where the carter had laid on with his whip, trying to keep her in line even as she scented her home pastures. Her eyes were fixed on the gray.

The gray was motionless, obstinate, and her intention was clear. She was not going home without her companion.

"You'd better not run off," said Ryan as he swung his leg over the saddle and dropped to the ground. He kept hold of the reins, and the gray rolled her spirited brown eyes at him as if to say, "I could break free any time I want to."

"Yes, you could," said Ryan, "but you won't."

The black horse was held by a heavy rope halter tied to a sturdy young tree. Rather than untie the stiff knot in the hemp rope, Ryan slipped the halter over her head. He patted her muzzle and ran his hand along her bony sides. "Go home," he said. "You've earned it."

The gray allowed Ryan to settle himself in the saddle before she set off at a slow trot. The black trotted at her side. Ryan looked behind him. Surely someone would see them. He urged the gray forward with his knees, feeling as though it would be somehow inhumane to actually kick her. She was no longer just a horse. She had become something more, an extension of the mystery, a representative of Avilion.

The gray settled into a slow canter, the black running alongside. They veered from the path and made their way steadily upward, and then down into a shallow valley where they were hidden from the army. The two horses picked up speed, crossing the valley and climbing again, passing beyond the tree line and up onto a high rocky ridge. They crested the ridge, and Ryan caught a glimpse of a high mountain lake, inky black beneath the blue sky, with mists swirling across its ruffled surface.

The horses came down from the ridge at a wild gallop, Ryan clinging helplessly to the gray's mane. He sensed that she was no longer trying to throw him, but she was running with wild abandon. Even the old and abused black horse seemed to have forgotten her hardships and was running with her tail and her mane flying in the breeze.

Well, Ryan thought, looking at her as she streaked alongside him, if I have never done anything else good in my life, I've done this.

The gray skidded to a halt on a pebbled beach beside the dark water. Mist swirled around her feet.

"Here?" Ryan asked.

From out of the mist, a hand reached up and grasped the reins.

"Here," a voice confirmed.

CHAPTER TWENTY ONE

Violet Chambray

The blue car was on fire. No one could possibly be alive inside, but Violet thought she saw someone moving around outside the vehicle. Maybe Mandretti had survived. A helicopter circled above the burning vehicle and lowered a rescuer on a rope. Another helicopter hovered nearby. The air was filled with the thump-thump of the rotors and the scream of the engines. Acrid smoke from the burning car filled her nostrils, but she had no time to dwell on her situation. Hands were pulling at her, dragging her through the passenger window of the limo, now lying on its side among the rocks.

"Come on. Hurry up." She looked away from the helicopters and into the face of Freddie, the driver, who had his hands hooked under her arms and was heaving her upward.

"Seat belt," she gasped.

Freddie leaned in and released the seat belt, and Violet collapsed sideways against Bors, who was jammed beneath her and apparently unconscious. He had slammed his head against the window and dislodged his eye patch, revealing a hideous scar and an empty eye socket. Blood trickled from his ear. This, she knew, did not speak well for Bors's future health.

Without a second thought, Violet used Bors's ribs and shoulder as a step to allow her to stand upright and squeeze her head and chest through the open window. Freddie moved in again, pulling her out of the vehicle and dumping her like a beached porpoise on the rocky ground.

She had no time to regain her breath or ask a question, or even check to see if she was bleeding, before Elaine was pulling at her arms.

"Get up; we have to go."

"Molly, Todd?" Violet asked breathlessly as she scrambled to her feet.

"I'm here," said Todd. "Molly's not so good. We'll have to let them take her."

"Who?"

"Don't know for sure," said Todd. "I assume it's the police. There are helicopters everywhere."

"The sword?" said Violet.

"I have it," said Todd.

"You?"

"Yeah, me."

"Come on," said Elaine. "The boys are coming for us."

"What boys?"

"Robby and Gavin, the ones who were here before," said Elaine. "We told them to wait, and they waited."

The battered green Land Rover with Elaine's faithful followers on board was coming toward them, making light work of the hill and the rocks.

"Don't let them see the sword," said Violet.

"Too late for secrets," said Elaine. "We need all the help we can get."

A helicopter made a swooping, circling dive down toward them as they scrambled across the hillside toward the Land Rover, and a muffled voice boomed through megaphone. Violet interpreted the words as "Stay where you are" and kept moving.

They came level with the Land Rover, driven by Gavin with Robby beside him, both of them red-faced with excitement and anxiety. To Violet's surprise, the abandoned hound dog still occupied the back seat, its tongue lolling out of its mouth and its eyes fixed on Violet.

Even as the Land Rover juddered to a halt, Freddie was beside the driver, hauling him from his seat.

"Hey," Gavin protested.

"No time," said Freddie, yanking Gavin aside and putting himself in the driver's seat. "Get in," he said to Violet.

She hesitated. She had been unable to vault into the back of the vehicle before the crash, and stiff and sore as she now was, she knew her abilities had not improved.

"Get out," said Freddie to Robby. Despite the thrum of the helicopter rotors, the crackling of the megaphone, and the sparks and crackles from the burning car, Robby seemed to understand Freddie's tone well enough to move with lightning speed into the back seat while Violet dropped down into the front passenger seat. Elaine sprang lightly into the back, followed by Gavin and then by Todd, still grasping Excalibur, all four of them fighting the dog for space on the back seat.

"Don't give them the sword; don't let them touch it," Elaine screamed.

"Why not?" Violet asked, but if Elaine made any answer, she could not hear what it was. The Land Rover appeared to have lost its muffler somewhere on the wild ride up the valley, and its crackling exhaust drowned out even the sound of the helicopters.

"Where?" Freddie screamed in Violet's ear, and she realized that Freddie had no idea where they were or what they were about to do.

She pointed to the river, wider now but hopefully still shallow enough to be crossed. As if to confirm her hopes, a herd of horses thundered along the river bank and then turned and splashed through the water. Their hooves sent up clouds of spray, but they did not slow their wild gallop. So, she thought, if the river could be crossed by a galloping horse, surely it could be crossed by a Land Rover.

As Freddie guided the Land Rover through the river, she watched the horses make their way up the steep hillside and disappear over the crest of the hill.

So much, she thought, for the fear that the horses wouldn't have the sense to get out of the way of the flood. Elaine had said that they would not move, and she had said it with such confidence. They were waiting, she said. Apparently, she was wrong; they were no longer waiting.

Freddie cleared the stream and did his best to get the Land Rover up the steep hillside, but it soon foundered, stopped by massive rocks.

The helicopters were still hovering above the river and above the last vestiges of the burning blue car. The pilot of one had come as close as he dared to the steep hillside, but he could come no closer. For the moment at least, Violet and her companions were beyond the reach of the law, but from here they would have to go on foot. And they would have to move fast, Violet thought, watching as the helicopters dropped down just inches from the ground and disgorged squads of helmeted-and-armed men.

The helicopters lifted away, and in the momentary quiet, Violet could hear Elaine urging them on toward the waterfall. They climbed in single file, Todd scrambling up ahead of Violet, agile despite the fact that he was holding the sword, and the dog following close on Violet's heels.

Rowan waited for them beside the waterfall, her face a mask of impatience. "Hurry," she said.

"We're hurrying," Violet said breathlessly. She felt someone push her from behind with large hands that grasped her backside and heaved her upward. She turned to look behind her.

"Freddie?"

"Get a move on," he said.

The expression on his face was the expression of a man moving in a dream. From the moment he had laid hands on the sword, Freddie had been a different man, a man on a mission. Violet knew that the sword was still talking to him, and the fact that he had a firm hold of her buttocks was neither here nor there. All he wanted was for her to move her backside up the hill.

They passed behind the waterfall, Robby and Gavin uttering cries of wonder, and Todd apparently speechless.

"Light," said Rowan, tapping Elaine impatiently with her carved staff.

Elaine was gasping for breath, her eyes wild and her dress torn and mud stained.

"Light," said Rowan again.

"I'm not sure if I can," Elaine gasped.

Rowan struck the girl hard across her face and spoke fiercely in a language that Violet did not understand. She could not understand the words, but she most certainly knew their meaning. Pull yourself together, girl, and give us light.

Elaine waved her hand, and a faint light flickered, illuminating the path into the deepest recesses of the cave.

"You follow," said Rowan to Violet. She tapped Robby, Gavin, and Freddie with her cane. "You stay here," she said, "and I will bring him to you." She looked down at the dog. He stared back with knowing brown eyes, and Rowan nodded her head as though she and the dog had reached some sort of agreement. The dog took a deep breath and settled into a sitting position.

Rowan turned her attention to Todd. "You," she said, "will carry the sword. It does not speak to you, and you will not be torn by any past loyalties. You are loyal only to the Lady Violet."

"Lady Violet?" queried Todd, raising his eyebrows and attempting to regain some of his usual insouciance.

Rowan smacked him with her staff. "Come," she said.

Elaine had recovered her breath, and the tunnel was now brightly lit, the sconces flaring as she ran ahead.

Rowan pushed Todd ahead of her. "Go now," she said, "and awake the King."

Marcus Ryan

The gray mare stood still, her flanks trembling from the wild ride across the moor. "Here?" Ryan asked again. This time, no voice answered him from out of the mist, and the stranger's hand was no longer on the reins. He sensed a presence close by and detected shadow within the mist. He urged the gray forward but she refused to move.

"Okay," he said, "apparently, this is as far as you're willing to bring me."

He swung his leg over the saddle and dropped to the ground. Now he was completely enveloped in the mist, seeing only the pebbles of the beach and the solid shape of a large rock. A gentle tug of wind blew the mist aside for a moment, and he saw the dark water of the lake. As the misty white tendrils snaked across the rock, it seemed to him that the rock itself was moving.

"Look," he said as vehemently as his limited Latin vocabulary would allow, "I don't have time for this. Whoever you are, just show yourself. Are you another guardian? Do I have to fight you? I will if I have to."

He knew that his speech was nothing but bravado. Whatever it was that was hiding in the mist was well beyond his ability to conquer. Was it a griffin like the one he had encountered the night before? Was it a dragon? Mordred had hinted at dragons. Perhaps it was one of the other perils that featured so strongly in the stories of the Round Table. It could be a demented knight able to fight without rest for days and nights on end, an enticing maiden who could administer a kiss of death, or a giant able to cross oceans in a single stride. Presumably, all of these creatures had once been created by Merlin to guard the gates to Britain, and presumably, none of them could be vanquished by throwing stones, the only weapons that appeared to be available on the inhospitable beach.

"Would you truly fight me?"

The rock had spoken. Yes, the rock was moving and it was speaking. What had appeared to be an outcrop now became a hand with long, gnarled fingers. The grass at the base of the rock moved, and Ryan saw feet. The cracks and crevices of the rock became long hair and a gray beard surrounding a face of immense age.

"I cannot yet move," said the rock, "but if I chose to fight you, you would die."

Ryan tried to frame an answer, a resounding challenge that would let the rock monster know that, whatever the cost, he planned to get the better of this creature. Come hell or high water or dark, evil magic, he would carry his warning through the gate, and Mordred's ambush would fail.

"Do not," said the rock, "waste your energy searching your mind for the language of the Carpenter's church. I can no longer fight against their God-Man, but I will not speak their language. My voice has long since passed from the land. I speak only to your mind."

Ryan opened his mouth to answer, but the rock intruded on his mind again. "You have a mission," it said.

"Yes," said Ryan.

"Show me," said the rock.

"How?"

"In your mind."

Ryan sent his mind back over the past few days. Professor Peacock dying in a pool of red wine, Carlton Lewis stabbed to death on a train,

Barry Marshall attacked at the altar of his church, Violet, Elaine, Crispin Peacock, Mordred …

"Enough," said the rock. "I cannot bring back the dead."

"But," said Ryan, "you can stop death. You stopped Arthur from dying."

"Then you know who I am?" said the rock.

"Yes," said Ryan. "You are Merlin."

"I am."

"And you are guarding this gate."

"I am," said Merlin. "I permitted this gate to remain open so that horses will be available to the King when he awakes, but too much time has passed. I am at the last of my strength. This pitiful creature that you see before you is all that remains of Arthur's great magician."

"So you couldn't fight me?" Ryan asked.

"I could," said Merlin, "but then I would have no strength left for the task ahead."

"But you're not going to stop me?" said Ryan.

"No." The rock appeared to shake its head. The stone tendrils of beard shivered, the granite shoulders moved, and the rock grew slightly in height.

Ryan heard the drumming of horses' hooves. Beyond the curtain of mist, the horses were moving and coming closer. They were all around him but still invisible.

"Tell me of Mordred," said Merlin.

Ryan thought about Mordred and the way he had presented himself, a modern Englishman, heir to a great estate.

"No," said Merlin. "I care nothing for his life beyond the gate. The sword is moving."

"Excalibur," said Ryan, interrupting the thought. "Have they found it?"

"It is found," said Merlin. "We have no more time. Tell me of the danger."

Ryan drew a mind picture for the magician. He showed him the war party and its encampment along the ridge. He showed him the sentries at the gate and then Mordred himself, waiting like a spider at the center of its web for the unsuspecting Knights of the Round Table.

"He will let the first ones pass," said Merlin, "and he will wait for Arthur and Excalibur. You are not mistaken. The gate will close and the war will be over."

"That's all that the people want," Ryan said, feeling the need to speak for the peasants and their miserable conditions.

"They will not prosper under any of the line of Mordred," said Merlin. "I know the evil of his conception and the evil of his descendants."

"But Arthur is old."

The rock shook itself and grew a couple more inches in height. Now Ryan could see the outline of a robe and feet in pointed slippers.

"Do you wish to discuss the philosophy of royal succession, or do you wish to save the King and all of Albion with him?" Merlin roared.

Ryan hesitated.

"Do you wish to save Ariana's daughter, the Lady Violet?" Merlin asked.

Ryan was unable to shield his thoughts from the magician. The rock emitted a creaking groan that may have been a laugh.

"Was ever a man so undecided?" said Merlin. "It was not that way when Arthur saw Guinevere, or," he added, "when Guinevere saw Lancelot, and that was a sad day for the kingdom. I will make your decision for you. You are not of Pendragon blood, but you will do well here. I will permit you to pass, and I will keep the gate open for as long as my strength will last, although I warn you, it may not last for long. When you return, I may be nothing more than another scattering of pebbles along this beach."

Ryan felt a gust of warm breath against his neck. The gray mare had reappeared through the mist and was nudging him with her velvety nose.

He hauled himself back into the saddle. Merlin, the great magician, was no more than a dark shape amid the encompassing mist, and the only true reality was the feel of the saddle beneath him, and the stomping feet and tossing heads of the herd of horses that surrounded him.

CHAPTER TWENTY TWO

Todd Chambray

Todd stopped at the entrance to the last cave. He could see that this final chamber had once been guarded by iron gates, but the gates were open now, and the girl in blue had gone on ahead to wave her hand and light the wall torches.

All of this was beyond Todd's comprehension. Despite the research he had carried out for Violet, the ancient, grainy pictures he had pulled from the internet, or even the flamboyant poesy of Mallory and Tennyson, nothing in his life had prepared him for the sight of Arthur and his knights lying in a row like colorful wax statues. He made an attempt to rationalize what he was seeing. Perhaps they were just wax dummies, because surely they were not the real thing. They were not knights from a parallel universe, sleeping the centuries away while waiting for the magical sword.

The sword Excalibur was silent in his hands. To him, this sword, for the sake of which people had already died, was nothing more than a modest creation of little artistic value, and he could not tell why it had such a profound effect on other people. Most certainly, if he was directing a production of Camelot, Excalibur would require a far more dramatic prop, something in bright gold with large gemstones, and perhaps some words carved along the blade.

Rowan, the old woman with the very creative hairstyle, turned to face him. "Place the sword in the King's hands," she said.

Todd surveyed the row of wax dummies. "Which is the King?" he asked.

Rowan looked at him impatiently. "You can't tell; you really can't tell?" she asked. "I wonder where your ancestors came from." She shook her head. "No, don't answer that. We don't have time to waste on idle speculation."

She pointed to a wooden pallet that was raised higher than the others, and to the inert figure of a knight, the only one who was not clasping a sword in his hands. "That one, he is the King."

Todd approached and looked down at the still figure of the King. Arthur was not a young man. His hair and beard were gray, but his shoulders were broad, and he had a barrel chest and sturdy legs.

"Place the sword in his hands," said the old woman.

Todd touched the knight's hands. He expected them to be cold and stiff, but they were warm, as though blood was still flowing in his veins. He placed the sword on the knight's chest and then moved the knight's hands so that they were clasping the sword.

He stepped back. While it was true that the sword itself was having no effect on him, everything else was serving to terrify him. Bad enough to have survived the wrecking of the limousine, and the hair-raising ride in the open jeep, or whatever the hell it was, but now they were deep underground in a chamber that was surely going to be flooded just as soon as the water rose high enough in the valley. He wondered how long Violet and Elaine planned to just stand there looking at those impossible undead bodies and ignoring the fact that they were all going to drown?

He edged toward the doorway, plotting his escape. He would sprint through the tunnels, and if the blond with the magic fingers was not available to light the lamps, he would use his cell phone as a flashlight. He would get out of the cave, out of the valley, and as far away as possible. He wanted to be back in Key West, playing Madame Arcati to an empty house, and going out drinking with his friends. He needed to get his life back, and he needed his therapist. If he did not go immediately into therapy, this whole experience would scar him for life.

No, he would not wait for Violet or anyone else to tell him to leave, he would make his own decision, and he would go just as soon as he was sure that putting the sword into the knight's hands had done nothing, absolutely nothing, which was obviously the case.

He stared at the King's hands. The fingernails were short and blunt and none too clean, and the hands themselves were large and bony, pitted with scars. As he watched, the scarred hands with the dirty fingernails twitched. He held his breath, waiting. The fingers twitched again, and then both hands moved, and the undead king took a firm grip of his sword.

He heard movement behind him, rustling clothes, clanking metals, and the sharp intakes of a dozen breaths. He turned slowly and reluctantly, fearful of what he might see. These men were dead. They had been dead for centuries, and surely the flesh was going to fall from their bones as soon as they moved. Surely their clothes were going to disintegrate, leaving nothing but a roomful of animated, naked skeletons.

But they were not skeletons. They seemed to be living, breathing, healthy men. They were sitting up on their wooden biers, stretching their arms, looking around with eager curiosity, and speaking to each other in low murmurs. The old woman answered them in soft, soothing tones, leading them to look in the direction of the King.

Todd looked back and saw that Arthur had opened his eyes, deep brown beneath wild gray eyebrows. He was looking round the cave with a quick, intelligent glance, taking in everything and finally allowing his puzzled gaze to rest on Todd for a moment. His glance slid away again. Obviously, he was not ready to deal with something so deeply unfamiliar as a man in a tweed suit.

The first sounds from his throat were cracked, like a man who had gone very long without a drink, but soon he had his voice under control. He spoke in a thundering, commanding bass tone. The words meant nothing to Todd, but the tone was easy to interpret. "Where the hell am I?"

Rowan answered him in one long, breathless sentence, pointing out the iron grill that had guarded the cave, the wooden pallets where the knights had slept, and then drawing his attention to a gaping hole in the King's breastplate. So, Todd thought, this was where he had received his mortal wound, the one that could only be healed by magic and a long, long rest. Arthur placed his hand on his chest and drew a deep breath. He smiled, and nodded his head, and sprang lightly to his feet, still clasping the sword.

He handled Excalibur with ease. Todd had labored to carry the sword up the hillside, but Arthur wielded it as though it weighed no more than a fencing foil. He held it above his head as he rallied his knights and directed them toward the exit of the cave.

The Knights of the Round Table passed before the King, each one lowering his head and clasping his chest in a Roman salute. Todd heard Violet whispering their names, although how she could know their names was one more mystery in a day of mysteries.

"Sir Ladinas of the Forest Savage, Sir Melion of the Mountain, Sir Gawain of Orkney, Sir Percival, Sir Lionel, Sir Bedivere, Sir Pelleas, Sir Edward of Carnarvon, Sir Dinadan, Sir Galahad the Pure."

Arthur lifted his head and looked around the cave.

"Sir Lamorak, Sir Griflet," Violet continued.

The King was becoming distracted and uneasy.

"He's not here," Violet whispered. "Who is going to tell him?"

"I will," said the old woman.

She pushed aside the remaining knights and spoke directly to the King.

"Who's not here?" Todd asked.

"Lancelot," said Violet. "He died somewhere outside the cave, a long time ago."

"But he's only just finding out," said Todd, "so it will be as though he died yesterday."

"There's worse news to come," said Violet. "Or at least I think it's worse news."

"What?"

"Guinevere," said Violet.

Several additional knights had already passed the King, each offering his loyal salute, but Arthur lowered his sword and turned away from them.

"Oh," said Violet, "I hope this isn't going to take long."

The old woman had taken hold of the King's arm, and she was showing him something concealed behind one of the deserted pallets.

"What is it?" Todd asked.

"Guinevere's bones," said Violet.

"But she was a—"

"I know what she was," said Violet. "Every story I have ever read says that Arthur loved her, but look where she died."

"Where?" Todd asked.

"She died alongside Lancelot's empty bier," said Violet. "She was unfaithful to Arthur even in death."

Arthur took no more than a moment to consider the remains of his wife. He reached down and took the wedding ring from the skeletal finger, crossed himself quickly, and then turned away. He gestured to the assembled knights to start moving out of the cave. His face was set in a grim expression, and it seemed to Todd that the High King was in a mood to do battle with someone. He was ready to put Excalibur into action.

Rowan grasped the King's arm. He slowed reluctantly and bent his head to listen to what she said.

"He has to know what's happened while he was away," said Violet. "He has to know about Mordred."

"Forget about Mordred," said Todd, "he has a bigger problem than that. What's going to happen when he gets outside? Think what he's going to see, helicopters, cars, hundreds of people. It's going to blow his mind."

"Rowan will take him back through the gate," said Violet. "It's really close, and once he gets to the other side, he won't need to understand what's going on here. As soon as Arthur and Excalibur are back on the other side, the gate will close, and he won't have to think about what he saw here. Maybe he'll think it was a dream."

"I wish," said Todd.

"Wish what?"

"I wish it was all a dream," Todd said. "How am I going to explain this to my therapist?"

Violet frowned at him. "You are not going to breathe a word of this," she said.

"I won't have to," Todd replied. "Do you really think that a couple of dozen knights in medieval armor are going to just pass unnoticed in front of the news helicopters out there? "

"Oh."

"Video at six," said Todd.

Violet shrugged her shoulders. "Well, it has to be done."

"What about you?" Todd asked.

"I'm not going to tell anyone anything," Violet said.

"But are you going with them?"

"With them?" said Violet. "No, of course not. I belong here."

"Are you sure?" Todd asked.

"I like my modern-day comforts," said Violet. "Now, please, can we get moving? Do I have to remind you again about the fact that we're all going to drown?"

Todd and Violet caught up with the King in the cavern behind the waterfall. Freddie, Gavin, and Robby had fallen to their knees, their eyes wide with wonder, their faces filled with a blind devotion to the barrel-chested man with the dragon symbol on his chest. The King, however, was not looking at his new subjects. He had stepped out from behind the waterfall and was staring out across the valley. Excalibur was in his right hand, and with his left hand, he was holding back the knights who were crowded behind him. Rowan was talking to him again. The King nodded his head.

"What's she telling him?" Todd asked.

"I don't know," said Violet. "I don't understand their language."

"Yes, you do," Todd said. "Concentrate; I know you understand them."

Violet closed her eyes for a moment, and then looked at Todd and smiled. "She's clever," she said. "She told him that the helicopters are flying dragons, and dragons are not his quest."

She listened again. "Okay," she said. "He's ready to move. He trusts her; he always has. You can say goodbye if you want to."

"I never even said hello," Todd protested.

"Neither did I," said Violet. "He doesn't even know I'm here. Well, it's too late now."

The King stepped away from the waterfall and onto the steep hillside path, with Rowan at his side. The knights followed, blinking in the sunlight. They hesitated as a wall of sound hit them. The air was full of noise, sirens from the dam, the roar of helicopter engines, and the rushing of water pouring through the sluice gates.

Rowan urged the King forward, and the knights, with fearful glances at the hovering helicopters, followed behind.

"That's the place," said Violet. "Right there, that's the gate."

"I don't see a gate," said Todd.

"It's somewhere in those bushes," said Violet. "See where the mist is rising? That means the gate is opening. This will be all over in a minute."

The tendrils of mist wrapped around the base of the bushes and spread outward, curling around Rowan's legs. Arthur hurried forward, sword in hand, obviously intending to be first. Rowan pulled him back.

"He has to be the last to go," said Violet. "As soon as he is through, the gate will close. The other knights have to go first."

Arthur turned to gather the knights around him. He touched one of the knights on the shoulder.

"Sir Melion of the Mountain," said Violet.

"How do you know these things?" Todd asked.

"Don't even ask," said Violet.

Sir Melion took a step forward. The mist boiled furiously upward around his waist as if to welcome him back to his own world. He turned and saluted the King one more time while the mist rose thickly to his shoulders.

As Sir Melion disappeared from view, Todd felt the ground tremble and heard a pounding of horses' hooves and a voice screaming, "Stop."

The King turned quickly and stepped away from the gate, his sword balanced and ready in his hand. Todd saw a herd of horses pouring over the crest of the hill above them in a flurry of dust. They were led by a jet-black stallion whose hooves flung aside mud and grass as he raced toward them. He was followed by horses of every color, running free without saddle and bridle. Only one of the horses carried a rider, Marcus Ryan, who rode astride a swift gray horse in the midst of the pack.

It was Ryan who shouted the warning.

"Stop."

Violet Chambray

Violet had not expected to see Ryan again. If Arthur was returned to his own world, there would be no need for them to continue their uneasy partnership. What could they possibly say to each other? If Mandretti had managed to survive the explosion of the blue car, Ryan would be wise to stay out of his way. If Mandretti had died, then surely someone else would demand a reckoning. Whichever way, she hoped that Ryan would find a way to vanish; wander off into some distant desert, looking for treasure, or submerge himself beneath a faraway blue ocean where he could search for pirate booty. Although he had been an unwilling partner, there had been moments when she had thought that they might be something more to each other. She had caught glimpses of a different future for them, but now that was impossible. All she could do now was to hope that he would be safe.

However, instead of disappearing, Ryan had flung himself back into the fray, screaming words of warning and scattering Arthur's knights as they prepared to go back through the gate and into their own world.

The horses milled around, whinnying and tossing their heads and drawing the attention of every helicopter pilot, and every sightseer along the road to the dam. And if they saw the horses, then they most certainly saw Arthur and his knights. She could imagine the paparazzi focusing their telephoto lenses as the black stallion trotted up to Arthur and allowed the King to vault onto his back. There was absolutely nothing inconspicuous about the broad-chested figure of the High King, resplendent in his red surcoat emblazoned with the Pendragon emblem, and with Excalibur held high as he gestured for the other knights to mount.

"What?" Violet screamed at Ryan. "What are you doing?"

"They can't go through," Ryan shouted. "Mordred is waiting on the other side with an army. He'll slaughter them as soon as they arrive."

"What about Sir Melion?" asked Rowan, who had her hand on the gray's reins and was listening to every word.

"Too late," said Ryan briefly.

"You told that man not to kill me," Violet said.

"Yes, I did," said Ryan. He looked around. "Where is he?"

"I think he's dead."

Rowan tapped her staff impatiently against Ryan's leg. "Concentrate, and save your reunion for later."

"Oh, it's not a—"

"I don't care what it is," said Rowan. "What are we to do with the King? We have to leave this place; there is no refuge for him in this world. Arthur will have to fight. How many men does Mordred have?"

"Too many," said Ryan. "He has his whole army."

"And Arthur's army?"

"They are gathering," said Ryan. "Arthur will have to lead them. We can't waste any more time. All you need to know is that there is one more gate, and I can show you where it is."

"Is it close?"

"Very close," said Ryan.

"The horse gate?"

"Yes."

"But we are not horses."

"I met a man," said Ryan, "who was more rock than man, but he could still speak."

"Merlin," said Rowan.

"Yes. He is weak, but he can hold the gate open for us."

The King was growing impatient. His knights had all found mounts and had gathered around him. Behind them the mist from the gate rose in a swirling cloud, but their attention was on the oncoming mechanical beasts, the flying dragons.

"They're all going to get themselves killed," said Violet.

Rowan took a deep breath and then struck the ground with her staff. A bolt of blue lightning struck the King's shoulder. He turned angrily, but Rowan held up an imperious hand and spoke swiftly. She pointed to the path that the horses had taken along the hillside, and the mounted knights began to move.

A brown horse with thin, delicate legs pranced toward them.

Rowan turned to Elaine. "He is for you," she said.

Violet watched in envy as Elaine vaulted lightly onto the horse, turned his head, and brought him into line with the other horses.

Another horse broke from the line, an old black horse with a gray muzzle and whip marks along her back and flanks.

"I think she's come for you, Lady Rowan," said Ryan.

Rowan smiled. "Yes, I think she has," she said. "How very kind of her."

She looked around and spotted Freddie, who had been staring openmouthed at everything that was happening.

"Would you mind?" said Rowan.

"Oh," said Freddie, "no, not at all."

He cupped his hands beneath Rowan's sneakered left foot and boosted her up onto the horse, where she perched sidesaddle.

All the time, the news helicopters had been approaching ever closer to the steep hillside, risking a fiery crash for the sake of an exclusive close-up. As Rowan trotted away, Violet looked up and directly into the lens of a news camera held by a cameraman who was leaning perilously from the open door of a blue-and-white helicopter. She saw the camera pan around to film the line of horses that streamed across the hillside.

In the valley below, an ambulance had succeeded in reaching the wrecked limo, and she saw Molly Walker being extricated from the back seat. As the medics tried to help her into the ambulance, the professor waved them away and stood with her face uplifted, watching as her impossible dream came true, and she was given one brief glimpse of Arthur and his knights.

Violet turned to Todd. "We have to get out of here without anyone seeing us," she said. "You have to keep the newspapers away from me. I know you can hide my identity. You can do your internet magic thing, can't you?"

"Oh, Violet," said Todd, "do you really think you're going back to Key West?"

"Of course," said Violet.

"What are you going to do with him?" Todd asked.

"Who?"

"Your new admirer." Todd gestured to the dog who had come to Violet's side and stood with his head pressed against her knees.

"I can't take him to Key West."

"I don't think you're going to Key West," Todd said. "You don't belong here. You've never belonged here."

"Violet?"

Violet turned and looked at Ryan. He sat easily on the gray mare, controlling her with no apparent effort. He extended his hand. "Are you coming?" he asked.

"Coming where?" she asked.

"To Camelot," he said.

He smiled, a smile that she had never seen before, and her heart lurched.

"Don't you want to know who you really are?" he asked. "It's now or never. The gate will close as soon as Arthur passes through."

"Just go," said Todd, standing beside her and trying to urge her upward with pressure on her elbow. "Don't think about it, just go with him."

Violet looked up at Ryan. This man, who sat his horse as comfortably as any of Arthur's knights, and whose strong arm was extending an invitation to adventure, was not the cynical academic who had been forced upon her a week ago. This was a different man, a man she didn't know. When the gate to Albion closed for the final time, he would be on one side and she would be on the other. She would have her home in Key West, with its shady porches, cool sea breezes, and the comfort of familiar foods, and he would have Camelot.

Violet looked at the impossible height of the saddle, and her own feet planted so firmly on the ground. How would he even lift her? He would try, and she would fall. No, it was better not to even try.

Someone grasped her around the waist.

"Wait," she protested, turning to find that Freddie was in the process of sweeping her off her feet. He was a little red in the face and short of breath, but he was succeeding.

"No waiting," he gasped as he dumped her onto the back of the gray.

She instinctively flung her arms around Ryan's waist. The gray, impatient with waiting, gathered her energy and then released it in a burst of speed that sent her flying across the hillside, with Violet clinging breathlessly to Ryan.

She risked one backward glance. Freddie and Todd were already lost from sight, but the dog was keeping pace with her, running with his mouth open and his tail streaming out behind him. They crested the hill and headed down into a deep valley enclosing a dark lake. As the mist of Albion swirled around her, Violet grasped for the talisman, the red stone that would permit her to pass through the gate, but then realized that she had no need of a talisman. She, Violet Chambray, child of Ariana, was already a daughter of Albion.

She tightened her arms around Ryan's waist.

Arthur held his mount in check and waited for them to pass before he spurred his horse forward.

On the shore of the dark lake, a mossy stone shivered and moved, and sent a sighing incantation into the gentle breeze.

"Cau'r drws," said the wind, and the last gate to Albion closed as the High King returned . . .

Would you like to know more? The story continues in Excalibur Rising Books Two, Three, and Four available in paperback from Amazon.

Find all the details at eileenenwrighthodgetts.com where you can sign up to receive Eileen's Newsletter and a free digital copy of Excalibur Rising Book Zero – The place where it all begins.

41354344R00137

Made in the USA
Middletown, DE
07 April 2019